# Soul Survivor

## Susan Plunkett

*To Kathee~*
*With love*
*forever!*

*Susan*

JOVE BOOKS, NEW YORK

HAUNTING HEARTS is a trademark of Penguin Putnam Inc.

SOUL SURVIVOR

A Jove Book / published by arrangement with
the author

PRINTING HISTORY
Jove edition / December 1999

The Penguin Putnam Inc. World Wide Web site address is
http://www.penguinputnam.com

ISBN: 0-515-12684-5

A JOVE BOOK®
Jove Books are published by The Berkley Publishing Group,
a division of Penguin Putnam Inc.,
375 Hudson Street, New York, New York 10014.
JOVE and the "J" design
are trademarks belonging to Penguin Putnam Inc.

PRINTED IN THE UNITED STATES OF AMERICA

10  9  8  7  6  5  4  3  2  1

*For Alexander and Elyce Fassbender with love and gratitude for the treasure of family you instilled in your seven children. Thanks, Mom and Dad.*

*The other day upon the stair*
*I saw a man who wasn't there.*
*He wasn't there again today.*
*I wish that man would go away!*
                    —Unknown

# Chapter
# One

Roxanne Griffith stared at the casket of the woman she'd spent twenty-six years hating and two years loving. Too little, too late.

Fragrant eucalyptus trees swayed among stately live oaks in the moody Northern California spring afternoon. Italian cypress, their tops waving, flanked the cemetery avenues. Not a blade of grass ventured into the flower borders ringing the secluded section reserved for the Griffith family.

The whisper of the wind through the trees matched the subdued comments of those seeking chairs beneath a royal blue canopy with white fringe.

"Thelma always had an agenda, especially when it came to her grandniece," whispered an octogenarian close behind Roxanne. "I wouldn't put it past her to have used Roxanne like an old shoe, then cut her out of the will."

"Well, if she didn't, Roxanne certainly earned every red, squeaky cent of that inheritance," agreed another.

"Shhh. Have some respect," chided a man from farther away. "It's impolite to whisper."

Roxanne nearly laughed aloud. How odd for someone to remember that tidbit of etiquette now. Although the whispers supported her today, they no longer mattered.

The whispers had started before her birth. She had learned to endure and, eventually, appreciate them. At least the whisperers had acknowledged her as alive and worthy of comment. In the mausoleum of the Griffith house Thelma had ruled with an iron fist, Roxanne had grown up in silent forbearance. The burden of the Griffith name had made her a possession requiring maintenance and polishing. But the brass knocker on the front door had received more attention and even greater affection than she ever had. In the darkest hours of the night she craved the love of another person, someone she loved in return. The years of deprivation made her fearful of pursuing such dangerous dreams.

Ensconced in a burnished black and brass casket suspended over the hole in the ground, Thelma Mae Griffith occupied her favorite position: center stage. The abundant floral arrangements, symbols of her cherished social prestige, paid homage beyond probably even Thelma's expectation.

The last of the Griffiths, Roxanne stood alone in the front row. The breeze brought the heady fragrance of roses, carnations, and florist greenery, replacing the miasma of Thelma's oldest friend, Lydia Camden's six-hundred-dollar-an-ounce perfume. Thelma had hated the scent and refused to let Lydia into the house when she wore it. Roxanne had silently agreed with her great-aunt's assessment but would have bitten her tongue in half before saying so aloud.

"We're ready to proceed," crooned the silver-haired funeral director.

"By all means, let's do so," Roxanne murmured. She was ready for the final act of this macabre play directed by Thelma from her casket a scant six feet away. Roxanne marveled that even now, her great-aunt had found a way to control the world, making it revolve, as always, around herself.

Honors for the graveside eulogy went to Former State Senator Quinton Norton, an old friend of Thelma's. She had campaigned and financially supported him for more than twenty years.

"Thelma Griffith was a pillar of the community that respected and appreciated her," Senator Norton started in the rich, somber tone that had impressed his colleagues at the capital for years.

Roxanne tuned him out; she knew every word of the speech. Under Thelma's editorial guidance, Roxanne had written and rewritten the eulogy six months ago. A stickler for protocol and detail, Thelma had been determined to oversee her own funeral—

even if it killed Roxanne. The good news was that Thelma hadn't wanted anyone coming to the house after the service. Her attitude had been to let them go home and drop canapés on their own carpets, not hers.

Staring at the bloodred roses, black lace, and snow-white gardenias draped over Thelma's ebony casket, Roxanne experienced a familiar burning sensation at the nape of her neck. It wasn't painful. Not even annoying. It was just *there*. Daring her to breach propriety by turning around and seeking the source.

*Of course people are staring,* she chided. *Everyone here is speculating, wondering if you took care of Thelma for the Griffith money. They're probably making bets on whether she left you everything or cut you out completely and gave it to the Humane Society. Or Quinton Norton's campaign war chest for U.S. Senator.*

Not a single person at Thelma's graveside service had any idea of how little the Griffith wealth meant to Roxanne. Money couldn't buy what she had ached for most of her life. It couldn't fill the holes in her life or give her the love she yearned for.

She touched the back of her neck and tried to ignore the sensation of being watched. But it wouldn't go away. The ripple of the fine hair at the nape of her neck kept her alert. She was being scrutinized. Sized up. Assessed.

The intensity of that gaze sent gooseflesh dancing down her arms. The temptation to tilt her head until she could see over her right shoulder nearly got the best of her.

Instead, she smoothed her close-fitting black skirt over the tops of her thighs, then deliberately laced her fingers together on her lap. If she had learned anything under the tutelage of the Griffith family, it was self-control. Discipline. Denial.

". . . benevolent supporter of the downtrodden. Thelma always stood ready to offer a hand up . . ." Senator Norton droned on.

A chair creaked, feet shuffled, and someone cleared his throat.

The eulogy continued, a recitation of how Thelma had wanted people to remember her, not who she really was. In the end it made no difference to Roxanne. This graveside service was her last obligation, the final duty, the action that stamped "Paid in Full" on the past.

The sense of being watched heightened as the mourners seated behind her grew silent. Not a sniffle punctuated Norton's pauses. A pall of resignation hovered beneath the blue awning holding back the sunlight. Limited to a hundred of Thelma's closest friends and associates, every member of the exclusive gathering owed Thelma in one way or another. Thelma's power, and the manner in which she had wielded it, guaranteed that she was, while not the most beloved of the cemetery's denizens, definitely one of its most respected.

Finally both Norton's drone and the service ended.

Roxanne unlaced her hands, her fingers aching from the death grip she'd held so long.

She stood, free to check over her shoulder and see who had stared at her throughout the service. But the sensation was gone. There was no one in that direction who might have had such an impact on her.

She followed the funeral director and left the front row of seats. The Astroturf carpet tugged at her high heels. The wind chose that moment to shift. The white fringe on the royal blue canopy snapped to attention. Gray clouds scudded over the sun and warned of the approaching fog typical of Palo Alto and the San Francisco Bay Area.

"My dear, if you need anything. Anything at all. Please let me know." Lydia Camden caught Roxanne's fingers in her gloved hands.

Roxanne managed a polite smile. Years of blending into the background and watching the cream of society with a silent hunger to belong had schooled her in propriety. Now, long after the hunger had abated, she belonged by default. And, like so many of the things she had once craved being a part of, it no longer mattered.

"You made the Griffiths proud," added Horace Blumenthal, Lydia's companion, as he adjusted his Fedora on his smooth, gleaming pate.

"I'm sure Thelma was here in spirit," Lydia said. "Smiling her approval at you."

"Thank you both," Roxanne said, suppressing a smile of her own at the way Lydia and her companion ogled each another. She hoped she had that much spice in her life at their age—if she lived that long. Of course, having *any* romantic spice in her life right now would be an improvement.

Like a sentinel guarding the gateway to the next world, a place most of the attendees were likely to see sooner than later, Roxanne held her position at the foot of Thelma's casket. She accepted condolences and assured Thelma's cohorts that all was well.

"Come, my dear, I'll take you home," Senator Norton offered with a slight smile rife with understanding. At sixty-four, he was a youngster among Thelma's close acquaintances.

The sensation of being watched returned, and Roxanne indulged the temptation to locate the source. She scanned the departing mourners. Not one prospect caught her sharp gaze. A slight motion beyond the throng shuffling away from the elevated casket grabbed her attention.

A man dressed in an elegantly tailored black suit, white shirt, and charcoal tie nodded acknowledgment. Roxanne guessed his age at the mid-thirties. His youth and charismatic half-smile were as out of place at Thelma's funeral as a wart on a baby's behind. Hands stuffed into his trouser pockets, he leaned against a decaying headstone with a casualness that belied the solemnity of the graveyard. His right hand rose from his pocket to his forehead. The salute matched the play of the wind in his thick black hair.

From where she stood, Roxanne couldn't determine the color of his eyes, but she could feel the way they roamed over her, bored deep inside of her. The compelling sense of power and strength he radiated went through her with the force of an electric shock. The jolt nearly stopped her cold. He wasn't just spice; he was rich, dark, hot chocolate.

"Who is he?" Roxanne asked Senator Norton.

"I can't say I know his name," the senator mumbled, turning a myopic, narrowed gaze on the dark-haired man. "However, he looks familiar."

"I thought I knew all Thelma's acquaintances. In fact, I'm sure of it. I wonder who he is," Roxanne mused.

"Perhaps he's a reporter." A slight hand gesture summoned Max, his chauffeur-cum-bodyguard, who, after catching the senator's nod toward the stranger, started after him.

"Leave him alone, Quinton. Anyone crashing this funeral ought to get his money's worth. Though Aunt Thelma would feign outrage, she'd be pleased beyond measure and we both know it." Besides, the funeral crasher had enticing eyes—even if Roxanne couldn't discern the color. The current from their brief eye contact continued running through her veins as she began to walk down the path toward the limousine.

Quinton heaved a sigh, signaled Max's return, and then turned his attention to Roxanne. "Few people know how close you and Thelma became the last couple of years. Even when you're ready for death, the finality of it is always a shock. How are you coping, my dear?"

"Fine," Roxanne answered. She shook her head in an attempt to rid herself of the disconcerting effects of the watcher's gaze. It seemed ludicrous to feel so alive at a funeral. "I really am doing fine, Quinton. By the time she died, Thelma was eager to go, and I was ready to say good-bye."

"You don't fool me, Roxanne. More than anyone else, I saw how you cared for Thelma. The last six months earned you a place in heaven. Thelma was a hard woman when she was healthy." Norton's eyes turned toward the casket. "Illness did not improve her disposition."

Roxanne didn't answer. The truth required no response.

Max opened the car door for Roxanne. She started to get into the car, then paused, lifting her gaze to Norton's. "Ironically, her illness drew us together." She got into the car and slid across the seat.

"It took looking death in the eye for her to appreciate you." Quinton got in and nodded for the chauffeur to close the door.

"It's a pity we wasted all those years. We might have actually been friends instead of . . . adversaries. Or whatever we were while I was growing up."

"You were family. You came back when she needed you. You were the only one willing to help. You're a Griffith."

God forbid that Roxanne could ever forget the burden of her name or the price inflicted by its awesome weight. "Yes," she agreed with a sigh. "I am that." By default. The questions she'd lived with were finally silent. No one remained to dispute her parentage. Consequently, the stodgy image of the Griffith family was about to change. Roxanne's duties were discharged, her obligations fulfilled. Aunt Thelma's funeral represented Independence Day. From now on, Roxanne would be herself first and a Griffith only when it suited her.

She glanced over her shoulder at the man who she was positive had watched her during the service.

He was gone.

Somehow, after so many lonely years, it figured that the first man to interest her would enter and leave her life in a graveyard.

•   •   •

Spencer Griffith saw more than he'd bargained for in the grave-yard. He'd come as a spectator for the living and as an emissary of the dead. The coincidence of identical last names had proven a bane for him and his family. For a few days, they'd had hope, not that Mitchell Maguire Griffith was alive, but that his remains were coming home to the heart of the family who loved him, home where he belonged. For a few days, Mitchell Maguire Griffith wasn't missing in action in Vietnam.

Their closure had lasted until the investigation at Hickam AFB in Hawaii proved, beyond doubt, that the remains were those of Captain Matthew Mayhew Griffith.

Roxanne Griffith, a stranger with an intimate knowledge of death and closure, was the beneficiary of the Remembrance Foundation's efforts. He envied her. Her father was coming home. His brother was still somewhere in Vietnam.

Ironically, Spence's role as the search group's public relations director, fund-raiser, and all-around-intermediary dictated he inform Captain Matthew Mayhew Griffith's family that his remains were coming home.

Spence tamped down his disappointment and focused on Roxanne. Newspaper photos on the society pages didn't do justice to her understated, classic beauty, Spence decided. Short, dark brown hair as shiny as her brown eyes framed her elegant face and accented her cheekbones. Her nearly six-foot height in heels sent her towering over most of the mourners at the funeral. She glided across the sea of perfectly manicured lawn like a bird skimming the ocean. Her smooth carriage suggested that she could walk on water and the waves would subside just for her passage. He knew high-fashion models who spent years perfecting the presence that appeared natural for Roxanne Griffith.

Spence shook himself. He had no business looking at her as though she was a prospective date. Hell, the woman had just lost her last living relative. At least on her father's side.

She'd lost her mother's relatives, the Boyles, before her birth. They had apparently abandoned Marian shortly after her husband went to Vietnam. Whatever feelings of connectivity the Boyles may have had for Roxanne apparently died with her mother in 1978.

According to the investigative reports, Roxanne's grandmother, Janice Boyle, had lived on the hard side of the law for over thirty years. From Spence's perspective, those circumstances made it fortunate that Janice Boyle walked away from her granddaughter.

Still, rejection was rejection. It fostered misery. Insecurity. If those things were part of Roxanne's life, it was unfortunate. He had the opportunity to do them both some good. Soon, he'd offer her what he assumed was some well-needed closure. The same closure he ached for but had yet to find.

This morning the wisdom of attending Thelma Griffith's funeral had seemed questionable. This afternoon Spence considered it a stroke of genius. He hadn't known what to expect when he entered the cemetery. But it damn sure wasn't what he found. He'd never attended a funeral where there wasn't so much as a single damp eye.

This one was the first.

Making his way back to his car, Spencer detoured around a pair of stately oaks spreading leafy black arms over the forest of granite sprouting at their feet. The gentle roll of the California terrain reminded him of a velvet sea, and the sunshine glittering off shiny flecks in the granite became the wave tops.

At the edge of the Griffith family plot, the fringe on the royal blue canopy waved him closer. The rows of chairs on the Astroturf carpet had lost their careful definition.

Spence approached the flower-bedecked casket waiting for the final journey into the ground.

"I hope you received this many flowers while you were alive, Thelma." He cupped a gardenia in his right hand, bent, and inhaled the fragrance. "You had an interesting collection of mourners. They obviously respected the hell out of you, but I don't think they loved you very much. From what I've learned about you, that's probably the way you wanted it, isn't it?"

The wind sighed an answer through the intricately woven floral garlands.

"Yeah, I thought so." After releasing the gardenia, he trailed his fingertips along the burnished brass side rail. "You were old school, old money, old morals. Duty came first. Responsibility was automatic. Family lay at the core of everything you did."

Spence shook his head, then loosened his tie. "You can rest easy, Thelma Mae Griffith. I'm going to tie up the loose ends you couldn't." He touched the foot of the casket. "I wish you could have lived long enough to experience what I've brought your niece. Let's hope she shares our values."

•   •   •

Captain Matthew Mayhew Griffith pondered the Abyss of Nothingness. How long he'd stood there, he couldn't say. It seemed forever, but that was impossible. *Forever* stretched in front of him, above him, and below him into the vast Nothingness. A spirit cast over the precarious edge upon which he teetered, Matt faced an inexorably slow disintegration that lasted throughout the course of eternity. Alone. Untouched. Unredeemable. Hopeless. That was the worst of it. The isolated hopelessness was hell of the worst kind for Matt.

It was more abysmal than fire and brimstone. Those implied the existence of *something* else, possibly even *someone* else. Pain and suffering equated a place where some entity cared enough to make him miserable. Here there was just nothingness—no people, no sound, no color, nothing to indicate the existence of anything else.

Time had lost all meaning in the sensory-deprived limbo he had occupied since he ceased being—being, well, anything. So when everything changed around him in what felt like the blinking of an eye, Matt had no concept of where, or even when, he was.

Light, warm and dazzling, flooded the nearly black world of his existence. The Abyss of Nothingness disappeared. The brilliance stripped away his impoverished spirit and revealed the famine-stricken plane of his soul. It wasn't the light as much as it was the sensation of love and acceptance inundating him from all directions that caused him to cower. But the light exposed him and cast no shadows in which to hide.

"Matthew Mayhew Griffith, account for your life."

Dispossessed of substance, he could neither tremble nor lick his lips as he had often done in his corporeal form. A citizen of the Afterworld, the compulsion to obey ruled him, regardless of how daunting the command. Matt recognized this as his defining moment, the heartbeat in Eternity during which his fate was written.

He had contemplated this opportunity since the beginning—the benign instant when a shaft of pure, white light had carried him from the physical realm. When the bliss-filled light faded, he had found himself perched above the Abyss of Nothingness. Near darkness and isolation were all he'd known until now.

"There isn't much I can say, other than it was terribly short." The response startled him. It sounded like his voice, but he wasn't sure it could be. He had no substance, nor had he a mouth with which to speak.

"It was long enough. I have reviewed your life, Matthew Mayhew Griffith, and found you squandered your talents and your emotions, allowing pitifully little compassion for those who cared about you. Have you anything to say for yourself?"

At the most crucial instant in eternity, he practiced a rare moment of restraint. All his life his lightning-quick mind had found ways out of any trouble his careless, glib tongue talked him into. This time was different. This time was for *forever*. Best he tread lightly and listen closely. "In what regard?"

"To your failures, Matthew, both omission and commission." The powerful voice penetrated every facet of Matt's awareness.

The brilliance he could not avoid left no room for avoidance, no place for a quick remark or a sidestepping quip. "I am guilty," he admitted, convinced he spoke the truth, but not sure exactly what it was he was confessing to. An impartial review of his lifetime undoubtedly revealed a plethora of sins. They just hadn't seemed more than peccadilloes at the time. Or maybe they had, but consequences weren't things he had taken much to heart— until his death—and now it was too late to change anything. "I would atone for them, if given the chance."

He would make amends, grovel, do anything to keep from being consigned to the Abyss of Nothingness.

"I'm sure you would, Matthew. We have examined your actions and the damage you've inflicted. We have watched and waited. Time has not healed the wounds your sins caused. Instead, the cuts have deepened and festered. The poison you sowed while alive tainted innocent souls."

"I can't help that from here," Matt retorted against the sting of condemnation. He'd never considered himself a detriment to humanity. On the contrary, he had deemed himself a cut above because of his intelligence and the esteem his family enjoyed in society. True, he could have done more for those around him than he had, but not doing so didn't necessarily—

"What is true is that there is nothing you can do to help or hurt from this side of the veil. Soon, one of those you harmed will join us. Your deeds caused injury repairable only in the corporeal realm. You cannot assuage the venom once you are in the Abyss of Nothingness."

Matt shuddered. The light around him shimmered. Fear replaced hopelessness. "I'll do whatever you ask to atone for my sins. What I can't change, I'll do my damn . . . utmost to make better. Give me a chance. Just one chance. I beg of you." And for the first time in his life, he really was begging, pleading, and praying.

The absolute silence that met his petition was deafening. Worse, the sense of love and benevolent acceptance had evaporated from the light. All that remained was a sterile brilliance that reinforced his isolation. Had he lost his only opportunity to avoid an eternity of nothingness?

"What you feel is the reflection of the love in your heart, Matthew." The voice was different, vaguely familiar, and infinitely sad.

The realization of how stingy he'd been with his love shamed him. There was nothing more to say. In a place where lies had no power and the truth shone like a million suns, he could not deny the poverty of his spirit. The line of excuses he'd relied on to help him out of one jam after another was exhausted, their effectiveness nonexistent.

"Your spirit may return. Use the time wisely. Redeem yourself by mending the wounds you callously and carelessly inflicted. Think love, Matthew. For someone beyond yourself. This is the only chance you'll have at redemption."

That voice. He recognized it. Almost.

"You may call upon me three times before Memorial Day. That is all the time you have to help them and yourself."

"Aunt Thelma? Is that you?" he asked, hopeful of an ally, even thought it meant a stern taskmaster.

As soon as he spoke, the benign light began shimmering. It closed in, pressing tighter and tighter, tumbling him in a vortex of color and chaotic sound.

Then everything stopped. Total stillness descended on him. He was in darkness again, only this time if felt solid and velvet-coated. Wherever he was, it wasn't the Abyss of Nothingness.

He said a small prayer that he wouldn't mess up the one chance he had to make things right for the people he had wronged—and himself. Damn, he should have asked who they were. Perhaps he might have an edge of figuring out how to play the situation.

Carefully, he decided. Above all else, he'd play it carefully.

Returning to the corporeal world had another up side. At last he'd find out how long the war in Vietnam had continued after he left it behind.

# Chapter Two

When Roxanne opened the big front door of the Griffith house the day after Thelma's funeral, the man from the graveyard was standing on her porch. He looked at her with an enigmatic expression. Her first thought centered on the rich, shining blue of the eyes that had stared at her so intently at the cemetery. The owner of the blue eyes studied her from the other side of thick, black lashes. Looking into them, she wondered how, even from a distance, she hadn't seen how blue they were. Her fingers tightened on the front doorknob.

Although his jaw was a bit too square and the dimple in his left cheek barely noticeable—until he smiled—she deemed him interesting to look at, but definitely not magazine-quality handsome.

Roxanne wanted to say something, ask him who he was and why he was there, but the words stuck in her throat.

"Spencer Griffith," he said in a bass voice as Roxanne just stood there staring at him. He shifted the cardboard box under his arm and then extended his hand. "No relation. I checked. I'm with the Remembrance Foundation." He smiled. "And I'm not soliciting a donation."

Still gazing into the sea of blue eyes nearly drowning her, Roxanne took his hand, then held tightly as his strong fingers enveloped hers. She must be drowning. Her heart was beating hard and fast and she couldn't breathe.

"Are you all right?" The arches of his eyebrows drew close and formed furrows in his brow.

Suddenly finding her voice, Roxanne managed to choke out an answer. "I'm fine, just fine." Speaking forced her to exhale. He wasn't just chocolate; he was a box of Godiva truffles. "I'm sorry, who did you say you are?"

"Spencer—"

"No-Relation Griffith," she finished for him. "I understood that part."

"I'm the owner of the hand you're squeezing like a lemon. You have a good grip, Miss Griffith. Lift weights?"

She released his hand as though it was a hot brick, which was exactly how it suddenly felt. "Sorry. It's been a difficult day."

"A helluva day?" The smile in his voice reached his eyes and made them sparkle like the sun reflecting off a deep blue ocean.

Roxanne returned his smile as she glanced across the front porch and into the yard. Long, late afternoon shadows bathed the yellow, red, and white tulip beds blossoming around a tulip tree with lavender, pink, and white blooms. A black Lincoln sat in the driveway. She knew a few reporters. None drove a big, new Lincoln. None could afford to do so.

"Yes," she agreed cautiously. "It's been a helluva day."

"I'm confident you'll view my visit here as something good. Although the timing may be questionable, considering that you buried your aunt yesterday."

Roxanne stepped back, still holding on to the doorknob, efficiently blocking his way inside. She realized abruptly this man, this stranger, knew a lot about her, things he had no right to know. "Are you a reporter or some sort of investigative journalist?"

"No." The grin broadened, revealing a line of white teeth.

"Then, besides attend stranger's funerals what exactly is your job and why are you here?" Judging by the clothes and the car, whatever it was, he did it very well.

"What I do for a living has nothing to do with why I'm here, Miss Griffith."

"Oh?" Roxanne hesitated, not ready to invite the stranger inside. "Please, answer my questions."

"I'm in the restaurant and packaged food business. My family owns a restaurant—Christopher's—in San Francisco." He offered a business card that seemed to come out of thin air. "We also own Christopher's in Seattle."

Still wary, Roxanne took the card and examined the embossed lettering. "Christopher's, huh," she mused aloud. That explained the clothes and the car. She had four desserts bearing the Christopher's label in the freezer.

"That's very nice, Mr. No-Relation Griffith, but you still haven't explained how you know who I am and why you crashed my great-aunt's funeral."

The full intensity of the blue eyes she'd felt watching her the previous afternoon focused on her. "I apologize for dropping by at what must be an emotional time for you. It's necessary we talk."

"I'm listening. Talk."

His hesitancy made her wonder if he was contemplating a retreat. "I think you'll consider what I have to say important and very personal. I'd prefer not to discuss it on your front porch."

He had her interest. What in heaven's name could be so important? He wasn't a relative . . . She bit her lip and shook her head. Aunt Thelma would roll over in her freshly dug grave if Roxanne invited a strange man inside on the help's day off. Roxanne's left shoulder lifted in a half shrug of apology. "I'm not in the habit of inviting strangers in."

"Look, Miss Griffith, I understand your reluctance. However, it's imperative I speak with you. I'm completely trustworthy, I promise. May I please come in?"

The longer she looked into his sparkling blue eyes, the more appeal the notion held. The woman who'd sworn to throw off the shackles of restraint imposed by the Griffith name urged her to open the door wide and invite exciting change inside. The voice of caution admonished her to look deeper. "So, why is it you know so much about me?"

"That's part of what I've come to talk with you about. If you'd prefer I can come back another time, maybe when you've got a friend with you?" His sensitivity to her reticence struck a chord.

"A friend," Roxanne repeated. She'd never made friends easily. Two years of nursing Aunt Thelma while at the same time trying to maintain her business and client base had left no time for anything else. Now, she was free and ready to pick up old friendships, but the sad truth was that she didn't really have any. The suppressed adventurer in her urged her to start now by taking a wild chance on the intriguing man with the smiling blue eyes.

"You find them in the strangest places," he said with a grin. "Sometimes they show up on your porch."

She weighed the possibility. "And what do you perceive is the basis for our friendship?"

"For starters, our last name. You aren't aware of the confusion that's caused recently."

"Really." She still wasn't convinced inviting him inside was wise.

"Interested?"

"Yes." In a spurt of sheer bravado she stepped aside and drew back the ornately carved door to allow him inside. "All right, you can come in and explain." Heaven knows the Griffiths would have considered a name mix-up a personal affront.

Buster darted across the foyer like a shadow fleeing the dawn. Curiosity may have killed the proverbial cat, but it wouldn't get Buster.

"You've obviously gone through a great deal of effort to speak with me, Mr. Griffith. Very few people would gate-crash a funeral, particularly one attended by so many geriatric dignitaries." She led him across the foyer, through the formal dining room. Hundreds of artfully arranged flowers from friends, acquaintances, and well-wishers decked a long, gleaming table ringed by sixteen padded, high-backed chairs with carved armrests.

"I hope you won't mind talking in the kitchen. I was just about to sit down to dinner when you rang the doorbell."

The expansive kitchen was an artful study in stainless steel and tile. Roxanne loved it as much as Inez, the housekeeper, did. With a spray bottle of window cleaner and a few paper towels, cleanup after an impromptu meal took only minutes.

Roxanne rounded the island, reached over to the stove and turned off the soup simmering on the burner, then took some bread out from the breadmaker. "Are you hungry?"

"Sure." He pulled out one of the swivel stools tucked beneath the island counter and sat down, carefully placing the cardboard box on the adjacent stool. "There's nothing like home cooking."

"How can you say that with a straight face? You own a restaurant." She brought down a couple of soup bowls and plates for bread.

"Where do you think the dishes we serve originally came from?"

"I never thought about it." Small wonder, she mused. Home cooking for her was a box of macaroni and cheese or a microwaved frozen dinner, not the elegant meals they served at Christopher's. Roxanne ladled up the vegetable soup. She placed the steaming bowl in front of him, then crossed to a long bank of cupboards and drawers to retrieve silverware, napkins, and glasses. "Coffee, soda, water, juice—what's your pleasure?"

He hesitated a few seconds before answering. "Coffee, if it's made. Water, if not."

A sudden seriousness in his voice made her glance over her shoulder. The smile was gone. He regarded her with the same acuity she had felt in the cemetery.

"I put on a fresh pot right before I made dinner." She poured two cups and set them on the countertop. She returned with steaming bread, butter, and a honey pot. She angled a stool around the corner so she could see him clearly. "Now," she started as she settled on the stool, "why don't you tell me about the name confusion and why you think we should be friends?"

"Sure."

But instead of expanding on the subject, he began to eat with tremendous gusto. "Great soup."

Roxanne stared at him from over her soup spoon. "It's Campbell's."

His eyes widened in surprise, then sparkled when he laughed. "Not a chance."

"Okay, you can tell the difference between canned and homemade. Is this a rating?"

"If it were, I'd give it four stars."

"Just four?" She shook her head and slathered butter over a piece of bread. "Inez will be so disappointed. I told her it was a five-star batch."

"If she makes a smooth white sauce, I'd offer her a job."

"She'd turn you down."

"Hey, I'd make it worth her while." He winked and took another bite of soup. "You don't think I'd try to hijack your cook and expect to get her cheap, do you?"

"I don't know you, so how could I speculate on what you'd do?" She offered him the bread plate. "Or what you're capable of."

"If I really wanted to hire your cook, I'd find a way, but that would be a very poor repayment for your generous hospitality, wouldn't it?"

Roxanne tilted her head, her defenses alert. She suspected this man would find a way to accomplish almost anything he set out to do. She'd let him in and offered him dinner, hadn't she? Time to get down to the purpose of his visit.

"So, Mr. Griffith, what exactly were you doing attending my great-aunt's funeral service?"

"I was checking you out, seeing how you were holding up, whether you were ready for . . . another closure so quickly."

Of all the things she might have expected, his statement caught her off guard. "What on earth made you think you'd know me just by looking at me?" Disappointment anyone thought her so shallow or transparent nurtured her suspicions of his motives.

"Emotions tend to run close to the surface during funerals," he said softly. "I didn't mean to imply—"

"Then you must have been disappointed I wasn't tearfully devastated." Death was a blessed release for Thelma. The only person more relieved than Roxanne when Thelma took her last breath was Thelma herself. Even so, Roxanne had cried for hours after Thelma was taken away. But none of that was Spencer Griffith's business.

He shifted on the stool and regarded her for a long moment. "All right," he said, setting down his spoon, "let's get down to it, then. There was a mistake because of our identical last names. Once things were researched and set right, my loss became your gain."

Roxanne stared at him. "What are you talking about? What kind of mistake could possibly . . ." Her voice trailed off, then became stronger as she realized why he was there.

"Look, if you're looking for money, just get out now." Roxanne began to rise off the stool disgusted with herself and her guest. Until this moment she'd considered herself an excellent judge of character. Over the past two years she had fielded more scams and creative solicitations for money than most people thought existed. Now she'd invited a con man into her kitchen and fed him dinner.

"Please, sit down. I'm not after your money, I promise. I'm actually here to give you something—a precious, priceless gift."

Spence's voice was deadly serious, and his bright blue eyes had become dark and stormy.

Roxanne frowned. She hadn't a clue what he was talking about. Although with the way he looked now, she was sure that whatever he wanted to give her, it wasn't a free dinner at his restaurant. After clearing her throat, she sat back down. "Okay. Talk quickly, Mr. Griffith. You've got five minutes to explain why you're here and what you want to give me, what this gift is that should be yours but is now, apparently, mine."

She met his gaze for a long moment. A hint of sorrow darted through his eyes before he began his story.

"My family takes care of its own. Sometimes things happen beyond our control to make it difficult. War is one of those things. My older brother got his draft notice the day before he graduated from college. That piece of paper put his life on hold. He came home on leave once before they shipped him off to Vietnam. We never saw him again. Six months later we received word he was missing in action.

"We prayed. Hoped beyond reason for his return after the war ended. But most of all, we waited for Mitch to come home. Five years passed. Ten years. Any chance of Mitch being alive got smaller each month."

Roxanne watched without comment, astounded by the depth of emotion he wore as easily as a tailored shirt. She couldn't imagine waiting that long for someone to come home.

"We lobbied congressmen and I went to Washington, D.C., three times to press for the recovery of men missing in action. I met other families of MIAs. We established the Remembrance Foundation. When relations improved between our government and Vietnam, we seized the opportunity.

"For the past ten years the Remembrance Foundation has worked with an international group trying to recover MIAs from Vietnam. We've had some successes. One of our investigators confirmed the remains of an American MIA. The investigator and I handled the diplomatic protocol and had the remains shipped to Hickam Air Force Base in Hawaii. The ID belonged to a pilot, Captain M. M. Griffith."

A glimmer of awareness soured the soup she'd just eaten.

"I had hoped the remains were my brother's. The dog tags were corroded, but you could still make out the last name with the naked eye. Closer examination and more complete testing concluded it wasn't Mitch. The next task was to locate this man's family and return him home.

Dread turned her hands to ice. He wasn't talking about *this* Griffith family. No.

"It took some investigation, but it wasn't difficult. The remains belong to your father. I've arranged to have his body, or rather what's left, brought back to the U.S., to you, Roxanne. Meanwhile, here are his personal effects." He picked up the small cardboard box he'd brought with him and placed it on the countertop.

Her father?

This man sitting in her kitchen, eating dinner with her, surely hadn't said he'd found her father's remains and arranged for their return.

She felt as though her brain had turned into mud. This wasn't really happening. "My father?" she whispered in a gush of air that left her lungs deflated and loathe to draw another fresh breath.

"Yes. The Remembrance Foundation has arranged for a ceremony honoring him on Memorial Day at Golden Gate National Cemetery. Of course, it's your choice where he's buried—with the rest of your family or in a military—"

"Vietnam," she rasped, then struggled for a full breath.

"I beg your pardon?"

"I said, bury him in Vietnam. That's where he died and that's where he should stay. I don't want anything of his anywhere near me. Not now. Not ever!"

Roxanne realized she was yelling but was too upset to care. The ignominy of the painful legacy her father had sentenced her with rose like a phoenix from the ashes of memory. "I don't want anything to do with that miserable excuse for a human being. And don't you *ever* refer to him as my father again!" She started to rise, then thought better of it. Her legs shook so badly she doubted they would support her if she tried.

"I don't understand—" he whispered, his gaze full of utter confusion.

"And you won't because I refuse to oblige you by explaining, Mr. Griffith. All you need to know is that I want nothing—nada, zilch, zip—to do with Captain Matthew Mayhew Griffith, other than to hope he rots in the worst part of hell there is."

She slid off the chair but held on to the edge of the countertop, her gaze fixed on him. "You've overstayed your welcome. Shall I walk you to the door, or can you find your way?"

"I'll find my way out," he answered sharply, obviously angered by her reaction to his gift.

"Don't forget your package." She pushed the cardboard box at him.

Spence lunged for it but succeeded only in knocking it to the floor. The top of the box popped open. An ornately carved black lacquered box slid from the corrugated container, spilling its contents across the slick tile floor.

A hiss, like air filling a vacuum, filled the kitchen.

The velvet darkness that had embraced Matt suddenly shattered in a burst of light. His surroundings reeked of familiarity, but superficial change gave him pause.

A sudden rush of nostalgia inundated him. If he possessed form or substance, he would have crumpled to his knees. As it was, his essence lay on the floor like a puddle of spilled milk. Still, his spirit reveled at being in his family home again. Home. Had any place ever been so sweet? Such a welcomed sight?

His recent brush with the Abyss of Nothingness gave him a deep respect for the powers governing the spirit world. Before he got too carried away, he remembered to offer thanks to those who allowed his presence in the most familiar, welcoming place he'd ever known.

The solidity of the tile floor should have imparted coolness, but Matt felt nothing, neither temperature nor the contrast of smooth Italian tile and rough grout beneath his prone form. Disappointment stung. He felt cheated. It was like sitting down to a hot fudge sundae and having it taste like sawdust. Still, he was finally home, so his disappointment was fleeting.

He looked around. *Home* had seen a number of changes since the Vietnam War, most of it bearing Thelma's touch. The kitchen was bigger. While much of the furniture was familiar, it was in different places. The arrangement gave the kitchen a completely new feel. Matt continued surveying the room from his ungainly position on the floor. He wanted to get up and explore the rest of the house but sprawled, halfway between his aviator wings and his dog tags, he lacked the strength to right himself. Like them, he had spilled across the tiles with the mementos of his life.

As his surprise at being home faded, awareness of his broader surroundings crept through.

He was not alone.

Beyond one of the corroded captain's bars and a cardboard box, a man and a woman stared at the items scattered across the floor. When she lifted her gaze, he saw his wife, Marian. Or was it? She had dark brown irises flecked with gold just like his sweet Marian. However, Marian's eyes had never held so much hate and anger. He shuddered involuntarily, taken aback by what he saw in the eyes of the woman who looked like Marian.

A cat as black and shiny as asphalt on a rainy night hissed from across the kitchen floor. Black slits of pupils in a sea of golden brown stared back at Matt. Slowly the cat unfolded his legs and stood, then began stalking him.

Spence flinched as the box hit the floor and the contents scattered across the tile. He couldn't pull his gaze from the meager collection that represented a man's life and death. He couldn't look at Roxanne. Hiding his disgust was impossible. Here she had all the closure he'd searched for for ten years, and she didn't want it. He simply didn't understand.

"I'm sorry, Miss Griffith," he managed, silently adding *So damn sorry it was your father instead of my brother they found in Vietnam.*

"Please leave." She turned her back on him and the memorabilia strewn across the kitchen floor. "And take that box and all the other stuff with you. I've lived my entire life surrounded by Matthew Griffith memorabilia. I really don't want or need any more."

Spence stood, shoved his hands into his pants pockets, then exhaled. "Maybe if you just—"

Roxanne cut him off, her tone cold. "Good-bye, Mr. No-Relation Griffith. I'll show you out."

Roxanne Griffith's voice held all the warmth of Alaska in January. Without a doubt, it was time to leave. He started for the kitchen door. "No need. I'm sure I can find it."

"Fine. Take all this junk with you." The harshness in her voice gave it a brittle, disembodied quality.

"I've delivered Captain Griffith's personal effects to his next of kin. What you do with them is strictly your business." With that, he turned and strode across the kitchen, careful to avoid stepping on the pieces of a man's life sprawled across the cold tiles.

The cat arched his back raising the hair along his spine, and hissed, as Spence passed.

Spence ignored the feline, wanting only to get away from Roxanne and out of her house. Bilious anger rose in his throat. Captain Griffith was her father, for God's sake.

This time when he passed through the dining room, the flowers took on a cloying scent, nearly choking him with their sweetness. The long shadows of early evening cast a heavy pall through the lace sheers screening the windows beneath the drapes.

Spence sat in his car in front of the park he had seen on his excursion to the Griffith estate earlier in the day. As the engine idled, he thought about Roxanne's strange reaction. His family would give damn near anything to find Mitch's remains and remove any lingering doubt about his fate. Although they all believed him dead, bringing Mitch home would provide the closure and the peace missing from their family for so long.

Roxanne Griffith was obviously not the woman he had thought she was. Instead, this woman could bury her aunt without shedding a tear, then shun the precious knowledge of her father's fate. If Roxanne had a heart, it was as cold as a bronze statue in the Antarctic, and just about as soft.

Still, he had a hard time reconciling the cold, bitter woman in the Griffith's kitchen with the woman at the cemetery. He'd seen the patience she lavished on her aunt's peers. That was no act.

He'd heard the ripple of comments from those same people before and after the service. Whatever Roxanne was, it wasn't a woman void of compassion. From the sound of things, no one had expected her to return to the family home after the diagnosis of Thelma Griffith's cancer. Several of the mourners had openly reiterated their shock upon learning Roxanne had moved back to take care of her dying aunt. A couple of them had expressed their wishes for a relative willing to do the same for them.

He'd seen and heard so many conflicting aspects of Roxanne Griffith, he didn't know what to believe. He thought he was delivering closure to her. Instead, she'd delivered him a bitter and unpleasant surprise.

The day had started with a number of misconceptions, beginning with his assumption that his visit would be easy, cut and dried.

This afternoon he'd thought she'd be eager to honor her father's memory at the Memorial Day service. If not eager, at least willing.

Then, *willing* also described what he'd hoped she'd be on another level. It had startled in him the cemetery. The electric sensation he'd experienced while watching her as Senator Norton droned on yesterday wasn't a fluke. He'd experienced it again the moment she'd opened the big front door. Sudden, sexual need had ridden roughshod through his system right up until she threw him out.

*Lust,* he rationalized.

He shook his head to rid himself of these thoughts of Roxanne. On the grass in front of him, he watched a father and son explore the physics of getting a glove on a baseball.

"Someday," he murmured, starting the car.

But life was passing him by with an endless flurry of business and family crises. *Someday* was getting farther away every year.

He shook his head to dispel his thoughts, started the car, and backed into the street. He had a restaurant to run. The evening crowd would be arriving about the time he got back to San Francisco.

# Chapter Three

Buster raced out of the kitchen before the front door banged shut.

Spencer No-Relation Griffith, entrepreneur, restaurateur, and chief meddler in Roxanne's life, was gone. Thank heavens.

Roxanne tried to ignore the disappointment that accompanied her thoughts, telling herself she was glad he left. She slid off the stool and turned her attention to the dishes and the memorabilia scattered on the tile floor. She wished Inez hadn't taken the three weeks off Roxanne had insisted she needed. It would be nice to have someone here to help deal with her father's things in particular and with the whole situation in general. Roxanne immediately shook off the thought. Inez needed the time away, although she'd probably retire when she returned. The housekeeper had certainly earned the generous inheritance Thelma left. Heaven and Roxanne knew Thelma hadn't been an easy employer, but she'd always compensated for her demanding nature with generous wages and bonuses.

Using the broom and dustpan Inez kept in the pantry, Roxanne swept up the pieces of memorabilia littering the kitchen floor. She dumped them into the black lacquer box, then, loathe to touch any of her father's things, used the toe of her shoe to push it back into the cardboard container.

"Too bad it wasn't your brother, Spencer Griffith. We'd both be happier." She left the kitchen and dropped the box onto the dining room table.

But she couldn't ignore it.

She stared at it in the midst of the flowers filling the table. In their florist vases the arrangements became a garden mourning the owner of the items in the black lacquer box.

As she stood there, the perfume of the blossoms became over-powering, choking her with the same intensity as her father's legacy.

She felt the presence of the Griffith family. It was, after all, their home, not really hers. She bore their name, but had never known their acceptance. They had never let her belong. Through the sound of the grandfather clock ticking in the foyer, she heard the censure of the three generations of Griffiths born under this roof.

"I'm an outsider. They didn't want me," she said to the card-board box stenciled with her father's name in block letters. "Because of you. *You* denied me. You got your pound of flesh from us. You carved it right out of our hearts. *You* put my mother through hell. We lived here; they allowed us that much. But they never let us forget we were second-rate charity-case relatives from the wrong side of the tracks. Mom worked her ass off trying to make them like her and accept me. Because of you, you son of a bitch, she's dead.

"Just when my life is taking on a positive direction, *you* turn up." She wanted to kick the box and all it represented. Would the burdens of having the Griffith name never end? "Spout praises for the man who killed my mother? In front of an audience? Not in this lifetime."

The litany of the Griffith value system echoed in her brain.

*A Griffith never turns on a Griffith.*

*A Griffith never passes an opportunity to socially advance the family or garner favorable recognition.*

*A Griffith never denigrates a family member.*

*A Griffith keeps family secrets within the family.*

But she had never been accepted as a true Griffith.

Years of doubt and the abrasion of obligatory family charity deepened Roxanne's bitterness toward her father. "Honor you? I seriously don't think so. If it's so damn important for Spencer

Griffith to have a ceremony, let him do it. I wouldn't waste my time spitting on your grave if it was on fire."

She turned away.

Tomorrow she'd burn the box and all its contents.

Marian was dead? Before tasting a full measure of life?

How?

When?

Matt's emotions curled in on him. Against all odds, he was home—too late. Marian's sweet, generous soul had moved to a higher plane. The certainty she experienced the full benevolence of the light tempered Matt's anguish of her loss in the corporeal realm.

During the timelessness perched over the Abyss, he'd envisioned her living in this house and making it hers over time. Roxanne should have grown up here remembering him with love not loathing. That was how it was supposed to be.

But it wasn't. In typical Griffith fashion, the house had followed the natural line of succession. The current landlord wanted to evict him.

"How can Roxanne hate me so much?" he wondered aloud. Even more important was the question he couldn't give voice to: Why did she blame him for Marian's death?

Lost in the anguish and mystery of Marian's fate, he wallowed in a puddle of self-pity. The only remaining member of his family hated him.

Matt was in worse trouble than he'd thought.

The cat yowled and raced from the room.

Later, he'd discover the fate of his beloved Marian and his parents. Now he had to focus on the living—his daughter.

Okay, he'd identified one of the people he had wronged. But if he was to make it right, he needed to know how he'd wronged her. He'd died before her birth. Hell, he hadn't seen her before today. He hadn't even had a chance to disappoint her.

He studied Roxanne from among the flowers. This elegant woman with the angry brown eyes was his daughter. She was beautiful. She was tall, perhaps as tall as he had been. Her mother had been tall, too.

If he had a bit more . . . what should he call it? Energy? Power? Vitality? Hell, if he hadn't felt so weak, he'd explore the house. There had to be a picture of Marian around here somewhere.

Family portraits lined the upstairs halls. At least, they had when he'd called this place home.

The longer Roxanne had glowered at the box containing the remnants of his military career, the greater her animosity had grown until it burst in a mind-stunning tirade. She hated him. Now what was he going to do? He'd counted on his family's help in righting the wrongs that had consigned him to the Abyss of Nothingness. He now realized that he had no family, except for the daughter who wouldn't take the time to spit on his grave.

He retreated into the darkest corner of the dining room, wanting to put as much distance as possible between him and Roxanne. The anger and the hurt he had apparently caused chilled him as he realized the difficulty of the task ahead.

For the next couple of days Roxanne buried herself in work as a way of escaping the depressing events of the past week. Late Friday afternoon, she hung up the phone, then switched off the computer. A sense of satisfaction rinsed away the weariness weighting her bones. She and her staff at Magic Wish could finally close the book on the WMP Technologies project they'd struggled so hard to complete. They had finished it late Monday night. The film footage, animation, graphics and voice-over blended into a cutting-edge-of-technology video worthy of an academy award for special effects.

A satisfied smile she felt in her toes became a gleeful grin, then a laugh that echoed in her home office on the second floor of the Griffith house.

Walter Penworth was ecstatic with the videos she had delivered this past Tuesday before Spencer Griffith knocked on her door. The level of his satisfaction was translating into a sizable bonus check because she and her staff had designed and incorporated the special effects they had discussed a scant three weeks earlier. Even better, he had invited her to a showing of what was tantamount to an infomercial for WMP Technologies' twenty-fifth anniversary. Attending as Walter and Meredith Penworth's special guest for the premiere of the video was a rare opportunity in itself. The prime exposure virtually guaranteed new clients for Magic Wish.

She and her animation programmers had struggled to complete the additions on time. The tasks hadn't proven overwhelmingly difficult once they'd finished the design phase. The glitch had been her concentration. It had eluded her since Thelma had taken a sudden turn for the worse last month, then died ten days ago.

When Roxanne's mind wandered, she had resolutely brought it back to focus on the task at hand. However, each lapse had cost precious time.

At times, she doubted her ability to pull off the ambitious project. Occasionally, she'd assumed a dangerously cocky attitude. Either way, subtle changes were creeping into her daily routine since Thelma's death. She equated them to the creaks, groans, and odd noises the ninety-year-old house made at unexpected times. Until recently, she had never noticed the arthritic sounds. She was so accustomed to having her aunt's staff around that the sudden emptiness was almost overwhelming.

The last few days had put her on edge. Sometimes it seemed as though the very walls were lamenting Thelma's demise, as though they were watching. The eerie sensations increased by the hour. She was, after all, the last of the *real* Griffiths and the curator as well as the beneficiary of the old house and its relics.

The light of the spring day faded from the sky. Roxanne turned off the lamp, then closed the office door. Her eyes burned. Fifteen hours at the computer had taken a toll. Next week she'd move back to the Magic Wish offices. The need to run her business from her home no longer existed. She looked forward to resuming the day-to-day interaction with her employees.

Hunger growled in her stomach.

Strange how Thelma's rigid schedules, the result of all her medications and treatments, had died with her. How easily Roxanne reverted to the old work habits that had helped start Magic-Wish and build her reputation as a computer artist and animator.

She reached for the light switches on the way to the kitchen, then paused. The lights were already on. Had she left them on? She didn't think so, but as preoccupied as she'd been with Thelma's death, and everything else that had happened lately, she might not have turned them off from this morning. She shrugged off the memory lapse and headed into the kitchen.

At the stove she adjusted the gas flame beneath the teakettle, then gathered together the makings of her evening meal. Not until she saw Buster in the opposite doorway did she realize she'd avoided the dining room. Again. Even from here she smelled the floral arrangements clustered on the table.

Tomorrow she would get rid of the cut flowers in the dining

room and arrange to donate the plants to the children's wing at the hospital.

Then she recalled the box she'd been trying to pretend didn't exist. The box and her father were synonymous. Both made her uncomfortable.

"We'll take out the garbage tomorrow, Buster. Then we'll both rest easier."

The staccato ringing of the telephone made her jump.

Buster continued staring into the dining room with the sharp intensity he used when stalking prey or studying an encroaching predator.

Roxanne reached the phone before the third ring.

"We need to talk," Spencer Griffith said.

"Mr. Griffith?"

"Call me Spence?"

"Why? What do you want?" she asked slowly, adjusting to the shock of hearing his voice. She'd hoped—and feared—she'd heard the last of him.

"I'd like us to start from square one."

"I don't think that's possible."

"Why don't we just talk and decide later if we want to know each other?"

The memory of those deep blue eyes begged a refresher. "I suppose we could work something out." Her irritation at his reasons for seeking her out had ebbed over the last couple of days. Despite the startling news he'd dropped on her like an A-bomb, she did want to see him again. She glanced toward the dining room where the nefarious box resided amid the saccharine funeral flowers. "Besides, you forgot something the other day. If you don't come and get it, I'm going to use it as kindling."

"It's spring. It isn't cold enough for a fire."

"I'll turn down the air-conditioning, put on a sweater, and pretend it's winter."

"Roxanne . . . you may change your mind later. Don't do something you'll regret."

Buster darted across the kitchen and hid behind the island. The fan of whiskers on the left side of his face twitched around the corner.

"Do I burn the box, or do you come and get it?"

"Let's talk about it."

"I've wasted all the breath on Dear Old Dad I'm going to

waste. Talk if you like. I'll listen—as long as he's not the topic. Just give me a yes or no." The china teapot she took from the cupboard was a Griffith family heirloom. She used it out of defiance—and because there was no one left to stop her or chastise her actions.

"Let's get reacquainted face to face, and we won't discuss your father."

She poured boiling water into the teapot, and then pulled a quilted cozy over it to keep it hot while the tea steeped. "Are you asking me out on a date?"

"If I were, would you go?" When she didn't jump with a response, he added, "Say 'Yes, Spence, I'd love to go out with you.'"

His imitation of her voice made her smile. "It's tempting, but I don't date men I meet at funerals. That seems so . . . so foretelling of the relationship, don't you think?"

"Progress already. We have a relationship. See what talking can do?"

When she let the grin tugging at her escape, a layer of protective armor slipped away. She couldn't help liking him. Dangerous, very dangerous. Her grin faded a little with a reminder that he was calling for one reason only.

She drew a controlled breath and wrapped her hopeful heart in disappointment. Regardless of his smooth words and abundant charm, Spence wanted something she was incapable of giving. Her upbringing didn't allow her to denigrate her father; her conscience didn't allow her to praise him. She was not a player in Spencer Griffith's Memorial Day plans. "The only 'relationship' we have is grounded in the accident of ancestors sharing the same last name. That's it."

"Will you forgive yourself for passing up the opportunity to find out?"

"Which opportunity are you speaking of? A relationship or talking with you face to face?" The ache she'd long ago recognized as loneliness began throbbing. Maybe she ought to go out with him. She knew the score. What could it hurt?

"Yes."

"Yes?" she asked, feeling reckless enough to play his game. The tea mug she took from the cupboard dangled from her fingers. "Yes, what?"

"Yes, I want a talking face-to-face relationship with you."

She laughed aloud. Not only was the man sexy, he had a brain and a sense of humor. She doubted there was a more lethal combination. But he was a man with an agenda in which she had no intention of participating. Forgetting that little fact might help his cause, not hers. "We won't discuss *him*?"

"Only if and when you want to."

She caught the ghost of her reflection in the microwave oven door. She hadn't had a date in nearly three years. She straightened. It wasn't a date, just a meeting. "Okay."

"How about dinner tomorrow night?"

"Tomorrow is Saturday. Do you think I have no social life?" Manicure night followed by popcorn and a rented video.

"You name the time and place. I'll arrange my schedule to fit yours."

She jammed the phone into the crook of her shoulder and held it with her chin as she rummaged through the cupboards. "I'm immune to guilt trips."

"Defensive is what you are, Roxanne." His soft laugh sent ripples over her skin. "Besides, you haven't read the brochure on one of my guilt trips. The lamentations alone will buckle your knees and bring tears of acquiescence."

Laughing in spite of herself, Roxanne selected a can of soup and reached for the can opener. "Why do I believe you?"

"Because you're a smart lady and have no reason not to. Besides, I'm honest, trustworthy, and——"

"Prepared? Were you a Boy Scout, too?"

"An Eagle Scout."

"Really?" She opened the soup. She'd never dated a Boy Scout, let alone a bona fide Eagle Scout. During her dating years, she seemed to attract men of the octopus genus.

"Have dinner with me."

The seriousness in his tone gave her pause. "I'll compromise. Lunch. Tomorrow. The Acorn on Main Street. Twelve-thirty. Do you need directions?"

"I know where it is. I'll be there."

"Okay." She hung up and looked toward the dining room. When had she turned on the light in there? Talking with Spence had rattled her more than she thought.

Spence assessed the Acorn with a professional eye. The health-food menu catered to New Age vegetarians and yuppies who prized a variety of specialty coffees and herbal teas. It made good business sense. The profit margin on beverages was high. Undoubtedly emphasizing them ensured profitability and a secure future. The line at the To-Go tea and espresso counter constituted a gold mine. The aroma of strong, fresh coffee blended with the hiss of steaming milk for a latte.

Luke Cathcart had done well. Seldom did a man and a marketing niche fit together as well as Luke and the Acorn.

Watching Roxanne wind her way through the tables, Spence wondered if she would have chosen the Acorn had she known of his connection with the owner.

"I'll be with you in a minute," Roxanne said, wiping her hands on her stained dish towel apron. "Meanwhile, have a seat at the back table, and Mavis will get your drink order."

Roxanne's cheekbones were rosy, her eyes bright as she straightened her apron. The fragrance of a dozen tasty dishes mingled with the assorted coffee aromas and the relaxing hum of amiable conversations.

Seeing Roxanne in a kitchen apron surprised him. He hadn't expected her to work here. Hell, the little he knew about her suddenly took a crazy tilt. As he approached the back table, he began planning a strategy for unraveling the enigma of Ms. Roxanne Griffith.

The décor combined the hippie influence of the sixties with the New Age of the nineties. Enough plants to start a greenhouse hung from the ceiling. Sturdy wood tables and ladder-back chairs seemed part of the wood floor.

Spence found the back table, settled on a chair. A waitress found him right away and took his order for coffee.

"Hello, Spence."

The sound of his name brought him around in his chair. At the adjacent table sat Candice Cathcart, vice-president of marketing for Griffith Enterprises—his employee and a close friend for years. Sharing the table with Candice was the owner of the Acorn. The high cheekbones, blond hair, and wide-set eyes identified them as mother and son.

Candice gave him a mock salute. "This is a surprise."

"A pleasant one, I might add," chimed in Luke.

"Candice," he said, nodding acknowledgment. "Good to see you again, Luke."

"Luke invited me out for breakfast," Candice said with pride.

Luke stood, leaned over the table, and stuck out his hand.

After a few niceties Luke and Candice resumed their private conversation.

Roxanne slid onto the chair across from him. "It's going to be a few minutes. One of the volunteers just called in with bad news. Her child is sick and she can't come in today."

"Volunteers?" In a tight labor market Luke got people to work free?

"Yes. Saturday is mostly a volunteer staff. Cuts down on over-head and gives the regulars a little time off."

Spence glanced at Luke, then back at Roxanne. "You work all week, then work here for free on the weekends?"

"Not every weekend, and my time and effort go for a good cause."

"Which is?"

"The proceeds support the job training center next door. It's open to unwed mothers to help them build a future for themselves and their kids."

"I see," he said slowly. Luke had turned nonprofit for a cause. Spence caught Candice's amused expression, then gave Roxanne his complete attention. "You're a weekend hippie chef."

Roxanne leaned back, smiling. "More like a one-Saturday-a-month salad- and sandwich-making dishwasher. But that's about to change. It was one of the cooks who called in. They've asked if I'd stay through the noon rush."

"I see." And this time he did. "What did you tell them?"

"I, ah, said I had a commitment I didn't know if I could get out of."

"Good thing we're not on a date. Commitments like this can be flexible." The relief flowing over her features relaxed her shoulders and disappointed him. "Suppose I fill in for your chef?"

Surprise, then skepticism, narrowed her brown eyes. The woman's emotions were amazingly easy to read. If only she were that easy to persuade.

"Why would you do that? Why would you want to?"

"Hey, you're calling the shots. If this is the way it goes, then okay. I can cook and talk at the same time." Had he ever met such a guarded, suspicious woman before? He doubted it, then wondered what had made her that way.

"You don't know the menu. Can you even cook?"

"Please," he scoffed, studying the menu for a moment. "I grew up in a restaurant, starting in the kitchen. Remind me to invite you over to see my diploma sometime." He hoped she'd take him up on the offer. The prized parchment had a place under the memento boxes on the top, back shelf of his closet. Said closet was on the far side of his king-size bed, which would undoubtedly see some action if the volatile Ms. Griffith showed the slightest inclination.

"You can cook and you'd fill in for a few hours?" Amazement glowed so brightly in her golden brown eyes that he wouldn't dare disappoint her.

"Show me the way to the kitchen." He stood and caught Candice's blatant amusement at the situation.

Roxanne hesitated and remained seated. "Why?"

"Because I assume that's were the stove and food are located."

"That's not what I mean. Why are you willing to do this?"

He resumed his seat, leaned back, and folded his arms over his chest. "Why do you think I'd lend a hand, Roxanne? Maybe I'm doing it to curry favor with you. Maybe so you'll think I'm a nice guy and have dinner with me. And just maybe because it looks like the only chance I'll have to talk with you before starving to death is to cook in the same kitchen you're working in. Take your pick."

Roxanne stood without meeting his gaze, then bussed the table. "You better know how to cook."

Candice pushed away the meal Mavis had just served. "I'll have whatever he's cooking," she said loud enough for Spence to hear. "I don't care what it is."

"One rubber chicken coming up for the lady at table three," Spence said.

Roxanne remained unconvinced and sought the owner's approval. "Look, maybe Luke ought to—"

"Any day Spencer Griffith cooks in my kitchen, he can fix anything he likes. Besides, this is my morning off and my mom is here," Luke said without turning around. "Thanks, man. I'll take over anytime you want out."

"Sure. I have a weak spot for a man spending time with his mother." He took a surprised Roxanne's arm and escorted her through the swinging doors.

The kitchen was small for the number of people it had to accommodate but well set up for convenience and efficiency. It was perfect for his conversational plans.

• • •

Spence spent most of the afternoon in the kitchen. Several times he had Roxanne and the staff laughing so hard that they had trouble keeping the orders straight. By the time Luke kicked them out with a couple of mocha lattes as payment for their services, Roxanne was eager to get off her feet. She wasn't ready to leave Spence for the day, but she didn't want to invite him home. City Park across the street seemed the best place to sit in the relative quiet of a spring afternoon.

As she and Spence stepped off the curb, Roxanne contemplated the task ahead. Under most circumstances, making an apology turned her stomach into a knot of snakes. Consequently, she seldom allowed herself into the uncomfortable circumstances of having to do so. This time was different. She drew a clean breath and accompanied him into City Park.

"I apologize, Mr. Griffith. Today didn't turn out the way either of us planned. You've spent most of it in a hot kitchen. I feel as though we took advantage of your good nature and your culinary skills." Roxanne could feel her cheeks burning as Spence surveyed her with a cool eye.

"And you insist on addressing a man whose good nature has served you so well as Mr. Griffith? After this afternoon we've graduated to a first-name basis, Roxanne."

"Fair enough."

On the trees, spring leaves in countless hues and shapes stretched for sun. Sweet-smelling blossoms unfurled their splendor. At the center of the park a sturdy bench ringed an ancient oak with giant, outstretched arms.

"By the way, you don't need to apologize for anything."

She had to hand it to Spence. He was a hard worker, disgustingly cheerful in the face of chaos, and the best cook she'd ever encountered.

"In fact, I should thank you," he continued, steering her toward the round bench beneath the oak tree.

"For what?" She brushed leaves from the bench, then sat.

"It's been a long time since I did any real cooking outside the family kitchen. I'd forgotten how much I enjoyed it." He grinned at her, then added, "And how tiring it is." He opened the tab on the lid of his mocha latte, then breathed in the steamy coffee and chocolate aroma. "Tell me this is as good as it smells."

"It is," she promised, watching him from the corner of her eye. Quick sips of her own mocha reconfirmed her pronouncement.

She leaned back on the bench, stretched her legs in front of her, then toed off her shoes, and let her gaze roam their surroundings. Parents watched children play in the fenced kingdom of the brightly colored playground. The sound of Little Leaguers wafted across the baseball diamond.

"I love spring," she murmured. "It's the time of year when everything in the world gets another chance."

"Some people and things need a second chance worse than others. The trouble is, you can't tell if they're worth it until you take the risk and try it."

He didn't mention her father, but they both knew what he meant. "The dead don't get a second chance."

"What if we don't know if someone we love is dead or alive? He might be living year after year in some hellhole of an internment camp. We won't know for sure until we have definitive proof."

The strained quality in his voice revealed deep feelings for his brother and roused her curiosity. She tried redirecting the conversation. "Your brother must have been quite a bit older than you. Did you and he get along?" She didn't realize she'd asked the question aloud until he leaned against the tree beside her.

"Oh, yeah. He and my dad were my idols." Spence sipped the mocha, then gazed across the grass. "See the little kid and his father near the ball field?"

She looked where he pointed. A boy about five threw a ball to his father, who talked and laughed with him. Their body language spoke loud enough for Roxanne and Spence to understand what they couldn't hear. "The boy isn't very good at throwing the ball yet, is he?" Roxanne said slowly. "He needs more practice. Still, he seems very young."

"No. He's not very good but that's not the point. It's not about how well you throw the ball—it's about never being too young to do that with his dad, or his big brother."

"Guess not." Spence's stillness as he watched the father and son intrigued her. She studied him and wondered what was going through his mind. The way he watched the man touched something deep inside of her, something soft and dangerous, something she hadn't known existed. "Did your father play ball with you?"

"Yes. Dad was a natural athlete. He could have been a major leaguer. My big brother, Mitch, was even better. He went to college on a baseball scholarship." He continued watching the pair while sipping his coffee.

"Impressive. Bet you were proud of him." And idolized him.

"Yeah, but nowhere near as proud as Dad. When Mitch was reported MIA, it broke something inside Dad no one knew how to fix."

Curiosity to understand Spence's motives overrode her growing discomfort. "I can't imagine the anguish a parent would experience under those conditions." Nor did she want to.

He nodded once. "Me, neither. It would have broken his heart if any of us kids had turned up missing and he couldn't find us. But there was more to it with Mitch."

He looked straight at her for a moment before continuing. "My dad wanted to play pro baseball. He also wanted to marry my mother. The Lazzaros, my mother's family, didn't want her marrying a man with an uncertain livelihood. Dad never took his shot at the major leagues. Presented with a choice by the Lazarros, he walked away from baseball and married Mom. Three months before he finished college, Mitch was born. Theresa arrived five years later, Carolyn four years after Theresa. By the time I came on the scene, Mitch was in high school and Dad had raised the capital to open the first Christopher's."

"The one in San Francisco?" The near whisper of her voice kept the fragile mood of revelation intact.

"Seattle. I grew up going to the fish markets at four A.M. to pick seafood for the restaurant, and barter with produce brokers for the specialty items that eventually became our trademark. My first memories are of riding my dad's hip in the chill of the night and the smells and sounds of the fish markets."

"That's too bad." At least the things that stank about her childhood didn't have olfactory triggers.

"There's nothing bad about it." He shook his head slowly as his smile grew. "Those are some of my fondest memories. I still like the fish markets. They remind me of him. It was the one thing that was always about him and me—no one else came with us.

"Mitch hated the markets," he added. "Besides, during Mitch's high school years, there was an unspoken agreement about his future."

"I know about those," Roxanne murmured.

"In high school Mitch had two jobs—academics and baseball,

in that order. He loved both and excelled. He was supposed to live out the ambitions and dreams he and my father shared. Dad didn't want any of the glory or the accolades, just the chance to give his kid a shot at a dream he understood."

"Regrets, huh?" Of course, she chided herself. The man was re-living his life, the life he had never had, through his son.

"No. Dad never regretted his choice. He always said the smartest thing he ever did in his life was to marry my mother. Loving her, loving us, didn't mean he lost his love for baseball. On the contrary."

She was batting zero and growing nervous. Spence had complexities and depths she wanted to explore. "You speak of your father in the past tense."

"I think he started dying the day we got the news about Mitch. From then on, he never watched another pro baseball game. He coached my Little League teams, and when a memory struck him hard and his eyes teared up, no one said anything. We knew he was thinking about Mitch and tried even harder. We all wanted to please him. And God, but he was an easy man to please. All he wanted from any of us was to try our best at whatever we did. That's all. We didn't have to win, not at baseball, not scholarships, not at anything."

A sad twist of his mouth reminded her of a smile, but his eyes were distant.

"Funny thing is, Roxanne, we discovered the harder we tried, the better our best became, and the more we won. I've wanted to tell him that I understand now, but it's too late. He had a heart attack and died when I was sixteen."

For an instant she closed her eyes and imagined Spence as a preschooler learning how to play catch, then later as a Little Leaguer, and finally as a broken-hearted adolescent holding an empty ball glove.

Her breath caught in her throat with the realization she would have walked through fire to have had a father like Spence's.

He turned toward her, the sadness fading from his chiseled features. "Ever been to a Giants game?"

"No." As a child, she'd begged to go to Candlestick Park to watch a live ball game. She'd wanted to lose herself in the crowd and pretend she was part of a family that yelled and lamented for the action on the field. Now that she had the freedom and money to go, the prospect had lost its appeal. The days of pretending were long gone. "Are you a fan?"

"Not a very loyal one, I'm afraid. When I can make the time, I sit in the stands. Want to go to a game?"

"Do I have to learn how to catch a ball first?"

"No, but it wouldn't hurt. I'll teach you. It'll give you a big appreciation factor." He grinned at her, his left eyebrow raised in question. "How do I let you drag me off on these tangents?"

"What tangents?" She swirled the last of her mocha in its covered cup, then finished it.

"I'd like to tell you about the Remembrance Foundation and how we search for our MIA soldiers in Vietnam."

She'd already heard more than she wanted to about MIAs. The families had her sympathy. She couldn't imagine the agonies of not knowing the fate of someone she loved year after year. The key word was *loved* and not applicable to her situation. "Not interested."

"You ought to be. From the sound of it, the results we achieved have messed up your life this week."

"Not mine. It was messed up long before you darkened my door." She met his steady gaze with determination. Spence would not steamroll or guilt-trip her into anything. Especially not where her father was concerned. The bitterness she harbored had heightened during Thelma's illness. "You said we wouldn't talk about him," Roxanne warned.

"We won't," he assured her. "I guess everything happens for a reason, Roxanne. Before this is over, maybe we'll discover the reason you wound up with something you didn't want. My family would give a great deal to have the kind of closure you have. That's why we help finance it. Why I go to Vietnam every year for the Remembrance Foundation and meet with the officials in Hanoi. Why it's important we get the right kind of publicity and public support. It's not just for us. Far from it. There are hundreds of families who will never know what happened to their husbands, fathers, brothers, or sons they loved."

"You can't miss what you've never known, Spence. I was better off with him in Vietnam. Regardless of what happened to him, I knew they'd save a seat for him in hell." Ready to end the conversation, she stepped into her shoes, stood, and took his cup. The garbage can was almost full when she stuffed the two cups inside.

Spence glared at her from the bench. "You're the one who mentioned your father, so tell me, how you can be so sure?"

She stopped in her tracks halfway between him and the trash-can. "Excuse me?"

"If the dates I have are right, you've never met the man." The blue in his eyes darkened with emotion.

"There is a God. I was spared being in the same room as he." She closed the distance between them. Anger welled from her toes. "Look, right now, you want me to like my father. I don't. I never have. I never will. The wherefore and why is my business. So just deal with the disappointment, Spence."

His eyes narrowed. His gaze felt like blue lasers boring into her. "Forget I asked why you dislike a man you've never met. And the disappointment of your rejecting him isn't mine alone. Unfortunately, your decision affects a lot of people."

"Ah, now we're getting to the heart of it. This isn't about my father or me. We're speaking about what *you* want—your precious Memorial Day ceremony. Sorry, Spence, but I'm not part of your agenda. If you and the Remembrance Foundation want to play honor guard to a man who had none, that's your choice. Don't expect me to show up."

"You made that connection, not me, Roxanne."

"No one asked you to find Captain Matthew Griffith. No one wanted him found."

"I don't believe that." He rose from the bench and towered over her. Whatever was going on in his head remained cloistered behind his stony expression.

"I'm all that's left of the Griffith family. *I* didn't want him found. Instead of criticizing my ingratitude for your altruistic efforts, you ought to be apologizing for the chaos and unhappy memories you've dredged up in my life. The door swings two ways—whether you want to acknowledge it or not." She hoped he'd see her point.

Spence, however, was unyielding. "Maybe if you looked at what's on the other side of the door, you'd get a different perspective."

Irritated, disappointed the upbeat mood of the day had deteriorated, she turned away. "Why are we even having this conversation? Why am I even talking to you? Obviously we have nothing in common."

"That's your solution? Write it off and walk away?" He caught her shoulder.

"I wasn't the one who walked away. I was the only one who stayed," she answered in a soft voice that helped keep a lid on her growing anger.

"Help me understand this, Roxanne. To me, family is damn near everything." The confusion creeping into his eyes leaked into his voice.

"And your point is?"

"Doesn't your family mean anything to you?"

"More than you'll ever know, Spence. Maybe you had a Donna Reed or Brady Bunch family. I didn't. That doesn't mean I didn't want it, it just means—" She hesitated. An explanation required dragging the past into the light of day, exposing it to a veritable stranger. "It means we don't always get what we want. It means you had no right to invade my life. No right to foist your needs, your pursuits, your . . . whatever, upon me and expect me to just gratefully buy into them.

"You don't know me. How dare you lay this at my door, then sit in judgment when I don't conform to your expectations."

"You're reading a helluva lot into what I've said. No one is judging you, except maybe you."

She brushed his hand away and squared her shoulders. Even dead, her father managed to remind her that she wasn't welcome in the Griffith family. *Family* implied caring. Love. Support. He had been the center of the Griffith universe, and now they were all dead and he was back.

Until this afternoon she hadn't known she possessed so much anger. Where had it come from?

"In a fair world, your brother would have come back instead of . . . him."

"In a fair world, neither of them would have gone to Vietnam," Spence said softly.

The sounds and smells of the park tempered the frustration grating her nerves. Being in public required manners, decorum, and civility. She assumed the polite mask perfected in childhood with the ease of donning an old sweatshirt. "Thank you for helping out at the Acorn."

"Where are you going?" Two steps brought him beside her.

"Home." She drew a deep breath. Under other circumstances, she might invest the time in knowing Spencer Griffith. But their differences were too vast.

"Why don't you let me drive you home? Your feet must be screaming."

For reasons she couldn't fathom, she had hoped for more than a dead-end with Spence. A pragmatist, she knew better than to try to change the man's perceptions of her. The last thing she needed was kindness or consideration from him. Besides, her newfound anger needed exploration. "I'd prefer walking."

"Then I'll walk with you."

"What about your car?"

"What about it? It won't start without me." He caught her shoulder and forced her to look at him. "I didn't intend to anger you, Roxanne. The least I can do is make sure you get home safely."

Obligation. She recognized it immediately. "I don't suppose I can stop you."

"No. You can't."

# Chapter Four

The longer Matt resided in his ancestral home, the stronger he became. Gaining power and substance here seemed a righteous thing. It was the one place where he gave love as well as received it. Home was where he'd known his greatest joys and sorrows. Ironically, he finally understood Scarlett O'Hara's affinity for Tara. He had the same affection for the two-story Victorian he'd secretly dubbed Griffith Gables.

Soon. Very soon, he'd have the strength to reveal himself to his daughter.

However, each time he contemplated the words to win her over, he faded into nothingness.

The term *coward* had never applied to him while alive. Dead, he didn't have the time or ability to delude himself. When it came to facing his daughter and her daunting hatred, his ectoplasm took on a definite canary yellow hue.

Try as he might, the old bravado, the daredevil who tempted fate until it crushed him in death, remained elusive. Hell, it wasn't just elusive; it was gone with a capital G.

Eternity in the Abyss of Nothingness was a definite unless he found a way to change Roxanne's loathing to love. Maybe love was stretching it. He might have to settle for amity. "Okay. Tolerance," he conceded to the cat stalking him from the kitchen doorway.

Matt tested his strength.

Every light in the house came on.

He was ready to take Roxanne on, too, except for the words. What did a man say to the daughter who blamed and hated him with a fervor as natural as breathing?

Strange how the physical emotions lingered after death. He could have sworn his heart skipped a beat, then started hammering like a bass drum when he felt Roxanne on the front porch.

She wasn't alone.

He had a reprieve.

Of course each reprieve, each delay, ate the precious minutes allotted to complete his tasks. And he still had not started looking for the other person whose forgiveness he needed. Whenever he considered turning his back on the momentous ordeals ahead of him, he thought of eternity in the Abyss. The price of avoidance was much too high and a bad bargain to boot. Matt took another egocentric step forward. Today he'd face his daughter whether either of them was ready.

The walk along sun-dappled sidewalks mellowed Roxanne. Spence asked about the homes they passed. For those she knew nothing about, he concocted humorous vignettes that made her laugh in spite of her ire.

When they crossed intersections, the glide of his hand across her shoulder blades turned the cool evening breeze into an inferno.

"How about a truce?" he asked halfway down the Griffith driveway.

"If I had a white flag, I'd wave it." Harboring anger around a cheerful, optimistic Spence bordered impossible.

"In that case, how about attending an old friend's party with me tomorrow evening?" Spence released her arm when they reached the front door.

Surprised he wanted to see her again after her outburst in the park, her defenses rose. However, for reasons even she didn't quite understand, she tempered the protest dancing on the tip of her tongue. "Have you discovered some common ground for us to explore?"

"The question isn't resolved, and won't be unless you go out with me. Besides, what can it hurt?"

"Sorry. I'm working tomorrow night." To her even greater surprise, she was sorry she couldn't see him.

"Is your schedule inflexible? Or is this your way of telling me I'm out of my mind for asking?"

The notion of changing anything about tomorrow night was ludicrous. In some ways, Walter and Meredith's anniversary party for WMP Technologies was a bigger night for her than for them. The exposure for Magic Wish alone was an opportunity too good to pass up for any reason. "Totally inflexible," she confirmed.

"Too bad. Meanwhile, think about having dinner with me next week, okay?"

She'd say no, but she knew she'd think about it. If she wasn't careful, she'd probably even talk herself into accepting the dinner invitation. In some ways, Spencer Griffith was a fantasy come true, complete with a sense of humor and the ability to cook any dish imaginable. He was also a very charming man with an agenda.

"I will." She paused and keyed in the alarm code before unlocking the door.

"Good. I know some great places for dinner."

"Spence," she said, turning against the door to face him. "You were a real sport today. I'm sure this wasn't how you'd planned to spend your Saturday. Would you like to come in for coffee or something?" Even as the words flowed, she hardly believed they came from her mouth.

A slow smile tempering the sharp angles of his face put a dangerous glint in his eyes and spoke his preference for the "or something" part of the menu.

"To drink," she added. Gad, but she was slow on the uptake. Playing Florence Nightingale and running a business on the side must have dulled her social skills.

"If that's your idea of a peace offering, I'll take a risk and go with the 'or something' right here."

Before she realized his intent, he captured her in the muscular prison of his arms. Through the mixture of aromas lingering on him from the Acorn, she caught the faint trace of his aftershave. Like a mountain bathed in the summer sun, he was solid angles and planes. Gingerly she relaxed into him, testing the delicious sparks awakening in her body, then savoring the glow.

Her gaze caught on his slightly parted lips. It surprised her that she wanted him to kiss her, wanted to discover if he tasted as good as he smelled. Her mind tumbled through the cobwebs of desire and climbed to a new, exciting plateau.

At the moment Roxanne wasn't sure who was seducing whom, nor did she care. His growing erection against her belly left no doubt that the desire was mutual. After three dateless years, her starving hormones wanted to feast on Spence.

"Aren't you rushing this part of the face-to-face relationship a bit?" The breathiness of her voice betrayed the desire yawning to wakefulness with a ravenous hunger. Yet as she reluctantly lifted her gaze from his tantalizing lips, and across the sharp planes of his cheekbones to his deep, blue eyes, she knew what he aroused in her was far more than mere sexual appetite.

"Am I rushing you?" His head lowered a fraction. The brush of his lips over hers weakened her knees. His mouth seemed hard and soft simultaneously. Impossible, she silently rationalized, then conceded that all sense of logic seemed to have left her.

"I've wanted to do this all day. Consider it another form of face-to-face communication," he whispered, lightly brushing her mouth with his again. Every nerve in her body jumped to life when his hand explored the length of her spine. Pure feminine instinct pressed her against him. Her belly felt afire where his erection pulsed on what she was sure was the wrong side of their clothing.

"Communicate with me," she challenged in a whisper. Rising on tiptoes, her head tilted slightly, she found the reward of his mouth. Her arms twined around his neck. Holding on to him kept her from crumpling or floating away; she wasn't sure which would happen if she let go. Her lips parted, yielding to the touch of his tongue. The carefully hidden sensual side of her she'd kept tucked away burst from its shackles into silver-white flames of need. Her breath caught in her throat. Fresh desire shivered over her skin.

The growl he unleashed into her mouth seemed to rise from his toes. She felt it reverberating up his thighs, and in the prod of his erection against her belly. The vibration climbed his chest, trembling against her sensitive breasts, continuing upward until it tingled against her lips. It made her crazy. Her arms tightened, drawing her breasts against his chest hard enough for her thundering heartbeat to synchronize with his.

The world ceased to exist while they tasted, explored, and feasted on each other's mouths. His entire body felt like molten steel, pouring over her, permeating her skin, and reaching into her heart. A sense of rightness pervaded the awesome excitement rippling through her and colored her passion a shiny gold.

The pressure of his hand riding up her hipbone, dipping into the valley of her waist, then sliding along her ribs made her whimper in anticipation. Silently she begged him to continue. With an ache foreign to anything she'd experienced, she craved the smallest intimacy he might bestow.

His hand stopped just below her tingling breast. His fingers flexed as though hungry to close around her tender flesh, to titillate and excite them both until Roxanne lost the last thread of reason she possessed.

He broke the kiss and whispered her name. The tenderness of it pierced her heart like a needle. Dazed, she blinked several times, then looked up into his puzzled blue eyes. When he released her, she reluctantly loosened her hold around his neck and knees shaking, leaned away from him.

He swore so softly that she didn't understand what he said. She stared into his eyes and wondered what had happened and why it wasn't still happening.

The feather brush of his fingertips over her cheek burned like a brand.

"See, we do have something in common. Think about dinner with me. I'll call you," he said in a cracking voice. "Soon."

Her fingers rose to touch the phantom fire on her cheek. Speechless, she watched him traverse the walk and yard, then the sidewalk on the way back to his car. She waited for him to glance over his shoulder, but he continued looking straight ahead. She suspected he was the kind of man who didn't look back. Heaven help the woman who ever wanted him to do so.

She was still light-headed when she entered the house. Lost in a maelstrom of sensual promise, she leaned against the closed door for support and absently flicked the deadbolt.

She might have dinner with Spence. The concession sent another wave of desire through her. From the way he kissed her, his idea of dessert just might be the hottest sex she'd had in years. Then, she hadn't had any sex in years. And she'd never experienced a kiss loaded with such volatility.

She tried to shake off the erotic image of undressing Spencer

Griffith. It wasn't easy. Overstressed hormones did strange things to the mind.

"You are on the edge of making the biggest mistake of your life!"

She agreed, until she realized she hadn't spoken those words.

Her eyes flew open wide. All her sexual fantasizing about Spencer Griffith became so much steam roiling from a soup pot.

Buster screeched and raced from the dining room and across the foyer. His claws scraped over the highly polished oak floor as he started his turn down the hall. When he hit the entry rug, he tumbled head over tail, scrambled to his feet, then raced down the hall.

Roxanne straightened and instantly felt the bite of the hand-carved door along her spine. Her heart lunged into high acceleration of another kind. For a fraction of a second, she thought the voice originated from a new form of conscience. Pressed against the door, not moving anything but her eyes, she frantically searched for the source of the booming proclamation.

Then the house lights turned on with a blaze. Radios and televisions blared. Just as abruptly the lights winked out and the ensuing silence echoed the cacophony.

Light and sound burst through the house again.

A few seconds later blessed silence settled in the twilight shadows of the corners and hallways.

All Roxanne could think was: Run.

She turned and fumbled with the deadbolt. It was stuck. Using both hands, she tried it again. The bolt remained frozen. It may as well have been welded shut.

Realizing the futility of her action, more desperate by the second to escape the unknown terror in the house, her gaze darted toward the dining room. The back door was on the far side of the kitchen. Frantic, she scoured the parlor on her right. The French doors may as well have been in France. The hall turned twice before leading to the outside. Ahead, the stairs led to entrapment on the second floor.

"Roxanne."

Wild-eyed, she searched for the intruder. How had he gotten inside without tripping the alarm? How did he know her name? Oh, God, a stalker maniac!

"Wh-what do you want?"

"Your friendship. Your . . . compassion."

*Spence, please come back. Please. Please. Please! Come back.*

"Wh-why?" If she broke a window the security company . . . She hadn't turned the alarm on. Maybe if she sidled close to the panel, then carefully activated . . .

"You look like you want to run. Don't bother."

The stairs lost their solidity. The risers shimmered in the center. The rich blue carpet running up the center changed to a sickly green, then became a splotch of mustard.

Any second Roxanne's heart was going to batter its way out of her chest and flee. She couldn't catch her breath. The final bit of starch melted from her legs. She sank to the floor, her terrified gaze glued to the anomaly on the stairs.

Matt had no idea where the sudden, potent sense of outrage came from when he witnessed Roxanne's irresponsible behavior on the front porch. He wasn't a prude. Far from it. The powers on high had already reminded him of the *ways, wheres,* and *whens* he'd sown his wild oats.

The early seventies had been a time of free love and flower power. Not until he'd reached Vietnam had he realized love was never free, not if you wanted it to last. The only power the flower or the weed offered was temporary oblivion. When the smoke cleared, flat-footed reality waited.

Seeing his daughter cowering against the door, Matt suspected he'd blown his best chance of winning her over. He shouldn't have lashed out at her. There were no second chances for a first impression.

So much for the carefully planned father-daughter chat to build their relationship. Maybe if he calmed her down a bit, she'd be more receptive. "Nothing is going to hurt you, Roxanne."

The horror in her eyes and the ashen pallor of her skin screamed her disbelief.

"Thelma?" she croaked.

"Thelma?" Was she kidding? "No. It's me. Your father."

Everything about her became as still as death.

He started away from the staircase, then hesitated.

"You—you're *his* ghost?" The lack of color in her face made her appear more *ghostly* than he felt.

"Yes. I had to come home."

She recoiled as though he'd slapped her and his spirits plummeted. "Really."

"Yes, really. How else could I get to know my daughter?"

"Why?"

"Aren't you glad to see your long-lost, lovable father?" He gave her his most winsome smile. "To know me is to love me." At least, it had seemed that way when he was alive.

In the heavy silence mounting between them the parlor clock chimed the half hour. Roxanne didn't even blink, but he sensed a change in her.

When the chimes faded into the walls and quiet reigned, she spoke in a chilled voice so controlled that Matt recoiled against the staircase. "You're real? Really come back to . . ." Her voice faded before she finished the question.

"Real as that damn cat stalking me since I came home." Just to prove it, he flexed his power with the electrical system. The lights flashed on and off. Televisions and radios blared. "Are you convinced I've returned?"

"I'd hoped I was hallucinating." As anger supplanted her fearful astonishment, hate slipped back into her eyes.

"We have a lot of years apart to make up."

"What do you mean?"

This was his opportunity to win her over. He'd appeal to her rationally, like an adult, which she was. Hell, she'd already outlived him. "We've got a second chance to know each other."

"I don't want to know you." Her eyes narrowed to angry slits. "Not in this lifetime, and God willing, not in the next, either," she whispered. "Go away."

She was a tough nut to crack, but she had to give him a shot. "Don't cop out on me here, Roxy."

The only sign of life was a slight tic around her left eye. "My mother named me Roxanne, not Roxy or Rox." Her chin lifted in defiance.

He should have realized her preference. After all, she was her mother's daughter. Marian had never used nicknames. From their first meeting, she had called him Matthew.

"Roxanne," he corrected with as much contrition as he could muster. "The truth is, I've got a little problem here. I've come home so you can help me out."

"Help you out?" she asked incredulously. "I can think of no reason why I'd help you unless, of course, it means you get sent back to wherever you came from. My money's on hell."

The element of surprise turned out to be sorely overrated. Hesitant to provide fuel for her anger, Matt kept his distance and settled on the stairs. "Have you no tenderness? No family loyalty? No respect for your father?"

A laugh born of stubborn bravado cut through the foyer. "Now—when you won't even do me the courtesy of staying dead—now when you want something, *now* you're my father?"

"Didn't your mother bring you up to respect your parents? Your elders?"

"My mother died while acting like a servant for your parents. Respect? How dare a Griffith speak to me of respect! Particularly where you're involved. Respect is earned. All you've earned is my antipathy. Contempt. Denial—the same legacies you left for me and my mother." She pushed to her feet, her hands clenched in white-knuckled fists. "This is my house now. You are no more welcome here than my mother and I were when we first came here. *Before* I was born."

Defiance darkened her eyes and ruffled his patience. He had no idea what had happened between Marian and his family. All he knew was the twisting anguish of their absence, particularly Marian's.

Conflict between Marian and his parents was incomprehensible. Judging by Roxanne's command of the house and her environment, her home life couldn't have been too bad. She'd grown up as a Griffith. As such, the family had supported her, just as they would have supported his wife.

Okay, so maybe he hadn't been the best husband.

And he'd died before he had the opportunity to screw up fatherhood.

However, given Roxanne's attitude toward him, someone had managed to paint a dismal picture of him. He wanted to blame Marian, but he couldn't lie to himself. Marian never said an unkind word about anyone. Considering what he had at stake in the afterlife, he had to make the best of the situation. "I can't leave, Roxanne. Not yet."

"Sure you can. Go out the front door, turn left, and keep going. I don't care where, just so it isn't here."

The force of her animosity overrode her fear and sapped his strength. Dismayed, he realized he was more at her mercy than he'd suspected. The trouble was, he doubted Roxanne had any mercy where he was concerned.

"Why do you hate me so?"

She took a step toward him, her eyes blazing and fixed. "You've earned my loathing. You think any kid wants to be born in a house where everyone hates her and her mother?"

"They didn't hate you." They couldn't have hated his child. His parents hating sweet Marian? Absurd. The notion of them doing anything but doting on their grandchild was incredible. Yet, even as he spoke the denial, the very air around him heated with objection. The fragile place in which he dwelled allowed no illusion, no falsehood of any kind. Even so, he couldn't imagine his parents estranged from Marian. Sweet Marian? Never. The judgmental vixen their daughter had grown up to be . . . possibly.

"Like hell they didn't hate us. You made sure they would before you left. You did a good job. *Daddy*."

The final address scratched like cat claws on his soul. No, Roxanne wasn't anything like Marian. Their daughter's eyes held no tears, just anger and something he couldn't put his finger on. Softhearted Marian could never stay angry with him; she'd never been able to hold a grudge. Her weakness was also her greatest strength. Harming Marian in any way was the equivalent of beating up Bambi in front of a kindergarten class.

"You inherited your mother's beauty, but you didn't get her heart or her gentle temperament."

Roxanne smiled a chilling smile. The early-evening light streamed through the dining room and parlor windows and leaked into the foyer. It caught in her eyes and turned them into hard chips of obsidian. "That's right. So take it to the bank, you'll never get anything from *me*. Leave."

"I can't."

"You can't stay."

"I don't have a choice."

"We've covered this ground before." She took another step forward.

"I won't be here long, if you help me."

She folded her arms beneath her breasts. "Does it freeze in hell?"

He didn't know, though he suspected freezing in hell was better than disintegrating in the Abyss of Nothingness for eternity. His energy depleted, he slunk toward the dining room. "We'll talk again. Later."

Roxanne stared at the stairs as they solidified. He was gone. For now. She would neither call out nor look for him. The totality of his absence made her think twice about whether he'd actually been there or was simply a figment of her imagination.

Time lost all meaning. She continued staring at the spot where her father's shimmering essence had appeared until dusk had faded the foyer into total darkness.

When the numbness ebbed, she again questioned whether she'd seen what she thought she saw, heard what she thought she'd heard. Years of self-reliance had molded a perversity into her character that rose to the occasion whenever circumstance backed her into a corner.

All forms of doubt dissolved.

Matthew Griffith's ghost was real. He was here.

"Get out of my house, Matthew Griffith. You don't live here anymore." Fists clenched, chin lifted, her voice gained strength. "Go back to hell and stay there. You'll get nothing from me."

When the echo died from the stairwell and halls, an oppressive silence thickened the air.

"The box," she whispered. He'd come with the box Spence brought.

A blazing fire would put an end to the box, Matthew Griffith, and Spence's grandiose plans.

Roxanne whirled on her heel and stormed to the heart of the problem.

The crystal chandeliers blazed over the flower-covered dining table. The ugly cardboard box with its tattered flaps stood out against the highly polished table and floral arrangements.

She grabbed the carton and carried it into the parlor. Carefully arranged wood and kindling filled the fireplace. Roxanne opened the glass doors, crammed the box on top of the logs, and then turned the key on the gas starter. Left-handed, she opened the flue. Right-handed, she flicked the starting lighter, then touched the flame to the gas.

With a whoosh, flames filled the fireplace. She closed the glass doors as the flames leaped around the cardboard.

Satisfied, she headed for the front door picking up her purse from the floor and a jacket from the closet beside the door on her way out. She didn't bother setting the alarm or locking the door. It no longer mattered if the house or contents were secure. The enemy resided within. Again.

She scooped Buster off the front porch. "Let's get out of here."

The cat remained in her arms until they reached the garage. To Buster, a trip in the car meant a visit to the vet. He squirmed free and took off into the night.

"Stay out of the house," she whispered, suspecting he would. She backed the car out of the garage, turned it around, and headed for the street.

She always thought clearer at the beach house. The vastness of the ocean helped her find perspective.

Hovering against the ceiling in the foyer, Matt watched Roxanne thunder out of the house. It took the last of his waning strength to turn off the gas log and quell the flames in the fireplace. He didn't care if she was pissed. She wasn't going to burn what little remained of his past.

Obviously, confronting Roxanne head-on hadn't been a good idea. All he'd won was her defiant animosity. He wouldn't make the same mistake again.

He pondered what it would take to win her over, what would turn her emotions from hate to love. Obviously, he couldn't order her to love him. Even so, love seemed the wisest course. Marian had told him it was possible to love someone she neither liked nor respected; after all, she had loved him. In the same breath, she'd told him she needed her head examined, too. Although teasing, Marian had spoken the truth. He wondered if she'd have found any satisfaction in him finally listening.

Then, that was straight-laced, striving-to-be-better-today-than-yesterday Marian.

He shrank into the corner of the dining room. Gazing at the flowers standing like centurions for the dead, the table reminded him of something else Marian had said when her grandmother had died. He had wanted to send a roomful of flowers. Marian had not allowed it, stating that death should at least be honest. The most important person at a funeral was the only one to whom flowers didn't matter.

"Flowers and guilt," he murmured. How had Marian been so wise about so many things at such an early age? When she'd married him on her twentieth birthday, she hadn't seemed young. His twenty-five years hadn't seemed old then, either. Had he known how little time he had left, he might have done things differently.

The bite of selfishness forced him to look at the past with a more objective and somewhat disciplined eye. When he did, he acknowledged that he wouldn't have changed anything. He'd betray Greg, his best friend, all over again. And he'd still trade his very soul to have married Marian. He'd wanted her with an unreasonable intensity. Marriage was the only way he could have her, so they had eloped to Reno and kept the marriage a secret. God, but it had been sweet. Exciting. Dangerous the times when they almost were caught making love in this house. Exhilarating, that's what it had been. Making love with Marian was the hottest sex and most soul-stirring emotion of his life.

The secrecy had lasted until Uncle Sam called his draft number and Marian turned up pregnant on his parents' front porch while he was in boot camp.

The shrill ringing of the phone sounded twice before the black box in the kitchen answered it.

The voice emanating from the machine belonged to the man who had kissed Roxanne on the porch.

Matt hovered over the machine and listened intently. It was possible, just possible he had an ally in this man. It was a good thing, too. He needed all the help he could get with Roxanne. He conceded he didn't know where to start mending fences or building bridges. Nor did he have much time in which to forge a relationship.

The answering machine clicked at the end of the caller's message.

Then silence filled the house. Not even a floorboard or attic joist creaked.

Spence hung up the phone and glanced at his watch. Nearly ten o'clock. It had been a full day. Perhaps Roxanne had gone to bed.

He settled behind his desk in the dimly lit office above Christopher's, turned the chair, and stared into the fog hugging San Francisco Bay. Downstairs, the Saturday-night crowd lingered. The post-theater deluge was due in a half hour. Once they were seated, he'd make his final rounds of the tables for the night.

He leaned back in the oversize leather chair and balanced his crossed ankles on the corner of the dark oak desk. Eyes closed, he thought about kissing Roxanne Griffith again.

She'd incinerated his soul.

Not since high school had he wanted a woman so badly or revealed his desire so quickly. The responses of her body had become a lure he had damn near followed over the edge. If he'd stayed on the porch with her a moment longer, he'd have kissed her again, then taken her so hard and fast she wouldn't have known what happened until they finished.

What a mess.

Things were coming unraveled. More precisely, he was unraveling.

He needed her on the podium on Memorial Day—patriotic and full of praise for the civilian efforts responsible for her father's return. How was he going to get Roxanne behind a microphone and making a speech for national and local television networks?

Six months earlier Spence had been angry when he learned the remains belonged to another family named Griffith. Upon reflection, he had no one to blame for his disappointment except himself. He should have known it wasn't his brother. According to others in his brother's squadron, Captain Mitchell Maguire Griffith never wore his dog tags in the cockpit. He took nothing of a personal nature on a mission. Family was separate from war. He hadn't wanted one to touch the other.

Politically, the search for MIAs was more sensitive than a festering boil on the rumps of both governments. The chances of the Remembrance Foundation continuing their search for MIAs rested precariously on the political whims of the countries involved.

Like motherhood and apple pie, everyone agreed with the theory that the families of servicemen should know the fate of their sons, fathers, husbands, and brothers. But no one wanted to finance the search. No one really wanted to do what was necessary. So the task had fallen on civilian shoulders supporting the Remembrance Foundation.

Roxanne didn't want to understand.

Clearly, she wanted no reminders of her father or the war in which he'd lost his life.

Her rejection rankled, but he had to find a way to change her mind. There was too much at stake for too many people to indulge her. He needed her Memorial Day.

Hell, the way his body throbbed, he needed her right now for a more personal, intimate reason. Today, he'd caught a glimpse of a very different Roxanne Griffith. This woman had made time to help and expected nothing in return. She'd given something she obviously considered more valuable than money—her time. Her zealous protection of the Acorn and the projects its profits funded bordered on fanatic. Roxanne Griffith knew how to make a commitment, then stand firm. If he weren't very careful, he'd fall in love with the stubborn woman he'd spent half the day working with in a hot kitchen. Then what?

"I need her at the podium Memorial Day, not more complications," he murmured, rubbing his temples. But he'd take the complications if Roxanne was part of the package.

A knock on the office door summoned him into the present. "Come," he called.

Dressed in a sleek black evening suit with a diamond and ruby peace sign on the satin lapel, Candice Cathcart entered the office and closed the door behind her. A fashionable diamond comb accentuated her blond chignon. Simple two-carat diamond studs adorned her earlobes. The picture of sophisticated elegance contrasted sharply with the mom in a jersey jacket and jeans sharing a table with her son at the Acorn earlier today.

"You look like you've had a rough day, Spence. Too hot for you in the kitchen?" Her smile alone commanded attention in a crowded room.

"Actually, I enjoyed it." He dropped his feet onto the floor. "Long day for you, too."

"Yeah, but worth it." She settled into the nearer of the two leather seats on the opposite side of the desk. "My boss cooked brunch in my son's restaurant and delighted the patrons. And yesterday evening over dinner I closed a deal to furnish Christopher's Frozen Desserts to an international hotel chain. The mere thought of my bonus makes me want to dance."

"Busy day is right," he complimented with a smile. Candice had a way of pulling those around her into her perpetual upbeat mood. "You closed the deal fast, Candice. Are you going to hit me up for a raise now?"

"The time to do that was before I got the signatures on the contract. This one is a done deal." She crossed her long, shapely legs and leaned back. At fifty-three, Candice defied time by looking twenty years younger without benefit of plastic surgery. She attributed her youthful appearance to choosing parents whose genetics helped them age well. "Actually I stopped by to see you because my curiosity was burning a hole in my composure."

Spence regarded his old friend for a long moment before shaking his head. "Lucky for you and Luke that Roxanne picked the time and the place. I just showed up. The only way I was going to talk to her was to put on an apron and pick up a soup spoon." He winked at her. "Have a good day with your kid, Candice?"

Candice laughed aloud. "Marvelous. Thank you very much."

"You looked as at home with the New Age hippie set as you do schmoozing a Nob Hill cocktail party."

"Thanks. All part of the fine art of survival for the single mother." She examined the diamond cluster on her right ring finger. "I know how to adapt. I've kept my hip-hugger big bell-bottoms, beads, and mood rings."

"I'd suspected you had spent a little time in Golden Gate Park during the Seventies but I had no idea you were a full-fledged member of the hippie movement."

"Ex-hippie. Correction: former hippie. I guess it's a mind-set, sort of like being in the Marines, but with a very different outlook." Candice laughed softly. A distant memory twinkled in her eyes. "Everyone was someone else at twenty-one. Even you, Spence, though I doubt you've ever possessed the ability to be a hippie. Basically, you're too straight-laced and responsibility-oriented,"

"I'll take that as a compliment."

"Only you would. So tell me about you and Roxanne the Ice Queen."

"Ice Queen?" He recoiled, disliking the label slapped on Roxanne.

"That's how the Acorn staff refers to her—to her face, Spence. To her face." Candice's hand rose in a gesture for him to stay seated.

"Why?" Christ, the woman could melt the Antarctic with a kiss. There was nothing remotely cool about her in the clinches.

"I doubt few people, other than Luke, could tell you how she got the name. I never asked. I suspected it was because she seldom dated. Luke says she's been volunteering a Saturday morning a month since her senior year in college, which was when he opened the place."

Spence stood and walked to the window, shoving his hands into the front pockets of the tuxedo he wore when he mingled with the restaurant patrons. "I need her on Memorial Day."

"Oh, that explains everything. The way you watched her, I'd have put my money on you needing her long before then."

"You're a crass broad, Candice."

"So what? I'm a helluva saleswoman. And I'm glad you recognize my sterling qualities," she teased. "Don't try to sidetrack me, Spence. You were talking about Memorial Day. There isn't a problem, is there?"

He drew a heavy breath, then let it out. "Afraid so. She doesn't want anything to do with her father or us."

"She doesn't even want to attend?" Incredulity faded her words.

After a long moment of silence, Candice rose and came to stand beside him. Together they watched the fog consume the coastal lights.

"I know what this means to you, Spence. To the family. You'll find a way to change her mind. You're the most persuasive man I know." She nudged him. "Even if you are a bit conservative."

Candice had never lied to him. He wanted to believe her now but couldn't quite convince himself.

# *Chapter Five*

Roxanne took a deep breath. The invitation to the Oceanus Country Club represented a milestone for personal achievement. She'd grown up hearing about the prestigious place. The Griffiths had been members for as long as Roxanne could remember. Tonight was the first time she'd climbed the carpeted steps.

As she approached the uniformed doorman, the parallel to Cinderella leaving the pumpkin coach for the palace peeked out of her fertile imagination. She shook it off. This was business. If Prince Charming waited on the dance floor, too bad. She didn't have time for him. Not tonight. This evening belonged to Magic Wish.

Dressed in a chic backless black party dress, Roxanne was ready for the night ahead. Although confident in her professional ability, her party skills were a bit rusty. Common sense coupled with a little luck and quick reactions would help her compensate.

At the cloakroom she exchanged her evening wrap for a claim check. The posh country club overlooking the ocean oozed elegance and old money from the mahogany walls to the gleaming oak floors. The mellow strains of a tenor floated through the rose-scented air.

The ladies' room caught her attention. She ducked inside for a last-minute bladder reprieve and grooming check.

Tiny butterflies beat their wings in her stomach. A full day at the beach hadn't restored her calm, nor had the night at the cottage left her rested. She had returned home only long enough to prepare for the Penworths' gala. On the way out of the house for tonight's big event, she'd spied the stenciled box among the wilted flowers in the dining room. A chill ran up her spine. The charred cardboard flaps told her how long the fire had lasted. He'd snuffed the fire and moved the box. What else had he done, and, more important, what else could he do?

No more avoidance, she decided. No more abdication of her home. For the first time in her life, the house felt like it was hers. She was not giving up. Especially not to the person who had taken it away from her to begin with.

*He* had to leave. Period. What she needed were real Ghostbusters to eradicate the unwelcome spirit.

"Ghost in a box," she murmured. That's what he was, and brought by none other than the well-intentioned, devastatingly sexy, closed-minded Spencer No-Relation Griffith.

She leaned toward the mirror. Another coat of lipstick wouldn't hurt. She dug the tube out of her small purse, touched up her lips, and then dropped it back inside. The gold case clinked against what she assumed was loose change.

On the way out of the ladies' room, she took a final look in the mirror. Just below the white crown molding framing the ceiling, the rose-colored watered silk wallpaper shimmered and started turning a sickeningly familiar mustard yellow. She whirled around to face the anomaly.

Her heart skipped a beat in apprehension, then plummeted to her toes.

*He* had followed her. Roxanne's heart accelerated with irritation for the intrusion.

"Did you drill holes in the girls' locker room in high school, too?"

The shimmer coalesced into the same form she'd almost made out on the stairs the previous afternoon. Tonight, the ghostly definition had a new sharpness.

The face that adorned the halls and rooms of the Griffith home all her life peered down at her. The flight suit bearing the name Griffith on a strip above his left breast dispelled any doubt of his identity. The uniform appeared old, tattered, and torn.

She had no trouble resisting the winsome grin his relatives had considered infectious. It was infectious all right. So were measles and mumps.

"Go away," she hissed, then closed her eyes and softly added, "Please. I've worked hard for tonight. Let me have my success or disappointment without you as a distraction."

"If I disappear, will you come home?"

Blackmail. Expecting compliance to a simple request was folly. In true Griffith fashion, he made sure he got something in exchange for any concession. "Isn't there some kind of code or a list of rules for ghosts? Aren't you supposed to stay in one place and rattle chains or something?"

"I'm learning the rules as I go. Coming to this party with you is more fun than chain rattling. Besides, I haven't found the chains. So, how about it? I'll stay out of the way tonight, and you come home afterward. Deal?"

"Like I have a choice?" She couldn't get through the evening ahead with him distracting her at every turn. "Yes. Just go."

When she opened her eyes, he was gone. But she did not trust that he'd actually left. No, if her father lived down to her expectations, he'd remain out of sight, but he wouldn't leave. Family stories had detailed his love of parties, and the Oceanus had been the site of many.

"Okay," she said more to herself than the meddlesome spirit she suspected of hovering over the stalls. "Pervert," she breathed.

"I beg your pardon?" asked a surprised woman standing in the doorway.

Roxanne snapped into the present. "Oh, not you. Sorry. My mind was wandering."

The woman nodded and gave her an understanding smile. "You've encountered the Don Juan with six hands groping more than canapés, too."

"No, not yet, but I appreciate the warning."

"You're welcome." The woman headed for the nearest stall.

Great, there was a masher to watch out for, too. For an evening she'd looked forward to with nervous gusto, it was starting on an ominous note.

As Roxanne approached the reception line, heads turned. The reaction to her presence added to her unease. She attributed the reason for the attention to her height. Surely, the other guests couldn't tell this was the first time she'd attended a country club function. A smile polished her façade and outwardly denied her breach of confidence. Spiked heels and a designer dress weren't her preference, but she wore both when the occasion mandated. Like tonight.

The smile lighting her face brightened when she spotted Walter Penworth among the greeters in the informal reception line. An energetic man in his late fifties, he had the vigor of a man half his age. Tall, stylishly attired in formal evening clothes, his stark white shirt matched his short, thick hair and accentuated his year-round tan. He wore rimless glasses that remained fixed on his patrician nose. Even in a social setting, Walter's brown eyes moved constantly. He was perpetually alert for the next discovery, a new technology, or an opportunity with his name on it. But when he gave someone his complete attention, as he did now, it felt like a gift.

Dwarfing her hands with his, he bent and kissed her cheek.

Her surprise must have shown, because he laughed.

"It's good to see you, too," she said.

"It's been a long time since a video excited me as much as the one you and Magic Wish prepared for my guests tonight. You've blended our company history with our vision for the future in a way that the stockholders will love. Once they see the full version, they'll be fighting to invest in our expansion into Texas. You're a genius."

The sincerity of his praise made her heart swell with pride. He'd believed in her since her college days, when the luck of the draw made him her business mentor. It had proven to be one of the most fortunate days of her life. "I had the help of my cohorts." She squeezed his hand and grinned back. "And a client who knew what he wanted."

"You look fabulous, Roxanne." Red-haired Melanie Penworth gave her a hug. "Walter has raved about the program you put together. I'm dying to see it."

Melanie and Walter had the kind of marriage Roxanne wanted—when she had time to find the right man. The Penworths shared a partnership that encompassed all facets of their lives. After thirty-three years of marriage, they still treated each other like sweethearts.

"My bride has no idea of the magnificent video you and your company created. I wanted to surprise her tonight." Walter slipped his arm around his wife's ample waist and drew her close. "Now that Roxanne is here, we can get on with the party."

"The food is not only a work of art, it tastes divine." Melanie gestured at the lavish ice sculptures towering over the heads of the party guests. "Walter called in a few favors when putting together the company's anniversary party."

"Are you pleased with the results, my dear?"

"Very little you do fails to please me," Melanie cooed.

Roxanne shook off the voyeuristic sensation she always got the first few minutes around Walter and Melanie. Okay, maybe she didn't want a relationship quite so cloying or conjoined.

"By the way, thank you both for the generous donation you made to the Leukemia Research Foundation in Thelma's memory." Roxanne eyed the crowd waiting to descend on them beyond the reception area.

"It was the least we could do. You've handled Thelma's illness, her care, and her death with a dignity and adroitness that humbles the rest of us."

"Here, here," Walter agreed, snatching two champagne flutes from a tray a tuxedo-clad waiter held.

Roxanne took a glass and let them toast her. "I don't know what to say."

"Let's drink to finding a cure." Melanie raised a flute, then followed her own advice.

Roxanne obliged, then spent the next hour meeting the Penworths' guests. Talking about her business took the edge off her nervousness. The more she mingled while discussing business, the more enthusiasm she had for the country club crowd.

She pinpointed the fanny groper roaming the tables and kept a distance. All the while, she felt watched. Thus far, Matt hadn't revealed himself in any manner, so she couldn't blame it on him. Still, not knowing what he might do, or when, kept her on edge.

Walter Penworth took center stage and used the microphone to gain the attention of his guests. After a brief anniversary tribute to WMP Technologies, he called for a dimming of the house lights. A large curtain opened behind him. At strategic places around the room, monitors winked to life with the WMP logo on the screens.

Video footage and graphics combined with dramatic animation and special effects. A brief summary of WMP's history preceded the innovative presentation of plans for a new communications technology as dynamic as the images and colors on the screens.

The ten-minute version shown at the party had half the detail and none of the proprietary information slated for the stockholders meeting tomorrow afternoon. Standing beside Walter and Melanie, Roxanne grew nervous when the lights brightened and absolute silence filled the room.

"Goodness gracious," Melanie whispered to her. "I feel like I've just stepped out of a science-fiction movie about our company."

"But did you like it?" Roxanne asked anxiously, keeping an eye on Walter as he returned to the microphone.

Wide-eyed, Melanie gazed at her. "Like it? I loved it! I'd *pay* to see it again. Now, you get up there and reap the praise Walter is sure to give you."

Several people began clapping. Within a heartbeat the room became a beehive of activity and accolades.

Beaming with triumph and pride at his young protégé, Walter extended a hand to Roxanne. "Ladies and gentlemen, please meet the genius responsible for the magic you've just seen. Roxanne Griffith, CEO of Magic Wish."

The applause became her heartbeat. Triumph had never felt so sweet.

Two hours later Roxanne's slim evening bag bulged with business cards. She shook hands and exchanged ideas freely. Power schmoozing was a skill she could thank Aunt Thelma for honing. And tonight, she did so.

The future of her business had never looked brighter.

Matt watched from the ceiling. The rich, smoky taste of power and money made him yearn for the substance of life. The mix of expensive perfumes, spicy aftershaves, exquisite liquor, and delicious food summoned memories that felt like yesterday. In reality, they were nearly thirty years old. Time had changed many aspects of the country club. But it hadn't changed the electric feel of the perpetual chess games the power brokers played. Each strategic move across the floor, every conversation, was part of a player's overall game plan.

Matt had learned the intricacies of the game from his father. He hadn't appreciated his talent to lead back then. He hadn't wanted the responsibility, either. Too late, he understood the gift he had squandered in pursuit of a good time. His father had called it I. I.—Intentional Immaturity. He'd been right.

Had Matt survived the Vietnam War, he'd be fifty-three and standing at the helm of his father's business. This should have been his life; the power brokers attending the gathering would have been his peers and members of his social set.

Instead, a strafe of bullets had knocked him out of the sky over Vietnam.

Nothing could change that.

The legacy of his birth now belonged to his daughter.

With a twinge of jealousy, and a sense of protectiveness that made him uncomfortable, he watched Roxanne navigate the shoals of a business party. Damn, she was cool. His pride in her invigorated him.

Then he watched the video his daughter and her small company had created.

He couldn't imagine what it took to make the short movie he viewed with the rest of the partygoers. They, too, were in awe of the kaleidoscope of motion and color depicting new technology. Not even Robert Heinlein or Isaac Asimov had projected such marvels. He wanted to see it again.

No wonder tonight was so important to her. Thunderstruck, he remained on the ceiling and continued his pitiful role of voyeur. The longer he watched her, the more amazing he found it that the talented, intelligent woman laughing and talking with industry captains was his daughter. Roxanne was the only legacy he and Marian had left in the world.

Christ, he was getting maudlin.

Being dead was the pits. Being a ghost observing all he had taken for granted and would never experience again was the ultimate bummer. Taking a passive, hands-off stance was insult upon injury.

While wallowing in self-pity he roamed among the guests and kept an eye on another man preoccupied with Roxanne.

Strange that Roxanne hadn't acknowledged him. The kiss the two of them had shared on the porch had generated enough electricity in their auras to light the house for a year. Perhaps Roxanne was upset with him, too. Or maybe she didn't know the front-porch kisser was there.

Matt would make book on the latter.

He sulked when the passage of time hit him. His twenty-eight-year-old daughter was three years older than he.

Even so, the front-porch lover was too bold and too old for

her. He had to be in his mid-thirties. At the moment, Matt couldn't do a damn thing about Roxanne's choice of men. If she liked middle-aged men, she'd go with him. Clearly, Roxanne made her own choices and managed her own destiny.

Belatedly Matt realized winning her cooperation was going to take more than charm, a glib tongue, and a quick guilt trip down loyalty lane. Roxanne wasn't at all like Marian. In fact, she wasn't like any woman he'd ever met. The man Roxanne had kissed on the front porch had watched her the past hour. Matt doubted that he'd met anyone like Roxanne, either. The man was all but taking notes as he marked her progress around the room. Matt considered himself an astute judge of people. Such a talent was essential if a man was to rely on someone to do his bidding.

The evening took on a fresh importance and became more interesting by the moment. Matt settled back to watch it unfold.

"I didn't realize you were Magic Wish. My congratulations on producing an amazing video."

Roxanne whirled around so quickly that her clutch bag slipped from under her arm. The clasp opened on impact with the floor. The contents tumbled out at her feet. "Oh. Spence. I thought you had a party to attend tonight."

He crouched and collected the paraphernalia from her purse; business cards, compact, claim check, aviator wings, wallet, lipstick, comb, tissue.

Old aviator wings?

Vietnam vintage. The corrosion pattern and telltale fracture of the left wingtip identified them as her father's. Spence's fingers closed around them. Surprise turned to satisfaction and the hope of more changes. Personal changes.

He dropped the memento into her purse.

For the first time since spotting Roxanne among the guests, a sense of ease settled over him. The wings were a reason for optimism. He hadn't expected a change of heart about Memorial Day so quickly, but carrying a talisman of her father couldn't mean anything else.

As they stood facing each other, the burst of sheer happiness from the sudden turn of events made him grin.

Then everything went to hell.

Roxanne yelped and reached for her posterior.

A champagne cork popped and flew through the air like a rifle bullet. It struck a target directly behind Roxanne.

The man let out a yowl and grabbed his head.

In what seemed an intricately choreographed ballet, the domino reaction spread to those around them. Two women spilled their drinks. Both jumped back to avoid the liquid arcing through the air. In the process, they dropped their champagne flutes.

The shattering glass sounded loud until the waiter the women bumped into lost control of the tray he balanced above his head. He might have recovered if not for the champagne-slick floor. It was either drop the tray and windmill his arms to regain his balance or go down with the stacks of dirty plates and glasses. He saved himself. The tray went flying.

The contents of the partially filled drink glasses coalesced into a vortex with food remnants and plates. Like the champagne cork a few seconds earlier, the dregs hit the same target with a resounding splat.

Stunned, the man let out a second yelp. Bits of food clung to his tuxedo. Cocktail sauce, avocado, and mustard dripped down his white shirtfront. Blotches of unidentifiable food scraps clung with the precision of a well-decorated Christmas tree.

To the open amazement of those surrounding him, not a morsel of food or a drop of liquid had landed on any other guest.

The sudden silence wasn't noticeable until it broke in a flurry of exclamations. Undoubtedly, the incredible incident would be the talk of the country club for years.

Spence took Roxanne's arm and led her away from the food-covered man ranting about the waiter's incompetence.

The incident robbed the color from Roxanne's cheeks. Her arm trembled under his hand. With haunted eyes, she searched the ceiling as though she expected it to fall.

"Are you all right?" Spence ushered her aside as an army of waitpeople hurried to the disaster site.

"Yeah. Serves him right, too," she said so quietly that Spence doubted anyone else heard. Still, she kept searching the ceiling as though inspecting it for cracks.

"Incredible." Spence caught a final glimpse of the man wearing some of Christopher's best creations on his tuxedo. "Are you sure you're all right? None of the dishes or broken glass hit you?"

Roxanne scanned the ceiling, then fixed her gaze on a spot in the far corner. "He wouldn't dare. It's against the Griffith code. We don't smear each other."

Laughter accompanied the sound of someone clapping. In seconds the room filled with spotty applause. Spence leaned closer to Roxanne. "I didn't catch that."

Her shoulders squared as she turned to him. Composure surrounded her. A hint of color returned to her cheeks. A trace of a forced smile lifted the corners of her mouth. Spence fought the impulse to lower his head a little more, just enough to brush away the strain with his mouth.

"I said, the guy was an octopus. He deserved what he got. He's been groping women all night."

The orchestra struck up a calming medley of dance tunes from the forties. Spence eyed the couples streaming toward the dance floor. "Why don't we see if we have dancing in common, too?"

"Can we go outside instead? I could use some fresh air." She nodded toward the French doors leading to the expansive patio facing the sea.

Together, they threaded the clusters of partygoers and made their way outside.

Fog gave the salty night air a mysterious quality. The patio lights illuminated white wrought-iron chairs and glass-topped tables drenched in dew. A damp chill rolled in from the ocean. Spence removed his jacket and draped it around Roxanne's shoulders. A slow version of "Deep Purple" wafted out from the open windows into the swirling fog.

"Have you noticed that the orchestra plays music older than most of the people who attend the club's functions?" he asked, leading her onto the open patio.

"No."

"We have music. We have plenty of space. Privacy. Fresh air. Will you dance with me here?" In the muted light she appeared frail in his tuxedo jacket.

"I haven't had time for dancing in a long while."

"Let's change that." He wrapped his arms around her. As if pressed by the fog, her body flowed against his. The feather-light impression of her open hands on his chest pulsed with his heartbeat as they swayed to the music.

"You've done yourself proud," he murmured. Damn, but it felt good to hold her. She was a complex, intriguing woman. Beneath her glib façade, she remained more distant than any woman he'd ever met.

"Thank you. Envisioning possibilities is the first step to solving problems." The dreaminess of her smile set him afire. He wanted to taste it and kiss her until they were both senseless and aching for more.

"I've envisioned a number of possibilities with you."

Her smile faded. "Is that so? Often, expectations exceed reality."

"You've already succeeded—and exceeded." It seemed prudent to tread lightly. Undoubtedly her recent change of heart concerning her father was still tender. She might swing the other way if the reasons for her change of attitude came into question. This was not the time to push. "Far beyond expectations."

"I had help."

He gathered her close and danced them around a table. Her initial stiffness in his arms faded quickly. "Even so, the results speak for themselves."

"I'm pleased." She took a deep breath and let it out with an air of contentment. "It was a risk."

"Scary?" Setting aside old prejudices and hostilities took courage. He decided she had plenty. After all, she'd gone from open loathing of her father to carrying his pilot's wings as a talisman at what had to be one of the most important evenings of her career.

"Downright frightening at times. It feels like your entire existence is hanging on the decision-making process."

The music evolved into a quicker tempo. Spence tightened his arms around her shoulders and continued the slower pace.

"This is nice," she murmured. "I can hear your heart."

"What's it saying?"

"Blub-blub. Blub-blub."

"Can you translate?" Her sense of humor delighted him.

"No. The heart has its own language." Her hands moved over his chest, and around his ribs. Like warm honey, her fingers splayed against his back. An intimate setting where they could get naked flashed through his mind. It looked a lot like his bedroom.

"I agree. The heart speaks loudly at times."

"Fortunately, the head seldom interprets the heart correctly, or it doesn't act upon it when it does. Something gets lost in between, which I suppose is good most of the time. It's a safety mechanism. Can you imagine the problems if people said exactly what was in their hearts? Devastating, that's what it would be."

He reared back slightly, causing her to look up at him. "How can you say that?"

"After a couple of glasses of champagne, it's easy. I open my mouth, and uncensored thoughts spill out." She looked evenly at him. "What would you have said?"

"Liberating."

"I'm already a liberated woman who answers only to herself. My heart knows which side the bread is buttered on. Besides, if we said what we really felt in our hearts, there would be even more broken hearts than there are now. Sometimes silence is a kindness of the first order." A small hiccup escaped her. She lowered her head and apologized just as softly.

He grinned. "You're tipsy." He hadn't thought her capable of yielding that much control of any situation. Again, he'd underestimated her.

"I'm working on it. How about you?"

"What about me?" He'd been too busy watching her to think about drinking.

"You're as sober as a judge, aren't you?"

"Depends on which judge you're comparing me to. Now, Judge Harkin—"

"I should have known you'd have an evasive answer." She rested her head on his shoulder and hummed with the music.

He fought the impulse to hold her tighter, stop dancing, and kiss her with all the need simmering on the back burner of his mind. "Did you drive here?" he asked after a moment, then couldn't resist dancing them closer to the ocean. The rhythmic surf blended with the music riding the fog.

"No. Walter sent a car for me," she answered softly. They glided over the fog-dampened patio with easy grace.

"I'll take you home."

"No, you won't. Besides, I'm not ready to leave yet. *He's* there." The music stopped. Applause broke the spell that had isolated them in the night. Roxanne stiffened and released him.

In the span of a heartbeat, they had stopped dancing and she was removing his coat. He caught the lapels and held them together until she silently agreed to continue wearing it.

"He's here, too." She glanced over her shoulder. Fog created muted prisms around the globes pretending to light the night. Beyond the concrete expanse, a long bank of windows and sliding doors looked in on the festivities. The orchestra started playing "Hey Jude."

"Who's here?"

"Dear Old Dad. Who do you think?" She looked back at him. Even in the thick, foggy shadows, Spence couldn't miss the consternation straining her features.

"How much have you had to drink?"

Her brow pinched in annoyance. "Not enough." She sighed. "Too much."

"I don't understand. I thought you'd come to terms with your father's memory, that you'd had a change of heart."

Total incomprehension pinched her brow and widened her dark eyes. "My god, what would make you leap to such an absurd conclusion?"

What indeed. "Weren't we talking about that when we came out here?"

"I was talking about my video tonight. Why would you think otherwise?"

He'd had enough games. He took her purse and rummaged through it, dropping some of the contents onto a damp tabletop. They clattered and rolled. In the bottom of the satin liner lay the prize he sought. He plucked out the aviator wings and held them to the light. "What kind of person carries a memento of someone they loathe?"

She stared at the pilot's wings for a long time, then shivered. "Damn it. He's getting stronger."

"Who?"

She slipped out of his jacket and walked into the darkness.

Spence scooped up the assorted items on the table and dumped them back into her purse, which he stuck into his jacket pocket. Confused, irritated, he followed her toward the ocean.

When he caught up, she was paralleling the rail of the lookout cliff above the beach. A wave of chill bumps rippled over her cold skin as he draped his jacket around her shoulders.

"I don't need anything from you." She tugged at the coat, ready to take it off again.

He stayed her hand. "You look dynamite in that dress, but there isn't much of it. One of the things I've learned about you is that you're as stubborn as a mule when you want to be. Leave the coat on, Roxanne. You don't have to impress me with your ability to stand on your own. You've already accomplished that."

Head shaking, she pulled the coat closer and stared into the night. "I see. And what else do you think you know about me?"

Sensing her turmoil, he stood close enough for her to touch him and remained silent for a moment. Fickle fog contorted the sound of the restless sea. "You're a complex woman," he said after a while. "Independent. Self-sufficient to the point of being unable to accept a kind gesture without looking for an ulterior motive."

He crossed his arms around her waist. When she neither objected nor responded, he continued. "You're a control freak when it comes to your emotions."

Her head shook slightly against his shoulder. He bent to her ear. "Sure you are. Want me to kiss you and prove it?"

When she started to object, he laughed softly. "But I am learning how to penetrate that wall you like to hide behind." He kissed the top of her ear and tightened his arms around her. He'd pushed this far; there was no time like the present to try for more. "Tell me what made you so fearful of the world. Why you retreat inside your shell when the emotions get too real."

"I'm not here for counseling, Spence."

"Good, because I'm not your counselor. Just a friend who wants to know what's keeping you from having a good time on what should be one of the biggest nights of your career."

"You," she said softly.

"Me?" He shook his head against the side of hers. "Not me, Roxanne. Tell me."

After a long moment she relaxed. She held her silence as the music changed to the love theme from *A Summer Place*.

"When I was a child, and my mother was alive, I used to pray my father would come home and make things better. Make things right," she said into the night. "Every kid wants to believe her parents have the power to make things better by ending the bickering, the censure, the snide comments and innuendo. As children, we want to believe fairness exists and someone on our side has the ability to impose it."

A half-dozen questions begged for answers on the tip of his tongue. The frailty of the moment kept him quiet in hopes she'd continue.

"What I didn't realize at four years old was that if he had come home, he would have made things better for himself. Not me. Not my mother. Matthew Griffith, son of Hayden and Pauline Mayhew Griffith, was self-centered and spoiled. He used people the way most of us use Kleenex. From all accounts he was charming and witty, but he could be vindictive and petty."

"He died before you were born. How do you know so much about him?" The question had nagged at him each time she referred to her father.

"When I was little, my father was a quintessential golden child. Even I revered him—before I learned how to read between the lines of the stories his family and friends, and even my mother, told over and over. That bubble burst when I was fifteen."

"What happened to burst your bubble?"

"Thelma needed storage space. Every five years she remodeled whether the house needed work or not. While I was rearranging boxes and antiques she didn't want to part with in the attic, I came across *his* high school yearbooks. There were a lot of letters in the box, too. They turned out to be correspondence from his college years. Some of the letters were to his parents. A few were to my mother. What a revelation reading them was.

"At fifteen I was pretty good at reading between the lines, particularly lines of bull. The more I read, the more I understood, and the angrier I got. He was a manipulator. I doubt he ever put anyone ahead of his own interests. Certainly not my mother. I think that's when I truly began to detest him.

"Last year Thelma bared her soul—and her conscience. Maybe it was the years, or the finality of death marching toward her. Maybe the veils of illusion fade when you confront mortality measured in heartbeats. Regardless, she answered my questions and told me everything I wanted to know about my parents, except about . . ." Her voice melted into the fog along with Spence's hopes of discovering the secret ingredient responsible for her reserve.

Her fingers wound around the cold metal rail, and she continued staring toward the fog-shrouded sea. "I'm angry at you, Spence. And resentful that you brought him back."

"Glad you're taking responsibility for your emotions." Annoyed, he released her and turned away.

She grabbed his arm. "Save your sarcasm for someone who appreciates it. I'm not talking about emotions. I'm talking about his *ghost*."

He stopped in his tracks, sure he hadn't heard her correctly. "His what?"

"You brought his damn ghost back from Vietnam."

"The hell you say. All I brought back was a box of tarnished, corroded mementos from a pilot." She wasn't just tipsy; she was drunk.

"I didn't put his damn wings in my purse. I threw the box and everything in it into the fireplace and started a nice little bonfire."

Disbelief became disappointment, then plummeted into the dark well of anger. He'd thought her courageous and open-minded. He turned around, daring her to face him. She hadn't moved. Light from the patio lamps and the chandeliers inside played over her the way an ethereal halo lit angels on television. "You expect me to believe a ghost put those wings in your purse?"

"I sure as hell didn't put them in there. And I don't care what you believe. I'm used to being a minority of one. But the facts don't change. Captain Matthew Griffith is here tonight. I've seen him, spoken to him. He's watching me. Probably watching you. He's a voyeur. He watched us on the porch yesterday afternoon, too. When I went inside, he confronted me. Jeezus, but I was scared. Later, I drove to the ocean and stayed at the beach house until I had to return to get ready for tonight."

"Your father's ghost decided to haunt the house nearly thirty years after he died? What'd he do? Take a slow boat from Vietnam?" Impossible.

"You brought him, Spence. You. Deny it if it makes you feel better, if it gives you the comfortable, fuzzy feeling that lets you put everything into logical categories. He's real. And he's here.

"We spoke in the ladies' room right after I arrived. Maybe manifesting in the rest room was supposed to put me on my best behavior. Daddy's watching. Be good. Or maybe he wanted to irritate me. Regardless, he found an opportunity, a lever, for blackmail."

She looked up at him. In the faint light he saw her eyes glistening with unshed tears. "Take the box and all his things away, Spence. Do whatever you want with them on Memorial Day, but get him out of my life. Please."

The story was outrageous. Unbelievable. Baffling. However, her sincerity stunned him into silence. The anguish in her plea pervaded everything around her and swept his objections aside.

"Do you believe in ghosts?" The flatness of her voice echoed a bleakness he'd seen in her eyes the evening he'd left the box.

"You're asking me if I believe your father's ghost came back in a keepsake box?" He doubted there was a correct answer.

"No. I'm asking if you believe in ghosts in general."

"I never gave it much thought," he said slowly. "I'd like to believe we brought your father's spirit back with the mementos from his grave. I'd like to believe you could converse with him. Maybe see him the way he was."

"Why?"

"I'd like to believe there's a possibility I'd have that kind of opportunity with my brother."

Roxanne tilted her head and stared up into the night. "Regardless of what you'd like to believe, the truth is you don't believe in ghosts, do you?"

"No."

"So you think I'm crazy at worst, unstable at best, for walking around with those wings in my purse. If there are no ghosts, I must have put them there."

He couldn't fault her logic. "I'm sure there's a reason—"

"Oh, there is." She removed his jacket, took her purse from the pocket, then laid the garment over the rail. "Good night."

"Roxanne—"

"Good night, Spence. I don't want you near me right now." She looked over her shoulder and met his gaze briefly. "Think about what occurred before we came out here. Who made things happen with the waiter, the fanny groper, and the spectators who escaped without so much as a drop or a crumb on them. Only Mr. Happy Hands ended up coated with slop. Think about it."

She turned away and walked back into the noisy party just hitting its stride.

Spence felt like his heart was dragging on her heel when she closed the door on him and the foggy night. He donned his coat and stared toward the ocean.

He'd think about it, all right. It was crazy, but not as crazy as the way he felt about Roxanne.

# Chapter Six

Roxanne picked up the cat from the front porch, then waved at the Penworths' limo driver as he pulled away. Every light in the house came on when she opened the front door.

Damn. *He* was home, too.

The cat writhing in her arms wasn't ready to forgive her for abandoning him yesterday. Once inside the house she loosened her grasp. Buster yowled, twisting from her arms in a bid for freedom. As soon as he hit the floor, he darted for the kitchen.

With a sigh she closed the front door, threw the deadbolt, and punched on the alarm. "You can come out now!"

"I'm not hiding." Amusement laced Matt's words.

Not caring if he followed, Roxanne headed for the kitchen, where she turned on the kettle and checked Buster's food and water. As a bribe into his good graces, she opened a can of tuna and gave him a tablespoonful. Given the Persian's current attitude, it might take the entire can.

The ceiling above the refrigerator shimmered. Well, if she had to share her space with a ghost, he may as well be useful.

"I want some answers." She dumped the rest of the tuna into a container, then tossed it into the refrigerator and placed the can on Buster's place mat. In five minutes he'd have the interior licked clean enough for the recycling bin.

"What do I get if I answer your questions?"

Roxanne thought for a moment while washing the tuna smell from her hands. "You get a day's reprieve before I call an exorcist."

The shimmers of his presence took shape. Bordering between transparency and solidity, Matt crouched on an invisible perch against the wall, his right wrist dangling over an upraised knee. "An exorcist wouldn't do any good. I'm not evil. And I'm not leaving."

"You aren't heaven-sent, either, so the length of our time together is open for debate." After drying her hands, she headed for the cupboard with the tea and teapot. "Why did you follow me to the Oceanus?"

"To be with my daughter on what turned out to be her big night," he said softly. She refused to acknowledge the wistfulness in his voice by remaining silent. "I want to know you, Roxanne, and for you to know me."

"I know you." She set up the tea. "Good-time Charlie. Allergic to responsibility. Smooth talker. Never put his money where his mouth was. Never found a woman he couldn't get into bed or a situation he couldn't charm his way out of." She glanced up at him. "How am I doing?"

His head tilted, the hand dangling over his knee waved. "So far, so good."

"You were brilliant but lazy."

"Guilty. Did you figure all that out by yourself?"

"Most of it. But Thelma confirmed it before she died." Roxanne prepared the tea, then carried it to the kitchen table. Here it was, 2:30 A.M., and she was having tea with her father's ghost. She needed a padded room and a straitjacket.

"I won't ask how you did your little trick at the country club with the spilled drinks."

"Hey, I kept my word. Other than you, no one knew I was there." A sudden impish grin erased any trace of worry. "Did you like it?"

Any form of encouragement invited the wrong impression. Bottom line—she didn't like him and wasn't about to let him try to change her mind. "Did you enjoy creating a spectacle? It was so . . . so . . ."

"Un-Griffithlike?"

"Yes." She bit the inside of her cheek to suppress a smile. Thelma would roll over in her grave if she knew what he'd done at the Oceanus. The idea of questioning Thelma's fate in the afterlife tempted Roxanne. But she wasn't going to ask. If Matt knew, he'd try to extract another sort of payment. She wasn't that curious about something she couldn't change anyway. "Why did you do it?"

"In my day I'd have taken him outside and taught him some manners." His chin rose in righteousness. "He was touching the ladies. He fondled your . . . your . . ."

"Ass?" How sweet it was to see Matthew Griffith disconcerted by a simple word choice.

"Bottom," he corrected. "I didn't want him manhandling my daughter."

His daughter? Lordy, but she couldn't think of herself in that light. "Neither defense nor retribution are necessary on my behalf. I can take care of myself." Still, Mr. Happy Hands had received justice of the first order thanks to a ghost.

"I'm sure you can. Presuming otherwise would insult both of us. In fact, after seeing the movie you made, I doubt there's anything you can't do. It was magic."

"You can save the charm around me. I'm not my mother or your parents. I'm not Thelma, either."

He stroked his chin and regarded her pensively. "You're the first woman I've come across who gets offended because I'm articulate."

Roxanne settled on the nearest chair and pulled out the adjacent one. With a small moan of relief, she kicked off her shoes. She pushed back and propped her feet on the empty seat. "Articulate is not the same as full of bull. Your reputation precedes you. I'll concede you're both."

She sipped hot chamomile tea while he prowled the kitchen. When she set her cup down, he was hovering cross-legged a few inches above the table with a steaming teacup in hand. The delicate china contrasted so sharply with his stained, tattered flight suit that Roxanne nearly smiled in spite of her pique.

"You have your mother's eyes. What happened to her?"

Roxanne closed her eyes and leaned back. "It's late. I'm tired. I don't want to go there. Besides, you haven't earned the right to mention her to me."

"What happened to my parents?"

"You really don't know?" Eyes closed, she massaged her temples against the faint ache gathering behind her forehead. "I thought you got all the answers when you died."

"If I knew, I wouldn't be asking the questions."

"I'm not talking about my mother or your parents tonight." The lingering euphoria from tonight's triumph was already fading. Relating the disaster that took all three lives would wipe away the last traces. She wasn't ready to give up the good feeling.

"What about Aunt Thelma? Will you tell me how she died?"

"Leukemia." Memories of Thelma's sometimes courageous, sometimes cowardly battle with the killer rode roughshod over Roxanne's weary defenses. "I didn't know what a marvelous sense of humor Thelma had until a couple of years ago. I miss her."

"She was a tough woman. Tough on me, anyway." Matt took a sip of tea. The liquid poured straight through him and splattered on the tabletop.

A hollow laugh escaped Roxanne. She managed to stifle it and tossed a napkin over the puddle. "You don't have a clue about her feelings for you. She loved you. You were the apple of her eye. Hell, you were the apple of everyone's eye, weren't you?"

"I suppose."

She sopped up the mess and dropped the napkin on the tray. "They talked about you until they died. All of them. Thelma was the only one who told me the truth. At least, the truth as she knew it." She stared up at him. The mischievousness that danced in his blue eyes so clearly in old photographs remained. Not even death had obliterated the force of his personality. Classic, square features and wide-set eyes made him attractive. When he smiled, he was disgustingly handsome. Natural curl gave his short, blond hair an unkempt appearance. "It always amazed me."

"What? That they talked about me? Missed me?"

"No. I can only speak for Thelma because she told me. She knew all your faults and intentionally turned a blind eye. When you didn't come back from Vietnam, those faults became the virtues of a saint. In retrospect, it's easy to see they never realized you were the only apple in the barrel, and the shine you possessed was due to their myopia."

"Ouch." He drifted off the table, straightening his legs until he floated less than an inch above the floor. Neither the table, nor the extra chairs, deterred him. "Surely I have some good qualities in your eyes."

Unnerved, Roxanne looked away. She thought for a long minute, sifting, sorting, and remembering more than she wanted to about her life in this house. "You have one."

"Only one? I guess that's a start. Name it." Defensiveness sharpened the demand in his voice.

"You're dead," she whispered. "Now I want you gone. Forever."

He was behind her, and she refused to turn her head even a fraction. She sensed that he had stopped in his tracks.

"It isn't as simple as wishing or wanting."

She hadn't thought it was. Too bad. "Why did you come back?"

"I'm here to . . ." He started pacing again. When his words failed, he stopped pacing. Unfortunately, he was in the middle of the table.

"To what?" Head tilted, she watched him struggle for an answer while trying to ignore the way the table sliced through his hips. The stories of childhood had painted him with a broad brush that endowed near superhuman traits to the Griffiths' golden child. Although Roxanne recognized that finding a nugget of enjoyment in his momentary discomfort was petty, she enjoyed it nonetheless.

"To win your respect. Forgiveness," he added slowly, then looked directly into her eyes. "I've come back to get to know my daughter and try to win her love."

Roxanne shook her head in disbelief. "Love? Don't hold, your breath. I'm the Griffith who didn't love you." The sharp laugh that tore from her throat sounded like a bark. In typical Griffith fashion he'd made no mention of loving her in return. "I guess there is Divine Retribution after all. You're proof. This is rich. You want something, so now I'm your daughter."

He had the audacity to look genuinely perturbed. "Of course you're my daughter. Who else's would you be?" He perched on the edge of the table. She would have to reach through him to get to her teacup. She decided to forego the tea rather than penetrate his specter.

A familiar burning started in her stomach and inched up her throat. "Gee, I can't imagine who might have brought up the question before I was born—a question that was kept alive until a couple of years ago. But at least you and I agree I'm your daughter up front. You look a bit anemic for a DNA test."

During the moment he was silent, he became more transparent. "Who questioned your paternity?"

She rose, hating the conversation, hating what it did to her each time she recalled that day in the doctor's office. "It's late. I'm tired. Talking about it changes nothing."

"Tell me, please, and I'll disappear for a day."

A Griffith always expected to pay a price for what he wanted, and knew how to dangle the right carrot. Weary, she nodded, then drew a deep breath and sat down again.

"When Thelma got sick, she didn't tell a soul. She was in the later stages of her illness before her doctor took matters into her own hands and called me. By then, her last hope of beating the leukemia or even buying a temporary remission was a bone marrow transplant. Her doctor, Dr. Grabel, asked me to come to her office to discuss Thelma's options."

She cast a sideways look at Matt. "Let me preface this by saying I moved out of this house the day I graduated from high school. For the next eight years I was on my own. Thelma and I saw one another two, maybe three times a year. It was a duty thing. We kept up appearances."

For the first time, she noticed an aura around him. She could have sworn it flashed a dull red, but she was tired and her eyes were most likely playing tricks. When his halo stayed a soft lavender-blue, then faded, she dismissed the notion.

"From the looks of things, you've lived here a long time. Why did you come back?"

"When I went to Dr. Grabel's office, she asked if I'd be willing to be tested as a bone-marrow donor. She told me I was Thelma's last chance.

"It hit me like a ton of bricks. Thelma and I didn't get along, that was no secret. But I never wished her ill, and I never wanted her to suffer or die. Whether I liked Thelma or not, she was my last living relative." Roxanne took a deep breath and let it out slowly. She hated reliving any part of that day in the doctor's office.

"You consented to the bone-marrow transplant?"

"Not then. I thought about it for a couple of days. This situation put me between a rock and hard place. I wondered how Thelma would face her friends if by some freak chance we didn't come up a match, and the news got out that I wasn't her grandniece. She was a fiercely proud woman. It would have killed her faster than the leukemia did."

"You really thought you weren't my daughter?" The sorrow in his whisper came from all directions.

"Until Thelma needed my bone marrow, I had hoped I wasn't. Imagine our shock when the DNA ended up so close that it was a near perfect match. We did the surgery, but even that wasn't enough. Ultimately, the bone-marrow transplant bought her a good year. We never spoke about it. It hurt too much. I hadn't wanted to claim this family any more than they wanted me. Suddenly, when all that was left of it was Thelma and me, and she was dying, it wouldn't let me go.

"The last year of her life, Thelma would look at me and start crying at the strangest times. Once, she asked if I wanted her seat on the board of the business your father started. She'd sold the company after he died but kept a strong hand in it as a major stockholder."

Roxanne forced her feet into her shoes, then thought better of it and took them off. "I didn't want it. I didn't want anything from the Griffiths. As it turned out, she sold her stock. In fact, she liquidated almost everything, except this house and the beach house. She knew I loved the beach house."

"What did she do with the money?"

Roxanne still didn't understand that irony. "The woman who could squeeze a nickel until the buffalo bellowed put it all in bank accounts."

Matt leaned forward, his eyes wide. "Bank savings account interest? She didn't invest it?"

Roxanne frowned at the surprise in his voice. "In matters of money, she was partial to Swiss banks. Speculation was that she'd mete it out to her favorite charities in her will."

"And?"

"I turned out to be her favorite charity." The first sting of tears burned in her nose and behind her eyes. "She never understood how degrading it was to be considered a charity case."

"She couldn't have meant—"

"How the hell would you know what anyone meant? My mother and I were charity cases in this house, and they never, not for one goddamn minute, let us forget it." Anger roared into life. "I was a kid. I don't know why we stayed here, other than

Mom believed you'd come back for her. After she died, the only reason I wasn't sent to foster care is because it would have looked bad. How would the country club set react? And what would their friends say?

"In the end no one outside these walls suspected that Thelma didn't believe I was your daughter, and no one within believed that I was."

"I don't get it. What the hell happened to make them think you weren't mine?" He ran his fingers through his hair and stared at her with an intensity that made him seem alive. "Believe me, Roxanne. There was never a doubt on my part about being your father. Your mother was a virgin on our wedding night."

Roxanne snorted and stood, leaning slightly on the table. "Now I know why there was a wedding night. Was that the only way you could get her into bed?"

"Yes," he hissed as though in pain. She couldn't see him and was glad.

"At least you didn't lie."

"I can't lie. It's an imposition of my being here."

"Obviously you didn't suffer that affliction twenty-nine years ago. *They believed you when you told my mother she wasn't having any kid of yours!*" she shouted. "Oh, I wasn't illegitimate. Not according to the law and society. She was married to you, but not one of them thought you were my biological father. The family treated my mother like a contagious leper." The images burned in Roxanne's head. She couldn't continue. Tears she'd refused to shed for over twenty years battered at her determination with spiked fists.

She left everything as it was and walked out. She had to make it to her room before she lost control. Crying in front of him would be the ultimate humiliation.

Matt prowled the kitchen. An hour before dawn he called upon the judgmental, yet benign, guardian who oversaw this final chance to save his soul.

"She has suffered the greatest injury a child can endure, Matthew," said the voice.

He looked around the brightly lit kitchen. Although he felt the ethereal presence filling the air, he saw nothing from the mystical realm. "And that is?"

"Abandonment. In her reality you abandoned her before birth.

Marian abandoned her with death. Without her parents she had no one."

"What about Marian's mother, Janice?"

"Marian's family took the buy-off money your father paid them and left town before Roxanne's birth."

Matt shook his head ruefully. "The arrest warrant on her mother for theft might have had something to do with it, too." He had hated the Boyles, not because of their social status, but because they were users. How Marian became the antithesis of her grasping mother still boggled his mind.

"Once Janice Boyle realized her daughter had no access to the Griffith money, it was easy to persuade her to depart for greener pastures." The voice paused, then added, "All Roxanne knew about Marian's family was their absence, which she interpreted as rejection."

"That left Thelma," Matt mused. Thelma's disdain for children had been legendary. "Roxanne had no one." The admission made her plight a harsh, painful reality.

"She had a guardian angel of sorts, but that is a matter we'll address at another time. You've summoned me for a specific reason, Matthew. State it."

"I didn't commit suicide. I didn't want to die and abandon her and Marian. Roxanne's a smart woman. She's got to know that."

"You're assuming she cares enough to give it thought, Matthew. Things are not as they were. You are no longer the golden prince in this house. You're just a bad memory."

Matt shivered at the pronouncement. "How did all this happen? How . . . Why did the family doubt Roxanne was my daughter?"

"Think hard, Matthew. Remember now the callous words you flung like stones across a bottomless pond." With those simple directions the guide's presence faded into the sterile overhead lights reflecting off the gleaming kitchen surfaces.

Irritation over being shortchanged in the guidance department flashed. But Matt couldn't afford anger. He'd already bartered a full day in exchange for learning Thelma's fate. He'd best use it to the fullest.

He went to the attic where the remnants of his childhood gathered dust in musty boxes. Nestled among the tokens of a life gone by, he let the events of nearly thirty years ago flow across his memory. As sharp as glass and as cold as ice, the brittle images coalesced.

How clear it all became from an omniscient point of view. Reliving the event from above also provided an uncomfortable objectivity.

A brash, egocentric man wearing Matt's face crooned sweet words to dark-haired, doe-eyed Marian. The words assumed a haunting familiarity. So did Marian's reactions; she wasn't persuaded to acquiesce and dug in her heels.

With a newfound chagrin Matt watched the man he'd been resort to intimidation, blame, and manipulation. Yet Marian had stood fast and denied him.

In retrospect, he had never anticipated the angry words he'd uttered would haunt him. And he damn sure hadn't expected them to live in infamy and hurt his daughter.

Out of habit he blamed the person closest to the problem. Marian.

However, the same power that prevented him from lying to Roxanne thwarted him now.

It wasn't Marian's fault. She hadn't made him speak those hateful words the family overheard so long ago.

In his self-centered mood he hadn't realized their arguments echoed through the halls or the consequences of anyone overhearing those angry words.

Matt shrunk into a ball between the moldering boxes holding the keepsakes of his mortal life as the past came alive.

*"Get real, Marian. It's the worst possible time to have a child. They're sending me to Vietnam when my leave's up. Viet-fucking-nam! I'll be gone a year. Your classes start in a few weeks. You can't go to college and take care of a kid."*

*"You don't know what I can or can't do, Matthew. Neither do I until I try, and if I try hard enough, I'll succeed. When you come home, you'll be a daddy."*

*"Shit! I don't want to be a daddy for years, Marian. The family has connections. We'll get you a safe abortion. In a hospital."*

*"Never! I'll go to Santa Cruz. Or I'll live in the Haight. I'll become a hippie, but I'll have my baby, Matthew. I'd rather die than have an abortion."*

*"I have a say in this, too. A baby will ruin our lives."*

*"You had your say the night you said we didn't need a rubber."* Long dark hair flying, Marian had grabbed her sweater and fled the parlor. She'd nearly knocked Thelma over on her way to the front door.

*"You're not having any kid of mine!"* he'd yelled. *"I'll divorce you for this, Marian. I'll disown the kid!"*

*The front door slammed with the force of an earthquake.*

From his current vantage point in the painful memory, Matt saw the stricken expression on Thelma's face. When he looked toward the top of the stairs, the tableau of his parents' horror at what they'd overheard had them clutching the banister and each other.

Why hadn't he noticed them then? Why hadn't he realized how they had interpreted what they had seen and heard?

Because he hadn't thought of anyone but himself, he realized.

Matt laced his fingers behind his head, caging his face with his arms. Marian had done the right thing. He had pressured her for sex without a rubber. When the consequences he never thought about became her reality, he'd opted for the easy way out.

Marian. Sweet Marian.

She'd been the first person to tell him. "No." At the time it had seemed impossible that she wouldn't go along with what he considered a reasonable solution.

Angry, hurtful words had come so easy then. As was typical of him in those days, he'd said what came to mind without considering the consequences.

When she hadn't returned to the house by midnight, he'd gone looking for her where she'd find a sympathetic ear, a soft shoulder, and rational voice.

Greg Detweiler, his best friend, had loved Marian. In retrospect he may have loved her better and more wisely than Matt. Without a doubt Greg had loved her unselfishly. He'd loved her enough to let her go, to convince her to give Matt another chance.

Until this moment Matt hadn't understood that Greg had acted out of love for them both. If circumstances had been reversed, he'd have seized the opportunity to win Marian to his side. He'd have said or done anything to sway her.

Tentacles of guilt wrapped around his soul and squeezed. He'd done just that to win her. He'd lied about his best friend. He'd cheated Greg out of the love of his life. And in the end he'd stolen Marian's heart. And he never loved anyone the way he loved Marian.

Losing her would have torn his heart out. He'd accepted fatherhood before he'd gone looking for her that night so long ago. She wasn't going to budge on the abortion issue. They'd find a way to handle a kid after he was out of the service. While he was gone, his family would take care of her and the child. That condition formed the basis of the bargain he and Marian struck in Greg's home.

Matt had agreed never to mention abortion again on the condition that she promised to stay in his parents' home until he returned from Vietnam.

Both had kept their word.

Imagining the price Marian had paid to hold fast to her promise filled him with angst. No one knew better than he how tightly his family banded together against a perceived interloper, or someone who wronged one of them.

He wanted to wail in anguish at the injustice.

The only person he could blame was himself.

He had vented his emotions and never looked back.

Marian and his family had lived with the consequences of his thoughtless, damning words and his self-centered reaction for the rest of their lives. As a family they should have consoled each other for losing him, then moved on and shared the treasure of his legacy—Roxanne's childhood. But they had experienced neither consolation nor joy with his and Marian's child. Knowing his parents and Thelma, he was certain the only thing they shared with Marian beyond the physical structure of the house was misery.

No wonder Roxanne was hard and bitter. Twenty-eight years around Thelma Griffith with a grudge would shrivel even the strongest spirit.

"God, are you listening?" His voice cracked with emotion. Crystalline tears flowed down his transparent cheeks.

Silence.

"I know you're there. I know someone's there. Tell Marian . . . Tell her I'm sorry. So damn sorry. She didn't deserve the mess I left her. I'm sorry, Marian. You were right. About so many things.

"God? You still listening? I need some more help here. I need to make things right with Roxanne. You've shown me why, now show me how to fix it."

Silence.

Matt faded into the walls.

At last he understood why ghosts wailed and rattled chains forged link by link, one transgression at a time. A ghost had an eternity to think about it.

After Memorial Day he wouldn't be a ghost. He'd be in the heart of the white light, or in the darkness of the Abyss of Nothingness. His certainty that the Powers on High had made a mistake when judging his fate dimmed a bit.

The memory of Roxanne walking into the fog replayed each time Spence closed his eyes. Three nights ago the mist had closed behind her, removing her from his reach. It was as though she had never been there, never touched his heart, and never looked at him with soulful brown eyes pleading for understanding.

The nights were the worst. The image of her disappearing into the fog hammered at him relentlessly.

He had tossed and turned, trying to figure out why he couldn't stop thinking about her. She had penetrated his well-honed defenses as though she'd had a map to guide her. She was an unnerving, straightforward individual. She was also the only person to reject the very gift he wanted so badly, for his family and himself.

She destroyed his peace of mind and jumbled his emotions. The longer he thought about Roxanne, the greater an enigma she became. Physically, she didn't conform to the type of woman he normally dated.

For starters, she was tall, almost six feet in those high heels she'd worn at the Oceanus. He hadn't dated a brunette since Angela Scarpelli walked out on him two weeks before their wedding day, an embarrassing event, but one he'd long since gotten over. The five-year-old experience left him wiser. Age added the element of caution. He had it all under control. Until Roxanne. The perverse woman electrified every molecule of testosterone in his body.

He had kissed Roxanne once, and knew if he kissed her again, it would take his last ounce of willpower to keep from pursuing the union his body craved. Oh, yes. He still wanted her.

Physically, the reason was clear. Lust. That was easy. Lust required no intellectual understanding, just a physical reaction, consent, and an opportunity.

Intellectually, she tantalized him. The imagination that had produced the enthralling video might prove even more fascinating in bed.

Mentally, she confounded him. The woman had thought processes so straightforward that they bowled him over at times.

Then she would turn on a dime and throw some incredible notion at him, and he'd stand there with his brain packed in ice.

Emotionally, she played havoc with him twenty-four hours a day. Since meeting Roxanne Griffith, he had plumbed new depths of uncertainty. He never indulged in self-delusion. At least, not consciously. He was too young for a midlife crisis, and far too old for any lingering adolescent craziness.

She made him question his actions and examine his motives concerning his involvement with the MIAs and their families. Until Roxanne, it had never crossed his mind that some families genuinely wanted their MIAs to remain lost.

The longer he deliberated, the quieter he became, and the harder he worked.

By late Thursday morning he had analyzed his actions with Roxanne and the way she responded. He had even run through the details of that amazing moment when spilled drinks and leftovers arced through the air as though propelled by an invisible hand.

She had claimed her father's ghost was responsible.

Each time Spence attacked the event from a different angle and recalculated the mathematical improbabilities, the entire incident became the more mind-boggling.

Once he decided the event defied the laws of physics, the question became personal. If he accepted that he had indeed brought back the ghost of Captain Matthew Griffith in a box of old, scarred mementos, then he had another question begging for an answer.

What was his responsibility in the matter and how did he carry it out?

Determined to resolve his quandary, Spence left the offices of Griffith Enterprises a little early on Thursday afternoon. It was past time he and Roxanne talked. The trouble was, there were so many things to talk about that prioritizing them created yet another new problem.

He arrived at her house no closer to finding the solution than when he'd left San Francisco.

Not until he stopped the car on the magnolia-lined street and turned off the engine did he consider the possibility she might not be home. For several minutes he sat motionless and tried to gather his thoughts.

The incoming fog curling over the Santa Cruz Mountains hurried the long shadows of twilight. He probably should have called first. As Spence approached the front porch, every light in the Griffith home came on.

While reconnoitering what he'd say when she answered the door, she pulled into the driveway. He stood at the bottom of the front porch stairs and watched her approach the garage. He slowed the car and nearly stopped when she was even with him, then apparently thought better of it and keyed the garage door open.

Spence cut across the yard and followed the driveway to the garage. When Roxanne emerged a few moments later, her gaze instantly went to the house.

"Have you returned for the box?" she asked, tucking her keys into the pocket of her fashionable charcoal-colored suit coat. He wondered if she donned her steely, businesslike attitude along with her clothing every morning when she dressed. Hell, she looked more like she'd attended a funeral today than when he first saw her in the graveyard.

"The box?" He hoped he wasn't the unwitting source of the displeasure tugging the corners of her mouth into a frown.

"Yes, the box. You know, the one you brought with my father's ghost in it?"

"Okay, you win. I'll take it." Her desire to be rid of the box was one of the things he had pondered, one of the problems he had yet to solve. Now, unexpectedly, it solved itself. Maybe he was making this entire situation too complicated.

"Good. I'll get it for you."

"So I can leave immediately?"

"Look, let's see how much you enjoy having a ghost dogging your every step, blackmailing you into concessions, nagging you endlessly for answers to questions he has no right to ask." She opened the gate to the backyard and waited for him to come through before closing it.

At the far corner of the yard a gazebo stood amid fruit-laden orange trees and lilac bushes bursting with lavender blooms. On the west side of the acre two patios and a cabana flanked a large freestyle black-bottomed pool and spa. Flower beds of roses, peonies, camellias, fuchsias, and other familiar annuals flowed through the sea of pristine grass. Flagstone walks wound through the parklike yard.

Spence put his hands in his pockets and looked around. "I'm impressed. My compliments to you, Roxanne."

"Why? I don't take care of it. Hiroshi does the yard. He has for years. The service comes in a couple of times a week and cares for the pool."

Another piece of information about her clicked into awareness. Not only did she not know how to take a compliment; she did not accept them if they were undeserved.

"Are you a good swimmer?"

"No. I paddle around in the pool a few times a year, mostly when it's very hot. I never cultivated the fine art of filling idle time." She walked over to the roses and cupped a bloom, bent, and inhaled deeply. The faint smile on her face revealed the enjoyment she found in the simple fragrance.

"Let's get the box, then I'll take you to dinner." He wouldn't let her shove him aside easily.

"Why?"

"Because we both need to eat. I'm hungry. You up for pizza and beer?"

She straightened, smiling, then faced him. "Pizza and beer? I didn't think the owner of a couple of five-star restaurants went in for such common fare."

"There's quite a bit you don't know about me, Roxanne. And there's a helluva lot I'd like to know about you. Pizza and beer are two of my favorites." He grinned. Matching her step, he caught her arm. "After all, anything other than pizza and beer and a ball game would be un-American."

"Un-American, huh?" This time when she smiled up at him, it reached her eyes. "Do we have time for me to put on all-American jeans and a sweatshirt? Or will malnutrition set in before then?"

"It may be a close thing, so hurry." He followed her into the house, surprised she hadn't used a key or touched the alarm keypad. "Is there a good pizza parlor close by?"

"Picasso's Pizza down the street from the Acorn has the best in the Valley. And believe me, as a computer programmer, I know good pizza. We live on it during development and deadline crunches."

She tossed her purse onto a white wicker chair with a blue cushion. White wicker furniture and lush ferns filled the entire sunroom. "Make yourself at home. I'll be down in a couple of minutes. The box is on the dining room table. You can get it when we get back. I'm not taking him to Picasso's."

"Okay." She had some strange ideas. If Spence played his cards right, he might discover how she drew some of her conclusions.

He wandered toward the front of the house. The place was larger than it had appeared from the street. That didn't surprise him. The old, stately homes of Palo Alto were renowned for their size and opulent, spacious yards.

Judging by the brilliance of the lamps, and the number of them, Thelma Griffith must have been nearly blind in her declining years. Every room was a well-decorated stage where the spotlights were always on.

Trophies filled a case in the library. A quick glance assured they were all riding trophies. Closer inspection indicated horsemanship was an old family endeavor. He filed the information away and continued to the front of the house.

He located the dining room easily enough. Freshly cut flowers filled an enormous Waterford crystal bowl on a long lace runner in the center of the polished table.

Instead of the box he found a chilled room with walls that seemed to watch his every move.

# Chapter Seven

Picasso's Pizza Palace smelled like heaven and was a lot closer. Located half a block from the Acorn, Picasso's was busy every night of the week. Roxanne grabbed the last available booth while Spence waded through a sea of Little Leaguers arguing over what they were going to order.

Picasso's attracted a variety of patrons. As a concession to the youth of the community, a video arcade and tables occupied the former smoking section at the rear of the building. The enthusiasm of the players spilled out along with the android voice of a conquered video game.

The family section clustered along the windows. There, the children had a view of the park, and parents monitored the passersby. Roxanne recognized a couple from her high school days. Between tending their boys, who looked around three and five years old, they watched the sidewalks. She couldn't help wondering if they were watching for ghosts from their own pasts.

In an alcove designed to accommodate the chaos of birthday parties and organized sports teams, adults in baseball attire talked amongst themselves, kids divvied up pitchers of soda and vied for the title of Loudest Talker. When the volume reached earsplitting, they toned down, as though collectively knowing the magic decibel that forced adult attention.

Roxanne relaxed into the corner formed by the booth and the wall. It was an excellent vantage point from which to observe the show around her. Although she frequently ordered out from Picasso's, it had been years since she had eaten a meal inside the pizzeria. When she dined alone, which was all the time except for lunch with coworkers and an occasional business dinner, she preferred take-out meals.

The way Spence laughed and talked with the kids in line touched a soft spot in her. All he needed was a baseball cap to be mistaken for a giant Little Leaguer. He fit in with the kids so easily she wondered why he didn't have several of his own.

Of course, he might have a couple of tykes and an ex-wife. Most men didn't wear a neon sign advertising their private lives, particularly if it was painful. Furthermore, she reminded herself, it was none of her business. Still, her interest in him clamored for satisfaction. And that was unsettling all by itself.

Carrying two frosty mugs and a pitcher of beer, Spence joined her. "Wait until you taste the combination on this pizza."

"Did you leave off the anchovies?"

"Yeah. No anchovies." He poured their beer and pushed a mug across the table. "I had him put on pickled herring instead. Is that okay?"

If she hadn't caught the glint in his eye, she might have thought he was serious. "Only if they serve horseradish with it."

She made circles on the frosty sides of her beer mug. "Have you always been into food?"

"Sure. Food consumption is the main reason people are alive today." He placed a folded napkin in front of her sweating glass.

"You get no argument from me on that." As long as she didn't have to cook it.

"When you grow up in the restaurant business, your world consists of food preparation, the financial bottom-line, and a clear understanding of long working hours."

"I see." She tried to smile, but her face felt brittle. "I have a confession."

"Are you sure you're in the right place? I'm not a priest," he warned, his gaze fixed on her.

"It isn't that kind of confession. Actually, I was curious about you, so I did some checking on Griffith Enterprises." Careful, she warned herself. Researching him constituted an open admission of an attraction she wasn't ready to concede.

"Should I be flattered?"

"No."

"Are you always this direct?" His smile disappeared behind his beer mug.

"Afraid so."

A slight tic in his left eyebrow betrayed his sudden mood shift to the somber side. "Did you discover anything interesting?"

"As a matter of fact, I did. Those long hours of hard work you mentioned have paid off for you and Griffith Enterprises—not to mention your family's two restaurants. But I'm curious about something else. Is building all that wealth the reason you don't have kids?" Recalling her earlier speculation, a hot flush of embarrassment crept up her neck. She reached for her beer. "Or do you?" She took a sip. The frostiness failed to cool the heat in her face. "Or would you rather I shut up?"

While he openly studied her, the angles and planes of his face assumed razor sharpness. The blue of his eyes remained focused on her. An inner struggle seemed to subside, softening his austere features. "I've never been married," he admitted. A tinge of the momentary struggle lingered in his voice. "But yeah, I plan on it. And kids. As many as possible. How about you?"

His unexpected candor took their acquaintance to a more intimate level where hopes and confidences moved into the light. "Right now, my business is enough. It looks like we're going to be busy for at least a couple of years." The deluge of calls she had received after Walter's party had continued through this afternoon. Even if chaos hadn't tugged her personal life in all directions, she still wouldn't have time to search for Mr. Right.

"Is this a case of 'Be careful what you wish, you might get it?' "

She licked the tip of her finger and made a check mark in the air. "You have that one right. The opportunity to grow my business is now beating down my door. And I'm grateful."

"What happens when you wake up one morning and realize the business isn't enough? That you want more. Things a successful balance sheet can't give you."

She watched the Little Leaguers settle at the tables. The first time that thought had crossed her mind she was holding Thelma's hand in the ICU. Thelma had been slipping away, and no one could stop the process. But Roxanne hadn't given an inch. Each day she sat with Thelma, read to her, and watched Thelma's favorite soap opera while brushing her hair. And each day she had massaged lotion into nearly transparent skin the texture of aged parchment while Thelma's strength ebbed. In one of those weak moments Roxanne had wondered who would hold her hand when it was her turn to die.

She shook off the memory and focused on Spence. He was strong, healthy, and made her feel things she had no business exploring. "Has that happened to you?"

"It happens to everyone in one form or another." He refilled their mugs. "Of course, when my family gets together for one of the many events we celebrate, you'd think the miracle of the century is that I'm not married."

"They think you're quite a catch, huh?" Great. Another golden child. Only this one had hair as black as sin and serious features that haunted her dreams. Her father merely stalked her days.

"Sure. And they have pictures and lists of women I should date to prove it."

Some of her incredulity must have shown because he laughed and continued speaking. "My father was Irish. My mother is Italian. When you put them together, you end up with a big extended family. In the restaurant business, that translates to a reliable workforce, delicious food, and fine booze.

"A few of my aunts and uncles are definitely Old World. A couple of them think my generation should be contributing to the world's population."

"It sounds like quite a conglomeration." She couldn't imagine a gathering of that many diverse relatives.

"Yeah, it is. We're a normal family with normal dysfunctionalities—none criminal that I know of. I'd like you to meet them."

"Meeting a seminormal Griffith family would be a unique experience." As soon as the words left her mouth, she wondered what had possessed her to say them.

"Great. We're celebrating my grandmother's ninety-fifth birthday next week."

She followed his perusal of the pizzeria. In a flash of insight she realized Spence wanted the slice of life surrounding them. The kids, the problems, the involvement. The close, core family. And he'd be good at it. He hadn't had any trouble talking to the kids in line and seemed to know what to say.

Roxanne squirmed in her seat. She had no idea what to say to kids. Her childhood had stopped the day her mother died. But she'd learn. To that end, she'd agreed to baby-sit a friend's three-year-old in a few weeks. The thought made her nervous. She swept it aside. There was enough to think about right here.

The Little Leaguers were munching on pizza. Two tables behind Spence a two-year-old demanded more soda at the top of his lungs. Someone broke the high-score record on the Death Invaders video game. Vociferous congratulations, along with the android voice promising retribution and issuing the challenge to resume play, sounded from the back room.

"A celebration of this magnitude calls for the gathering of the entire clan. That means the Griffiths, Kellys, and Lazzaros, all in one place. The results are a lot like this pizzeria tonight, only without the video games."

Paulo delivered the pizza personally. With a flourish he placed two olive oil cans in the center of the table and bridged them with a wooden platter holding the pizza. Roxanne stared at the steaming pile of Canadian bacon, onions, tomatoes, pineapple, olives, and several other ingredients she didn't recognize embedded in the mountain of cheese.

She didn't have to worry about where to begin, as Spence started right in by tucking a plate under a slice of pizza oozing cheese strings. Fortunately, Paulo had brought forks.

"Tell me about your family." Roxanne used the side of her fork to cut through the thick slice.

"What would like to know?"

"Why don't you begin with your grandmother, the one who's having the birthday."

"Let's just say that Grandma Lazzaro didn't get to be ninety-five by holding in her emotions and letting stress build up."

"You mean she says what she thinks."

"Exactly. Like you." He gestured with his beer.

"I don't say everything that's on my mind. If I did, I wouldn't have any friends." She grinned and bit into her pizza. For a moment, she forgot everything except the mouth-watering explosion of flavors packed into that single bite. Pizza had never tasted so good. "Marvelous choice, Spence," she said between bites. "Continue."

While devouring the pizza, he talked about his grandmother, and his cousins. When he spoke of his older sisters, his eyes brightened. Clearly, he was close to both of them.

His elaborate descriptions of his most colorful relatives made her laugh until her sides hurt. She had never met a man as open or candid as Spence. When he spoke of his family, he wore his emotions on his sleeve for the entire world to see. There was nothing guarded, or middle-of-the-road, when he shared his insights of the people he loved.

But he saved his greatest tenderness for his mother and, in so doing, wormed his way a little deeper into Roxanne's heart.

By midnight the cleanup crew had started sweeping the floor, and the last of the die-hard customers dribbled away. The Little Leaguers had gone home hours earlier. The dishes from the salad bar were gone, as was the ice; the water drained. A pair of the high schoolers who worked behind the counter began refilling dried pepper medley, cheese, salt, and pepper shakers.

Roxanne and Spence had consumed their beer, another mug of soda each, and polished off the last crumb of pizza. It was time to leave. Paulo was closing up. Besides, tomorrow was a busy day for them both.

When they returned to the house every light was ablaze. Spence pulled into the driveway, got out, and opened Roxanne's side. Together they walked up the front porch. She turned the knob and pushed the door open.

"Is your alarm broken?"

"No, the alarm works fine. So does the dead bolt. *He* can take care of any burglars brave enough to invade the house he claims as his territory. You might have noticed, he had no trouble handling the groper at the party the other night."

"I suppose that's one way to look at it."

"You may not believe in ghosts right this minute, Spence. But you'll change your tune after you've had his box for a little while. He's a blackmailer and a nag." She grabbed the newel post and called up the stairs. "And, as you can see, he's afraid of the dark. The utility company loves him. You will, too," she added, turning back to him.

"I'll let you know how I make out." Spence still had difficulty accepting the notion of a ghost.

He followed her into the dining room. The light streaming through the crystal chandeliers cast colorful prisms on the French silk wallpaper. The room was exactly as they had left it when they went for pizza.

Roxanne pushed her fingers into the back pockets of her jeans. "Did you move it?"

"The box?"

"Yes. It was on the table this morning."

"No, it wasn't here earlier. Could your housekeeper have moved it? Maybe put it in a closet?"

With each headshake of denial, emotion colored her cheeks. As he watched, her features resumed the tension that had melted away over the last several hours. The change saddened him. Her left eyebrow rose a fraction as her eyes narrowed, her gaze fixed to a place on the wall near the kitchen door.

Although Spence saw nothing, clearly Roxanne did. Her eyes became golden agates and her entire body assumed a rigid, defensive stance.

The hair on the back of the Spence's forearms rippled to attention.

"Either you're leaving, or I'm leaving," she said softly. "If I go, I'll donate this house to a rehab center. While it would please me immensely, I doubt you'd be thrilled."

For the next several minutes it was so quiet Spence heard his heartbeat between the faint tick-tock of the grandfather clock.

"I don't care. I want the box," she ordered through clenched teeth. "Now."

Spence was growing increasingly uncomfortable at this one-sided conversation. Apparently, so was she. Her fingers had curled into white-knuckled fists.

There seemed little choice but to start believing in ghosts. It was either that, or believe the sane, intelligent, witty woman with whom he'd shared a pizza was more than a few ingredients short of a finished recipe.

Without warning, Roxanne shoulders slumped, and she exhaled a deep breath he hadn't realized she'd taken. "Let's check it out," she said.

Hopeful she was finally speaking to him, Spence followed her into the brightly lit kitchen. On the island where he had placed it the first time, sat the box. It looked unaffected by Roxanne's attempts at incineration despite its singed flaps and charred sides.

Roxanne removed the smaller black lacquer box from the scarred cardboard container. She opened the lid and one by one removed the contents.

"What are you doing?" Spence asked.

"Making sure he doesn't stay behind."

"Oh. And just how do you do that?"

"Remember the wings you found in my purse at the Oceanus club? *He* put them in my purse—I didn't. That's how he got there. It's as if he hitchhikes on a piece of the past. He needs an artifact to ground him, or move him to where he wants to go. All he has to do is find someone who's going there."

She glanced up at him. "He went to work with me on Tuesday. That's when I realized how he travels. He probably would have gone Monday, but he'd already bartered a day of leaving me alone for a few answers."

She whirled around. "Go pound sand."

Spence settled onto a high stool. This was getting bizarre. "You were right, Roxanne. The pizza is giving me nightmares, and I haven't been to bed yet." And that was part of the problem. Each time he went to bed he made love to Roxanne in a fantasy world without boundaries.

"I've been told that to know me is to be confused." She returned the items, then closed the lid. With the box tucked under her arm, she walked over to the kitchen table and put out her hand. "Give it."

Head shaking, foot tapping, she wiggled her fingers.

Spence stared with the same macabre fascination with which he had watched the horror movies with Jason in a hockey mask during his adolescence. His heart nearly bolted from his chest when an old, barely recognizable military ID card materialized on the flat of Roxanne's open hand.

"Jesus H. Christ," he croaked, unable to blink. Watching the corroded metal pilot's wings materialize out of thin air and hearing the subtle *clunk* as they dropped on top of the ID card disoriented him completely. He gripped the side of the island to keep from falling off the stool.

If he wasn't seeing it firsthand, he'd never believe it. The truth struck with a force that made his heart pound in his eyeballs.

"And the other one," she demanded. "The picture."

Dry-mouthed, Spence gaped at the mildew-stained relics. A fungus-eaten picture encased in a zipped plastic bag appeared over the wings and the ID card. As part of his brain assimilated what he'd seen, another part relaxed. She wasn't over the edge—unless he was, too.

Only later did he realize how Roxanne had taken advantage of his stunned state. Within a few word-frenzied minutes, she had the box packed and the cardboard container taped shut so nothing could escape.

"This should take care of it," she said with conviction. Her hands lingered at the taped edges.

He wasn't sure about Captain Matthew Griffith, but the ordeal certainly squelched his doubts concerning the existence of ghosts.

"Is he . . . the ghost, that is, in the box, too?" Spence eased his knuckle-aching grip on the island. He couldn't remember anything rattling him as thoroughly as Roxanne's authoritative command of a ghost he hadn't believed in when they entered the house.

"No. He's faded into the walls. It's his way of sulking." She braced the box on her hip.

"Sulking?"

"Like a spoiled child who didn't get his way." She finished her survey of the kitchen ceiling and wall joists before meeting his gaze.

"What do you expect me to do with him? Send him to his room if he throws a temper tantrum?" As the words tumbled forth, he realized he had no idea of what to do with the box or the spirit Roxanne believed attached to it by some paranormal umbilical cord.

"You could send him back to Vietnam," she suggested.

A hollow laugh caught in his throat. "Not an option. You have no idea what it took to bring him out. Even if I could, I wouldn't. There's too much at stake. Too many families still wanting closure and the comfort of bringing home even this much of their MIAs."

"Then I guess you'll have to figure out something on your own. I don't want him here." She extended a hand, signaling an end to the impromptu date and the conversation. "Maybe you could turn him over to Customs and lose him in the red tape."

"What a miserable fate that would be." Spence caught her hand and walked through the house, down the front porch steps to his car. He locked the box in the trunk, then leaned against it.

"Now what, Roxanne?"

"Now what, what?"

Despite the tumultuous events in the kitchen, he hungered for the taste of her mouth. It would be torture if he kissed her and agony if he didn't. He chose the sweeter kind. "How about if you say something like: 'Thank you for a fun evening, Spence. And thank you for taking away the box. May I kiss you good night?' "

A roulette wheel of emotions moved over her face, ranging from startlement, to surprise, then amusement. Fortunately, the ball came to rest on what he could only hope was red-hot desire.

He gathered her hands and drew her into the vee of his spread legs. "And then I say something like: 'I thought you'd never ask.' "

"Then you say: 'That's all I've thought about for the last hour.' " He coaxed her arms over his shoulders.

Roxanne smiled knowingly, her eyes twinkling in delight for him and the game. He didn't care which when she picked up the challenge by adding, "And you say: 'I've wanted to kiss you all night, too. That's why I'm playing Sir Galahad and taking your ghost. Why I plied you with pizza and beer.' "

The embrace tightened at the small of her back and brought her soft curves flowing across his body. Her arms fastened around his neck as her balance slipped away. The angle lined them up hip to hip, chest to breasts. Mouth to mouth.

His body was already reacting to her nearness, demanding, the need growing with each heartbeat.

"Then I say, 'It worked, because I definitely want to kiss you.' " Her fingers slid up the back of his neck and through his hair. "Oh, yes, I do," she breathed, then touched his lips with hers.

The slow journey of the tip of her tongue along his lower lip sent sweet fire through him. He let it burn; savoring the erotic path of flame she created, instinctively drawing her closer. As soon as his splayed fingers pressed her lower back, her moist, warm breath against his cheek quickened.

He seized her mouth. Her arms tightened around his neck, her fingers plowing into his hair. Braced against the car trunk, Spence drew her entire weight against him, all the while exploring every inch of her back. His mouth tasted and tested hers.

Restraint, he admonished, then promptly forgot the warning.

His fingers molded, then clung, to the shapely globes of her buttocks. Their hips ground together. The heavenly agony of her pubic bone sliding over his erection forced him to shift. In one urgent movement of primal need, his knee split her thighs.

Roxanne cried out against his mouth, then accommodated the intrusion, making the contact with his leg even more intimate.

The heat of her sex penetrated the fabric separating them. With each heartbeat the sensation grew hotter, searing him.

One of them deepened the kiss; Spence moved them in the age-old erotic dance of courtship. He wanted her. Craved her. Had to have her.

Then she stilled. Her mouth remained pressed to his, only she no longer returned his kiss. Slowly, reluctantly, her hands moved back to his shoulders.

Every fiber of his being wailed in protest.

Their ragged breathing spoke volumes about the chemistry between them. "I'm sorry." Her words sounded as shaky as he felt.

He tried to douse the wildfires of disappointment, but the need burning him to a cinder had only one cure—the woman in his arms. Logic cried it was too soon for him to make love with her. His body had only one response: It was never too soon.

She rested her forehead on his chin. The scent of the pizza parlor and the underlying fragrance of her shampoo filled his nostrils.

And he wanted her even more.

Her fingers dug into his shoulders when he withdrew his thigh from between hers, then settled her on the ground. Both shook so hard, one of them was bound to fall if he released her.

"He's right, isn't he?"

Spence exhaled a shuddered breath. "Who the hell is *he*? And what is he right about?" He gathered her against his chest and rocked them to keep the ache from consuming him.

"*He* is sitting on the top of your car, watching us."

"Shit." The damn ghost. The entity he could neither see, nor hear.

"He says all you want is to get into my pants."

"I don't want to get into your pants. They wouldn't fit. What I want is to get your pants off you." He moved his hips as a reminder of just how badly he wanted her. "But, you already know that, don't you," he breathed into her ear.

"I can't . . ."

He kissed her forehead. "Can't what? Get wild and naked in your front yard while *he's* present?"

She groaned and leaned into him. "I didn't even think about . . ." Her voice trailed.

For several minutes they held each other. Releasing her a final time was sheer torture for Spence. He straightened; it would be a while yet before the ache in his loins subsided to a tolerable state.

"I'd better go," he said, bent and brushed a kiss across her lips.

"Yeah, I guess so." She pushed against his shoulders until she caught her balance, then gave him an apologetic half smile.

He flicked the tip of her nose with his forefinger. "I'll call you."

"Sure."

He got into the car and started the engine.

She stood on the lawn. Behind her, the house lights blazed.

He started backing out. "I don't suppose it matters if he rides on top of the car or inside it."

She said nothing, just stood there, watching while Spence backed the car down the drive. When he reached the street, she was still standing in the same spot. It took all his determination to keep from racing back up the drive and kissing her senseless.

She was still standing there when he drove down the street and into the night.

"You're making me real sorry I brought you back, Griffith. Real sorry."

Matt lounged in the backseat of the spacious Lincoln. Small wonders his chauffeur was in a surly mood. He hadn't gotten what he wanted. Although he didn't know it now, Spencer Griffith would have been a lot sorrier if Roxanne hadn't noticed him and put an end to the passionate liaison.

Matt congratulated himself on his diplomatic tactics.

He hadn't said a word to Roxanne, though a tirade about necking in public twisted his tongue into knots. So, maybe it wasn't *public* public. It was outdoors. Anyone driving down the street could have seen his daughter perched on Spence's thigh and . . .

He changed position and looked over Spence's shoulder rather than finish that thought.

Matt had exercised great restraint, and it grated him sorely. Trying to win his daughter's amity was difficult at best. It required a forbearance he'd seldom used when alive. Roxanne's belligerence added another complication to the mix.

Determined to keep things simple, he had chosen the most direct, unobtrusive way to interrupt the lovers. He had hovered cross-legged over the top of the car and watched. Nothing more.

And that's what he'd continue doing. Watching. He hadn't earned the right to direct interference or parental lectures—no matter how much his fledgling paternal feeling prodded him in that direction.

The only potential ally Matt had was in the driver's seat. Until Spencer Griffith crossed the line with his daughter or proved unworthy in some other fashion, Matt would literally remain in the backseat and learn what drove the man.

Matt had to admit that Roxanne had assessed his limitation partially correct. The items in the box were conduits of sorts. Wherever one of them went, he could go, if he chose. What she failed to realize, and he did not intend to reveal yet, was her own importance. She was part of him, too. She also lived in the house he'd grown up in, the house that held memories of him. In dissimilar ways, they each had a piece of him.

Consequently, he could go home any time. And go home was exactly what Matt had expected Spence to do. Unless the man lived above a restaurant, which hardly seemed likely.

Perched on Spence's shoulder, Matt took on the role of observer. He was about to find out what kind of man his daughter necked with in the driveway.

Roxanne stood on the dewy lawn until the night chill penetrated her awareness. Hugging her arms against the cold, she turned toward the house. It seemed bigger with all the lights on, and emptier now that Spence had taken away the last ghost. Consequently, the house assumed a cold and impersonal aura.

She climbed the front steps.

"It's a house. That's all." She resumed the nightly ritual of locking doors and setting the security alarm. It took nearly fifteen minutes to turn off all the lamps and overhead lights.

After a quick shower, she climbed into bed and stared at the ceiling.

The things she didn't want to think about slid into her brain. They all looked and sounded like Spence.

"He has an agenda," she reminded herself for the umpteenth time. Once Memorial Day passed, Spence would be moving on to his next interest. "Don't get carried away."

If *he* hadn't materialized tonight, she might have done just that. Logically, she owed Matt a debt of thanks. Physically, she wanted Spence so badly, she wondered if the ache would go away.

"What the hell am I going to do?"

No answer penetrated the silence.

# Chapter Eight

The enthusiastic demand for Magic Wish's computer animation and video services turned the offices into organized mayhem. Roxanne put in an order with a temp agency for an experienced receptionist and an office administrator.

Late Friday night she loaded her briefcase and laptop and went home to pack an overnight bag. She had only one destination in mind: the beach house.

It was the place where her thoughts seemed clearer and she found solutions to even the most complex problems. In retrospect, it was amazing Thelma hadn't sold the beach house long ago. Purchased a year before the horrendous car accident that killed Roxanne's mother and paternal grandparents, Thelma had never visited the place. From the time Roxanne was old enough to take the bus to the coast, she had spent as much time as possible there.

Friday night traffic bogged down in the mountains. A stop at the grocery store posed another delay. But she didn't mind. Already, the ocean breeze had blown away a layer of tension.

Shortly after seven o'clock, she turned the key in the front door lock. It took another half hour before she had the groceries unpacked, dinner started, and her work spread across the kitchen table that doubled as a desk.

An *Elton John Greatest Hits* CD played softly in the living room. The night air stirred the curtains on the opened window and carried in the scent of ocean and fog.

By eight she had finished her soup and sandwich and was well into the first of four proposals she needed to draft by Monday. The sudden, shrill warbling of her cell phone sent her entire body into a muscle-crunching lurch and left her heart racing.

She emptied her purse onto the floor, rummaging the contents as they mushroomed across the Berber carpet. The phone rang a second, then a third time before she managed to find it.

"Yes? What is it?" Only a handful of people knew her private cell phone number.

"You're a difficult woman to locate on Friday night."

Spence. He was part of the reason she'd wanted to get away for the weekend. He may have her number, but he didn't know where she was.

"Is *he* giving you trouble?"

"I haven't seen hide nor hair of him. Are you sure the box is his anchor?"

"I saw him leave with you." She shrugged and started to gather up the spilled contents of her purse. "I haven't seen him since."

"Nor do you want to, right?"

"Absotively, posilutely, one-hundred percent on the money."

"Speaking of money, here's the $64,000 question. Can I see you tomorrow?"

The tension knot she was trying to rub out of her shoulder tightened. "I'm buried in work."

"I promise to be a distraction."

Roxanne could not prevent the sudden smile tugging at her mouth. "Yeah, you would be." And a very sexy distraction, too. Heaven only knew what would happen if he kissed her as he'd done last night, this time without interruptions. A split second of thought, and she knew. "It's not a good idea."

"It's not a good idea because you don't want to see me? Or it's not a good idea because you would rather work? Or it's not a good idea because I frightened the hell out of you last night and you're running scared?"

The latter skated dangerously close to the truth. She stood and walked to the window, where she peered out into the darkness. The rhythm of the tide riding the back of the storm beat against the sand. "Yes, to all three. Let's not play games, Spence. When it's all said and done, and we're looking at the naked truth, you want something from me. Something I'm not prepared to give."

"You're right. I do want something. I want a great deal from you, Roxanne."

"No. The answer is no." Because she didn't trust herself to remain firm, she pressed the button and disconnected the call. As an afterthought, she turned off the cell phone. No amount of simmering desire or charm would coerce her participation in the Memorial Day service. She could not be that much of a hypocrite for anyone.

After a few moments she grabbed her sweatshirt and went outside. In the thick, starless night she let her thoughts drift with the sound of the waves.

"Coward," she murmured.

Spence hung up the phone and looked around his office above Christopher's. Roxanne had him pegged; he intended to play the angles. A tinge of guilt nibbled at his conscience. Wanting to spend time with her was a purely selfish pursuit. Part of the trouble was his desire for something more tangible than her time. He wanted her naked body next to his with an unreasonable intensity; he also wanted her at the Memorial Day ceremony.

What he had intentionally omitted in their long discussion of his family at the pizza parlor were the myriad demands, requests, and expectations that fell on his shoulders as the *de facto* head of the clan.

Spence sighed as he made a final notation on a document he had been drafting and tossed it onto a growing stack of problems and questions he'd spent the afternoon and evening resolving. With an equally high pile waiting in the in-basket, Spence settled behind the desk. For the next several hours he'd review the personnel problems that went hand-in-hand with being related to half of the restaurant staff.

Shortly after 2 A.M., he dropped the folders into the center file cabinet drawer and locked it. Monday, the operations manager would distribute envelopes containing his disposition of each request or problem. Those who wanted a personal explanation could make an appointment, but all knew it was an exercise in futility. Although Spence listened, he seldom changed his mind, not because he didn't understand, but because he did. Part of his business philosophy was to know his employees as well as family.

And because most of the Christopher's staff actually *was* family, albeit extended, he had a unique insight into each of them.

Griffith Enterprises, although far larger and more complex from a business standpoint, was much easier to run. Only two employees were extended family and those only during the summer school break. He would rather negotiate with an egotistical bureaucrat than argue with an aunt over one of her children.

He turned off the light on the desk and put on his coat. Before he reached the office door, the phone rang. A flash from his optimistic nature sent him hurrying back to answer. Roxanne may have changed her mind and couldn't sleep.

Only it wasn't Roxanne. Sergeant Graystone of the Richmond Police Department informed him that Brian Lazzaro, his third cousin, was in detention for curfew violation. Brian had given Spence's name and number instead of his mother and stepfather's.

It was going to be a long night.

The world had become very complicated over the last thirty years. Matt wasn't sure he liked the changes, but he admired the way Spencer Griffith coped, juggled two businesses, and addressed the problems of a squadron of relatives.

Not a man easily impressed, Matt had admired precious few people in his life. Now, in death, he found another to add to the short list. The way Spence had handled Brian's parents had done the trick.

It would have never occurred to Matt to look beyond Brian's rebellious disobedience. He would have dealt with the act itself, the sneaking out of the house. Spence had addressed the boy's isolation, the sense of abandonment Brian had felt since his father's abrupt move to New Jersey. Whenever his stepfather attempted to rein him in, Brian rebelled, just as he had tonight.

Spence had worked a deal with the authorities that put the entire family into counseling.

The encounter at the Richmond police station gave Matt plenty to ponder. He considered Spencer Griffith a cross between a Mafia strong-arm and a sixties sensitivity trainer.

Gradually, he understood the man who wanted into his daughter's pants also wanted into her heart. Matt contemplated Roxanne's life, his predicament, and Spence's character until making a decision shortly before dawn.

He did not act on it until Spence got out of the shower and

wrapped a towel around his hips. Steam coated the expanse of mirror plastered to the wall over the double sinks. Just as Spence lifted a towel to wipe the mirror, Matt began to write.

Roxanne planned to spend the weekend with a laptop and a CD player.

Not only did she intend to sort out the increasingly chaotic mess of her personal life, but she also needed to attack the mountain of paperwork the Walter Penworth video continued to generate.

The knock on the door disrupted all three.

She blinked several times to clear her vision, then rose and stretched her arms high overhead to work out the muscle kinks on her way to the foyer.

Spence stood on her porch. Three dozen roses rested in the cradle of his left arm. Two bottles of wine dangled from his right hand.

"How on earth did you find me?" And why wasn't she disappointed that he had? His serious expression made her hesitate.

"Are you going to invite me in?"

Still, she vacillated. "I don't know." She sensed doing so could jeopardize more than her weekend work plans. The prospect filled her with a mixture of excitement and trepidation.

"You still haven't told me how you found me," she said, slowly perusing him. Under the black leather bomber jacket he wore, a white T-shirt hugged his chest like a glove. Faded jeans caressed his hips and thighs the way she had ached to do in the driveway.

When her gaze finally rose to meet his, Spence answered her question. "Your father made his presence known."

Roxanne took an involuntary step backward and gripped the edge of the door as though it was a shield. "My father?"

"He drew a map. I gotta tell you, Roxanne. I'm not used to having directions appear in the condensation on my bathroom mirror. But I wasn't about to look a gift horse in the mouth, either. In this case, maybe I should say finger."

"My father?" she repeated, her heart plummeting to her toes. "He doesn't know about this place. He can't. They bought it after . . . after they learned he was MIA. How could he know about it?" What else he did he know about her? And how did he find out?

"That wasn't part of the exchange. Obviously, he does, but you don't have to worry about him showing up. We struck a bargain."

The situation worsened by the minute. "Great." A bargain between the Golden Griffith boys boded ill all the way around.

"Don't you want to hear what it is?" Worry—or was it concern—narrowed his eyes slightly and left the traces of a frown. Whether it was for her or him, she didn't know.

"I don't know, Spence. Do I?" Any time two men with separate agendas combined forces and focused on a woman, that woman needed to tread very, very carefully.

"Why don't I come in and tell you about it? These flowers are getting thirsty." His eyebrows lifted in expectation, hope shone in his eyes.

Roxanne continued staring into those deep blue eyes for a long moment while her thoughts strayed. The prospect of kissing him again sent a trill of excitement coursing through her veins. The allure of tasting him, feeling his hard, eager body pressed against hers, robbed some of the strength from her knees. She gripped the door a little tighter to keep from swaying, and sought a diversion. "Are the roses and the wine bribes or conciliation?"

"Your father has made sure I believe in ghosts. I hope you'll accept my apology along with the flowers." His shrug of apology jostled the red, yellow, and white roses that filled his arms. "I didn't know what color you preferred, so I got some of each."

Roxanne leaned her temple against the side of the door and stared at the roses. "I don't suppose I have a preference. The only time I've received roses was . . ." She rolled her head against the edge of the door. It didn't matter.

"Was, when?" he coaxed.

"When somebody died." The admission added to her unease.

"Neither one of us is dying today, and it's too late for the flowers. However, the blooms will last longer if they're in water."

With a sigh, Roxanne opened the door a little wider. She knew when she was conquered. Only in this case, opening the door didn't feel like defeat. "You're the expert; I'll leave it to you."

Accepting the flowers, actually taking the fragrant multicolored blooms from his arms, would lend a personal significance to the gift she wasn't ready for. So instead of taking them from Spence, she ushered him into the kitchen. A quick rummage of the cupboards produced a vase large enough for the lush bouquet.

Arms folded, her hip braced against the countertop, she watched Spence arrange the flowers. It struck her that there probably wasn't anything he couldn't do, and do well. Maybe even handle her father's ghost. "So you met him and he made a believer out of you."

"I wouldn't say I met him, because I didn't actually see him. But he made his presence known when I least expected it." The twinkle in his eyes softened his features when he grinned at her. "I'm not used to sharing my bathroom with a man—dead or alive."

She doubted he objected to sharing the same space with a woman, and probably did so on a regular basis. And why not? Given his money and position, women undoubtedly followed him as though he were the Pied Piper. It wasn't just his social status and personal magnetism; he radiated sex appeal, had a devastating smile, a charming, witty personality, and a body that promised a woman ecstasy. And that was before they learned he could cook and had a Dunn & Bradstreet rating.

And he brought a woman roses as a form of apology.

"Where is your ghost now?"

"I left him at my place. I don't think it makes any difference where the box is, Roxanne. It seems as if he can pretty much go where he wants." He shrugged. "Before I came down here, he asked me to spread a map of San Francisco out on the kitchen counter. He's looking for someone, which is why he hasn't returned to your house, not because I took the box." Spence lifted the vase from the sink. Sprigs of fern and baby's breath blended tastefully with the red, yellow, and white blooms.

"Explain this bargain you two made, please." She prepared to listen between the lines.

"It was more of an agreement." He placed the vase stuffed with flowers next to the sink, and leaned his hip against the countertop, imitating her stance. "I agreed not to make love with you today if he gave me this address, and he agreed not to leave the City until I got home."

Roxanne stared at him in disbelief. Double blackmail—Griffith style. The man who wanted to be her lover and the ghost who was her father trusting each other stretched even her imagination. There seemed no end to the lengths these two men would go to achieve their agendas. Then the similarities of those agendas struck her.

If she loved her father, or at least had tender feelings for him, she would have no qualms about eulogizing him Memorial Day.

That fulfilled Spence's agenda perfectly. And a profession of affection, particularly a public one, was exactly what Matt had said he wanted.

Irritation heightened her wariness. "What makes you two think I'd go to bed with you in the first place? A few flowers? Some wine to dull my senses?" The irritation was turning into aggravation. "It's clear neither one of you has a very high opinion of my morals or standards. For your information, Spencer No-Relation Griffith, I'm not for sale. Neither you nor your ghostly friend can bribe, or coerce, or manipulate me into singing his praises at your precious Memorial Day ceremony. It's not going to happen, Spence. If that's what you're looking for with all this fluff, tuck it under your arm and go home. You're wasting my time."

Arms folded across his chest, he looked at her for a long time. The heady scent of roses permeated the kitchen. The faint sounds of Celine Dion leaked from the living room. In the distance the rhythm of the ocean kept time with the tension growing between them.

"What are you afraid of?" he asked softly.

"Nothing." The word flew off her tongue without thought. She had spent a good part of last night asking herself the same question. The glimmer of an answer slipped awkwardly into her awareness. Him. Emotion. Entanglement. Disappointment. Abandonment.

"If you want me to leave, I'll go. But let's get something clear up front. Yeah, I want you on the dais Memorial Day. The Remembrance Foundation and the families supporting it need the positive press for political reasons. But your absence will not deter us. We'll honor our dead and our missing. We'll console each other and ourselves. We'll go on, just as we have for years. Given your feelings about your father, we're better off with your absence than with the hostile, negative press your presence would attract."

"I would never jeopardize what you're trying to do. I resent any implication that I would." His blunt appraisal stung. What kind of person did he think she was?

"I'm not implying you would. I'm trying to make a distinction you seemed intent on misunderstanding."

"I'm sorry. Please, finish." She felt the chip perched firmly on her shoulder bearing her father's name grow the size of an ancient Redwood.

"I came here to see the intriguing woman I spent last Saturday with in a hot kitchen. The woman who listened to the tales of my family over pizza and beer. Who responded to my kiss in her driveway last night."

The swift, sure arrow of honesty penetrated her defenses. "Well, you're scaring the hell out of her," she whispered. He had a way of making her feel vulnerable.

"Do you want me to leave?"

Roxanne closed her eyes and slowly shook her head. She didn't want him to go. "Stay." When she opened her eyes, he was watching her with an intensity that sent a wave of gooseflesh over her body. "Would you walk with me along the beach? We can talk. Or just walk. Your choice."

"Yeah. That's a good place to start."

Roxanne wasn't sure just what they were starting, but she had no doubt they were embarking on new territory. Her limited experience with the opposite sex had proved disappointing in the past. It was her fault and she knew it. Letting a man close enough to trust became more difficult with each failed attempt at a relationship. Before taking over Thelma's care, she had guarded against the disappointment that her love affairs always seemed to bring by avoiding intimacy altogether. The last couple of years she hadn't had time to think about why she never dated a man more than two or three times. Or so she told herself.

They walked along the beach for over an hour. A storm off the coast whipped the waves into a foamy frenzy. The wind carrying the spray off the crest of the surf persuaded them to fasten their jackets.

Again, Spence's accounts of extended family members he never identified by name made her laugh. It wasn't what he said, but how he presented each vignette or painted the circumstances leading to some dramatic event.

Roxanne was laughing when they returned to the house. She hadn't felt so unfettered in a long time, if ever. They brushed off the wet sand clinging to their jeans and went inside.

"Can you stay for dinner?" she asked, hanging her jacket on the hall tree.

"There are things at the restaurant in need of my attention." He thrust his balled fists into his jacket pockets. "I'd better go."

The warmth of the house became stifling. She wondered if his lips were cool like the sea breeze or as hot as the memory of their last kiss. "Another time maybe," she murmured, willing her feet to remain planted. She would not fall into his arms and kiss him senseless while losing her mind at the same time.

"How about a week from next Saturday? There's a stable a mile or so down the road. We can get a couple of horses to ride on the beach."

His searching gaze stilled when she met it; she could not look away. "I'm game." Sounds romantic, she thought. Sounds like a real date. Sounds like she was biting off more than she could chew. And it felt like the two weeks she'd known him were alternately the longest and shortest in memory.

"Good."

The silence stretched between them for several minutes.

"Spence . . ." Her voice faded and she looked away, embarrassed. Damn, she was about to ask him to kiss her. It was tempting to reach for him knowing that was all it took to get what she wanted. But a chaste good-bye kiss wouldn't douse the fire of need burning away her caution.

"It's dangerous," he whispered, closing the space between them in two strides. He did not touch her, merely stood so close that she felt his body heat and the excitement of shared desire.

"I know." The pulse of his heart thudded against her fingertips as she pressed her hand to his chest. "*You're* dangerous."

"I'm harmless. Today." The back of his fingers caressed her cheek, leaving a cool trail along her heated skin. "Just a kiss, Roxanne."

"Just a kiss," she agreed, then lifted her mouth to his. This time she let her emotions tumble. For a few minutes she wanted to feel the strong, ripping current of raw passion. She yielded, giving herself over to the need building to a higher pitch with each increasingly ragged breath. She couldn't help the little rush of air shuttering through her lips as he brushed them with his.

His lips were cool, though the heat of his body burned through her clothing, searing her with its intensity. He seized her mouth in a blinding kiss, and every coherent thought fled her mind.

His tongue danced with hers, teasing, inviting, blending the taste of him with hers until she didn't know which was which. When he pulled her body hard against his, a cry of yearning escaped her. She clutched at his shoulders, her fingertips pressing into the soft leather of his jacket.

Her mind had fallen into an ever-expanding whirlpool of color and erotic sensation. With each nuance of the kiss, each motion of his aroused body, each glide of his hand, she fell deeper.

His fingers slid down the curve of her back, kneading their way over her buttocks, then gripping, holding her against his heat. She responded by releasing his shoulders and twining her arms around his neck, stretching the length of her body against his.

Desire flared, adding a new, frenetic dimension to the kiss. He lifted her and backed her against the wall.

Suddenly he tempered the kiss, taking time to leisurely explore her mouth, and then draw her into him when his tongue retreated. Quaking, she reined in her fiery need and savored what he offered. His gentleness stoked the raging fires of passion.

A small cry escaped her when his hand closed over her breast and goaded her aroused nipple into aching hardness. Oblivious to everything beyond the need to make love with him, she arched against his hard body.

Lost in the sensation of fire pinning her to the wall, the urgency to feel him, to touch his naked flesh, she tugged at his shirt. And kept groping for the hem until she pulled it free from his jeans. She slipped her hands beneath the soft fabric.

His flesh felt like freshly forged velvet steel. The heat of him made her greedy fingers throb. She couldn't touch him enough.

Spence slid his hand along the side of her leg, then lifted her thigh. Without thinking, Roxanne braced herself on his shoulders and lifted her legs until she could lock her ankles behind his hard buttocks. The sudden gasp at the electric sensations charging through her might have broken the kiss had he not held her head in place. He moved slowly against the building heat, hurling her into a level of need she never imagined existed. She wanted him inside her. Now. Filling her. Loving her. Giving her his tenderness, his passion, his strength, his . . .

Then he wasn't kissing her anymore. His forehead rested against the wall for a moment. The hip-grinding passion between them stilled, but their fiery need continued building. The ragged saw of their breathing penetrated the sound of blood pounding in her ears.

After a moment he lifted his forehead and met her gaze. He

looked as confused and needy as she felt. "It's time for me to go," he said in a raspy voice.

"Go?" Stunned, disoriented, she gaped at him while trying to comprehend what was happening.

He released a shaky breath. "Yeah. Otherwise, I'll enjoy breaking a promise far too much."

Reality crashed on her awareness. She lowered her left, then her right leg, nicking his shin, then stepping on his foot before regaining her balance. "I'm not very good at this sort of thing."

"Oh, yes, you are, Roxanne. If you were any better . . ." He leaned close. Heated breath washed over her cheek. Unbidden, she moved into the kiss.

The rigidity of his stance and the measured control of his breathing promised the kiss was nothing more than a simple good-bye. Even so, there was nothing simple when his mouth touched hers.

"I want you," he breathed against her mouth.

"I know."

He kissed the tip of her nose, then straightened. "Don't give an inch, do you?"

"You kiss as good as you cook," she managed with a smile. Given the way her insides shook, she must have organ damage from the desire seizure she was almost surviving.

"We've barely started on the appetizers." Reluctantly he stepped away and tucked his T-shirt into the waist of his jeans. "My specialty is dessert."

Roxanne's mouth became dry. She just bet it was.

Matt's return to the house in the middle of the week didn't surprise Roxanne. It was almost as though she had been expecting him. If asked, she could not have said why.

By Friday, Matt had wandered the corporeal realm for nearly three weeks. Roxanne was far too busy and too tired to care if he made an appearance at Magic Wish—as long as he behaved.

Since her last encounter with Spence at the beach house, he'd phoned daily. Meanwhile, she'd barely had time to resent Matt's presence. The demands of her business grew each day. Even though the long work hours left little time for sleep, the workdays passed in a blur.

When she did sleep vivid fantasies of Spence and a dessert tray filled her dreams. She awoke perspiring and aching in a way she hadn't experienced before. She knew the driving need wouldn't abate until she and Spence had sex. That they would seemed as inevitable as the sun rising in the morning. The admission frightened her. For with Spence, it wouldn't be just sex. He wouldn't let it be. She sensed that he wanted more. Much, much more.

It terrified her.

# Chapter Nine

The calendar flipped to the first week of May. Judgment Day approached Matt at the speed of light. He'd used up twenty days. The halfway point in his time as a ghost loomed on the next sunrise. The events of Memorial Day would seal his fate for all eternity.

Besides building his strength, he'd made progress on a personal level. At least, he considered it such. Roxanne had become more complacent about his presence at the Griffith home and his forays to Magic Wish. He preferred the slightly more favorable notion of complacency to teeth-grinding tolerance.

Matt's time on Spence's shoulder had reacquainted him with a number of lessons he should have learned in life. Being omnipresent in someone else's daily routine became a double-edged sword. There was more to Spence than just libido. So much more that Matt began to comprehend what a dismal failure he'd been as a son and a husband. He took consolation in reminding himself that Spence was ten years older than he'd been at his death. He'd had time to mature.

Roxanne had dubbed Matt a "Good-Time Charlie." Today, Good-Time Charlie had the blues big time.

When he watched her now, he saw her work with single-mindedness he'd never possessed, or considered cultivating. The vast differences between their personalities made him marvel that she was his daughter. The only time he'd mustered that much diligence, his airplane had gone down in flames and his life had depended on his wits.

Then, it had been too little, too late. He didn't know *how* to focus his resources because he lacked the requisite knowledge. That had been his fault, too. He'd listened with half an ear during the emergency survival briefings. He hadn't believed the enemy capable of shooting him down. Besides, he'd led a charmed life. Luck had always ridden his shoulder, and in his cockpit. Between his luck and his reflexes, twenty-five-year-old Matthew had felt invincible. He'd taken chances, done things his way, even when his superiors had told him he was dangerous and threatened to ground him.

And now he knew why there were no old, bold pilots. No one was invincible. Neither luck nor reflexes could compensate for inattention. Eventually, luck and charm ran out, giving way to harsh reality.

Matt's luck and charm hadn't kept him alive, and, he realized, they also weren't getting him anywhere with Roxanne. He needed a new approach.

After a thorough examination of his twenty-five years as a mortal, he conceded that he didn't know how to change a lifetime of self-centeredness, just that he had to. While contemplating how to make changes of so great a magnitude, he did his best to keep from incurring more of Roxanne's animosity. Without a doubt, he was on his last chance—for everything.

Open honesty was a damn hard road even when one was incapable of lying. What he'd perceived as a handicap initially, he began to regard as a helpmate. Honesty became the lens through which he scrutinized the world. The colors of life were infinite.

But honesty alone wasn't enough. He took a chapter from Spence's book of life, the one titled *Fairness*. It was a lot to digest in a short time, and he found himself embroiled in recriminations for his sins of the past.

Now he waited on the threshold of another important step, a very risky one. He bided his time until Roxanne shuffled into the kitchen later that night and turned on the teakettle. Seeing her in an open bathrobe with only a skimpy T-shirt that stopped short of her belly button and a scrap of what passed for panties disconcerted him. A man shouldn't have to watch his daughter parade around the house half-dressed.

And that was the point, he realized, swallowing a condemnation of her habits that had been burning the tip of his tongue. It was her house. She lived alone. She was free to dress any way she wanted.

Roxanne leaned against the counter beside the stove and continued reading what Matt recognized as a proposal. The totality of her concentration, coupled with an ability to perform mundane tasks without conscious effort, never ceased to amaze him. It made him proud, though he could claim no credit for the way she turned out. It was all Marian's doing.

"I need your help," he told Roxanne when she settled at the table with her tea, a package of Oreo cookies, and a box of cat treats. "Please," he added.

She set the proposal aside and regarded him speculatively while she sipped her tea. The sound of the cellophane tearing around the cookies summoned Buster. He bounded in and sat obediently beside her chair. A cookie for her meant a bacon treat for him. Roxanne gave Buster the treat, then petted his head.

"What do you want?" she asked flatly.

"I need to find someone." He'd had no luck locating Greg in San Francisco. Asking Roxanne was a desperate measure.

"Does he have a name?" One-handed, she split the Oreo, then began nibbling the cookie away from the white filling.

"Gregory Detweiler."

Roxanne sat a little straighter and popped the cookie into her mouth and chewed. All the while, she watched him with eyes that reminded him of Marian more each day. "There's a name I haven't heard for a long, long time. He was persona non grata in this house. Did you know that?"

The news stunned him. "No, I didn't. He and I grew up in each other's homes. He was my best friend. What happened?"

She ate two more cookies, fed the cat another treat, sipped her tea, and looked everywhere except at him.

"I need to find him," he said when it became clear she wasn't going to answer his question.

"Why?"

Honesty. Fair play, he reminded himself. Patience. Don't give her a reason to turn away. "He's the other person I must make peace with before I leave." The desire to pace the kitchen pulled at him. He fought it, suspecting that his pacing agitated Roxanne.

Small wonder. Thelma had been a pacer, too. The faster she had paced, the greater her wrath.

"Does this mean I'm off the hook? You're giving up?"

"I won't give up on you, Roxanne. You may act older than me, but you're still my daughter. That means something to me."

"What, exactly, does it mean?"

"It's hard to explain. Half the time I feel I ought to be protecting you, but you don't seem to need it. Therein lies the rub. I want you to need something from me." The sudden rise of her chin sent him scurrying for clarification. "Other than my absence."

"This is rich. You want me to need you, so you're asking for my help in finding Greg Detweiler? What's wrong with this picture?"

"One doesn't necessarily have anything to do with the other."

"How convenient for you. Tell me, though, how well is Mr. Detweiler likely to take someone poking around in his life?"

"He's my concern. It's something I have to do. We were best friends once, the closest thing I had to a brother.

"Greg was a pacifist. When our draft numbers came up, he was this close to high-tailing it to Canada." A fraction of an inch separated his thumb and forefinger. "I talked him out of it."

"I'm sure he thanked you for your expert guidance countless times," she murmured, then fumbled another cookie from the package. "This ought to be interesting. When you find him, give him my regards."

She stilled suddenly, lost in a memory; the Oreo poised between her mouth and the table. Her brown eyes softened. "Greg Detweiler attended Mom's service. It rained. He dared Thelma's wrath when he picked me up and held me during the church service. And later, in the cemetery, he held me beside her casket, and we both cried until everyone else left," she said softly, then set the cookie down and gave the cat another treat.

"How did your mother die?"

She bit into an Oreo. "You haven't earned the right to know. The telling is too painful."

*Painful* was envisioning Greg standing at the grave of the woman they both loved while holding the daughter Greg would have loved as his own if given the opportunity. "Did your mother and Greg . . ."

She closed the cat treat box and set it on the table beside the cookies. "Did they what?"

"Were they close? Did they date?"

She shook her head. "I was too young to notice things like that, but I seriously doubt it. Your parents and Thelma hated Greg. Mom tried not to piss them off. And there was something else." She ate the Oreo as though it was fuel for thinking. "I can't put my finger on it now."

"If you remember, will you tell me?" It would have been the most natural, logical thing in the world for Greg and Marian to become a couple. Marry. Have more kids. And it would have sent Matt right into another kind of abyss. Thinking about Greg and Marian together, as they had been for two years before Matt found a way to change things, made him just as jealous today as he'd been thirty years ago.

"Why are you turning a yellowish-green?" Roxanne asked between nibbles on her cookie.

"I'd rather not say."

"Figures. One-sided all the way. You want answers, but you aren't willing to give any."

He hadn't realized he was an ethereal mood ring until now. "Jealousy," he mumbled. "Stupid, huh?"

She shrugged uncertainty. "Can I ask you something?"

"Ask."

"Was Greg Detweiler in love with my mother?"

The straightforward question reminded him of how many skeletons even a ghost had in his proverbial closet. Much as he would have loved to color his answer, he could not. "Yes." Her questions were like needles. He wanted to pace, to do something to assuage his growing unrest.

Roxanne's eyebrows shot up. "Did she love him?"

The needles became knives carving away the insulation time had layered over his past. "Yes. They dated for two years." No man could ask for better friends. But a triangle always left one man out.

"No wonder the prospect of them outliving you makes you jealous. What happened? Why did she marry you instead of Greg?"

When he didn't answer, suspicion pinched her brow. "I mean,

really. If they were in love and they dated for two years, why'd you marry your best friend's girl? What am I missing?"

"I loved your mother, Roxanne. I loved her more than I loved my best friend." *I loved myself best of all.* "The answers to your questions are part of the reason I'm here."

That part of Matt's past belonged in the silent darkness he was sure to reclaim in the Abyss of Nothingness. He'd have eternity to ponder his actions which was partly why he didn't want to talk about them now. The other part was because it simply hurt too damn much. Maybe some secrets of the heart should never become more than whispers in the night.

"And you aren't going to answer, are you?"

"Your mother married me because she loved me. Had she wanted to marry Greg, no power on earth could have stopped her."

"Not even you?"

"No. Like you, Marian was a strong woman in the ways that mattered. I realize now that her greatest strength was love."

"Yes, it was," she agreed softly.

He remained silent on his perch atop the chair.

Roxanne heaved a sigh and carried the cookies, cat treats, and tea tray to the sink. "When you've finished doing whatever it is you're doing here do you go back to wherever you came from?"

"Yes." And the time he had left was frightfully short.

"You're sure Greg's alive?"

"Yes." Although the reason for his certainty eluded him, he had no doubt about Greg. Admittedly, his old friend might not have much time left here, the guardian would have told him if his quest for atonement was futile.

"In that case, I'll help you find Greg Detweiler." She rinsed her cup and placed it in the dishwasher. "It shouldn't be too difficult."

"Thank you."

"No thanks necessary. My motives are purely selfish. Greg Detweiler is a good man. He deserves the opportunity to . . . express his feelings for you."

Damn, but she was like him in at least one way: She didn't give an inch to an adversary. "Fair enough. I'm a man who understands self-motivation."

"I agree with you on the part about your understanding self-interest. As for you being a man? The jury is still out." Roxanne snagged the half-proofread proposal from the table and headed for bed.

Matt remained in the brightly lit kitchen and wondered how he'd begin to make amends to the man he'd once considered a brother.

The next morning Roxanne left Matt an address and phone number for Greg Detweiler on the dining room table before leaving for work. The accompanying note indicated the address was eleven years old.

Saturday morning Roxanne realized she was a fool for agreeing to ride a horse anywhere, let alone on the beach with Spence. Last weekend at the beach house, hormones had short-circuited her brain. What other explanation could she have for accepting Spence's invitation? Telling him she'd never ridden a horse hadn't crossed her mind. Fortunately for her, he hadn't invited her to take off her shoes and do a fire walk.

People rode horses every day; even kids rode. How hard could it be to sit in a saddle while the horse did all the work?

She wasn't sure she'd wanted to find out and began praying for snow Friday evening. Rain might not deter Spence from bringing the horses.

The morning fog retreated from the coast early. The postcard-perfect day reminded her that whoever was in charge of granting her petitions had said no.

Of course, when Spence arrived, she could tell him she'd never ridden a horse. Sure she could. She had even picked up the phone and punched in his number with the intent of admitting she'd never ridden. But conceding there was something she couldn't do without even trying wasn't in her makeup and so she had hung up before he answered.

"I can ride a horse. Sure I can," she assured herself as she watched Spence leading two horses up the road.

"My money's on you making any horse do exactly what you want."

Roxanne whirled around. *He* was here, floating in the center of the living room.

"I'll share the old house with you, but give me some space here at the beach house, okay?" Lord, she didn't need this distraction.

"The Griffiths were big on riding. You had riding lessons.

What're you worried about? It's like bicycling," he encouraged. "Once you learn, it comes back."

She glanced at the clock. "I got the name, not the frills."

"What's that supposed to mean?"

"It means forget riding lessons. I've never ridden a horse, let alone taken riding lessons. When I wanted them, Thelma said no. When she wanted me to take them, and dancing lessons, and modeling lessons, I was in high school. I said no. I had a job and didn't have time for them."

"A job? You had a job instead of riding lessons?" Matt's aura flashed crimson.

"Yes. I needed a job."

Matt glowed like a red Christmas bulb. "Then tell Spence you don't know how to ride."

"It's no big deal." Then she remembered Superman, Christopher Reeve, an experienced horseman, and knew it could be a very big deal. The biggest. But then again, she wasn't going to jump with the horse, just let it walk. Slowly. On the soft sand.

Matt disappeared after Spence tied the horses to the front porch railing and walked through the front door she held open.

Spence didn't slow until he had her in a loose embrace and planted a quick, thorough kiss on her mouth.

It happened so quickly; Roxanne had no time to react, just enjoy the lightning strike crackling through her veins.

"Ready?" Spence asked.

"As I'll ever be," she murmured, pasting a smile on her face and pulling on her jacket. "Sure," she said brightly remembering that she was supposed to enjoy this. "I've been thinking about it all week. Let's head 'em up and move 'em out." Her competitive nature trampled her reservations.

"That's the spirit." He held the door for her, then closed it behind them.

They approached the horses, both of which seemed disinterested in the venture.

"I figured it may have been a while since you've ridden, so I got the roan for you."

"How considerate. Thank you. I can't remember the last time I was on a horse." Certainly not in this lifetime. Now she had only to discern which horse was the roan. They both looked like plain brown horses to her.

"Would you like some help mounting?"

"Uh, no. Thanks. You go ahead." She paused, pretending to adjust her jacket. The horse seemed enormous. She kept an eye on Spence as he mounted, then copied each move. She had to lift her right leg higher than anticipated and didn't make it into the saddle the first time.

"You sure you don't need a hand?"

"I'm fine." She put more spring in her next attempt and felt triumphant when she plopped into the saddle. Immediately she tucked her toes into the stirrups and gathered the reins. All the while she kept one hand wrapped tightly around the saddle horn.

From the lofty perspective of the saddle, the horse *was* enormous. Fortunately it had its own "go" button and followed Spence's mount along the cliff.

She'd watched enough television to acquire the rudimentary rein functions: tug the reins in the direction desired, pull to stop.

"I can do this," she breathed, her bottom bouncing like a piston on the saddle.

Spence turned in the saddle. The temptation to yell at him to turn around and hold on to the horn with both hands nearly got the best of her.

"We'll take the long way down. It's an easier ride."

The way her fanny slapped the hard leather, she doubted he saw her nod of agreement. The current pace was fine; a little slower would be even better. Walking beside the horse was the most preferable.

The concentration required to stay in the saddle conjured bits and pieces of countless conversations centered on horseback riding. One of those tidbits sent her experimenting with the stirrups. If she went with the flow of the horse's gait and sorta stood, she didn't bounce as much. And wasn't there something about using her thighs?

Applying the theory of riding from atop the horse was risky. The responses to the changes she attempted were immediate. By gently touching her heels to the horse's flanks, she coerced him into a position beside Spence's mount. A flicker of confidence bolstered her confidence.

She felt, rather than saw, Spence's concern. When she had enough control of the horse to lift her own gaze from the creature between her legs, she afforded Spence a quick glance. That was all.

"What?" she asked, wondering if she appeared as inept as she felt.

He grinned at her. "Just thinking."

She didn't dare ask about what.

"There's the trail to the beach." He nodded at a valley winding down to the sand not far ahead. "Lead the way."

With a bit too much enthusiasm, her heels touched the horse's flanks. He took off at a trot.

Panic set in. She gripped the saddle horn and tried to lock her ankles around the horse. Never mind her legs needed to be six feet long to have a chance at doing so.

The horse responded by lurching into a full trot jarring enough to rattle her back teeth. Her mount descended the winding trail toward the sea at what she considered reckless speed. Everywhere she looked, Roxanne saw deathtraps. Rocks poked out of the sand. Bleached deadfalls carried far up the valley by savage storms waited to trip the unwary. Indistinct snarls of hazards reached out from the various plants lining the trail.

She gripped the saddle horn and tugged as though she could downshift the horse into a slower gear. The press of her ankles against the horse's sides sent them galloping across the dunes.

With each fanny-bruising placement of the roan's hoof, she became more convinced she'd be a ghost by the time this ordeal ended. The horse would tumble and crush her if she managed to avoid the mire of obstacles reaching out of the ground.

*I'm going to die.* The thought froze her. Time stopped. Only the sound of her frantic heart and the pounding of the horse's hooves on the uneven ground filled her world.

"Relax, Roxanne. Let the reins rest in your hands. Unclamp your thighs before you break the poor horse's ribs."

"Poor horse, my ass!" The beast was trying to kill her. Secretly she was glad to hear a familiar voice. Through her panic, Matt's presence offered real comfort.

Ahead, the trail veered sharply to the left at a cluster of man-sized boulders.

"You're going to be okay, Roxanne."

She saw him working the reins at the horse's head and gave him slack when he tugged. The roan's ears twitched, then his entire demeanor changed and the gallop returned to a trot.

With Matt's encouragement she settled into the rhythm of the gait. Little things Thelma and her friends had discussed ad nauseam popped into her mind.

"That's it, Roxanne," Matt encouraged. "Relax into the rhythm. I'm not going to let anything happen to you."

The horse slowed to a walk when they reached the dry sand. Roxanne glanced behind her. Spence was coming out of the turn.

"I've got the hang of it now," she managed, though she doubted anyone could hear over the drumbeat of her heart.

"The hell you do. I'm not leaving until you tell Spence you can't ride. Damn it, Roxanne, I'm not going to let you risk yourself for the sake of daring or pride. One daredevil idiot in the family was enough!"

The horse snorted and stepped lightly toward the hard-packed wet sand. She let the beast choose his direction. It was the least she could do considering she'd almost gotten them both killed.

"You've got a reckless streak I hadn't suspected." Spence was grinning when he caught up to her. "I've never seen anyone with your style before. What desperado taught you how to ride?"

There was no acceptable answer. The way her body trembled, she couldn't even manufacture one. The aftereffects of a massive adrenaline surge still heated her veins. A fine coat of perspiration covered her skin.

The roan snuffled, tossed his head, then settled into a slow, steady pace along the edge of the surf.

"This is more what I had in mind," Spence said. "It's hard to talk to you when you're galloping away from me."

"We could have talked at the beach house," she grumbled. She certainly would have preferred it to this near-death experience on horseback.

Shaking his head in dour disapproval, Matt disappeared.

Left to her nonexistent skills, Roxanne gripped the saddle horn again. This time she consciously fought the urge to put a leg-lock on the horse.

"I had no idea you were such an accomplished horsewoman."

"Things aren't always what they seem."

Spence urged his mount beside her. "What did you say?"

"Nothing." She looked around half expecting to see the specter of her father hovering in the crisp spring air. No sign of him lingered, yet she felt his presence as well as his reluctance to leave her alone on the horse.

The clear day had summoned beach-goers from all over the

Valley. Children in shorts and adults with their trouser legs rolled
up around their knees dared the incoming waves. They cringed,
then laughed when the water caught them and the spume splashed
their clothing.

Roxanne remembered another time, long ago. At five years old
she'd had few cares. She still had her mother. And her mother
loved the ocean. Back then she had been the shivering little girl
daring and racing the waves, catching the spume in the air, and
laughing with the carefree abandon too often lost when childhood
fades.

She rocked in the saddle as the horse ambled along the beach.
The near disastrous gallop through the vale had tempered the
beast's exuberance.

"You look a million miles away."

She glanced at Spence and smiled at his scrutiny. "In some
ways perhaps I was. I was just . . . remembering. See the little girl
over there? The one in the pink top running to her mother?" A
powerful wave crashed on the shore. The leading edge crept farther and farther up the beach until it splattered against the horse's
hooves.

Spence smiled and angled his horse higher on the wet sand
with Roxanne's following diligently behind. "Did you chase the
waves as a child, Roxanne?"

"My mother and I came to the beach as often as we could. I
think I inherited her love for the ocean. I remember her saying
the answers to life's questions became clearer when she looked
out across the sea.

"You see things in hindsight that never crossed your mind as
a child. Maybe that's as it should be." She watched the little girl
outrun the next wave. The child's mother swept her up in her
arms and swung her through the air, turning them both in circles
before hugging her tightly. The sound of their laughter rivaled
the call of the gulls circling overhead.

"There isn't a day you don't miss her, is there?"

She turned in the saddle and look squarely at Spence, amazed
by his insight. "How did you know? I seldom speak of her."

"I feel the same way about my brother. When I was a kid, I'd
stare across Puget Sound, expecting Mitch to come sailing home.
I'd watch the ferries dock. People streamed off, a few walking,
most in cars. I'd imagine that one day he would get off the ferry
and come home. We'd get our baseball gear, and everything

would be fine again." He looked away, a tinge of color inching up the sides of his neck. "Silly, huh? He left on an airplane, not a ferry."

"Not silly at all," she said, wondering if he had spoken of this to anyone else. It seemed such a painful admission for him. "When we're kids, all we know is the want, the need, the desire for the truth when we suspect a lie. If we admit it's the truth, we have to accept the loss." She gazed out at the breakers, remembering, admitting the years had not erased the pain of loss, merely dulled its razor edge.

"How did you lose your mother?"

She had not spoken about the horrible day for more than twenty years. And even now it was so painful, so personal, a lump formed in her throat. The salty spume stung her misting eyes more sharply than a moment earlier.

"Maybe I shouldn't have asked," he said softly.

"No," she said with a sniff, "I can't think of a better place to talk about my mother than here."

The shrieks of children behind them startled her horse. "Easy." She was unsure whether she was speaking to herself or the horse. She resisted pulling on the reins and instead, patted the side of his neck. The smell of wet horsehide stung her nostrils.

"The Griffiths used her, you know. I was six when she died. Even then, I knew something was wrong, terribly, terribly wrong. We'd lived in that big house with my grandparents my entire life." She released a deep breath and looked at Spence for a moment. "Thelma didn't move into the house until . . . until after the funerals. When my grandparents died, the house became Thelma's and so did the family problem: me. But I digress.

"My grandparents were major sponsors of the symphony, but they hated San Francisco traffic. My mother would take them, then wait, and drive them home when it was over. It wasn't that they couldn't afford a chauffeur; they had one. But they also had my mother, and because she wasn't on salary, she didn't require overtime for waiting around a parking garage while they attended the symphony.

"It wasn't the money. They did it to punish my mother, to remind her she was a Griffith in name only. She wasn't entitled to the benefits, like going inside the symphony hall or, God forbid, accompanying them as their equal. And my mother willingly did whatever they asked. She was trying to earn their love, or maybe trying to earn their acceptance for me. She failed on both fronts. I have no idea why she stayed there. Maybe she believed my father was still alive and he'd come home. I don't know."

Two boys raced down the sand, jumping and dodging the waves in their pursuit of a third, older boy.

"To make a long story short, one night, instead of coming home from the symphony, my grandparents went to the morgue and my mother went into the hospital. At the time, all I knew was that my mother didn't come home.

"Like you, I kept watching the road, waiting for her to turn into the driveway. Waiting as only a six-year-old can wait, I sat by the door, looking out the window, sure the car would pull in any moment.

"Inez, the housekeeper, took me to school. As soon as I found an opportunity, I'd cut school and walk home. I had to. My mother might return. I didn't want to miss her."

The touch of his hand on her shoulder forced her to look at Spence. She hadn't realized she was crying. The blur of tears mercifully clouded the sympathy she glimpsed in his face and the anguished specter of her father over Spence's shoulder. "My mother didn't die right away. She went into a coma. After a month Thelma had the machines turned off."

She looked out to sea without focusing on anything. "Thelma made the right decision. I know that now. But they should have let me see her, Spence. They should have let me into the hospital to say good-bye. It was a closed-casket funeral, so it was easy to believe there'd been a terrible mistake. My mother was coming come. She wouldn't abandon me."

"Don't," Spence said softly.

She lifted her hand, knowing if she didn't continue she'd lack the courage to delve into the painful memory again. "Sometimes, one answer leads to a thousand questions. That happened shortly after I moved back in with Thelma. I researched the accident through old newspapers. I even went to see the officer who stayed with my mother until they got her out of the wreckage. He's retired now."

She drew a shaky breath and tried to clear out the vivid images racing through her mind. "A car cut off a big rig on the freeway. The truck swerved, hit the center divider, then jackknifed across the road. The trailer turned over and slammed the car my mother was driving into the underside of an overpass. My grandparents died instantly. My mother was pinned in a low spot of the wreckage. The officer I spoke with remembered her because she asked for my father during the three hours it took to free her."

The sound of screaming children jolted her.

The horse shied away from the approaching children turning until he faced the way they'd come, then completed the circle.

"Easy," Spence called.

Unprepared for the sudden movement, Roxanne dropped the reins and grabbed the saddle horn to keep from falling. She might have recovered if the boys hadn't run straight at the horse, tossing sand as they passed.

The horse whinnied and reared his front hooves a couple of feet from the ground. No sooner did they alight than one of the boys shouted again and the horse bolted.

This time Roxanne *knew* she was going to die.

# Chapter
Ten

Heart-stopping terror seized Roxanne. Every tidbit of riding sense she'd just acquired bounced right out of her ears. Now her only goal in life was to hold on to the horse any way possible; that meant using her hands, legs, and feet. Even the saddle seemed to work against her. Each kidney-crushing lurch forward threatened to unseat her.

Fear and the smell of the sweat—hers and the horse's—fed her panic. Ahead, the beach narrowed. Massive, black rocks grew out of the sand. A vision of the jagged spires turning into knives with the sole purpose of shredding her and the runaway horse flashed through her mind.

"Help me!" she cried. Not for an instant did she consider the consequences of calling on the only person she knew could help her. Even if she had, no price was too great to avoid death.

Then her father was with her, wresting control of her body and the horse. Icy slush replaced the blood in her veins. The arctic chill that accompanied his presence emanated from inside her.

Unbelievably, her death grip on the saddle horn loosened. Her legs relaxed enough for her feet to ease away from the horse's sides. Her back bowed and she rode low over the horse in the same manner a jockey crosses the finish line. Her back teeth stopped rattling against each other, and her heart began to slow to a somewhat normal pace.

The sensation of having her father take over her body for a few minutes was an unexpected yet incredible experience. Most amazing of all was the hope she'd live long enough to get off this horse.

Spence caught up as her horse slowed to a walk. "That's it. Ease him back."

Poised on the brink of hysteria, Roxanne wanted to laugh, but her body wasn't her own. A new fear wafted from the cauldron of terror bubbling over in her mind. What if she couldn't reclaim her body? What if . . .

"You're doing great," Spence encouraged.

Yeah. Really great. Mounting a horse she had no business getting near had darn near killed her. Stupidity of the first order not once, but twice. She wasn't going for a third time.

Nervous, tossing his head in wide-eyed terror, the horse stopped, then danced in place. Terrified, she immediately dismounted and backed away.

As soon as it was evident Roxanne wasn't going to try and remount, Matt returned control of her body, whereupon she collapsed onto the sand. With effort, she caught herself before landing facedown. Her entire body shook from the chill of Matt's possession and the adrenaline that still coursed through her.

She inhaled the sharp tang of the kelp snarled along the beach, and felt the coarseness of the sand on her hands. A fine mist of salt water stung her face.

Most of all, she was aware of the horse—huge, sweating, and way too close. His rapid breathing drowned the sound of everything else. He took several steps away from her, as though sharing her need for distance.

"Easy, girl. We'll take it slowly from here out." Spence's assurances fell on two sets of deaf ears.

Her heart thundered in her chest. "Thank you," she whispered. *For saving my life. For giving me back my body. For . . .*

"While I found riding in this fashion a unique and exhilarating experience, might I suggest you stick with cars?" Matt advised from the sand in front of her. "The alternative is riding lessons, starting at square one. You didn't inherit the Griffith gift with horses."

Dry-mouthed and twitchy, not knowing what to say, all she could do was nod and stare at him. She had called on Matt for help, and he had answered by saving her.

Spence crouched beside her. "That was a helluva ride. For a few minutes there, I didn't think you'd stay on."

A few minutes? Was that all? It felt like hours.

"Tell him." Matt reclined to lean on one elbow while hovering just above the sand.

Foolish pride and arrogance, the very traits she disliked about the ghost who'd rescued her, were responsible for this near-disastrous debacle. "I can't—"

"Yeah, you can. What's the worst that can happen?" Matt challenged.

"You don't have to do anything right now, Roxanne. Just catch your breath. Relax. You're as pale as a ghost," Spence said.

"You don't understand." She caught another breath, still addressing her father. It didn't seem possible for her lungs to absorb enough oxygen.

"You want to get on that horse again?" Matt demanded. "Listen to Spence. Take a deep breath and think this through. He makes sense, even if his concept of ghosts is based on Casper the Friendly Ghost."

She lowered her head. Crazy that's what this was. Insane. "Go away. I need to sort this out."

"I'm not going anywhere," Spence answered. He cupped the sides of her face and forced her to look at him. "You could have been seriously hurt if you hadn't gotten that horse under control. What the hell happened?"

She stared at him, not quite comprehending. "The kid—"

"Not the brat with the sand. Jeezus, you scared the hell out of me! One minute I thought you were losing it, the next you took charge like a Kentucky Derby jockey."

The cradle of his hands kept her from shaking her head in denial. "I can't ride a horse."

Spence blinked in blatant disbelief. "The hell you say. You just showed some riding skills most of us will never acquire."

"Not me. Him." Her gaze slid from Spence to where Matt reclined above the wet sand. Her adrenaline had finally shut off, leaving her disconnected from her emotions, temporarily suspended before the inevitable crash ahead. In that neutral moment Matt's smug smile didn't irritate her nearly as much as it usually did. "I've never been on a horse before, and I'm not getting back on this one," she said in a rush.

Matt curled into a sitting position. "Promise?"

"Promise," she whispered to her father.

Spence released her face but continued staring at her. "It's damn hard to believe you've never ridden. You managed to save yourself twice today."

Roxanne tried to stand, but her shaky legs weren't ready to support her. She sat on her heels and turned her attention on Spence. "He did it, not me," she said, gesturing toward Matt. "It was my body, but he controlled what I did. That's why."

Still and silent, Spence didn't so much as blink into the sting of the onshore wind. "By *he*, I'm assuming you mean your father."

"Yes. He warned me not to ride. He was right." She grew more uncomfortable by the moment. "It was a stupid thing to try. I knew a little about horses. Thelma was a master horsewoman. She talked about riding all my life. I didn't figure it could be very difficult—"

"Because Thelma did it?" Matt interjected with utter disdain. "Boy, you either think a lot of yourself or not much of the people who fed and clothed you and put you through school."

She wheeled on Matt. "The trust fund my mother set aside for me helped me through school. Not Thelma. Not anyone else."

"This has to be the worst idea I ever came up with. Talk about being alone in a crowd." Spence stood and took a few steps before turning on her. "Can you walk home or should I carry you?"

"And break your back? I don't think so. I can walk." All she wanted at that moment was to crawl straight into the safety of her own shower where not even Matt trespassed. The longer she sat on the wet sand, the more pronounced the aches in her body became.

Spence looked over his shoulder as he approached the horses. "I'll take the horses back. You're sure you and your father can make it home okay?"

"I'm fine." Just fine. So fine, she had the urge to simultaneously scream and cry. "And he's not coming with me!"

Matt raised his hands in capitulation before he melted into the sand and sea.

All things considered, Roxanne wished she could do the same.

•  •  •

Spence gathered the reins of Roxanne's mount, then swung into the saddle of his horse.

She might be fine, but he sure as hell wasn't. He was pissed down to the marrow of his bones, those same bones that had experienced the quaking fear of watching someone he cared about skate the rim of death.

Today was the topper. He'd seen the changes in her riding, and heard her claim of never having ridden before. Something saved her, and it sure as hell wasn't he. Damn, he'd never felt so helpless as when watching Roxanne race into the depths of panicked hysteria.

When her horse bolted down the beach, she had looked exactly like an inexperienced rider galloping toward disaster. Fearful for her safety, he'd urged his horse at top speed in pursuit. Just as it seemed he might catch up, she stopped screaming and everything changed. She'd handled the frightened horse like a pro and brought him under control.

If he hadn't seen the change with his own eyes, he might disbelieve her claim of her father's ghost possessing her body.

"Possession," he muttered, then swore under his breath.

Accepting the reality of their invisible chaperon was difficult, but he was managing. Barely. The annoying three-way conversations she'd conducted on the beach continued to irritate him. Consigned to hearing only part of what was going on was frustrating to say the least.

Spence angled the horses toward the stables, careful to keep a wide berth from the sand-throwing kids he wanted to take to task. The trail to the stables was only a half mile down the beach. He tugged on the leader rein in his hand and urged his mount to a trot. Sensing the familiarity of the stable, the riderless horse almost overtook him.

Spence's mind raced in circles.

The lingering roil of fear and his growing anger were a potent combination. Wallowing in righteous rage and letting it build had definite appeal. He could no longer discern whether he was angry because he'd had twenty years scared out of him, or scared because he was so angry she'd misled him.

Throwing her father's ghost into the recipe complicated everything. Ignoring her assertion of Matt's presence was a helluva lot easier than confronting it.

Much as he preferred denying the existence of ghosts, he

couldn't. Capt. Matthew Griffith had seen to that. When the impossible writing had appeared on his bathroom mirror last weekend, skepticism vanished. In light of what had just happened, admitting he'd brought back a ghost was undeniable. The sledgehammer of reality struck home at the heart of his beliefs.

He hadn't believed in ghosts—until he delivered Matthew Griffith to the unwilling, unsuspecting Roxanne. What had started as a benevolent act for closure had evolved into something he barely comprehended.

What he did understand was that he bore responsibility for this karmic chaos. But just what that responsibility was, he hadn't a clue.

The trouble worsened when he realized he had no idea of what a ghost could do or how to get rid of one, other than have it exorcised. But how did he exorcise a ghost that went wherever he damn well pleased?

Roxanne's account of what Spence construed as *possession* sat crosswise in his rational mind. It stretched his imagination, but he'd seen the radical changes in her horsemanship. That, he couldn't deny. Whatever happened had saved her from certain injury, possibly even death.

But possession . . . It left a vile aftertaste and sent a chill down his back. Possession conjured thoughts of evil and exorcism. Exorcism summoned visions of an old horror movie like the one where the girl's head spun on her spine while she spewed nasty things. This was different. More like the one where the bogus medium lets a dead lover's spirit possess her body long enough for a dance and a kiss.

Spence urged the horses up the trail, his stomach churning.

No, from what he'd seen, it was possession, and he had to believe it because of the abrupt change and rescue.

He turned in the horses, paid the man, then strode over to his car, his mind still churning.

Regardless of how strange and perplexing the situation was, perhaps some good might still come of it. If Roxanne recognized how close she had come to disaster and her father's role in saving her, she might reconsider. The side of Spence that perpetually sought opportunity with an optimistic eye wondered if Roxanne might soften concerning the Memorial Day ceremony.

Anger brushed the thought away. Even if she praised her father's virtues in a full-page newspaper ad, she damn sure owed him a full explanation of what happened and Spence was going to get it. Until now, he'd had no idea of how many facets there were to anger, and he was discovering more by the minute.

"You're a masochistic idiot, Griffith," he said to the man looking back at him from the rearview mirror, then started the car. He ought to walk away from her. He ought to. But he couldn't. Not yet.

Roxanne stood in the shower and let the hot water massage her battered body. Each time she touched her buttocks, she found a new spot she was sure was black and blue.

For a day that had started out questionable, it had gone downhill faster than she'd thought possible. If she had made a list of her worst fears, she'd have experienced most of them today.

Fear of falling off the horse wasn't the worst of those infamous moments now permanently etched into her memory. The sense of helplessness she'd experienced while her mount raced toward the rocks had crushed something fragile and valuable deep inside of her.

She folded her arm against the shower wall and rested her forehead upon it. Hot water massaged her lower back.

A self-sufficient woman, she abhorred helplessness particularly in herself. She hated herself for that moment of stark terror and weakness when she'd called on *him* for help.

And he'd come without question, without bartering for a return favor, without reservation.

A banging on the bathroom door made her jump. Instantly every muscle in her body tightened.

"Roxanne? Are you okay?"

Oh, God! Spence. He'd come back. She'd hoped he'd gone home so she wouldn't have to face him or attempt an explanation.

"I'll be out in a few minutes," she said just loud enough for him to hear.

The shower began losing steam, prompting her to turn it off and get out. She toweled off slowly, then prolonged her stay by drying her hair. After finishing, she moisturized her face. When she ran out of excuses and hygiene projects, she put on her heavy terry robe and opened the bathroom door.

Spence stood in the bedroom doorway, his back to her.

"I didn't think you'd come back." *And I'd hoped you'd give up and leave,* she added silently.

"You thought wrong. Wild horses couldn't have kept me away." His head lowered a fraction. "No pun intended. I put a pot of coffee on. We need to talk."

The mirrored closet door opened on oiled hinges. She reached inside for the mismatched sweat suit on the shelf. "What do we need to talk about?"

"You."

"I don't think so." She stepped into the pants and pulled them up under the robe.

"Your father's ghost."

"Not interested." She tucked her feet into a fuzzy pair of slippers. "Don't turn around."

His entire body stiffened, but he remained fixed in place. "Me then," he said.

She ducked into the closet, dropped the robe, and quickly pulled on an old, burnt-orange University of Texas sweatshirt. "In that case, I'm listening." She left the closet, closed the door, then shuffled toward him. "You can move now; I'm dressed."

Instead of retreating into the living room, he turned around and grabbed her shoulders. "Clarify this for me. You don't want to talk about you. Or the ghost. Or what happened, or why. Is that right?"

She had run out of adrenaline. Only the dregs of stubborn determination fortified her. "Yes."

"But you're willing to listen if I pour my guts out to you. If fact, you'd like it, wouldn't you? Did you think I wouldn't notice most of our conversations are one-sided? Not this time, Roxanne."

Her stomach did a flip. The anger in his voice was a drop in the bucket of what she saw on his face and in his eyes. "Look, I didn't ask you to come back here—"

"No, you would have preferred I went away and didn't come back at all. That I abandon you like everyone else in your life. Then you wouldn't feel threatened if I got too close. You wouldn't have to worry about keeping a distance between us."

She paled. His summary was right on target. Almost. "I never wrote my mother off. Never!"

"That's right. You loved her without reservation or conditions."

"I don't want to talk about this."

"I do."

"Too bad." The power of his fingers splayed across her shoulder blades kept her from jerking free. Defiant, she glared into the midnight blue ice of his eyes.

"What are you afraid of?"

She glared at him, her mouth pressed into a line. The pressure of his hands around her shoulders eased after a moment.

"I'll tell you what I was afraid of today," he said without the edge that caused his words to slash at her defenses. "I was afraid you were going to break your goddamn neck, or worse. After it was over and I was driving back here, I wondered why the hell you didn't tell me you didn't know how to ride. What possessed you to try to fake it?"

She'd asked herself the same question repeatedly and still didn't have a logical explanation. Her sense of fairness entitled him to an answer. Still, irritated as she was, explaining what she barely understood seemed impossible. She started to turn away, but his fingers renewed their hold on her shoulders.

She took a breath and tried to sort out the emotional snarl. "Last Saturday I wasn't thinking very clearly. Horseback riding on the beach sounded like fun." She lowered her gaze to stare at his chest. "It sounded sorta, well . . ."

"Romantic?"

The admission rankled her. "Yes. I didn't think past the moment, and that bothered me all week. I'm not an impulsive person by nature."

"But you still didn't say anything when I brought the horses." Though softly spoken, confusion and a tinge of admonition gilted his words. "I'd like to believe you wanted to impress me, that you considered me worth the effort." His thumb ran along her jaw. "I am, you know."

She looked up, uncertain, then detected the hint of his smile. The man teased at the strangest times.

"But that never crossed your mind, did it?"

Head shaking, she retreated to the safest place she knew: silence.

"Besides being brutally honest, you're an intelligent woman, Roxanne. You plan, and you use logic. The unpredictable unnerves you, so why'd you take such a chance?"

The question had rattled around her brain for the last hour. "It didn't seem like such a risky thing until the horse decided to take off down the hill. For years I listened to Thelma and her friends talk and talk about riding. Even after Thelma's condition deteriorated and she seldom left the house, her friends visited and they talked horses. In all that time, not once did I want to ride. Ever. But when you suggested it, I suddenly did.

"When you hear the same things over and over you begin to, you know, own them. You've heard it discussed ad nauseam. After a while, you believe you can do or be whatever it is. It becomes a kind of reality, a pseudo-truth."

"Pseudo-truth, huh? An interesting concept. I'll have to remember it."

"Yeah, you do that. And while you're at it, remember that at no time did I endanger anyone but myself. No one would have had to answer for my stupidity."

"You endangered the horse."

She gaped at him in disbelief. "The horse? Are you talking about the brain-damaged animal that tried to kill me by running into a rock wall? That horse?"

"And me."

"You? How did I endanger you?" Absurd. How did he draw that conclusion?

"I damn near had a heart attack!"

"A heart attack?" There was no question about his sincerity, yet the entire conversation had taken on a surrealistic quality.

"Did you feel helpless when the horse bolted? You must have, given your admitted lack of expertise. How the hell do you think it felt watching you? I was responsible for you, Roxanne."

It was too much. She lunged under his arm and into the openness of the living room. "No! You were never that. I'm responsible for me—no one else."

"First, last, and only, right?"

She whirled around to face him. He leaned against the doorjamb, his arms folded across his chest, the angles and planes of his face sharp enough to slice her to ribbons—that is if his gaze didn't do so first.

"It's time for you to leave, Spence. You know where the door is. Don't let it hit you on the way out."

"I'm done walking on eggshells around you, and I'm not going anywhere yet."

Exasperated, she threw her hands up. "What do you want from me? I told you why I did what I did. Do you want me to say I was stupid? Okay. I was stupid. I was wrong for not warning you I'd never ridden. But an apology isn't enough, is it?" Anger inched her closer to him with each staccato admission. "I know this game. You want a pound of flesh because I scared you out there, and that's what really irks you, isn't it?"

"Yes, damn it, you scared me." Without warning, he trapped her against his chest, his arms like tensile steel bars holding her against his length. "You're one scary lady."

Inexplicably, liquid heat suffused her traitorous body. She shoved hard against his shoulders, wanting to deny his power, afraid of her weakness to his physical allure.

"I'm scaring you right now, Roxanne, and it has nothing to do with what happened on the beach," he said softly, the anger supplanted by a familiar, mutual hunger on a primal level. "I see it in your eyes. I can feel your heart pounding."

"You're dreaming. What you're doing is irritating me, Spence. That's all." And damn it, yes, he was scaring her because she wanted him so badly. She questioned her resolve to walk away if he released her. Somewhere during the three weeks since she met him and now, the want had become need. Hormone-driven, basic sexual desire was manageable, but need . . . Needing anyone for anything led down one road—Disappointment Avenue.

"Prove I don't scare you. Kiss me," he challenged.

"What? You get some perverted—"

He caught her open mouth in a blistering kiss. Dark and heavy his mouth ground over hers, his tongue claiming her with an undeniable urgency. The excitement hardening behind the barrier of his jeans shot down to her toes, then surged along her body with the speed of an electrical current. Her ability to resist Spence vanished, replaced by a need that throbbed through her, demanding fulfillment.

Instead of heeding the distant voice crying for her to pull away, she leaned into him. In that moment anger, fear, helplessness, even anxiety evaporated. All that mattered was Spence and the fire his hands created as they moved down her spine, finally stopping to cup her bottom. He brought her hard against the proof of his desire.

It was heaven.

It was madness.

Her half-hearted efforts to break the kiss pushed him to a deeper, more urgent level of carnality. The primitive persuasion of his mouth and body overwhelmed her feeble objections. Roxanne quivered with sensual awareness. His hand dived beneath the waistband of her sweatpants, and he groaned as his fingers pressed hard into her bare bottom.

Sanity struck with the force of a lightning bolt. She jerked back and stared into his dilated blue eyes. She'd already used up a year's quota of stupid today. If she continued the way she was going, she'd exhaust next year's, too. She held his gaze, blaming herself for their escalating passion. She knew better, knew he'd wanted her as badly as she wanted him.

"Let it happen. Make love with me, Roxanne," he rasped, his fingers flexing against her naked buttocks, his hips rocking against the building heat.

Tempting, so tempting. Had he asked to have sex, she might have weakened and agreed. But making love struck a dangerous chord. She suspected saying yes would change everything. And if it did, she ran the risk of losing her heart when all he wanted was her cooperation on Memorial Day.

Spence was a man who knew his appeal, and apparently, he knew her weaknesses almost as well as she. He wouldn't be the first man to seduce a woman to get what he wanted. Never mind his assertion it didn't make a difference; she knew it did. Spencer Griffith wanted her on that podium Memorial Day. He needed to keep the search for his brother alive. At any cost. She'd be another casualty of a war that still raged on.

She lowered her gaze, not wanting to succumb to the desire evident in the deep blue of his eyes.

"I've had enough danger for one day." And enough stupidity, she reminded herself.

"Danger is right. We're on the brink of genuine intimacy and maybe a whole lot more. Right now this is feeling one-way, as if I'm falling all alone here. But the only thing scarier than taking a chance is letting it pass us by."

Oh, God, his words were as potent as his kisses. She didn't want to acknowledge either. "Nobody is falling anywhere, Spence, least of all into bed. We're still ticked off at each other, so get your hand out of my pants and let me go."

Instantly he released her, causing her to grapple against his chest to catch her balance. His arms raised as though someone had put a gun in his back and told him to stick 'em up.

Adjusting her clothing, she retreated, careful to divert her gaze from his eyes and the erection straining against the metal buttons of his jeans. There seemed no safe place to look at him, so she turned away and attempted to gather the frayed threads of her composure. "You said you made coffee?"

"Yeah," he said with a sigh. "Go put some underwear on and I'll take you to eat."

She looked down, assessing her worn sweat suit, debating.

He walked across the living room as though in pain. "I couldn't sit across the table from you knowing you were naked under that."

"I don't know if I want to go—"

He stopped in his tracks on the way to the kitchen. "Knock the goddamn chip off your shoulder and give a little, Roxanne. If you do, you might end up looking in the mirror and seeing the woman I catch a glimpse of every now and then."

She held her ground, wondering how far he'd seen into her and how he'd managed to do it. She took a breath and let it out. A physical pummeling couldn't have made her ache more.

She went to change clothes. Maybe they'd find some neutral ground in a restaurant. Then, considering the tension mushrooming between them, maybe not.

# Chapter
# Eleven

"Okay, what do you want?" Roxanne slammed the front door of the big house and half the lights went out. It was nearly midnight, and she was physically and mentally drained. For the first time ever, she hadn't been able to relax at the beach house. Dinner with Spence had exhausted her and the drive home hadn't improved her mood.

She dropped her overnight duffel onto the bottom stair, then turned toward the kitchen. Mentally she made a note to speak with Inez about closing up portions of the house until she decided what to do with the old place. Other than her bedroom and office upstairs, the kitchen was the only room she used. Lately, she was seldom home long enough to make more than a quick meal and coffee in the morning.

"You bellowed, my dear daughter?"

Halfway across the dining room, she nearly tripped over her own tired feet. "Jeez, get off my shoulder."

"I'm not on your shoulder."

"Well, keep your distance. It sounds like you're talking in my ear."

"We are cranky tonight, aren't we."

If the *we* he referred to was Spence and her, then the answer was a definite affirmative. "*We* have just had the Mother of all bad days." She opened the freezer. "But then, you know about most of it already, don't you? I have the unique misfortune of being indebted to you not once today, but twice."

"Forget it." He sat cross-legged on top of the refrigerator, his feet dangling over the shelf containing the ice cream. She hesitated, then reached through the specter of his shin and grabbed the container.

"I can't." She slammed the freezer door. "And you won't."

"I already have. There are some things a man just does for his kid."

She shivered and set the ice cream down. It was hard to believe he was her father. For starters, he looked about twenty, not the twenty-five he was when he died, nor the fifty-three he would be if he had survived. He certainly didn't look ... fatherly. Given what she knew about him, it was even harder to believe in his newfound streak of altruism. "Please don't try to recapture either one of our lost youths, and spare me the obligatory father-daughter chat."

"I agree we're beyond that. How about a bowl of ice cream? I saw some hot fudge in the cupboard."

She stared at him in utter disbelief, her hand suspended over the carton of ice cream. "When you can keep your tea from running straight through you, you can try solid foods. Until then, just remember, having isn't as good as wanting."

"Who told you that line of bull?"

She finished dishing up the ice cream. "I saw it on *Star Trek*. A rerun from your time, I believe." She returned the carton to the freezer and went in search of the hot fudge he'd mentioned.

"The pointy-eared guy, right?"

She put the hot fudge in the microwave. "Yeah, the one who makes sense."

Matt studied her from the center of the island, which he had come to regard as his command post. He wasn't sure, but she appeared a bit thinner than when he first arrived. Tonight she lacked her usual vigor, moving around the kitchen as though sleepwalking. "What happened?" he asked after several minutes.

She shrugged and continued drizzling hot fudge over her ice cream. "I don't remember."

"You don't remember what happened this afternoon?"

"I thought you meant in that *Star Trek* episode." When she

sighed Matt saw the mask over her emotions weaken faintly. A hint of her vulnerability peaked through. However, before it took hold, she banished it as surely as she did the jar of hot fudge his mouth watered for to the refrigerator. When she joined him at the island with her sundae, he noticed the stains of fatigue reflected in the shadowy half-moons beneath her eyes.

For the second time today he genuinely wanted to help her, to ease the invisible burden stooping her shoulders as she toyed with the hot fudge sundae. Would wonders never cease? Whatever was happening was changing him, too. Because he didn't have a body to consider, maybe thinking about her came easier. Or maybe he genuinely wanted to help his daughter. His daughter. Fatherhood still sat a little lopsided but he liked it more every day.

"Spence was angry. He's still angry." She dropped the spoon in the bowl. "I get no reprieve, either. Tomorrow, I'm supposed to meet his family—all ten thousand of them. It's the matriarch's ninety-fifth birthday." She stared at the ice cream puddling around the hot fudge. "As for today, I don't want to talk about it."

"Why not? I might be able to help you. I'd sure like to have the opportunity to try anyway." He'd do whatever possible to put a real smile on her face.

"What is this new 'I want to help you without asking for anything in return' thing you're doing? Sort of goes against your nature, doesn't it?"

He imitated her by folding his arms across his chest. "You believe it, or you could take me at face value."

"Which is?" She lifted her eyebrows the same way Marian had when she'd questioned his motives.

"I'm worried about you, Roxanne. If I can help you, at least I'll be productive in some way. I don't seem to be doing myself much good. Half the time I don't know what I'm doing here or how I'm supposed to do it. The rest of the time I'm trying to figure out what's happened to the world I knew. Maybe I can't give you deep insight, but I'll damn sure give you honesty." He grinned and flashed Roxanne a wink. "Fortunately for us both, I don't have a choice there."

"You think I'd be easy to lie to?" Not a hint of emotion touched her words or clouded her eyes as she tilted her head.

"No. You're an astute cynic where I'm concerned. And you're your mother's daughter. Like her, you'd probably catch me every time I so much as bent the truth." And for the inability to lie, he sent up a silent prayer of thanks.

"I don't want to talk about what happened after I got off the horse or about Spence," she said after a moment, then picked up her spoon and took another bite. "I'm never getting on a horse again."

"What happened with Thelma and the riding lessons? I'd have placed a hefty bet she'd tie you to a saddle before you were seven."

"I think giving me riding lessons at an early age was the equivalent of sanctioning an intrusion into the Griffith realm. She didn't want me there."

She studied the ice cream dripping from the tip of her spoon. "She didn't want me here, either. I wasn't like most of the kids I went to school with. Oh, I had the clothes and all the trappings; it wasn't anything obvious. In fact, my name was always first on the list for trips—the longer the better. Overnight trips were one issue Thelma and I actually agreed on. I never missed an opportunity to leave and she'd gladly write the check to have me gone.

"My junior year in high school . . ." Her voice faded. The ice cream continued dripping from the tip of the spoon she still dangled over the bowl.

"What happened, Roxanne?" he crooned, hungry to know about her life.

"Between my junior and senior year I went to Pennsylvania for three weeks on an American History Studies program. I loved going and being on my own." The excitement of discovery echoed in her voice and flashed a brief smile. "Something changed that month. I think Thelma realized she only had another year to put up with me. She'd intimidated and guilt-tripped me into doing what she wanted.

"I'd never been gone for three weeks before. I think she realized how big this house was without someone to share it, even if we seldom spoke."

"It shouldn't have been that way," Matt said softly.

"Yeah, well. When I came home, she wanted me to learn to ride."

"What did you bribe you with?" Matt asked.

Roxanne grinned. "You did know her well, didn't you?"

"Know her? Hell, I'm probably the reason she didn't like kids."

"A new car of my choice. *If* I took riding lessons and ballroom dancing. It was tempting for about thirty seconds. Heaven knows I wanted my own car, but there were too many strings. Besides, I already had my driver's license. When it was our turn to drive somewhere, she'd give me the keys to one of the cars rather than associate with any of my friends. As long as I didn't do anything to stain the Griffith name, Thelma didn't care what I did—until that fall."

She stirred the ice cream and took another bite. "It was like she realized she hadn't lived up to the Griffith protocol. I'd be graduating high school and her control. By the time she offered me Stanford—and yes, I had the grades and the SATs—I'd already accepted a scholarship and had Pell grants lined up for U.C. Berkeley.

"She wasn't doing it for me. Not really. She was doing it for her and the Griffith image, but it was too little, too late for both of us."

"Berkeley is a good school. I'd say you did fine for yourself. But Ballroom dancing . . . Did you take the lessons?" Matt mused, recalling the lessons his parents insisted he take.

She shrugged, then regarded him so seriously he didn't even dare shimmer. "Thelma had no idea Freddy Solis and I were the hottest dancers in school. Freddy was a fringer, like me."

"Fringer?" he asked.

"Someone who didn't quite fit in but came from too much money and power to exclude."

He nodded, understanding more than the terminology.

"Freddy and I attended the big school functions together. Everyone thought we were an item. We were, but not romantically. We were in love with each other and mathematics. Freddy's dad gave me my first job as a gofer on the production floor of his company when I was fourteen. The rest is history.

"As for the riding lessons, Thelma got tired of pressuring me and backed off. I went my way. She went hers. We came together when social necessity dictated. End of story."

The lack of rancor in her voice further saddened Matt. "That was wrong. You were my daughter. You were entitled to whatever they could—"

"Yeah, well, they didn't think I was entitled to jack. They weren't convinced I was your daughter. Maybe if I'd been a blonde with big blue eyes or had your nose, mouth, or mannerisms, instead of my mother's, things might have been different. But it was what it was, and now it's over. Frankly, I like the cliché that says 'that which does not kill me makes me stronger.' Things could have been much worse. I always had food to eat. I went to school, had a place to sleep, and learned how to work for what I want in life. I'd say I made out very well."

"I'm proud of you, Roxanne. You grew up to be one helluva fine woman."

She stared at him as though he'd struck her a physical blow.

Dimly he comprehended she'd lived on the precipice overlooking an abyss as desolate and empty as the one he faced in the Otherworld. To a kid, it'd be the equivalent of living in a candy store and never allowed to taste anything.

She slipped off the stool, her gaze never leaving him. Then, without a word, she left the kitchen.

Matt dropped his head in his hands. Hadn't anyone ever told her they were proud of her? Good God, hadn't anyone told her they loved her since Marian's death?

The things he'd taken for granted all his life—love, understanding, forgiveness, support for whatever he ventured, pride in what he achieved regardless of how small—she'd known none of after Marian's death. He couldn't imagine what life had been like for his six-year-old daughter. It amazed him that Roxanne had survived, let alone flourished in the emotional desert of a house ruled by Thelma the Iron-Fisted. But Roxanne had found a way, and she had done it according to her own terms.

For the first time in memory he lamented a dismal circumstance other than his own. He had questions demanding answers and nowhere to turn. Those with the explanations were dead, too, and well beyond his reach.

Unable to tolerate the confines of the house, he stalked the grounds. Oddly, he longed to rattle the chains forged by his misdeeds one link at a time, but his daughter needed her rest. And if the past of this house didn't haunt her, it damn sure haunted him.

He waited until Roxanne's bedroom light winked out before leaving. He had business to take care of, and time was slipping away.

Matt roamed the streets of San Francisco's Mission District, drawn by his old friend, Greg Detweiler. Funny how, when the time was right, the essence of one spirit recognized another. Or at least it was until the first time he'd faced Greg. Recognition was a one-way street. Greg had walked straight through him. He hadn't seen him, hadn't wanted to see him, nor would he be happy when Matt figured out how to change that circumstance.

Greg lived in the attic rooms of an old row house. The condition of the apartment his formerly wealthy friend called home saddened Matt. He couldn't help wondering what had become of the Detweiler money and property and why Greg lived here.

Matt invaded the small living space by moving directly through the closed door. The freight-train volume of snoring from the other room proclaimed Greg's presence.

Although the two men had grown up knowing each other's personalities as well as they knew their own, they were no longer kindred spirits. Greg's inability to see or hear Matt added to the difficulty of his task. How could he make amends if he couldn't communicate with Greg?

This far from the touchstones of the past, his daughter, and their home, Matt's strength ebbed. He lacked the power to move or pick up an object. On his last visit he'd tried writing on the bathroom mirror as he had with Spence. Nothing had happened. At the time his failure had baffled him. If he was to salvage anything from the opportunity Heaven bequeathed, he had to act fast.

"Guardian? Are you here?"

"Yes, Matthew, I am with you."

"Tell me how to reach Greg." This second of three interventions was the only shortcut possible.

"A tormented man seeking peace through the reparation of other's lives sees little beyond his goals."

"Is that want he is? Tormented?"

"Can you not see it when you look at him?"

Matt hesitated. He hadn't wanted to see Greg in torment, and he damn sure hadn't wanted to see him living on questionable resources in a seedy part of the City. What had happened to Greg's dreams of seeing the world as an airline pilot? For that matter, what had happened to the airlines Old Man Detweiler started?

"I see a man I wouldn't recognize if I was alive. In this form, I sense him as though he were a ghost, too."

"Mr. Detweiler has squandered many years of his life, but he has performed great kindness, too."

"Are you saying Greg won't be contemplating the Abyss of Nothingness?"

"His present direction leads into the heart of the light. He has a beautiful soul, Matthew. It is scarred with remorse, pitted by disappointment, fractured by loss and grief, but it shines with love. In part, that is why he trod a self-destructive path for many years. But neither the alcohol nor the drugs gave him peace."

Matt studied his sleeping friend. On the street Greg looked much older than his fifty-three years. Sleep didn't change that impression. "Why did this happen? He had everything going for him. He survived Vietnam. I don't get it."

"I know you don't." Sorrow softened the affirmation and further isolated Matt.

"Wait a minute here. Are you telling me I did this to him? I'm responsible?"

"He is responsible for his choices and the state of his soul. But it is highly doubtful Mr. Detweiler would have made the choices that brought him here without you, Matt."

Only now did he comprehend the brevity of physical life. Eternity was, well, forever. Infinity. It was beyond the grasp of the corporeal mind. Having stood at the Abyss of Nothingness, a desolate state beyond mortal imagining, Matt envied Greg's direct path into the light.

"Given the same set of circumstances, you would have made different choices," the voice assured him. "Greg will enter the light because he has *earned* his place here."

"Do you read my thoughts?" Disregarding the walls lined with bookshelves and boxes, Matt paced the length of the attic rooms. In his agitated state, he barely noticed the mountains of newspaper clippings and the vintage Vietnam photographs.

"Does it matter?"

When he stripped the situation down to the hard reason, nothing mattered except making full use of the opportunity at hand. "What do I need to do to reach Greg?"

"You may communicate with him through your daughter, Matthew. Roxanne is the key. The catalyst. The solution. To everything."

"Great. I'm dead."

"Yes, you are."

His mind worked at a frantic pace, not ready to give up. "I can't bring her here. Hell, I wouldn't think of coming to this part of the City if I were alive. No, I damn sure can't bring Roxanne here."

"The location makes no difference."

"Will he see me then?"

"Not at first. It is up to you to open that door."

"How?"

"You are a free-thinking individual, Matthew. Use your head, and your heart. The solution will come to you."

"You're sure?"

"Self-doubt is uncharacteristic of you."

"Yeah, well, this is uncharted territory for me."

A soft laugh rippled through the dark room. "I'm sure it is. Responsibility has a way of forcing a man to think ahead and consider the consequences of his actions."

Without another word the Guardian departed. The darkness of Greg's room closed in on Matt. Even the feel of the air reminded him of the Abyss. Spirits both of the living and the dead filled this area of the City. While he could neither see nor hear them, he sensed them moving through the walls of the old house and out on the street. Their restlessness stirred him and fed his unease. He was the outsider here. He hadn't died on these streets or in the alleys. He didn't belong.

Any sane mortal sensing what he did in this part of San Francisco would run for his life. But he couldn't run, and he couldn't die again. He could only persevere toward his goal. Right now *fumble* more aptly described his progress.

Hovering over Greg's chest, Matt watched him sleep and contemplated how in Heaven he was going to arrange a reunion between Greg and Roxanne.

Roxanne debated going to the Sunday evening birthday party for Spence's grandmother. The list of excuses seemed flimsy each time she reached for the telephone. Finally she decided she owed it to Spence to show up. Settling into the commitment left her with a clear mind and a nervous stomach.

She whittled her "Must Do" pile to a manageable height, then got into the shower. The gift she'd purchased earlier in the week sat on her dresser. The bright wrapping and big old-fashioned floppy bow begged for attention. Satisfied with the present, card, and wrapping, she faced another challenge: what to wear. She'd

never attended a function of this nature and had no guidelines
from the past. In the end she opted for basic black because the
festivities were at Christopher's. Although the restaurant did not
enforce a dress code, an air of formality was implied, and few
diners ventured inside wearing shorts and sandals.

Not until she was dressed and preparing Buster's food did Roxanne realize that her resident ghost had remained uncharacteris-
tically quiet.

"Where are you?" she called. "We need to talk." What she
wanted was Matt's promise to stay away from Christopher's tonight.

Matt watched Roxanne from his command post in the center of
the kitchen island. He didn't want her to see him, didn't want to
talk to her right now. She might ask him something and be willing
to bargain for the answer.

The habits of a lifetime were difficult shackles to cast aside.
No more bribery, no more deceit, and no more blackmail and
bartering with Roxanne. That's what he'd decided last night in
the yard. From now on, she came first no matter what the cost to
himself.

But in the cool light of a spring day, with summer approaching
too fast, the urgency of his own self-interests provoked a relapse.
Maybe not a complete one, he rationalized. He just wouldn't tell
her he was going with her tonight. He wanted to see Roxanne's
reactions to Spence and his family. Then he'd visit Greg again.
There was a great deal he had to learn about the life his former
best friend was living in the bowels of San Francisco.

Roxanne gave her car keys to the valet, drew a deep breath, and
entered Christopher's. Stepping inside was like entering another
world. Street noise gave way to soft classical music as a seductive
blend of delicious aromas enticed her farther into the restaurant.

The place reflected Spence's personality. Rich, heavy wood
paneling framed by finely carved wainscoting and crown molding
gave the entry a rich, polished air. It reminded her of a parlor
instead of a restaurant waiting area. Then, that was probably
Spence's intent.

She crossed the maroon and blue paisley carpet and approached
the maître d' at a polished walnut podium illuminated by a brass
light.

The young man's smile was so genuine, Roxanne responded in

kind. "I'm here for a birthday party," she said. "Is Spencer Griffith available?"

"And waiting," came a voice from behind her. He took her elbow and gave the maître d' a dismissive nod. "I was wondering if you'd changed your mind."

Good grief, the man was devastating in a white dinner jacket. In the soft light that seemed to come from nowhere, his black hair shone and turned his eyes into sapphires.

"You look gorgeous." The words went from her hormones to her mouth without passing through the filter of her brain.

An instant smile brightened his face and deepened the faint laugh lines around his eyes. "That's my line."

"No line," she murmured, suddenly uncomfortable. She offered the present for his grandmother to him. "Here."

"Hold on to it for a moment." He led her around a corner and up a flight of stairs. At the end of a short hallway he unlocked a door and ushered her inside, then closed the door.

Bewildered, Roxanne glanced around the office. It took two seconds to realize the strong, polished, subtle authority of the room was a continuation of the statement below.

She met his gaze and had to lock her knees to keep them from buckling. The echo of last night's erotic dream rushed through her mind. The aftereffects lingered in the sensitive areas in her body. The room suddenly grew too warm and Spence's hungry gaze too inviting. "I don't think we should be here," she whispered.

"Why not? It's my office and we aren't scheduled for dinner for another twenty minutes." He put his hands into his trouser pockets. "The truth is, if I take you in too soon, I'm afraid they'll overwhelm you and you'll run out of here screaming."

The twinkle in his eye promised he was making light of what lay ahead, but not too much so. "Will I regret coming?"

"Good God, I hope not. I want you to have a good time."

So did she. She needed to let her hair down a little. "If I match your relatives with the stories you told me about them, will you tell me if I'm right?"

"Most certainly, but I won't give you any hints."

"I'm looking forward to figuring out which cousin got caught on the MUNI in his underwear at three A.M."

Spence laughed softly. "You'll get bonus points if you match on that one."

Roxanne smiled, savoring his unintentional hint. Then his enigmatic smile made her wonder if he knew exactly what he'd done and intentionally misled her. "I'm getting the feeling you have a very sick sense of humor."

"I resemble that remark." He walked over to a picture window overlooking the rooftops and the bay beyond.

Roxanne set the gift and her purse on the arm of a soft leather couch the color of walnuts and joined him. Hands curled into cool, sweaty fists in her coat pocket, she was careful not to stand close enough for temptation to strike a victory on either side. Logically, she knew this was the smartest way. That her body didn't agree changed nothing.

Beyond the roofline of the restaurant the last traces of twilight lingered on the horizon. A thick fog bank lay waiting for just the right time to creep over the City.

"About yesterday," she started. "I'm sorry I upset you. It won't happen again."

"Oh, I'm sure it will, just not with horses." He smiled at her and flicked his left eyebrow. "Nice coat you're wearing. Got anything on under it?"

"Of course," she said, startled.

"Too bad."

Now she did laugh. "Do you act like this around your family?"

"We're not that kind of family. When we had to share beds while growing up, we slept. If you and I shared a bed, we wouldn't waste time sleeping."

"You might be disappointed. Did you ever consider that?"

"I'm willing to take the chance. Is this an offer?"

"No way," she said through a laugh at his hopeful, lecherous grin.

"Afraid you'll be disappointed?"

"It's a possibility," she conceded, loving the way he bristled, then shrugged off the notion.

"Not a chance. I'll even give you a satisfaction-guaranteed promise. In writing."

The laughter faded as the heat simmering between them flared with the talk of lovemaking. Roxanne returned to staring out the window.

"Have you ever been in love, Roxanne?"

His question caught her off guard. "Never," she answered. "You?"

"Yeah. Came within two weeks of going down the aisle."

She gazed at him from the corner of her eyes. He continued peering into the night as relaxed as if they were discussing the color of the shingles on the roof. "Two weeks, huh? Did you change your mind, or did she?"

"We stumbled across some irreconcilable differences. Angela walked."

"I guess you both were fortunate it happened two weeks before instead of two weeks after the wedding." Yielding to temptation, she looked squarely at him. "Are you on the rebound?"

He shook his head in denial. "It was years ago. Five, to be exact. I mention it now because it's inevitable one of my cousins, aunts, or uncles will mention Angela."

"Why? Do I look like her?"

"Not even close. For starters you're a lot easier to kiss, especially in those spiked heels." He turned slightly.

Roxanne retreated a step. "Then why?"

"I haven't invited anyone to a family event since Angela. In their zeal to marry me off, they may speculate."

"What? That we're an item? Didn't you tell them the only reason I'm here is out of morbid curiosity to see the people you described in all your stories?"

He laughed, not the slightest bit embarrassed. "They'd believe that, *then* they'd speculate."

"About what?"

"Little things."

"Like?" God, this was like pulling teeth.

"A wedding date. How many kids we're planning. Little things like that."

"I see." She wanted to, but she didn't see at all. "Why?"

"You haven't spent much time around big families have you?"

"None." And as little as possible around her own until Thelma got sick.

His grin returned. "Then, I guess you will see." He checked his watch. "Are you ready for an adventure?"

"That's why I came."

He reached for her coat and helped her out of it. "You look good enough to be the main course in a very private dinner."

"Don't start." Already her heart was quickening.

"Trust me. I haven't." He folded her coat over the arm of the soft, leather couch. "You might want to stay close to me until you get your bearings."

"Thanks for the warning." There was no reason for nerves. She'd addressed CEOs of major corporations and pitched her business to some of the most powerful people in Silicon Valley. This was just a family. And she was nervous. "I don't suppose they wear name tags?"

"Afraid not." Laughing softly, he led her to the door.

# Chapter
# Twelve

The banquet room accommodated eighty-nine. As they approached the door, Roxanne was certain the birthday guests exceeded capacity by a factor of two. She'd attended conventions as crowded, but nothing quite as eclectic.

Oak paneling, oil paintings of old San Francisco, and fifteen tables shrouded in dark blue tablecloths with an overlay of ecru lace set the formal tone. The mix of people and ages surpassed her naïve expectations. Most amazing was that all of them were related in some convoluted way. For a woman who claimed no living relatives, the prospect was daunting.

"How many people are here?" Roxanne asked as they entered the room.

"Eighty-three, including us. Grandma was born here in San Francisco, but she's lived in the Seattle area for over eighty of her ninety-five years. This is where she wanted the party, so this is where we're having it." Spence waved at a middle-aged woman with a smile that matched his. "Get ready for the crush. You're about to meet Aunt Constance—my mother's oldest sister."

The logistics of such massive preparations for tonight's party staggered Roxanne. "Do I get a scorecard or a family tree?" What she wanted was a digital camera and a computer to catalog the relatives for later review. In truth, her curiosity about his family fostered a strange excitement.

"You get something better. Me."

Even more frightening than the sincerity she saw in his eyes was the trill of joy dancing through her. Before she could explore it, the family noticed their arrival.

The flurry of introductions and countless names were impossible to track. Inevitably, a few slipped from memory and she had to ask Spence to repeat them. The speculative glances and appraising stares she drew were more blatant than Spence had warned.

A young woman in a string tank top and jeans so long they draged behind her heels held a baby and shared a laugh with a boy of ten, a man easily older than God, and another woman a few years older than Roxanne. No one seemed to notice the difference between the young mother in casual street clothing and the designer suit worn by the other woman. The baby waved drool-coated fists and bounced with the laughter.

Roxanne paid special attention to the grand matriarch and guest of honor. Had Spence not mentioned her age, Roxanne would have placed Amelia Lazzaro in her late sixties, early seventies, certainly not ninety-five. The woman was positively energetic. One look into her blue eyes and Roxanne knew the genetic source of Spence's expressive eyes.

The most interesting guests were Spence's sisters and mother. Not a faint heart in the bunch, they radiated strength. While talking with them, she lost track of Spence.

She recognized Candice from the Acorn and marveled at how a designer dress and upswept hair transformed her into socialite.

"Collectively, the family can be a little overwhelming," Candice said, thrusting a glass of wine into Roxanne's hand. "Let's find our seats."

"Are you related, too?" Candice seemed to know everyone in the room.

"No, but there have been times when I wished I was. Luke would have loved growing up with all these cousins, aunts, and uncles around. They might bicker amongst themselves, but heaven help any outsider who threatens one of the family." Candice steered her to a table near the front of the room. "Of course, there is a price to pay. The birthright comes hand-in-hand with the expectation of self-sufficiency, hard work, and personal success. That's what drew me to them. I took a large professional and financial risk going to work for Spence when he launched Griffith Enterprises ten years ago." Her smile imparted a warmth that touched Roxanne. "Best decision I've ever made. Not only is Spence the best boss and friend I've had, he's made me a wealthy woman. But you probably realize what a jewel he is by now."

"Luke said you were a heavyweight in the sales and marketing field," Roxanne affirmed. "I didn't know you'd expanded into personal politics."

Candice laughed. "I don't need to sell Spence, nor would I. He'd be mortified."

"To know Spence is to love him? Is that your meaning?" Roxanne voiced the message she'd read between the lines since she walked into the room.

"Close, Roxanne, real close." Candice indicated a chair, then settled into the one beside it. "As long as you don't cross him."

"So, what happens when Spence doesn't get his way?" His dark side had to be as dangerous as his sunny side was bright.

"Back up there. Like most of us, Spence likes to have his way, but he gets over it if it doesn't happen. However, he doesn't get over being crossed, as in lied to, used, or outright betrayed."

"Who does?" Certainly not her, which was why she trusted so few people.

"Depending on who you ask in this room, you could get some interesting answers," Candice said softly enough for only Roxanne to hear.

"I see you found our table and a friend," Spence said in Roxanne's ear.

Startled, she turned in the chair she'd just settled onto. A few short inches away from her mouth, his lips parted. The lingering essence of his aftershave penetrated the perfumes and food aromas in the air. For an instant there was only him and her—no one else. Every cell in her body acknowledged the certainty that if he kissed her now, the hot, moth-to-the-flame desire bubbling to the surface would take on life. If it did, nothing beyond satisfying the primal need, the need that kept drawing them closer and closer would matter.

The sound of a baby crying brought her back into reality. Still, she couldn't drag her gaze from Spence's tempting mouth. All she had to do was lift her chin an inch and he'd take her lips . . .

Candice jostled her shoulder and brought her down to earth. Roxanne retreated a few inches. So did Spence. She met his gaze and saw a reflection of the hunger gnawing at her most sensitive places.

"I'll be back, shortly. Gotta get this going," he said in a thick, strangled tone. Without another word he straightened and walked away.

Uncertain what had just transpired between the two of them, Roxanne reached for the ice water in front of her place setting. Her nerves danced on the hot griddle of near disaster. Had she kissed him, she'd be dancing in the fire.

"So, are you planning to increase your hours at the Acorn on a permanent basis?" Candice offered the breadbasket and an amused understanding.

Roxanne stared at the round of sourdough bread in the basket, then looked at Candice. "Huh?"

"That's what I thought. Want some friendly advice?"

"Uh, sure."

"Have some bread, and stay away from the wine. You're going to need all your wits in this crowd."

It took several minutes for Roxanne to pull herself together. Somehow and in some indefinable way, something had shifted within her. She put a piece of bread on her plate and watched Spencer prepare to address the gathering.

"Welcome to our celebration honoring the wisest and loveliest woman in the family," Spence said loudly from beside his grandmother's chair.

The room hushed. Even the baby in the back stopped crying. Roxanne assessed Spence's audience, noting the rapt attention he commanded.

"Thank you for coming from as far away as Milan, Italy." Spence gestured toward a couple in their sixties sitting with Grandma. "And from down the street." Without a break in his welcoming speech, he reached down and picked up a little red-headed boy who had run around Grandma Lazarro's table with his arms outstretched. "And the side tables," he added. Amid the laughter, the boy rested his head on Spence's shoulder and popped his thumb into his mouth.

The naturalness of Spence's action dispelled any cause for comment. Roxanne followed the line of Spence's gaze to a woman draped by a blanket at the side of the room. A baby's foot bounced in the air and fanned the edge of the blanket. A young man in a neat white shirt and tie juggled the twin of the boy Spence held into the nearer of two highchairs and started to rise. Spence had only to shake his head to convey the message that he and the redheaded escapee were content.

Roxanne felt, as well as saw, the familial bonds shared by the diverse group. She no longer cared which one of them had ridden the MUNI at 3 A.M. in his skivvies. The baseball player who reminded Spence of his dad became unimportant. The couple who had survived a terrorist bombing years ago in an Athens airport could have been any elderly couple among the attentive listeners. They might be seated next to the aunt on her seventh marriage. Whoever they were, it no longer mattered.

Young and old, travelers and locals, they gathered here for one reason: the matriarch's birthday. Incredible. Thelma would have paid a fortune to command such a tribute for any reason.

The thickness forming in Roxanne's throat became a lump. Next Sunday marked the twenty-second anniversary of her mother's death.

*"We're a family, Roxanne. That's so important. When your daddy comes home from the war, everything will be wonderful."* Her mother had braided her hair and put pink elastics and Pop-beads at the ends.

*"Will we be part of Grammy and Grampa's family, too? And will Aunt Thelma like me then?"* Even at five she'd doubted her great-aunt would ever like her. But if they were a real family with a daddy, maybe Aunt Thelma would be nicer.

*"Oh, yes. You'll see,"* her mother had assured with a special smile that had always banished a little girl's fears.

Roxanne blinked away the memories.

His speech done, Spence carried the redheaded toddler to the highchair beside his twin. An army of waitpeople distributed giant salad bowls and silver serving tongs to each table. The easy laughter and camaraderie became intoxicating.

Out of the blue Roxanne understood why she had returned to take care of Thelma. It hadn't been because of some misplaced sense of obligation or duty. The reason had deeper roots, so deep she hadn't recognized it.

Thelma had been family. Roxanne's only family. Even as an adult she'd still sought the love and acceptance of a family and the sense of belonging it engendered. The years spent alone hadn't assuaged those fundamental needs, only disguised them, leaving a part of her empty and afraid.

Ironically, in the last two years of Thelma's life, they had learned to be a family. Not because of a leap of faith or even a newfound love, but because of science. A DNA test. The answer to a prayer Roxanne had given up on long ago.

"Are you all right?" Candice asked, her furrowed brow fraught with concern.

Roxanne nodded, then placed her napkin on her empty salad plate. "Excuse me for a moment." Clutching her small purse like a lifeline, she left the table and, with a forced calm, walked to the door.

In the open space of the hall she drew a ragged breath and headed for the ladies' room with as much haste as decorum allowed. Something was unraveling inside her and she didn't know how to stop it. The most she could exert was temporary control. The tears she hadn't finished shedding for Thelma, or for herself, blurred her vision.

In the confines of the nearest bathroom stall, Roxanne locked the door and sat on the lid of the toilet. Bent over with her purse in her lap, her face in her hands, she pressed her fingertips against her temples and tried to keep the dam from bursting.

Until tonight she hadn't grasped the real meaning of being a family. It didn't matter if the family consisted of only two members. To the contrary, the totality of loss of one of them became keener in the face of total aloneness.

But after Thelma's death she shouldn't have been alone. Not ever, she lamented. Where was her mother's family? Why had they abandoned her and her mother years before her death? Why hadn't she known them?

The old wounds cracked and bled their own pain. She hated it—hated that it still made a difference. Defensive, she suddenly resolved to use the time and resources now in plentiful supply to hunt down the Boyles. And when she found them, she'd look them in the eye and ask why they turned their backs on her and her mother.

Roxanne sniffed hard, then exhaled through her mouth in an effort to force herself into composure.

No, she wouldn't look for relatives who didn't want her.

Besides, what difference did the reasons for the total abandonment of her mother's family make? It was a long time ago. There was no sense in deluding herself—the Boyles had chosen to make a life separate from hers. Nothing she did could change the choices they had made.

*That which does not kill me makes me stronger.* She was strong. The old cliché fortified her resolve to pull herself together. A counselor at the hospital had warned about the moments when grief and loss struck from nowhere. Roxanne hadn't believed it would happen, hadn't wanted to admit she genuinely cared for Thelma. She had loved her, and still loved her, which made her vulnerable to the pain of loss running roughshod over her emotions.

Obviously, she'd been wrong. Again.

For the first time she admitted that while accumulated grief hadn't killed her, it injured her. The accompanying pain amassed over the years was finally lashing out, trying to escape.

But she couldn't let it happen. Not yet. Not here. Later, she admonished. At home. In the dark. Under the pillow, so no one, especially herself, could hear.

"Roxanne? Are you in here?"

Oh, God, Candice was looking for her.

The lump in her throat kept her from opening her mouth. Better silence than a sob that Candice would ask her to explain.

Mercifully, the ladies' room door whooshed shut, leaving her alone with the faint hum of an exhaust fan stirring the silence.

Slowly she uncurled her spine and lowered her hands until they dangled over her knees.

Suspended less than a foot in front of her, her father stared back. In a cross-legged position, his shoulders slumped, his hands clenched on his ankles. Silent, crystalline tears streamed down the gossamer specter of his cheeks.

The torrent of her sobs welled dangerously close to the surface. At the sight of his grief-stricken face, she nearly lost control and cried aloud.

The outer door opened again. Two sets of footsteps crossed the carpet, then clacked on the tile flooring.

Matt faded into the cold tile wall, leaving her alone with her unwanted quandary of emotion.

"In answer to your question, no, Spence isn't serious about her," said an authoritative voice. "He needs her for Memorial Day. Having a family honor a reclaimed MIA in front of the military apologists and politicians is important. I heard she refused to attend the ceremony. We'll see. You know Spence. He always gets the job done, no matter what it takes."

The clank of two stall doors closing and the bolts sliding into locked positions interrupted the conversation.

"Sounds like you have a case against her" came the softly spoken response from the far stall.

"I just don't get it. Spence hands her the very thing the rest of us would give our eyeteeth for. What's her response? She doesn't give a damn. Not about her father and definitely not about the rest of us looking for our MIAs." The bitterness in the woman's tone built with each word. Roxanne thought if she touched the metal wall separating them, it would burn her fingers.

"Sounds like you haven't gotten over the disappointment of it being her father instead of Mitch," suggested the other woman.

"It seems so damn unfair for her to turn her back on something we want so much. It should have been Mitch." The flushing of a toilet punctuated her statement. A muffled thud indicated the close of the adjacent stall door.

"We all want Mitch brought home where he belongs" responded the woman in the far stall. Another toilet flush and door thud followed.

"Spence will keep the search going."

"Yeah, we can count on him. Even better, he knows how to get what he wants. Let's see if Roxanne Griffith does."

Roxanne stopped breathing and listened as though her life depended on it.

"What do you mean?" asked the softer-spoken woman.

"If she's here because she's interested in Spence's money—which she probably is—she'll undoubtedly try to seduce him."

"Yes, but Carolyn, didn't you think the way they looked at each other before he started his speech tonight was incredible? I'm not sure you're reading this right at all."

"I know my brother. And you're right. He'll be all too willing to play hide-the-salami with her."

Roxanne barely breathed, her heart twisting in the silence.

"Don't be crude. If he didn't really like her, he wouldn't have brought her."

"Could be, but my money says he's softening her up for a little friendly persuasion that will lead to her inclusion in the Memorial Day ceremony. But it might be too late. Word is circulating. Before dessert the rest of the family will know what we know. Once they get the story Miss Roxanne Griffith will wish she'd stayed home."

Sink water snapped off and the pull of paper towels followed. "Where do you think she went?"

"Who cares? She doesn't belong here anyway."

High heels clacked against the tile. Like a distant echo, the thick carpet in the sitting area muted their steps.

The door whooshed closed.

Roxanne clutched her purse against her forehead for several minutes before mustering enough strength to leave.

To think she had almost believed Spence when he said he didn't want her presence on Memorial Day. That she had believed him when he said he cared about her. Fool. Fool. Fool. She had wanted to trust him and thus, had played right into his game.

In the hall she turned her back on the banquet room and blended with the patrons milling around the restaurant waiting area. She threaded her way across the room, then out the front door and into the crisp chill of the evening. There she dug her claim check from her purse and handed it to the parking valet.

"Roxanne? What's wrong?" came Candice's strident demand from behind her.

"Are you part of it?" she snapped, looking down the street for the valet with her car. The last thing she wanted to see in Candice's eyes was the betrayal. So Roxanne didn't look.

"Part of what? What happened?"

Roxanne patched up her defenses for a final stand. "Tell Spence I said nice try. It didn't work."

"What on earth are you talking about?"

Hurt pinched the anger roiling through her. "Did he really think bringing the pressure of his family down on me would change my mind about Memorial Day?" The sight of her car emerging from the parking lot promised an escape from the ordeal. "You can tell him I said he can go to hell with my father and stay there for all I care about either of them."

"Roxanne, there's been a misunderstanding. Please, let's talk this through. Spence wouldn't—"

"The only misunderstanding is him thinking he could seduce me and manipulate me. And use his family to pressure me into doing what he wanted." She grabbed the keys from the valet, shoved a five into his hand, and hurried around to get into the car. "And you can tell him that he and his entire family will be sunbathing in Siberia before I change my mind about Memorial Day."

She got in the car, slammed the door, and then checked traffic through her blurry eyes. She couldn't get out of San Francisco fast enough. Not until she turned away from Christopher's did she have reason to look across the passenger side.

The faint specter of her father sat in the seat. The safety belt stretched snugly across the seatback. Matt sat so low in the seat, he became part of it.

"Go away," she ground out. "Please. I can't handle any more tonight."

Matt faded a little, but not completely. The crushing sorrow radiating from her kept him from leaving. Later, he'd find a way to make his presence known to Greg Detweiler. Right now Roxanne needed something. He wasn't sure what, just that he wasn't leaving her alone in her misery.

Though he didn't understand what had sent her fleeing to the ladies' room in the first place, the message they had overheard left no doubt about what Roxanne faced if she had remained at the party.

For Matt, it didn't add up. He was sure he'd missed something if for no other reason than he considered Spence a stand-up guy.

However, he missed nothing in Roxanne's message to the blond woman in front of the restaurant: He and Spence could both rot in the Abyss of Nothingness. From what he'd seen of the other man's life patterns, Matt doubted Spence would face such a grim fate in the Otherworld. Unfortunately, his own future was beginning to look more ominous with each passing day.

Regardless of his fate, tonight he'd remain beside his daughter. She needed someone, whether she knew it or not.

Her calm control during the drive home added to his unease. She said nothing and kept her hands tightly fixed at the ten and two o'clock position on the steering wheel. She didn't even play the radio. Most unusual.

Once home Roxanne strode through the front door he opened, climbed the stairs, and went straight to her room.

Matt paced through the downstairs while she showered, and showered, and showered, until he was certain the water had to be as cold as ice.

At first he sensed rather than heard her tears. When she actually cried aloud, he cried with her. No one should be that desolate, that alone, that isolated. Especially not *his* daughter. She should have had everything the Griffith position and money symbolized. The laughter of her husband, their kids, or at least friends should echo from the walls of the house. Jeez, she ought to have friends. But if she did, they stayed well hidden and kept their distance from the house. Judging by her work and the messages spoken into the box beside the telephone, she had a wealth of acquaintances. But she had no Greg Detweiler in her life. No one shared Roxanne's hopes, her fears, her longings, and certainly not her confidences. No one claimed her love, nor did she allow anyone close enough to love her.

Matt continued pacing long after he sensed his daughter had cried herself to sleep. It tore at his heart to wonder how many other nights she had done the same thing.

"Because of me and my arrogance. Thoughtlessness. Immaturity. Self-centeredness." He ended the dreary recounting before he got too carried away. He already felt morose. No point in pushing his mood over the edge. That would come soon enough.

He paced the backyard, including the bottom of the swimming pool, while reviewing everything he'd seen in the banquet room of Christopher's.

There must be something he could do to help Roxanne. He owed her that much. He owed her mother even more, but a dead man had few ways to make restitution.

This was bullshit. Pure, simple, unadulterated crap.

Spence had seen Roxanne leave the banquet room. He had kept an eye on the door expecting her to return any moment. But the moments ticked by and Roxanne hadn't returned.

Earlier, she'd caught the attention of his family. After she disappeared from the party the questions started. He'd had no answers when asked where she was, what had happened to her, or the inevitable inquiry of when she was coming back.

He'd wondered if she'd taken ill. If so, did she need help?

For a fleeting moment, he'd wondered if she'd planned to embarrass him by making an appearance, then leaving without an explanation. He hadn't wanted to believe he'd misjudged her that badly.

He'd searched the entire restaurant for her before discovering she'd claimed her car and driven away. A quick check of his office where the gift she brought lay beside her coat on the arm of the couch indicated she'd left quickly.

Not until Candice cornered him with the bits and pieces she'd reconstructed did he understand the possible motive for Roxanne's departure. Then, and only then, did he catch bits of conversation and faint whispers of ingratitude, jealousy, and irritation.

"I guess your friend showed her true colors," Carolyn said with a smugness that grated on Spence. "Making an appearance is what it was all about, and a lot more than she's going to do on Memorial Day."

"Memorial Day has nothing to do with tonight or why I invited her," he answered.

"She's a self-centered bitch, Spence. You're better off without her."

"Is that why you're circulating half-truths about her?"

"Hardly half-truths," Carolyn snapped. "Truth. She turned you down flat for the Memorial Day ceremony. All she cares about—"

"Carolyn—" He locked his jaw on the words he might regret saying later. "You don't know what the hell you're talking about, so shut your poison-spewing mouth and keep your distance from me tonight." He turned on his heel and walked away.

This had all the ingredients of a long night.

The orchestra played tunes from the past nine decades. Old and young danced and sang when they knew the words. Stories told a hundred times blended with new tales of adventure, embarrassment, and hilarious circumstances. As with most family gatherings, wine and Irish whiskey flowed freely.

Spence danced with Granny Amelia and his mother. He managed to smile at the appropriate times and held up his end of the few conversations he couldn't avoid. Inside, he fumed.

Spence ended the bash at 1:00 A.M.; otherwise, it would have lasted until dawn. The twist of fate that had sent Roxanne home in tears made this the longest party he'd attended in his life.

Once the last of the family departed, he turned to the very personal, unfinished business of Roxanne Griffith. It wouldn't wait until morning. Tonight was a turning point, and he had to find out in which direction he and Roxanne were headed. It damn sure wasn't the one she'd taken by running away.

He telephoned her twice from the car. Both times he reached her answering machine. A third attempt as he left the freeway met with the same results. He pulled into her driveway and got out of the car.

The resident ghost touted his presence by burning all the lights.

Spence balled his fist and beat on the door. "Roxanne. Open the door."

She might ignore his calls, but she damn sure wasn't going to ignore him. Not after what happened earlier tonight.

He pounded hard enough to rattle the door frame the second time.

And a third time.

Suddenly the door opened with a crash slamming back against the wall.

Light blazed across the foyer and up the stairs. His gaze followed the rise of the banister to the top of the stairs.

Roxanne stood in a scrap of panties, a skimpy T-shirt that didn't reach her navel, and an open, flowing cotton robe. The hem danced at her bare ankles. In the glaring bright light, her face looked red and puffy, like she'd fallen asleep after crying for a long time. His gaze fixed on the soul-gripping misery evident in her brown eyes.

Fists balled at his sides, he climbed the stairs two at a time.

"Get out." Her words were more a plea than an order.

"As soon as you tell me why." He scaled the last six steps as she retreated. "You owe me that much."

"I don't owe you anything. You bastard. You set me up for your whole family to gang up on." Anger gave her voice strength.

The front door slammed shut hard enough to vibrate the windows.

Neither gave it a glance.

"I know your excuse for leaving, Roxanne. Now, I want to know why you left without talking to me." He advanced on her even as she retreated across the landing.

"Are you disappointed your little plan didn't work?" The wall behind her stopped her retreat.

He advanced until he braced his hands on either side of her head and looked into her bloodshot eyes. He would have his answers tonight. "Why, Roxanne?" The tension in him tightened another notch. "Why?"

"Why what? Why did I do the smart thing and get the hell out of there before I was roasted on the spit of your family's holy pursuit? Why didn't I march back into the banquet room and confront you in front of them? Why didn't—"

Livid as he was, he couldn't let her continue. "Why the hell do you believe everyone—even a couple of women you eavesdrop on—instead of me?" His bellow rattled the house, and he didn't care if the neighbors six blocks away heard. He wanted answers. Now!

Her mouth opened, then closed. Her golden brown eyes darkened with anger. "Those women had no ax to grind. No hidden agenda, Spence. One was your sister, Carolyn. She knows you far better than I do. Both were speaking from experience, from—"

"They spoke from ignorance," he said softly, willing her to understand how binding his word was. "Had they known I'd let you off the hook—"

"Let me off the hook? Sure. The same way you'd release a trout if you were hungry. You never let me off any hook. What you said is that if I wasn't going to behave and say nice things, you'd rather I didn't attract any bad press."

"Get something straight here, Roxanne. If I tell you it's Easter, you can start coloring eggs. Come hell or high water, I'll make it happen."

"Yeah, I believe it, Spence. Like I believe you told your family I'd be there Memorial Day to eulogize my father and sing the praises of your wonderful MIA recovery program. Well, there's no Easter bunny, so get your eggs out of my basket. I'm not part of the hunt."

"Answer my question." If he wanted answers, he had to set aside his anger and not let her bait him. She was too good at sidetracking him.

"I answered it. Now get out of my house."

"You didn't answer it."

"What do you want to hear, Spence?" Her voice softened as though she was out of fight.

"The truth. Why do you believe everyone—except me?"

He met her gaze for a long time before she answered. "Because they don't have an agenda where I'm concerned. You do. Now go away."

Head shaking in denial, he squared his shoulders. "Not good enough to get rid of me, Roxanne. Try again."

"I can't say it any clearer. You want something from me; they don't," she admitted in a whisper. Tears swelled along her lower lids. "I'm tired, Spence. So tired."

"Yeah, I know, baby." He gave into the desire ripping through his veins and lowered his head a few inches. Staring into her glassy brown eyes, then down at her lips, he held his distance. He needed answers. Damn, he needed her. "But you have to know what I want from you has nothing to do with Memorial Day. It's something far more important."

"Wh-what do you want from me?" Her chin tilted her mouth closer to his.

"Your heart." His lips grazed hers. Fire shot through him. His tightly coiled body was ready to claim hers. Clearly, her emotions teetered on a precarious fulcrum. He wanted to make sure she didn't decide to shut down and throw him out.

"No."

"No, what?" With the tip of his tongue, he lightly teased the lingering moue formed by her denial.

"Uh-uh." Another denial, another denied entry. The hand she placed on his chest wound into the pleats of his shirt. Her fingers neither drew him closer, nor pushed away, just held on.

She smelled of soap and shampoo, clean and intoxicating, sexy and desirable. His palms remained flat against the wall. He was moving too fast for her. Christ, if he touched her now, he'd lose everything.

"I want your heart, Roxanne, your loyalty. Your love. But to-night, I'll settle for your body," he breathed, aching to kiss the lips responding to every nuance of his testing.

Yearning knit her brow and softened her eyes. Her vulnerability lay exposed. "Tell me, when we're having sex, will you make me feel like I belong somewhere?"

The words ripped at him. "God, Roxanne."

Her fist tightened around the wad of his shirt, but the fight was gone from her. "Will you take away the loneliness for a little while?"

He kissed her jaw, then her ear when her chin lifted. "Yes. For as long as you want."

He felt the catch in her breath as he laid a trail of kisses along the side of her neck. The quick, steady thrum of her pulse thudded against his lips.

"Will you go away in the morning and never come back?" she asked in a breathy voice.

He stilled, then caught her earlobe between his teeth. "Not a chance."

"Too bad."

"I won't go away now, either." God, he could taste her desire.

"Then make me feel it all, Spence." Her hands came alive, gripping his jaw and the sides of his neck, pushing, twisting until her hot, moist breath pulsed against his mouth. "I want hard, fast sex. That's all. Just intense sex. Make me—" As though tipped over the edge by her own words, her mouth finished the plea.

Spence didn't know whether to weep with joy or gnash his teeth against the raw sexual hunger and the desolation he had seen in her eyes. The desperation in her kiss touched his soul. He answered with need. They'd have hard, fast sex. God, yes. Every fiber in his body screamed for it. Then he'd make long, languid love to her, more intense than desperate sex. Far more dangerous, too.

Lost in the endless kiss where they took turns devouring each other, his hand brushed aside her flimsy robe and found the swell of her breast. He needed to touch her, feel her skin against his. He slipped a hand under her cotton sleep shirt. Then he possessed the prize—excited satin skin, warm and eager, her breast filling his hand. He stroked her turgid nipple until she moaned and clutched at him.

He pulled her from the wall, shedding her cotton robe, and savoring her cool, soft skin. She moved so easily, so willingly into his arms that he trembled with the power she gave him.

Quickly the kiss turned primitively carnal. He rocked his hips against her and groaned when she arched into him, then lifted a delicate foot and ran her arch along his calf.

In a heartbeat, he swept her up and carried her down the hall.

Only later would Spence realize that he'd found Roxanne's bedroom like a homing pigeon came to roost. Her room was the only one in the house with the lights out.

Intent on keeping the rest of the world at bay, he heeled the door shut. In the darkness his only thought was to find the bed and get naked.

Now.

# Chapter
# Thirteen

A soft sigh escaped Roxanne. "Why don't you put me down?"

"Now that I've got you? Not a chance."

"It's dark in here. Aren't you worried about tripping over something and killing us both?" Despite her protest, the sense of being physically safe in his arms quieted the misgivings niggling at her defenses.

He inched forward while she tugged the pins from his shirt studs. "Trust me. I won't drop you."

"Not more than once, you won't." She slid her arms around his neck and inhaled. Through the lingering hint of his spicy aftershave and the distinctive Italian aroma of Christopher's, she caught his scent. And wanted a taste. Right now, she couldn't wait to get him naked.

"My eyes are adjusting even as I pant over your body."

"Pant away," she whispered into his ear, "just so you kiss me."

Kiss her, he did, like a starving man at a feast.

He placed her on the rumpled quilts of her bed, his knee insinuated between her thighs. She wanted the kiss to last forever. The intimacy filled the dark spot in her heart that had grown wider with each passing year.

For now she wouldn't think about the price she'd pay in the

cold light of morning. Tonight she'd step out on the edge and brazenly live for the moment. For once, she was taking what she wanted, when she wanted it. She gave in to the seduction of his mouth and let him draw her deeper into this world where need reigned supreme.

Cuff links bounced above her head. She pushed his shirt over his shoulders and, with a little help from him, got rid of it. A generous pattern of springy hair was the only softness about his hard chest. She teased the silky-feeling hair, liking the way it slid around her fingers and the harsh sounds he made while she stroked him. Heat radiated from the hard sinew and muscle defined on his long bones.

The thud of one shoe, then the other, sent him into a frenzy to get rid of his trousers. "Still want it hard and fast?" he asked against her mouth.

"Yes. Oh, God, please tell me you have protection." The sinuous motion of his thigh between her legs begged for more intimacy. She fumbled with his belt and trouser fastenings.

"I do."

She wasn't sure if she was relieved or disappointed he was prepared for whatever came his way. Before she decided which, it no longer mattered.

He let his full weight settle on her. "I started carrying some after I met you. If you can't figure out why by now, I'll explain later." He pulled her forward and stripped the scanty shirt from her body. "Much later. After I touch you in all the ways that have been running through my mind since I first saw you."

Roxanne shivered in anticipation. She'd take what he offered and indulge the ravenous thing inside her. She nipped his mouth, testing, tasting.

Without warning, the teasing turned serious. His tongue pushed into her mouth. His big body tensed over hers. Roxanne caught a handful of the hair at the back of his head and held while she made her own heady exploration of his mouth. Her back arched, thrusting her breast into his hand. He taunted her nipple until she thought she'd scream.

"I need to touch more of you," he said in a voice so heavy with need that Roxanne whimpered in agreement.

She could make out his face in the glow of the outdoor house lights filtering through her open drapes. He watched her with an intensity that reached into the core of her being. In that secret place, her power and vulnerability dwelled side by side behind the veil of their protector, Fear.

Tonight, Fear had taken a holiday.

Slowly, as though memorizing every curve, his hands were on her breasts, shaping, stroking, and molding. Part of her she had beaten into a submissive corner roared to life with a ravenous hunger. His thumbs built the fire of desire by toying with her aching sensitive nipples. Everywhere he touched became a mix of sweet agony and painful ecstasy. She relished each move, every nuance.

Dimly she realized that sex with Spence would be different. She still had her panties on and already she'd experienced pleasurable depths she'd only hoped to know before tonight.

"Spence," she breathed as his mouth found her breast. She gave him her body knowing he was claiming something more—a piece of her heart.

His fingers glided along her abdomen, dipped into the well of her belly button, wiggled beneath the little panties, and found the nest of curls hiding her sex. The heat of his touch penetrated her skin. The sweet, dangerous fire threatened to consume her. Deliberately she parted her legs and extended an invitation she insisted he accept.

Their breathing sounded rough in the near darkness, almost controlled, but on the verge of unbridled passion. All it took was the right touch. And they were quickly approaching the point where any touch was the right one.

Roxanne tugged at his upper arm and shoulder, wanting more, needing more. "Spence," she breathed, aching for him to do something, anything. He stroked her, barely caressing her, not yet taking what she wanted to give, what his erection against her sensitive thigh throbbed to claim. "I want you," she begged.

"You have me." He slipped a finger into the tender, dewy folds of her femininity.

And she went wild. Primal hunger possessed her. She was his. Wrapped in eroticism, she rode his hand, clutched at his body, trying to draw him closer and closer while kissing him as though she'd never get enough of Spencer Griffith on any level. He was nourishment for her starving spirit and a heady narcotic for her aching heart. For in those moments of intense, unbelievable pleasure, she doubted she'd get enough of him and the way he made her feel.

A cry started deep in her soul and burst with a colorful explosion of sweet-tasting light. She climaxed hard and fast. In the astonishing aftermath, her eyes closed as she floated back to reality. She ran the tip of her tongue over her bottom lip. Yes, light did have a taste. It tasted like Spence.

Gradually she became aware of him looking at her, and she opened her eyes. "It's been a long time. Even then I never felt . . ."

The glint of thinly tethered desire burned in his dark eyes. "You're about to come again." He caught her behind the knees and lifted her legs. "With me."

Wild excitement set her afire all over. "I want—"

"I know exactly what you want." He moved over her, entering her with one sure, swift move, filling her, pushing her back into the bed quilts.

Roxanne let out a cry that became a laugh. "It seems you do." Thank heavens, because she'd already forgotten. Spence and the dangerous, delicious sensations he created stirred her cowering emotions to life, filling the sphere of her universe.

Looming over her, he stilled, his chest heaving as though he'd run a long distance. "Hold on," he ordered in a gravelly voice.

She had wanted it hard and fast. He gave it to her. He carried her to the edge again and again, stretching her endurance and firing her desire until she couldn't stop touching him, tasting and kissing anywhere her mouth could reach, then kissing, nibbling and devouring his mouth in return. Fast. Hard. Desperate.

When she didn't think her body would hold together another second, he took her over the edge to glory so swiftly she couldn't even cry out. He climaxed with her, calling her name as he buried himself in her a final time.

Nothing had ever been like this. Nothing and no one. Roxanne basked in the wondrous euphoria of their lovemaking.

She clung to Spence with her arms and legs. If only she could dwell in this moment forever, heaven would truly be hers. No questions, no responsibilities, no consequences. Just bliss packaged in the hot flesh of a man who knew the difference between wild passion and out of control. That was them, she decided. She was out of control; he was wild, hot passion. Both were perspiring, their breathing settling into a ragged state.

"Spence?" Her fingers buried in his hair, she drew his earlobe between her teeth and tasted the saltiness of his perspiration.

"Hmmm?" Beyond taking a deep breath that pressed his chest more firmly against her breasts, he didn't move.

"Did you just take me to heaven?" Her left hand followed the contours of his back and kneaded his muscles with the pressure of her fingers.

"Next time you won't have to ask." He kissed her neck. "That feels great. Don't stop."

"I won't. I don't think the rest of me can move anymore, though. That was . . . incredible." Her stomach growled.

"You can move, you just don't realize it right now." He raised his head. "Did you eat anything when you came home?"

"No. I . . . was busy. I'm not really hungry."

"I am and you have to be. I noticed you didn't eat anything at the party. Do we go to the kitchen, or do I dine on you right here? God, you're all dessert, woman."

Gooseflesh rippled up from her toes to her head and made her scalp tingle. Another rumble of her stomach sent a shock wave through her.

"That's it. To the kitchen." With a groan he pushed away. "I'm not done with you tonight. Let's feed you so you can keep up."

She pushed at him. "I'll keep up with you any day of the week." Physically depleted as she was, her words were sheer bravado.

Perched on the side of the bed, he spun around and grabbed her, hauling her across his lap.

Roxanne laughed. God, what fun this man was in bed.

"I'd like you to keep up with me *every* night of the week," he breathed, then bent them into a tangle of limbs as he kissed her.

The heady essence of the kiss dulled the meaning of his statement. It hardly seemed possible for passion to rise so quickly. When he broke the kiss, all levity had vanished. The sense of need was as strong as when he'd carried her into the bedroom. Bracing her hand against his chest, she felt the racing thud of his heart.

"What's happening here?" Her head spun as if she'd had too much champagne. Laughter bubbled in her veins, and tears of emotions stung the corners of her eyes. She couldn't remember when she'd felt this good or even if she'd felt this way before.

"Something real, Roxanne. Something rare." Instead of kissing her again, he brought her to her feet as he stood. "Now, let's take care of the other hunger." His hands ran down her ribs, into the vale of her waist, and over her hips before he let her go. He found his trousers and pulled them on as she slipped on a robe.

Minutes later they entered the brightly lit kitchen. Buster the cat yowled from atop the far high stool at the island. He bounded to the floor and sulked into the dining room.

"Is this what you planned for dinner? Peanut butter and"—he picked up the jar—"peach jam?"

Roxanne laughed, settled her bottom against the edge of the high stool, and admired him in the bright light. Clad only in his black tuxedo pants, all he lacked was a bow tie to pass as a high-classed male dancer. The lush pattern of hair she'd explored tapered to a line down his abdomen and disappeared beneath his waistband. Her gaze lingered, entranced by the bulge of his sex before she came to her senses. "It's a peace offering from Matt Spence."

She tore her gaze from the planes and sculpted contours of Spencer's torso and searched the kitchen, sure *he* was here.

"Show yourself."

"Have you any idea what time it is?" Matt manifested in the middle of the island and opened the peanut butter jar.

"Jesus H. Christ!" Spence stepped back, pulling Roxanne away from the mysterious lid apparently turning on its own.

She laughed, then pushed him away. "Get used to it, Spence. You brought him. It's not like you have to see his torso protruding from the table when you drink your morning coffee."

"Damn. I knew he was around, but . . . Damn." His fingers ran through his hair as he stared at the bread floating out of the loaf bag.

"He's an acquired taste. I don't suppose you can see or hear him?" Roxanne admired Spence's fortitude and the way he tried to take Matt's antics in stride.

"No. Afraid not." Spence backed away as though reconsidering.

"Only you can," Matt said. "That's a problem we need to discuss later. I take it Mr. Griffith's visit has improved your disposition?" His angelic smile radiated innocence and light, but his expression telegraphed that he was thoroughly pissed.

Roxanne smiled back with intentional sarcasm. "Much. What's griping you?"

"I don't think I like the idea of my daughter making love with a man."

"We were having sex, not making love."

"Jeezus, Roxanne," Spence hissed. "You talk to your father about your private life?"

Roxanne grinned at Spence and tilted her head toward the ghost. "A woman would be okay?"

The bread flew across the island countertop.

Oh, she was enjoying this. Matt was flummoxed, and Spence had a ringside seat to the circus he'd dropped on her doorstep. It served them both right.

"How about an omelet?" Spence asked, reaching for the refrigerator while watching the bread fly. "Or maybe a few scrambled brains—make that eggs?"

Roxanne laughed. "Either one is fine. Shall I make toast?"

"Uh, got another loaf of bread? Or can you get him to deal us in on the fly?" He opened the refrigerator and whistled. "I didn't peg you as a shopper."

"I'm not. Inez loves to grocery shop. Looks like she went overboard Friday. Monday is actually her first day back since Thelma's death, but she hates to come to work in a house without food. Heaven knows I don't grocery shop. She'll be delighted if I eat any of what's in there, especially the vegetables." She joined him at the refrigerator.

"In that case, how about a veggie omelet?"

"You cook it. I'll eat it." She slipped her arm around his waist. "I don't cook much beyond a scrambled egg now and then or macaroni and cheese."

"Not a problem." He cupped her jaw and kissed her long and hard. "I want you for dessert," he breathed when they ended the kiss.

"Forget the omelet. How about cheese and crackers? Let's grab a couple of bottles of iced mocha, and go back to my room where we've got some privacy."

"Flexibility and diverse tastes. I like that in a woman." He kissed her again, this time with the same kind of hunger they'd shared earlier. "Get the crackers. I'll get the cold stuff. Got any fruit?"

"I'll bring it." She outlined his bottom lip with the tip of her tongue.

The lights went out all over the house.

"What the hell? Did we blow a fuse?" Spence asked in the darkness.

"No. Our ghost did. He's unhappy, so he left," Roxanne said

with a sigh. "He did that a lot when he was alive, too. Like a little boy who didn't get his way, he picked up his toys and went away." She went to the wall switch and turned the overhead lights on. It shouldn't matter what Matt thought. The trouble was, she no longer thought of him as a sperm donor. He hadn't volunteered for Vietnam. And he damn sure hadn't wanted to die over there. Worse was the growing belief Matt genuinely loved her mother— as much as he was capable of loving.

"How do you know so much about him?"

"Thelma. My mother's diaries." She wheeled around and gathered crackers from the cupboard. "Keeping a personal diary was a popular thing to do back then."

"Are you telling me my name isn't going to be immortalized in your daily memoirs?" He set down the tray holding cheese, fruit, mustard, wineglasses, napkins, and utensils on the countertop beside her.

The delicious sensation of his hands sliding around her torso and enfolding her against the hard wall of his naked chest muddled her thinking. "I keep track of my daily appointments and contacts."

"That's business. This isn't," he whispered. "This is very, very personal." For emphasis, he nibbled the crook of her neck and shoulder. She put the crackers down and settled her hands over his.

"No, I don't keep a personal diary." Who needed a book filled with blank pages? The emptiness would say more about how she lived than any words she might write. What she needed was this moment. Spence. She guided his roaming right hand to the swell of her breast and pressed her buttocks into the ridge of his arousal. "Wouldn't you rather be in me than in a diary?"

His hand closed around her breast avoiding the peaked, aching nipple begging for attention.

"I want both," he breathed into her ear, then kissed the angle of her jaw. "We aren't two ships passing in the night."

It seemed more like a collision on the high seas. The question of survivors remained unanswered. With her body singing and aching simultaneously, all she wanted was more. And he gave it, cupping the fullness of her breasts in the palms of his hands. She moaned, reaching back and grabbing his hips. The response thrust her aroused nipples against his thumbs, which moved back and forth, teasing, titillating, and taunting her with sensual promises.

"Spence," she breathed, feeling the world around her become one of total sensation and desire. Their bodies swayed and rocked to the rhythm building in a slow crescendo.

"Slow, this time. You're gonna want me so badly, you'll beg." His thumbs and forefingers closed on her nipples and tugged.

A small cry escaped her. She tried turning in the circle of his arms, hungry for his mouth and the joining of their bodies, but he held her back to him and spread his big palms over her breasts.

"Get the crackers, Roxanne. Our dining room is upstairs." He kissed her neck below her left ear.

Her knees nearly buckled when he released her. The excitement Spence created with his touch and his soft, seductive words was worth any consequence she faced tomorrow.

Roxanne was a big girl. Hell, she was three years older than he and had grown up in a world moving faster than anyone in the late sixties and early seventies thought possible. He never thought about women having sex lives or base needs. That was a man thing. Girls either put out or they didn't. Some you dated, others you married.

But now sex was less taboo, more out in the open than during the years before he had married Marian. After he married Marian, he'd never so much as looked at another woman. This small character gem may have been his saving grace. Surely if the Powers That Be had added adultery to the long list of his sins, he'd have gone straight into the Abyss of Nothingness, with no chance of redemption.

He had trusted Marian explicitly. She'd never stray. She had kept her word in all matters regardless of personal consequence. She had known what she wanted, and her needs had been so simple—him and a family.

How ironic that their daughter needed the same things her mother had needed, but didn't know it. Roxanne knew what she wanted. And for tonight, at least, she wanted Spencer Griffith.

Well, she got what she wanted, but Matt didn't have to hang around. The rest of the night belonged to him and his old friend Greg.

He supposed Roxanne could have done worse than Spence. At least the guy had some social standing and knew how to work.

Who was he kidding? Spencer cared about Roxanne and she

couldn't see it. "Can't see the forest for the trees," he reiterated, leaving the house behind.

Just like Greg.

In Greg Detweiler's sparse apartment, Matt had little power, and he sensed he was not alone.

In the small hours before dawn, Matt roamed Greg's rooms. Try as he might, he could not levitate a single item, contact Greg through his dream state, or otherwise make his presence known.

Years of hard living had carved deep lines into Greg's features. Matt wondered how blatant his own sins might have shown with the passing of the years had he survived Vietnam. The nagging sensation he was somehow responsible for the path Greg had chosen refused to dissipate.

Friends since kindergarten, they'd had only one serious fight. Staring at his sleeping friend all these years later, Matt finally understood another truth. It wasn't that he had won Marian's heart. Greg had no control over her feelings and had acknowledged as much. No, it was the underhanded way Matt had betrayed Greg that had cut so deep.

The longer Matt watched Greg sleep and listened to the disturbing rumble of his breathing, the greater the urgency to speak with him. With each visit to the attic room of the old San Francisco row house, Matt needed Greg's forgiveness more and more for reasons unrelated to spending eternity in the Abyss. His friend deserved better.

Had Greg married? Had children? He'd have made a great father. Mr. Involvement, Matt mused. Mr. Organization.

Since their first meeting, Greg had taken more interest in the welfare of those around him than in his own endeavors. Of course, Matt hadn't realized it at the time. To five-year-old Matt, Greg was the perfect friend. He went along with the program. Greg took chances with gusto when Matt goaded him hard enough. And with the heart of a true friend, Greg looked for ways to help his friends. And if a cookie was broken in half, Greg had always given Matt "the big half."

Matt curled in on himself and began rocking in the air above Greg.

Greg's connections had made it possible for them to fulfill their dreams. Dreams as big as the sky. Both boys had soloed in an airplane at sixteen.

Next to his wedding day, Matt considered soloing in the Cessna

150 the most important and memorable event of his life.

On the high school football team, Greg had played wide receiver. Although he'd had a strong, accurate throwing arm, he'd balked when Coach Reeves tried talking him into trying out for quarterback. That was Matt's position. In Greg's book a man didn't cross some lines or compete in a friend's territory.

The memories of the thousand little sacrifices that became a habit for Greg to make and Matt to accept flowed through Matt. He hadn't appreciated Greg. Not like he should have. He'd loved him, but he'd never put him first. And Greg had never put Matt second.

Desperate to make his presence known, Matt tried to rouse Greg. Perhaps in the thin spot between awakening and sleep, Greg might see him. He might acknowledge him. He might even remember his old friend who betrayed him.

Shortly after the first light of morning grayed the sheets over the windows, Matt gave up his attempts to reveal himself. Even if Greg had an open mind and believed in ghosts, the uneasy presence of so many other entities posed insurmountable interference. This far away from Roxanne and the home from which he drew strength, he didn't have a prayer of reaching Greg.

Just as the Guardian had said, he needed Roxanne's intervention. She was the crux of everything, he admitted to the fog rolling beneath the Golden Gate Bridge. How much more would she hate him when she knew the secret he loathed sharing with anyone? If the only avenue of communication with Greg required Roxanne's presence, he'd have everything on the line. Every good feeling he'd coaxed from his daughter might turn to stony hatred if the truth came out. And of course, it would. There was no hiding the way he'd betrayed his best friend, or how he'd lied to Marian.

If he moved forward, Roxanne would have to know all his secrets.

Matt hovered at the edge of the water and contemplated his options, on rather his lack thereof.

Around him morning traffic built as the City came alive for the dealings of another day.

How blind he'd been about so many things.

Twenty-twenty hindsight lent a clarity that made him feel foolish. Everything hinged on Roxanne—which was how it should be. She bore the distinct burden of being the only true innocent in the debacle he'd made of his life. She was his daughter, but never his child. Until now, when it didn't matter to anyone except to her. Now, when she'd already learned how to deal with family secrets grounded in lies and conjecture. He could not answer for his parents or Thelma, only for himself and the horrendous omissions of his life. Those omissions had shaped the misery of his daughter's childhood.

He'd never given much thought to the types of poverty a child might endure. Growing up as the only child in a privileged household, money equated an absence of need. After seeing Roxanne amid the trappings he had savored as the finest parts of life, he realized the worst poverty a soul could endure was the poverty of love.

In the midst of affluence his daughter had grown up impoverished.

Small wonder she had gazed upon Spencer Griffith's enormous extended family with the wonder of a child going to Disney World for the first time.

The fog and the sea merged in a slowly roiling gray entity.

Another day and he was no closer to changing his destiny.


Spencer Griffith never lied to himself.

He awoke with Roxanne curled against him and the sexual hunger of a man celibate for too long. He had no doubt where he wanted their relationship to go—straight to the altar. He was in love.

She had given him a glimpse of her vulnerable, sheltered sensuality as well as the gift of her trust.

Eyes closed, he concentrated on the sensations created by the press of her body against him. His sex acknowledged the effects of her presence even before he was fully awake. He savored the desire throbbing through his veins whenever she was near. Having her naked and in his arms brought to mind all the sweet things they'd done to each other a few short hours earlier.

"You're a sheep in wolf's clothing, Roxanne," he whispered, then kissed the top of her head.

Slowly he extricated himself and slid out of bed. She barely moved when he tucked the blankets around her.

He dressed while watching her sleep. Not until he searched for his shoes did he look around the room. When he did, his gaze caught on the most prominent feature of Roxanne's retreat: a dresser-top shrine to her mother. Carrying his shoes, he went to the dresser and studied the pictures and small tokens encased in glass. It was easy to see the similarities between mother and daughter. The shape of their faces, long, graceful limbs and their smiles were nearly identical.

Plastic hospital bracelets for Miriam and Baby Griffith sat in front of a picture of a newborn. Beside it was a small portrait of mother and daughter taken in one of the four-shots-for-a-quarter machines he recalled seeing in the mall when he was a kid. On the wall beside the dresser was a framed colorized version of the same photo. The detail was exquisite, but then Roxanne had undoubtedly done it herself. Images, special effects, and computer magic were her business.

There were other pictures, all of Marian, many with Roxanne and one of Marian and Matt, with Matt in his dress blues. The way the two of them gazed at each other made the hairs on Spence's arms tingle. Marian's love for her husband and daughter reached out from the pictures regardless of how faded or grainy the quality.

A worn photo album rested atop the glass encasement.

The temptation to thumb through it tugged at him. He resisted. This was Roxanne's private tribute to her mother. If, and when, she was ready to share it with him, she would do so. In the meantime, he'd respect her privacy. Already, he suspected she had allowed him deeper into her world than she'd planned.

He found a pen and paper beside the telephone on the nightstand, then hesitated while debating whether to wake her. He opted for writing a note that made it clear he wasn't disappearing. He'd pick her up for dinner.

He propped the note against her toothbrush where she couldn't miss it, then headed for his car.

Tonight, he'd batter down a little more of the thick walls protecting her heart. It might take some convincing before she acknowledged her feelings for him, but the one thing she couldn't deny was her desire for him in bed.

He grinned.

Yeah, she wanted him, all right. She might call it sex, but he knew the difference between driving, needy sex and lovemaking. Earlier, they'd experienced both.

Roxanne woke slowly from the best sleep she'd enjoyed in years. The pleasant aches and pains in her body were souvenirs of the wild, then tender, sex she and Spence had shared until dawn had lit the morning fog.

She stretched, reaching for him and found nothing but the expanse of cool sheets. She rolled over, tucking her arm under her cheek.

He was gone.

Disappointment took a bite out of her lingering euphoria. She should be relieved. This was exactly what she'd said she'd wanted last night. Now there were no awkward moments. No questions. No obligatory, hollow promises to die silent deaths.

Then she looked at the clock. Most of the morning had passed. She was late, late, late for work!

She jumped out of bed and raced into the bathroom. She read the note Spence had left against her toothbrush.

Dinner. That meant he wanted to talk.

Moments later hot water sluiced over her body. She lowered her head under the spray and tried to think of ways to avoid seeing him again.

Spence had the gift of a glib tongue, just like her father. She was not her mother. She was not gullible and ready to change her life or risk her heart on an easy smile and pretty words whispered in passion-heated moments.

Roxanne was still contemplating the reasons she had let her guard down and had sex with Spencer when she finished drying her hair. She opened her dresser drawer, her gaze flitting over the childhood mementos of her mother.

She was stronger than her mother had been. At twenty-eight, she was neither as young nor as naïve as Marian had been when she gave birth at twenty. Roxanne took pride in holding the reins of her life and future through the company she was building. But she wanted to have it all. *All* meant a family. And as much as she wanted a husband and family, she abhorred the notion of being that vulnerable.

*Wanting what you fear. Fearing what you want. Paralyzed while life rolls by,* she admonished, then closed her eyes.

The paradox she faced continued to baffle her. While she did not want to risk her heart and fall in love, she could not bring herself to consider a loveless marriage.

Spence deeply frightened her. Going to bed with him had changed things, and if it was a mistake, she had no one to blame

but herself. She'd known it last night and ignored the consequences.

This morning she vowed it wouldn't happen again. She'd taken
care of her physical needs, and that was the end of it.

The only thing they had in common was their last name. That
was it. His perceptions of life differed from hers. Neither of them
was likely to change.

Besides, he was dangerous. He made her feel things far too
intensely, things she'd prefer ignoring.

She dressed, carried the tray of dirty glasses and snack remnants to the kitchen, then left the house without her morning
coffee.

Despite her resolve, all she could think about was how sweetly,
wildly, and thoroughly she and Spence had explored one another's bodies.

# Chapter
# Fourteen

On the way to Griffith Enterprises, Spence stopped at home long enough to shower, shave, and dress in a business suit. Already running an hour late, he went straight into a meeting he managed to attend on time. Shutting down one aspect of his life to concentrate on another had come easily over the years. Odd it should be difficult now that he knew exactly what he wanted.

Cloistered in his office with the buyers and two top executives from an East Coast supermarket chain, Spence had trouble concentrating. It didn't help that all they had to iron out were a couple of details from the deal essentially completed the previous Friday afternoon.

Everywhere he looked something reminded him of Roxanne. Even the acrylic paperweight on his desk, which encased an old, scruffy baseball his father had given him, evoked a memory of the shrine in Roxanne's bedroom. He fought the temptation to dwell on the rich, sensual memories of the steamy, intimate hours he had spent with her.

The buyers signed an agreement to put Christopher's frozen desserts into their East Coast supermarkets shortly before the lunch scheduled at the restaurant. Thanks to the efficiency of his executive administrator, the arrangements ensured everything moved smoothly even on rare occasions, like today, when Spence was running late.

At Christopher's, Spence's cousin Virginia shuttled him aside for a private conference before he reached the reservation podium. "Have you heard anything new yet? Have they found them?"

Spence stared into Virginia's agitated brown eyes while she searched his face as though the key to the universe lay hidden in his features. "Found who? Heard what?" he asked.

Virginia, a wispy reed of supermodel proportions with the disposition of an Irish rebel, glared at him. "Your niece and your cousin. I don't understand. Didn't anyone tell you about them not going home after Grandma's party? Both are gone, and the whole family is looking for them."

"Which niece? Which cousin?" There were times when being the de facto head of a large family had drawbacks.

"Carolyn's daughter, Erin, is missing. So is your cousin, Brian Lazzaro. They spent most of the party together. Whatever they've decided to do, they've managed to do it well enough to disappear."

"Great." He caught Candice's eye and motioned her away from their guests. After hearing his brief explanation, Candice assured him that she'd take care of their guests and escort them to their hotels after lunch.

In his office over the restaurant, he phoned his sister Carolyn. "Has anyone notified the police?" he asked her while loosening his tie.

"No. They won't do anything except label Erin as a runaway. And if I did notify them, I'd have them looking for Brian Lazzaro on kidnapping charges. There's no telling what he's—"

"Cool it, Carolyn, they're both minors. Brian's a good kid. So is Erin. Let's not rush to judgment before we know the facts. For starters, where would Erin go if she ran away? Have you checked with her friends?"

"Yes, yes, yes, and Brian's, too. While you were off doing who knows what with who knows who—"

"Back off, Carolyn. I'm your brother, not your husband. I don't have to put up with your crap. You can place blame later. Right now I'm interested in finding Erin. Let's start with why she and Brian ran away." He ran his fingers through his hair and stared across the rooftops toward the bay. "What did you and Erin fight about?"

"You're always so damn sure it's my fault—"

"If it makes you feel better, say it's my fault, Carolyn. Tell me what you two fought about."

"What makes you think we had a fight?"

He bit his tongue. *Don't go there,* he admonished. "Bait a different hook, Carolyn." He ran the night through the filters of his memory, concentrating on Carolyn and Erin. Yeah, he had seen Erin and Brian with their heads together in a corner. Erin had been doing the talking. Brian's expression had consisted of a disapproving scowl.

"Are you going to help find her or not?" Carolyn demanded.

"What did you fight about?"

Silence filled the connection for a long moment before she answered, "This summer. Going to Alaska."

"Where was Dave last night? Didn't he come down for the party?" Knowing Dave, he wouldn't have missed it, but Spence didn't recall seeing him there, and he'd have remembered despite his personal turmoil. If Dave had attended Erin wouldn't have left his side.

"I told Dave not to come."

Anger tightened his gut. "Since when is your husband not part of this family?"

In the silence that followed, Spence could hear trouble expanding on an exponential basis. "Did Erin know you didn't invite him?"

"I thought it would be better for everyone if Dave stayed in Anchorage," countered Carolyn in a huff. "And no, Erin didn't know I asked her father not to come. I may as well tell you now. I've decided to file for divorce, Spence."

He swore under his breath, surprised, then dismayed. His sister's tendency to orchestrate sweeping changes without considering all the ramifications was legend. So were her temper and her rush to judgment. Later, he'd examine the reasons for her life-altering decision. Today Erin needed attention.

"Divorcing Dave is a big mistake, Carolyn, but it's yours to make. Have you contacted him about Erin?"

"No. It's none of his business."

"The hell it isn't. Erin is Dave's daughter, too." Spence took a deep breath and let it out slowly. "Something else is going on here, and right now I don't have time to dig it out of you. But later, Carolyn, later you're going to give me some answers."

"I don't owe you any explanations."

"You damn sure do. Number one, you're my sister and Erin's my niece. Number two, I'm your boss. Number three, I'm the one you always call to get you out of a jam.

"If we're going to find Erin and Brian, I need to know why they're running. I have a pretty good idea for Brian, and I'm beginning to get the picture for Erin."

"What does it matter? She's only fourteen, for God's sake. In a strange city. She doesn't know San Francisco. Not that I'd feel any better if this were Seattle, but at least I'd know where to look."

"For starters, we bring in the police—"

"No! I don't want her to have a record."

"—I have friends at SFPD who can help," he continued. "As for Erin having a record, that's the least of our worries. Let's just hope she stays with Brian. He's got some street savvy."

"He's a bad influence. I never should have taken her to the party. He's talked her—"

"You don't know anything of the kind. Why'd she run away, Carolyn? And save the bullshit. I don't have time for it."

Carolyn sighed heavily. "I told her we weren't going to Anchorage this summer, that I was filing for divorce instead."

"*Great.*" *Popped her bubble, then stabbed her with the pin,* he thought bitterly. "Did it ever occur to you that at fourteen, Erin can choose to live with her father, Carolyn? My money is on her exercising her legal choice right now, with Brian helping her. He's probably looking for some freedom, too. Now, are you going to call Dave, or am I?"

"I'll call him." Defeat thumped in her words like a lead footfall.

"Good. Tell him to use my cell phone number if he needs to reach me. I'll be out of both offices until we find Erin and Brian." He hung up feeling as though he'd been flogged. Damn, but his sister could be a bitch!

The euphoria of lovemaking, or hot sex, as Roxanne labeled her liaison with Spence, lasted until she got into the car. Traditionally, Mondays were late mornings at Magic Wish. Even so, she was still late. Lunch was an hour ago.

"I need your help." Matt's seat belt clicked in the hasp.

"Good afternoon to you, too." Roxanne watched over her shoulder as she backed down the driveway. Why Matt bothered with the safety belt, she had no idea, nor did she intend to ask.

"Or do ghosts care whether it's morning or night?"

"I prefer the light."

"I noticed. So did PG and E. They sent a thank-you card with this month's bill."

"A little increase in the electric bill won't overtax the estate."

"The estate doesn't pay the bills. I do. As for taxes, let's not spoil a beautiful day by thinking about them. That's the CPA's job, and heaven knows I play her plenty." She stopped for a traffic sign and glanced over at him. If it was possible for a ghost to appear fatigued, that was how he appeared. He looked, well, washed out. Paler.

"What gives?" She turned down the boulevard, joining the flow to the freeway.

"Remember when I told you I needed to make atonement to two people?"

"Yes. What's the matter? Isn't Mr. Detweiler welcoming you with open arms?"

"Greg can't see me. Or hear me. I can't even levitate simple objects around him. There are too many other ghosts where he lives."

Roxanne shuddered. She couldn't imagine living with more than one. Getting accustomed to having Matt materialize in the middle of the table or dangle in midair was difficult enough. How anyone coped with more than one ethereal entity was beyond her comprehension. "Surrounded by ghosts. What a gruesome thought. How has he kept his sanity? Or is that a moot question?"

"He can't see them. Some are as old as San Francisco itself. There's one from the Gold Rush looking for the men who robbed and killed him. There are two or three from the earthquake."

"Loma Prieta?" she asked surprised.

"Has there been another big one since 1906?"

"Yes, but not as bad in terms of destruction and the amount of people killed." She glanced at him then over her shoulder before signaling for the lane leading to the freeway on-ramp. "What do you want from me?"

"I won't ask you to go where he lives. It isn't safe for you there, and I don't think I can protect you."

She turned and accelerated up the ramp. "You're assuming I'm foolish enough to do anything you ask."

"Oh, I assume nothing where you're concerned, Roxanne.

There's a lot of your mother in you, but like it or not, there's a lot of me in you, too."

"Don't flatter yourself." Despite her denial, she supposed he was right; admitting it didn't sting as bad as it had a couple of weeks ago. Maybe she was softening. Besides, she did owe him for saving her on the horse, even though, true to his word, he hadn't mentioned it. Like a canker sore, she felt the presence of the unpaid debt. "All right. What do you want from me?"

"Write a letter and invite him to the house. Greg might come at your request, particularly if you mention your mother."

"But not for you?" The sorrow in his voice touched her. She understood aloneness and loneliness—and the difference between the two. She couldn't turn her back on a man suffering the pain of both.

"No. I don't think so."

"I don't know about this. You want me to invite a man I haven't seen since I was six, into my house so you can—what? Haunt him?"

"Make peace with him," Matt said.

"I don't know. Let me think about it." The notion sat crosswise to common sense. But then again nothing seemed to make much sense these days. There was no telling what she might be letting herself in for. But she did want to help Matt. Though she couldn't say why.

The old photos of Greg with the Griffith family smacked of debonair, understated elegance, not some part of the city that was unsafe in broad daylight. "Where does he live?"

Matt gave her an address in the Mission District. "The City has changed a great deal in the past quarter century. Roaming the streets early this morning, I felt the passage of time since my death. That was a first."

"But you do know you are dead, don't you?" she asked as gently as possible.

"I am painfully aware of it, daughter of mine."

Daughter. A tight band formed across her chest. Childhood longings ran down the familiar trails of her memory. She would have given anything for him to have returned and called her "daughter" just once after her mother's death. This morning the endearment held a specialness she couldn't deny, and all the protective barriers she'd honed weren't enough to shut him out.

"I'll write the letter," she heard herself say. She was getting soft. No, she chided herself, she was making a payment on a debt. That was all. She'd be damned if she owed him for anything, even saving her life. The sooner he collected in full, the better she'd feel. "I'll do it as soon as I get into the office."

Writing a letter to lure Greg Detweiler to the old Griffith house proved more difficult than Roxanne had anticipated. After all, what did one say to a man she hadn't seen for twenty-two years, a man who had been in love with her mother and who had grown up with her father? She gave it her best shot, and in the end offered Greg Detweiler the one thing they had in common: her mother. She invited him to join her in marking the anniversary of Marian Griffith's death.

Once she finished the missive, she set it aside for mailing, and then focused on designing a new animated video with two of her employees. They worked through a late lunch of delivery pizza and deli sandwiches.

Shortly after five, the admin from heaven she'd hired a scant two weeks ago knocked on the door of the development room. "There's a call you may want to take," she told Roxanne.

She excused herself and went through the side door and into her office. "Roxanne Griffith speaking. How may I help you?"

"You can forgive me for not taking you to dinner as promised," Spence said.

Roxanne glanced at her watch. Damn. She had less than half an hour until their dinner. "Oh, yeah, I got your note. Glad you called. I sorta got wrapped up in a project."

"Yeah, well, I'm that way myself. My niece and cousin are missing. Looks like they ran away together."

Niece and cousin. All this family stuff was mind-boggling. "Is this anything like, well, incest?"

"They're distantly related by marriage. We're not talking Romeo and Juliet here, although they are awful damn young. They're a couple of unhappy kids who see leaving as the only means of gaining any control over their lives."

"What can I do to help?" The offer was out of her mouth before she'd thought it through.

She listened intently as Spence summarized the events, starting with the departure of the teenagers shortly after the party and ending with his belief their destination was Alaska. "The airlines are clear. They didn't fly out of the city. We checked Oakland,

San José, and Sacramento, too. Same for the buses and trains.
My guess is they either hitched a ride north, or they're laying low
until the right opportunity comes along."

"Do they have money?" The thought of any kid on the streets
hiked her anxiety level ten degrees. Thelma had always told her
how fortunate she was to have a nice place to live and food on
the table. Roxanne had believed it with all her heart. She hadn't
wanted to be an item in a television news story about runaway
teenagers and orphans abandoned by their relatives. Regardless
of how tense things got between her and Thelma during her teenage years, she'd never considered running away. No, she'd already formed a plan when she walked away the day she graduated
from high school two weeks after her eighteenth birthday.

She'd had an apartment lined up and a job, money in the bank,
and a summer semester of college staring her in the face. Thanks
to her mother, she had a small trust fund to cover her tuition and
books, with a little left over to help pay for the basics.

"Erin closed her savings account before she and her mother left
Seattle. Carolyn said she had nearly four thousand dollars in it.
That tells me Erin was on her way down the road before she and
her mother left Seattle. I suspect she found a kindred soul in
Brian, who is equally unhappy with his home life."

"I can't imagine they'll find any solutions on the streets. What's
her father doing? Or is he out of the picture?" Roxanne wondered
if either teenager knew how fortunate they were someone cared
enough to worry or look for them.

"Dave is definitely in the picture and damn near out of his
mind. He and his friends in Anchorage are watching the airport,
just in case they show up. If the kids don't turn up soon, he'll
get some of his friends to wait at the docks and bus depot to keep
an eye out for them. Anchorage isn't a place people from the
lower forty-eight hop in the family car and visit on a whim.

"I wasn't calling to solicit help, Roxanne. I just wanted you to
understand why we won't be going to dinner tonight. Go home.
Be safe. Think of me."

"Sounds perfectly boring. How about I help you look for
them?" God, how long had it been since she'd done anything
proactive for someone else? Being around Spence fed her appetite
for a sense of belonging even though her logical mind proclaimed
it a forbidden fruit. If she relied on no one, she'd avoid disappointment.

In the far reaches of her mind, she wondered if Matt was game for a little night work.

"It'll be cold and tiring," Spence warned. "There's no telling what we might turn up. I'd planned on going door to door in the Mission District."

"Don't worry about me. I can take care of myself." And she'd made sure of that over the years by taking courses in self-defense. For the last decade she'd belonged to a local judo dojo and studied the Gentle Way with regular practice and meditation. Mastering the art of self-defense had saved her from disaster twice in the last eight years.

"Yeah, I'll bet you can. I'll pick you up in an hour. Does that give you enough time to wrap up what you're doing?"

"Sure, but why don't I meet you in the City. It'll save time, and I suspect time is of the essence." She sat at her desk and grabbed a pen. "Give me your address." She scribbled his street number and directions in the Marina District, then hung up.

"Why?" Matt materialized in the center of her desk.

She lurched back in her chair, startled by his presence. "Darn you!" She slid her hand beneath his apparition and caught the paper with Spence's address between her fingers, then slid it to the edge of the desk. "Why, what?"

"Why have you decided to become Miss Civic Duty and look for these kids?"

"None of your damn business." She'd already asked herself the same question. Probably because the two teenagers in search of something better than they had at home reminded her of herself. God knew she understood domestic misery. She wasn't sure if she had stayed with Thelma because she was smart enough to comprehend the finiteness of the situation or because she lacked the courage to strike out on her own.

In the end Roxanne was her mother's daughter. She stayed because she wasn't a quitter. A masochist, perhaps, but not a quitter.

"Just make sure you're falling in love with the man, not his family."

"Falling in love?" Preposterous! "Are you out of your mind?"

"You slept with him. That implies commitment. Caring. Love."

"In your day maybe it did. Today things are different." But not that different, admonished the small voice of her conscience. Matt was right. She'd jumped into bed with Spence Griffith, and when she got out, she looked at the world a little differently. She ought to thank Matt for pointing out her character flaw. If she allowed it to persist, it might become fatal to her independence.

"Tell me you could walk away from Spence right now and never have a twinge of remorse over not seeing him again," Matt goaded.

She couldn't. And that left her vulnerable. Surely, there was a way of preserving her autonomy and dating Spence. There, she'd admitted it. She was dating him. In truth, she wanted to sleep with him again. To have wild, wonderful, and slow, erotic sex with him. In those moments she thought of nothing beyond him and herself. Those dangerous, daring interludes had consequences she hadn't wanted to consider and still refused to confront.

"I wrote your letter. Now, if you don't want to help find these kids, go away and don't hinder us." She reached into the bottom drawer of her desk and retrieved her purse. "Of course, if you help, you might chalk up a few Brownie points."

"I suppose that's a possibility." He appeared to contemplate it seriously. "I'm not here for search-and-rescue duty, but I am going your way tonight."

"Right. You just happened to . . ." Her voice trailed with the realization he'd spoken the truth. Not only couldn't he lie, the letter she had written to Greg Detweiler bore an address in the heart of the Mission District. She sorted through her out basket. The letter was gone. Her efficient admin had already taken care of mailing it.

Inadvertently she'd played right into Matt's hands. "I'm looking for runaway teenagers tonight, not looking up the ghosts of your past," she warned.

"Must I remind you who the ghost is here?"

"Hardly." She bit back an explicative she was ready to launch at him when she saw the state of his dejection. There was no satisfaction in trading barbs with someone who fought back half-heartedly.

She almost asked him about what had upset him to such an extent, then caught herself.

Watching him fade into thin air, she tightly clamped her jaw shut. She realized she cared about Matt although she didn't want to. Damn him, somehow he'd charmed his way past her defenses.

Regardless, nothing he said or did compensated for the misery her mother had lived with or the legacy of doubt and isolation he'd left her.

Determined to shut out any tender feelings for Matt, she gathered her purse and jacket, checked with the programmers, she'd worked with all day, then went out to her car.

As she pulled out of the parking lot, she noticed the seat belt on the passenger side remained snugly against the door frame. She was alone.

# Chapter
# Fifteen

Matt found Roxanne and Spence in a battered '86 Toyota Celica cruising the streets of the Mission District. The car, like the area, was in the process of "becoming." As coffeehouses and bagel bars moved into the area, the socioeconomic base improved, as did the property values in what was one of the most expensive cities in the world in which to live. In contrast, gray primer freckled the dull, metallic blue paint of the aging Toyota hatchback. Matt wondered where they got the car, but not enough to reveal himself and ask. It was probably Spence's idea of blending into the neighborhood. Amazingly it worked, they attracted very little attention in the aged heap.

The old, unsettled spirits increased Matt's unease. He drew strength from Roxanne's presence. Whether touchstone or talisman, he'd never deny his ethereal connection with his daughter. Sadly, he doubted she'd ever acknowledge it.

Of late he grew maudlin when reflecting on the fate of the wife he'd never see again and the daughter he'd lost even before her birth. If a man's immortality lasted only as long as the memories of him lingered in the minds of the living, Matt's promised to be short and infamous.

He assumed a spectator role. From atop a streetlight he watched the activity around the row house where Greg Detweiler lived. The bottom floor consisted of meeting rooms for what Matt assumed were self-help groups. As near as he could ascertain, derelicts, most dressed in discarded clothing, frequented the house. Men came and left. Some stayed only long enough for a meal in the kitchen at the rear. Others stayed and pored over books or huddled around the two computers in the back room.

Tonight the house lights were ablaze. The temptation to drift inside nagged at him. The strength he garnered from Roxanne's closeness egged him on. He might even be strong enough for Greg to see him. The Guardian hadn't mandated Roxanne's physical presence in the same room with Greg and him.

And if he did manage to have Greg see him, then what?

Being a ghost was such an inexact state. So was his ability to manifest. Lately, he suspected his strength was tied directly to his daughter's opinion or mood about him.

No doubt, any goodwill he'd generated with her would go to hell in a handbasket if she was present during a rehashing of the past with Greg. In order to maintain the scant progress he'd achieved, the confrontation had to be one-on-one. He needed personalization.

If he mustered the strength to manifest inside the row house, others, besides Greg, might see him, too. Many of the derelict souls and spirits surrounding him lived dangerously close to the veil shielding the Otherworld.

Prodded by the same self-interest that had motivated him while alive, Matt remained true to his nature. He needed Roxanne's help. Thus far, he'd tried orders, demands, anger, and bribery. Only generosity spurred by genuine emotion had unnerved her; even then she recovered quickly. It was time for a new tactic. Guilt, he decided. It had always worked with her mother.

There was an impediment, though. Roxanne had nothing over which to feel guilty. The tight shoe was actually on his foot. The trick was getting her to slide into the mate.

He'd further ingratiate himself to her. That would work. Oh, yes. If she wouldn't help him out of love, then all was fair. Wasn't it? Damn, it didn't feel right, but the discomfort didn't stop him from going forward. He materialized on the front hood of the Celica. "I'll check the alleys, if you like."

"Holy Hannah!" Roxanne's coffee splashed onto her wrist as she tried to recover her shattered composure.

Spence slammed on the brake. The car behind them screeched to a halt. "What? Do you see them?" Spence demanded over the blare of horns.

"Sorry, no," Roxanne admitted, shaken. "What I see is the Ghost of Christmas Never sitting on the hood of the car. I didn't mean to startle you."

"Since this predicament began unfolding, I've done a little reading up on ghosts and haunting." Spence waved off the guy blowing the horn behind them and started forward again. "From what I've read, your father is one peculiar spirit, Roxanne. Have you decided whether he's haunting you or the house?"

"It feels like me." She looked at Matt. For once he remained silent. No help there. Lord, but viewing the world beyond the hood of the car through the filter of her father's Vietnam era–flight suit was disconcerting. "Which is it?" she asked Matt directly.

"At the moment, does it matter? I've extended an offer you can accept or refuse. Which will it be?" He leaned through the windshield and studied the pictures on the flyers.

Her natural aversion to having any portion of Matt's ectoplasm penetrate her body sent Roxanne pushing as far back into the seat as possible.

"Has he given any indication what he wants? Why he came back now?" Spence nosed the car into a parking place.

"All I know is that you and he arrived together. He wants the impossible." Belatedly, she questioned what Spence wanted, other than fabulously hot, incredible sex. She opened the car door and practically fell onto the curb. The Celica was much closer to the ground than Spence's Lincoln. She regained her balance and managed to extricate herself from the door, seat, and seat belt with a modest amount of grace.

"Wait for me," Spence ordered as he got out of the car and slammed the door. Matt swayed above the hood and studied the man who had dragged his daughter to a part of town sensible people avoided even in strong daylight.

"Why is he here now?" Spence rounded the car and took her arm. "What does he want?"

"He says he'll check the alleys for us."

Spence studied the street the way a soldier scoured an enemy minefield before picking his way through it. "Can you trust him?"

Roxanne shrugged. "He can't lie. Or that's what he tells me."

"Do you believe him?"

In the brief moment she hesitated, Matt realized the importance of her answer. He'd taken other people's trust for granted. If they didn't give it willingly, he'd always been able to talk them into placing their faith in him—whether he deserved it or not. Now that he did deserve it, now that he was earnest in his dealings, he realized what a precious thing he'd taken for granted without appreciating the true value.

"Yeah, I guess I do."

A flicker of the trust he wanted to see blazing in her eyes quickly passed from view when Spence moved forward and blocked his line of sight. Had it been real or just hopeful imagination?

"Then take him up on it. If he's willing and you trust him to do it, I'd just as soon not take you down any dark paths."

"Smart man." Matt headed for the nearest alley. Evidence of man's base depravity lurked in the depths of the alleyways and side streets. Much as he abhorred exploring the dank, dark minipits of hell, he preferred doing it instead of his daughter.

A sense of urgency gripped Roxanne as she spoke to passersby and handed out flyers with Brian's and Erin's pictures and statistics. The streets were a sad collection of people, some of whom preferred to remain among the anonymous homeless. Others chose to live here with the purpose of making it a better place. And even more drifted onto the streets, never meaning to stay but somehow never quite finding the right impetus to leave.

Spence and Roxanne distributed flyers and spoke to people on the street and in local businesses until shortly after midnight. Roxanne had to admit they conducted a much more thorough search of the area with Matt's help. Yet, when she conceded the value of his endeavors, she immediately understood the magnitude of the debt she'd incurred tonight. The running balance sheet with her and Matt's names at the top was becoming dangerously lopsided.

The old Celica waited half a block ahead. Roxanne was ready to go home. Neither she nor Spence had slept much the previous night. The lack of rest was catching up with a big yawn.

Then she noticed the address on a brightly lit row house. Her yawn died in midstretch. Greg Detweiler's house. Or at least the house number was the same one she'd written on the envelope.

"One more stop," Roxanne said.

"No. Not here. Not now." Matt blocked her way up the stairs. She'd either have to walk through him or forget indulging her curiosity.

"Why not?" she asked Matt.

"What gives?" Spence asked from right behind her. "Are we knocking on this door or not?"

"Matt says no. He wants us to skip this house," she said softly, studying the misery in the distinct lines of her father's face. She'd swear he'd aged fifteen years since the first time he manifested in front of her. The reasons for the changes must have been monumental. Funny, she'd always thought ghosts just . . . were. In a bizarre way, it made sense for him to stay the age he was when he died. She never considered the possibility of a ghost aging or worrying. Maybe stress followed an individual into the grave. Because he spent most of his time in her presence, she couldn't keep wondering if she was the cause.

She shook off the dismal thought.

"If Greg sees you now, and talks to you, he might not come to the house. I can't take that risk," Matt explained. "This is important to me, Roxanne. Vitally important. Do it my way, okay?"

"He might help pass out flyers," she pressed, remembering the lopsided tally sheet both kept and neither mentioned.

"Put some on the top step under the corner of the mat. I'll see to it." He retreated to the side of the porch and gestured toward the worn bristle mat. "Please."

Mercy, she was getting soft. Now all he had to do was say please and she caved in. Still, if she was responsible for the changes in his appearance the least she could do was give a little.

"What's it going to be, Roxanne?" The weariness in Spence's voice indicated the toll the night of futile searching had taken on him. "Knock on the door, or let's get in the car. We should go back to the house and see what kind of night the others have had."

All the while Roxanne continued staring into her father's sad, blue eyes. She exhaled in submission. "I'll leave a few flyers under the doormat. It's late. I hope Erin and Brian have found a safe hole to crawl into."

"Thank you." Matt retreated through the porch railing.

"Leave me alone for the rest of the night, and we'll call it even." It was far from even. She owed him big time for the help with the search alone, but there was no point in conceding the upper hand without a struggle.

"Even." He saluted her, then faded.

It was getting easier to reach détente, and less satisfying. She wasn't sure if that was good or bad. Right now she was too tired to decide.

"I take it you're bartering favors with your father," Spence said.

Ironically, by talking into thin air, she had blended in with the street people settling in for the night. "I was. I think we're alone now." She slid the flyers under the edge of the doormat and turned on the step. Spence blocked the stairs. In the glow of the porch light and the streetlamps, she saw the unmistakable flare of desire in his face. Awareness of the sexual fission between them sent a thrill from the crown of her head to the tip of her toes. An un-disguised impishness in his sudden grin commanded a responsive smile in return.

"Yeah, we're alone with half a dozen spectators we can both see." He slid an arm around her waist and drew her down the stairs beside him. "Does *alone* mean you're speaking to me when you're talking?"

She nodded, her smile broadening, admitting that he handled her one-side conversations with an entity he neither saw nor heard extremely well. Given the circumstances in reverse, she doubted she'd be as accommodating.

Both kept a sharp eye on the sidewalks during the drive across the city to Spence's home. "How street smart is Brian?"

"He knows the ropes. Until today I wasn't sure that was a good thing. He's been a handful since his mother remarried a couple of years ago." Spence accelerated when the light changed to green. "Brian's dad, Jack, dropped out of the picture about then, too. Guess he thought the family was overwhelming. Maybe we are, but he still had, and has, an obligation to Brian. The kid worshipped him. Jack should have recognized that and stayed close to Brian even after the divorce. Instead Jack transferred to New Jersey without saying a word and took the woman he'd been seeing on the side with him. Brian still hasn't gotten over his father leaving.

"I thought Jack was a good father, until then." He glanced at Roxanne. "He didn't do well at keeping the fidelity part of the marriage vows, but he'd always been a devoted father."

"Until he left and slammed the door on Brian. That's tough on a kid," Roxanne mused. "I've seen it in epidemic proportions with the women at the Acorn picking up the pieces of their lives. Throwaway kids. Throwaway relationships. Let's have a good time until things get too real."

"Is that why you don't let me get too close, Roxanne? You think I'll walk at the first ripple in the pond?" She felt his gaze and continued looking out the side window. "Or are you telling me that you'll walk? Or should I say run?"

She closed her eyes. He had a way of shooting the truth like a bullet, with her as the bull's-eye. "It's late, Spence. I'm tired. I don't want to have this conversation."

"We will have it, though. Tomorrow. The next day. Soon, Roxanne. Last night changed things."

She shook her head in denial. If they did rekindle this conversation, it wouldn't be until well after Memorial Day, after she was sure he wasn't interested in getting something entirely different. "Last night changed nothing, Spence. It was one night. We had sex. That's all."

"It changed things. You came with me tonight."

"Helping look for a couple of runaways has nothing to do with you and me. The least I could do was hand out a few flyers and ask some questions. I've done it before. Unfortunately, there will be occasion to do it again. Anyone would have done as much."

"No, they wouldn't. Face it. You wanted to be with me, even if it meant pounding the street in the Mission District. You're crazy about me, Roxanne, and it scares the hell out of you."

The sudden acceleration of her heart warmed her. She wiped her damp palms on her Levi's-clad thighs. "You have a pretty high opinion of yourself and a pretty low one of me. You also don't know the difference between lending a helping hand and infatuation."

"Is that what you think is going on between us? Infatuation?"

She refused to look at him. "Infatuation, chemistry, lust—in the long run it's all the same. Six months from now you won't remember my phone number, let alone my face. Look, Spence, I'm tired. It's been a long day. Tomorrow is only a few hours away. Drop it, will you?" Finally she turned her head enough to look out the windshield. "Let me out at my car. I won't mislead you by offering to help again tomorrow. I'll just go to work like a good girl and take care of my own life. What you do with yours isn't my concern."

"Are you trying hard to piss me off, or is this your way of

telling me last night didn't mean a damn thing to you?" Jaw set
in aggravation, he drove past her car, turned into his driveway,
then pulled into his garage. Before she got out, he toggled the
garage door closed.

"Why are you doing this? Open the garage door." The direction
of their conversation made her squirm; she was eager to end it.
The walls of the brightly lit garage were lined with cupboards
and neatly arranged garden tools. At the rear a workbench
stretched into a back room.

"You're an expert on my motives and plans. You tell me," he
snapped. "Better yet, come inside. We need to talk, Roxanne."

He closed his car door and headed for the small door leading
into the house. As though taking it for granted she'd blithely
follow him anywhere, he unlocked the door. Roxanne waited until
he realized she wasn't following before she spoke.

"No, we don't. You need to push the little button beside the
door frame there and let me go down the driveway. I don't mind
helping you look for a couple of kids. But I do not intend to
dissect my reasons for not wanting to get involved, or have a
cozy chat with members of your family tonight. I've had my fill
for the week. Thanks anyway."

He hit the button. The garage door started up. "You can run
from my family, but you can't run from me, Roxanne." As the
door rose, he crossed the length of the garage and intercepted her
at the rear of the Celica.

"I can find my car." He was as dangerous to her heart as he
was devastating to her self-restraint. He saw too far into her
thoughts. He had a way of disarming her before she'd even drawn
her weapon. But she had his number, too. He wanted her in his
house, then in bed as badly as she wanted him. There, she gave
him everything and in turn took all he offered which, she was
beginning to realize, was even more than she had thought initially.

"You're a strong, independent woman, capable and competent
of achieving anything you set out to do. It won't hurt your fem-
inist image if I walk you to your car to make myself feel good,
will it?"

Laughter lurked in his blue eyes. She looked away so she
wouldn't weaken and smile. "How could I possibly deny you
anything that made you feel good?"

"In that case, come in the house. We'll send away any family
members who might be hanging around, then make each other

feel exceptionally good." He gathered her in his arms.

"What an interesting way to end the evening: literally evicting your worried relatives so we can have sex." The rest of her protest went unspoken. He caught her mouth in a long, languid, wet kiss before she even realized his intention.

Instead of refusing to play the seduction game, she reveled in the carnal delight of his kiss, her heartbeat climbing as he drew her into a seamless embrace. The response of his tensing body was enough for Roxanne to wish they were naked and in bed.

One kiss, she bargained as the flames of need leaped higher. Just one.

Like Fritos or Dove Dark Promises, one was delicious, but it didn't slake her growing appetite, merely goaded it.

"Tell us both the truth," he whispered in her ear. "You wanted to be with me tonight."

On tiptoes she caught his earlobe in her teeth, then tugged. "Yes. I wanted to be with you to search for Brian and Erin. Other than your grandmother and mother, you're the only one in your family I like. I was hoping we'd find the kids and the sphere of *likables* would expand by two more." She gave his earlobe a playful nip. "Good night, Spence. Call if you need my help."

He held her loosely and grinned. "I need you, all right."

"I know. For Memorial Day." Falling back on her first and best line of defense strengthened her resolve.

"That's not what I meant."

"Maybe not, but tonight you needed my help with the search," she added, extricating herself from the temptation of his arms. And Matt's, she added silently.

"We can play search. Hide-and-seek, if you want. Ever played strip hide-and-seek?"

The notion made her smile in spite of the situation. "That's ridiculous."

"Don't knock it until you've tried it." He let her steer them down the driveway toward her car.

"Are you serious?" Certainly, there was no such game. Was there? Immediately her imagination leaped into a vision of the two of them darting through the house and leaving a trail of clothing along the way.

"Completely. Interested?"

Unable to maintain her stern veneer, she laughed aloud. Interested? Of course, and all the way home she'd think about how they might play such a game. Maybe by the time she pulled into her driveway, she'd decide if the winner was the one who lost all her clothes first. "I'll take a rain check on the game playing. Thanks for the offer, though." With the press of a button, she unlocked the car.

Spence spun her around and pinned her against the door. He caught both her hands in his, then laced their fingers together, the car keys still cupped in her right palm. "But you are playing it, Roxanne. You keep hiding from me and I keep seeking. Each time we come together, we strip another layer away. The real question is which one of us will wind up naked first."

All levity vanished. The bare truth glowed like a beacon in the night. *Not me*, she promised herself, then kissed him anyway.


Spence watched her drive into the night. He'd never met a woman as skittish and fearful of a relationship as Roxanne. If he hadn't caught glimpses of the soft heart and generous spirit inside her defenses, he'd consider her every man's fantasy in the flesh. She wanted no ties. Just sex. Hot. Fast. Exhausting and exhilarating.

Thinking about last night with her kept him standing in the driveway long after Roxanne drove out of sight.

He was still contemplating ways to penetrate the titanium-like defenses around her heart when he entered his house.

His mother sat at the kitchen table with Carolyn and Alice Sutton, Brian's mother. Looking into their faces, he grudgingly admitted Roxanne had pegged the situation accurately. There was no way he could tell the women to leave so he and Roxanne could play noisy sex games.

Judging by the pout on Carolyn's face, the determined set of Alice's shoulders, and the tension riding the cinnamon-scented air, Ester Griffith had played referee most of the night. Spence couldn't think of a worse job.

"Well?" Carolyn demanded. "Any luck?"

"The good news is, no one has seen them in the Mission District. We'll keep looking tomorrow." Spence poured a cup of coffee, snagged one of the fresh cinnamon rolls the women had brought, then joined them at the table. "You three look like you've been chewing on lemons."

"What do you expect? Our children are out there," Carolyn snapped. "God, I can't believe you turned looking for them into a date."

"Then don't." He felt like fresh meat in a shark tank. "And don't make an ass out of yourself by attacking me." He sipped coffee and continued staring at Carolyn.

"That woman isn't interested in helping find Erin. She's after you and your money," Carolyn snapped.

"That's a relief. I was afraid it was just my body and good looks she wanted." He bit into the cinnamon roll.

"It's your money."

"Carolyn, please," their mother said softly. "We don't need this bickering."

Relief for a burden shifted onto another set of shoulders shone in his mother's dark blue eyes. The hint of a grateful smile touched the corners of her mouth. Tall, statuesque, with a steel backbone, she hardly appeared old enough for grandchildren. Soft, black curls lightly peppered with white framed an unlined face with a flawless olive complexion. "This is a difficult time. We need each other," she added in her typical forthright manner.

"Have any of the other search groups picked up their trail?" He took another bite from the cinnamon roll.

"No. It's like they've disappeared into thin air," Alice said into her coffee cup. "Once Brian decides to do something, he always does a thorough job. Guess it's a family trait."

"He and Erin have that in common, along with their dysfunctional family life." Carolyn's uncharacteristic concession forced Spence to take a closer look at his sister. Traces of mascara smudged the thick lashes beneath her bloodshot eyes. Fatigue deepened the normally faint creases at the corner of her eyes and around her full mouth. He could count on one hand the number of times he'd seen Carolyn in tears, including when she broke her arm at age thirteen.

"These kids will need help when we get 'em back. Have you notified Jack?" he asked Alice.

"Why? He couldn't care less." Alice rolled her eyes in blatant skepticism.

"What's with you two?" Irritated, he stood, then walked away from the table. "You both bitch and moan that the men in your lives aren't helpful or responsive, but you exclude them at every turn." He glared at Carolyn. "Did you call Dave tonight?"

"I didn't see any point in it. You'd already talked to him. All I could do—"

"He's the father of your child. He loves Erin as much as you do. Bottom line, Carolyn, you're in this together." He whipped the cordless phone from the counter, stormed back to the table, then set the phone in front of her. "Call him."

"It's after midnight." She folded her arms and stared at the phone as though it were a cobra ready to strike.

"You think he's not walking the floor? You think he's not worried? He's alone, Carolyn. There's no family up there to console or support him, or take the brunt of the anger and fear he's feeling." He leaned on the table. "Call him. Now."

"He doesn't need any family to comfort him, Spence. He has solace, comfort, and a lot more on the side. He might be walking the floor, but not alone."

Silence stretched into a long moment, filling the space around them. "An affair?" He'd never pegged Dave for an affair.

"Yes." Tears spilled down Carolyn's cheeks.

"You're sure?"

"That's why I told you I was considering divorce, Spence. So, yeah, I'm pretty damn sure." She sniffed and took the tissue her mother offered.

Shit! "Did you confront him?"

"I don't need to. The bitch he's been sleeping with called me." Carolyn stared at the table.

"And you based the assumption Dave was having an affair on her phone call?" God, why did women trust each other so easily?

"She gave me details, Spence."

"So without discussing it with him, without confronting him, you're divorcing Dave because some bimbo calls you on the phone and says she slept with him?"

"She gave me specifics! Of course I believe her."

"Hey, maybe Dave is having an affair. What do I know? But the only way to know for sure is to ask him. Meanwhile, think about those specifics *objectively*, not emotionally. Just how specific were they? Hell, any man can claim to have gone to bed with you, Carolyn."

"I've kept my marriage vows," Carolyn retorted.

"I'm sure you've been faithful," he said softly. "But aren't you the one who told me there was more to marriage than being faithful?" He set the phone in front of her. "Communication, isn't that what you said it takes? Communicate with Dave about your daughter and your marriage, Carolyn."

Carolyn glared at him, started to object, then thought better of it and picked up the telephone. "You're a righteous asshole, Spence. And a busybody."

"And I'm right."

The chair scraped over the wood floor as she stood and stabbed the phone buttons. "We'll see." Head down, she walked into the darkened cove of the breakfast nook.

He turned on Alice and withdrew a cell phone from the inside of his jacket. "On the other hand, Jack is probably asleep in a comfortable bed with his latest bimbo. Call him. Wake him up. He's Brian's father. He may have walked away, but the responsibility is still his." He extended the phone to Alice. "Do it. Now."

"It's after midnight," she warned, and reached for the phone. "But you're right. Brian wanted Jack's attention. Maybe it's my job to see he gets it." She cast a meaningful glance at Carolyn, then started punching in numbers.

Spence sighed. "Fine. Their mom and I will see you in the morning. Make yourself at home, just stay the hell out of my bathroom." He directed a knowing glance at Carolyn as he opened the kitchen door for his mother. "You'll never need to shave your legs badly enough to use my razor."

Carolyn shot him a surly look, then turned away. "Dave? This is Carolyn." Damn, if she got any paler, she would fade into the woodwork.

"Jack Lazzaro, please," Alice said, leaning both elbows on the tabletop. "Wake him up. This is his son's mother, Alice Sutton."

Spence left the kitchen and putting an arm over his mother's shoulders, led her down the hallway to the guest bedroom. "You must've had a helluva night with those two."

"Thank goodness you finally came back. I thought I was going to be refereeing them until dawn. Mercy, but I'm tired." She put an arm around his waist.

"Yeah, me too." But he wouldn't sleep. If only the path to Roxanne's heart was as clear as the ones he saw for Alice and Carolyn. God help them all if Brian and Erin didn't turn up soon.

# Chapter
# Sixteen

"I got your message." Clad in jeans, running shoes, and an old San Francisco 49ers sweatshirt, Spence leaned against the door of Magic Wish's brainstorming room. Had his hair been longer or his ear pierced with an assortment of baubles, the Magic Wish employees might have mistaken him as one of their own.

Roxanne relinquished her seat at the main computer console to a young, blond man in ragged sweatpants and an MIT T-shirt. "I'm glad you decided to come by in person. We might be able to expedite this." She led him into her office. The fragrance of the two dozen roses he'd sent over Tuesday morning to thank her for helping with the search met them as soon as she opened the door.

"Did I thank you for the flowers?" She dragged a second chair over to the computer table abutting her massive oak desk.

"Yes, you thanked me Tuesday, when I called. And last night when you called my cell phone." He adjusted the chair she'd scooted in front of the computer screen. "What are we looking for?"

"Not for. At." She settled into the chair, feeling the electricity of his nearness more keenly than ever. Three days apart had only increased his attraction. "We all help in our own way, according to our strengths. This is mine. I suspected you hadn't exploited this avenue to look for Brian and Erin. My crew and I spent Tuesday afternoon on the Web. We surfed, dropped into chat rooms, made contact with people we knew and trusted on the Net.

"To make a long story short," she said, then winked at him, "we tapped into—I guess you'd call it—Nerd-Net."

"Nerd-Net? Never heard of it." The easy way he smiled belied the fatigue etched in his face and the half-moons of sleep deprivation beneath his bedroom blue eyes.

"Well, there aren't a lot of us sophisticated entrepreneurs in the ranks. When we Nerd-Net folks go on vacation, the first thing we make provisions for is our computer and a sky link to the Net. To us, it's mental life support. Anyway, a couple of programmers on their honeymoon answered our query. I've been communicating with them since yesterday afternoon. I think they've found Erin and Brian, but I need you to look at the pictures they sent for confirmation." With a few keystrokes she brought the picture onto the screen. The young man wore a tux. The woman wore a blue sequined evening gown.

"Son of a bitch. Carolyn has a dress. . . ." His voice faded when Roxanne enlarged the young woman's face.

"The picture on the flyer didn't show the mole on Erin's neck mentioned in the description. Is this Erin?"

"Yes." He was leaning so close to the screen, she thought he'd reach into it and try to pull Erin through.

She clicked twice and the young man filled the screen. "This looks like Brian to me."

Nodding, Spence stared at the screen. "Different haircut. He lost the earrings. Damn, they look like they're in their twenties. Where the hell are they?"

Roxanne folded her arms and leaned back in the chair, enjoying the astonishment transforming Spence. "The last place anyone would look for them."

"Obviously. We haven't found them, but you did. Where, Roxanne?"

"They're on a cruise ship bound for Seward, Alaska, registered as Mr. and Mrs. Derek Armstrong." She held up a hand when he started to sputter. "I did some checking. The Armstrongs put an ad on the Net to sell their tickets at the last minute. They didn't expect any takers a day before the ship was supposed to set sail, but they got one. Brian bought the tickets for a thousand cash, no questions asked. The Armstrongs were happy to recoup that much of their investment."

She stayed his hand as he reached for the phone. "Wait." She picked up a paper from her desk. "Here's the itinerary. Brian and Erin are having a good time and don't know we've spotted them. What do you want my contacts to do?"

"Enjoy their honeymoon." He studied the itinerary, then checked his watch. "How would you like to go to Alaska this afternoon?"

"Sorry, I've got a date tonight."

Though he remained stoic, disappointment flashed in his eyes before he looked away. "Apparently, so do I. In Ketchikan." He checked his watch, then reached for the phone. "May I?"

Roxanne gave a kick against the side of the desk and sent her chair rolling away. "Help yourself." She stood and headed toward the door. "Good luck with the kids, Spence. You have to hand it to them. Besides being an ingenious way to run away from home, it's certainly the most comfortable." She grinned, recalling their night roaming the Mission District together. "They are more savvy than anyone suspected."

"Thank you, Roxanne, and my thanks to your crew. You're right. No one thought about searching online." He regarded her with a need that grabbed hold of her heart and twisted until all her private places tingled with anticipation.

"You're welcome. We were glad to help." Sheer willpower turned her away. What was there that made him so hard to resist? He wasn't the first man who attracted her. But he was the first one she had trouble keeping at a distance. Spence was also the first man to threaten the safe constructs that kept her from succumbing to the glib tongue of a seductive man. That made reinforcement of her defenses imperative.

"You sure you don't want to go to Alaska tonight?" His light, teasing question was at odds with his intense gaze.

"Like I said, I have a date." She'd cut her tongue out before telling him she was baby-sitting. "It wouldn't be fair to leave him stranded. Maybe some other time." She opened the office door.

"I'll hold you to it, Roxanne. We'll go together. Keep September open. Autumn in the Chugach and Brooks ranges is worth seeing. The geese start flying south then, too."

Even before she could ask if he was out of his mind, she realized he was completely serious. Without a word she backed out of the office, closed the door, and then leaned against it. Her heart beat like a jackhammer. Perspiration beaded on her forehead. Dry-mouthed, she smelled fear in the air. Hers.

The notion they'd be seeing each other in September sent her reeling. She hadn't dated a man for longer than a month. And if he got close enough for her to have sex with him, she never went back for seconds. Until Spence she hadn't had a reason. Planning a trip months away . . . It boggled her mind. That kind of togetherness was terrifying. She couldn't fathom it. No way. Besides, they had the Halstadt video due in mid-September. The idea of it happening without her was unimaginable.

"Try again in January," she said to the closed door. "Hell is more apt to freeze then."

"Well, if you don't want the handsome hunk in your office, I do," Jenna said from across the hall.

Roxanne scowled at the smartly dressed receptionist with artistically coifed blond hair, tastefully polished acrylic nails, and a tailored Evan Picone suit. A ringer for a cover girl, Jenna was perfect at the front desk. The further she strayed from her post, the more inept she became. "Don't you have something to file or a phone to answer?"

"I'm on break. Mrs. McCorkle is at the front desk." Jenna's gaze focused on the office door separating Spence from the rest of Magic Wish. "I'd like to file him, and if he calls me, the answer is yes. Not only is your Mr. Spencer No-Relation Griffith a hunk on the hoof, he's extremely wealthy. He's just what I've been needing to spice up my life." Jenna folded her arms and emphasized her ample breast. "You sure you don't want him, Ms. G.?"

No, she wasn't sure, and she wanted to punch Jenna's clock for provoking the angry jealousy rising in her craw. She would not give in to it. No way would she run after any man or defend territory. Her mother had tried to hold her ground. All it had netted her was misery and, eventually, death.

"If he wants you, Jenna, take him. I certainly won't get in your way. In fact, I give him to you." The bitterness in her words surprised her. This was what she had wanted, right? Salvation lay in Spence actually giving Jenna a tumble and forgetting about her. Enduring the equivalent of a paper cut on her heart now was better than the pain of loving and the inevitable abandonment later.

Whom was she kidding? Whether Jenna turned his head or not,

there was no way Roxanne could escape Spencer Griffith and remain unscathed. In fact, she wasn't even sure if she could break things off with Spence, regardless how much she told herself she needed to do just that. Maybe letting Jenna have him *was* a good idea.

"Thanks. I knew I was going to meet some interesting people on this job." Jenna turned down the hall to the coffee room. "Alaska tonight, huh? I could do that."

"Right." Roxanne turned back to the brainstorming room and the Halstadt project. In the future she'd watch Jenna's eavesdropping tendencies—and close her office door. Presently, part of her lamented turning Spence down. Still, she reminded herself, a bruised heart was small price to pay for emotional safety.

Roxanne and two of the programmers were unraveling a graphics problem when Spence burst into the brainstorming room like a ball of thunder. "I need to speak with you, Ms. Griffith. Now."

The force of his command compelled an equally forceful response. "Excuse me?" She shot out of the chair, knocking it backward against the far table. "This isn't Griffith Enterprises, Spence, and I'm not one of your minions awaiting your beck and call. If you want to speak with me in a rational tone, I'll be glad to listen. Otherwise, make an appointment with Mrs. McCorkle. She'll give you a number."

"I'm leaving in a few minutes. The choice is yours, Roxanne. Do you want to have this conversation in front of your employees or in your office?" Clearly livid, he raked the four programmers staring at him with a scathing glance.

"I don't want to have this conversation at all." She looked past Spence. In the hallway Jenna winced and ran a bright red acrylic nail through the air beneath her lifted chin. At the moment cutting Jenna's and Spence's throats seemed a good idea. "But it looks like you're going to insist."

He followed her into her office, then slammed the door, leaving red-faced Jenna in the hall and the programmers craning their necks in concern.

"You've disrupted my entire work staff, Spence. Why?"

"Get something straight, Roxanne. I'm not a possession you can give away. Where do you get off telling the barracuda manning the front desk you gave me to her? That crosses the line, and it really pisses me off."

"If this is your pissed-off mode, how do you react when you really lose control?"

"Answer my question." He glowered with the heat of a volcano ready to erupt.

Furious at the power play he instigated in front of her staff, her eyes narrowed. "Yes, I see you're upset with me. But you're not exactly following the Dale Carnegie course for winning friends and influencing people."

The phone on her desk rang.

Spence strode over to the side of the desk and whipped the receiver from the cradle. He said his name, then listened. A quick flurry resulted in him scribbling notes on a pad.

"Hey, anytime you need a phone, feel free to drop by and tie up mine for an hour or so." She leaned against the closed door, trying to appear more casual than she felt. Who did he think he was answering her phone? Not her admin assistant, for sure. "This is only a place of business, and I'm just the owner and CEO. My phone is available any time."

His fulminating glare scorching the air between them provided a small triumph. At least she'd gotten her point across. "Take the whole office." She threw her hands up in disgust. "Obviously you're busy, so I'll consider this conversation over."

Without responding, he hung up the telephone and finished jotting notes on a pad. He folded the paper, then stuck it into the back pocket of his jeans. All the while his attention remained on Roxanne.

Caution silenced the tendency she had to run her mouth when upset. Across the office an angry, tired, stress-ridden grizzly bear glared back with blue fire in his eyes. It had been a terrible week for Spence, and now he was on his way to even more turmoil. She didn't envy him taking Erin and Brian off the cruise ship.

The realization Spence had to carry out the delicate but distasteful task struck Roxanne like a bolt of lightning. The prospect of dealing with two sensitive, defensive teenagers quelled her ire. Regardless of what he did, he'd be in a difficult situation with the kids, their parents, and the authorities. "When's the last time you had a good night's sleep, Spence?"

"The night before I met you," he answered in a dangerously soft voice.

Rattled, she had no response.

"You've disrupted my life as severely as your father's ghost has affected yours, Roxanne. Tell me, what kind of game are you playing? I'll admit I don't get it. Is this push-me-pull-you tactic supposed to keep me at arm's length? Meanwhile you're dangling something you have no intention of delivering. Is that the plan?"

She wasn't playing any game. She wanted to look away in denial, but couldn't. "I don't know what you're talking about."

"The hell you don't. You busted your ass. You disrupted your company's work flow and set your work schedule back I don't know how far. And why? To search for two kids who aren't even related to you. That's no small thing. It says you care." He rounded the desk, stopping right in front of her, his gaze never wavering from hers. "Or is that part of the game, too?"

"No game. I just wanted to help. Those kids have a lot more guts than I did at their age." She shoved her fingers into the front pockets of her chinos and held fast. "I wasn't brave enough to run away."

"There are lots of ways to run away, Roxanne. You've stayed in one place, but you're running nonetheless. At least Erin and Brian know what they're running to."

"That's ridiculous. I'm not running." She straightened against the door.

"No? Then you were just being helpful again when you made a gift of me to the gold digger at the front desk?"

Oh, God. She'd gone too far when she let her tongue rule. Mentally she sought wiggle room. Physically, if he took another step, he'd be inside her clothing with her. Her traitorous body adored the prospect. She inhaled the faint scent of him and the tang of his aftershave. "I told Jenna I had no claim on you, Spence, no plans for anything. If you don't like her, don't go out with her."

He flattened his palms against the door above her shoulders. "Let's get something clear. If you want me to take a permanent hike, say so now and I'm gone."

The emotion riding the depths of his blue eyes warned this wasn't the time for glib retorts. Bottom line, she didn't know what she wanted. More accurately, she was afraid she did know. The direction her heart wanted to take led down the primrose path of risk into the bonfire of disappointment. But answering was a moot point. Ambiguity kept her from committing either way.

"Your silence is an answer, too. I'll see you Saturday afternoon. Your place. We're going to talk, Roxanne, so think about what you want and what you want from me." His head tilted as his mouth lowered to hers. "Get used to the idea we aren't just about sex. Next time we're in bed, we're making love first." The tip of his tongue touched the seam of her lips, parting them. "Two days, Roxanne."

The aching tenderness of his seductive kiss melted her reservations and her knees. Gone was the pique. The irritation over the way he dictated an agenda vanished. And the shadow of fear chilling her heart whenever he got too close receded.

Returning his kiss became essential. Desiring him was as natural as breathing. She didn't fight it, just yielded to the carnal need screaming through her veins as it did each time he was near.

The light touch of his Levi's against the back of her hands coaxed her fingers from her pockets. She reached for him. The soft texture of denim washed a hundred times turned harsh under her sensitive fingers. Clothing became a barrier. She sought closer contact with his body. Her fingertips slid around his hips, cradling him. She found his back pockets, plunged her hands into their depths, and then pulled him against her.

Roxanne's sudden, unmistakable message wrung a groan of longing from Spence.

The hard, physical contact increased the tension building between them. She couldn't get close enough to the core of his heat. Her left hand followed the contour of his back, slid under his sweatshirt, found the waistband of his jeans and wiggled under his shirt until she found warm flesh.

She was ravenous for the unbridled passion he shared without reservation. The tempo of the kiss deepened. As they took turns tasting and teasing, her hands mapped the landscape of his well-muscled back and shoulders. The sheer act of breathing ground her breasts into his chest with a nerve-tingling eroticism.

"Break your date tonight," he rasped against her mouth.

"Break your date, *please*," she corrected. Lord, but he was a single-minded, dictatorial man. He was also the most exciting man she'd ever met.

"Please."

Before she answered, he was kissing her again. Wild, the kiss broke and resumed. Roxanne tried to pull his shirt over his shoulders but couldn't remove it while his arms were extended. God, they were so good together naked.

Spence ended the kiss, but he wasn't finished. His warm lips laid a trail to her jaw below her ear and coaxed her chin up to expose her throat. "You're driving me out of my mind, Roxanne." He kissed her exposed throat with a controlled passion that made her want to weep.

"I can't . . ." She found the waistband of his jeans.

"Can't, what?" His parted lips blazed a heated line from the hollow in her throat to the tip of her chin.

Roxanne moaned. "Cancel. He'll cry."

"Better him than me."

"He's only three." A tug at his jeans evoked a responsive grinding of his hips against her. "Oh, God, Spence. I want you."

"Three? You have a date with a three-year-old?" He put his forehead on hers, then pushed until she looked into his emotion-filled eyes.

"Yeah." Fatigue and relief vied in the turmoil evident in his blue eyes. Her fingers slid between their bodies, intent upon opening the metal buttons imprisoning his erection. She had his shirt bunched under his arms, exposing his bare torso.

It suddenly dawned on her his hands hadn't left the door. She froze.

"Three, huh?" He kissed the corner of her mouth and let the tip of his tongue tease her into moving her head in a silent plea for more.

"Touch me," she demanded in a raspy voice.

"If I do, I won't stop until I'm inside you."

She shivered in delight at the prospect. "Then kiss me," she whispered, abandoning his waistband for the warm expanse of flesh above.

"With pleasure."

A hard pounding on the door startled them both.

"Ms. Griffith, I need to see you." Jenna's professional tone was as urgent as it was controlled.

"Can't it wait?" she answered, unwilling to relinquish Spence's intoxicating nearness. Her forehead rested on Spence's chin for a brief moment while she collected her wits.

"No. We must see you right now."

Spence kissed the tip of her nose. "I gotta go, too. I have a plane to catch." He backed away, adjusting his clothing. The best he could do with the tail of his 49ers sweatshirt was camouflage the ridge of desire in his jeans. "Saturday evening we're going to continue this. And have a serious talk."

Roxanne stepped away from the door. For a split second she considered adjusting her commitments and accompanying him to Ketchikan. Sanity prevailed. She opened the door, then stepped back onto Spence's foot.

"What is going on?" She stared at her entire crew, all nine of them, including the mail and copy room boy who came in after school had finished for the day.

"I was . . . concerned," Jenna stammered, her nails glistening in the light as she wrung her hands.

"We all were," added the programmer in the MIT sweatshirt. "Hey, we take care of one another, right?"

Nonplussed by their intervention, Roxanne nodded.

"Take good care of her." Spence's possessive hand on her shoulder lent a sense of comfort. So did his silent message of understanding. "Thank all of you for the work you did finding my niece and cousin. Because of you"—he squeezed Roxanne's shoulder, but she couldn't look at him without the fire in her body showing on her face—"we'll be having a little family reunion early tomorrow morning."

"Bummer, I wouldn't want to be them," muttered the high school copy boy.

Gooseflesh replaced the sudden absence of Spence's hand from her shoulder. She started to turn and sought his gaze. Though he remained silent, she read the promise of sweet, yet serious confrontation. Fatigue lingered around his eyes.

Without a word or a backward glance, he strode through the parting ranks of Magic Wish employees and down the hall. Roxanne watched him disappear around the corner. The ringing of a phone sounded like an alarm. Something had changed, but she wasn't sure what or how.

She closed the office door and tried to pull the fragments of her composure together. Thoughts of Saturday and Spence filled her with excitement and dread. She'd been right. He wasn't going to settle for sex. He wanted more. When she stripped the situation down to the bone, the question of whether or not she was willing to trust him with her heart remained.

If Matt had known how difficult it was to find redemption in the afterlife, he'd have made other plans. Maybe he'd have made different choices.

Nothing was coming together.

A dozen scenarios of what might happen Sunday kept him preoccupied. The odds against him spending eternity disintegrating in the Abyss of Nothingness seemed higher each time he considered his predicament.

If Greg didn't come, there was no chance of Roxanne learning the secrets best kept in the past. The flip side of the coin was that this was his last chance at reaching Greg. A lack of communication meant failure. Period. No chance of atonement. No hope of understanding and forgiveness.

Even if, by some undeserved miracle and the goodness of Greg's nature, they resolved the past, Matt still risked losing Roxanne.

Suspended inches below the powerful kitchen lights, Matt turned the lose-lose situation of his fate over in his mind and searched for new angles. Somehow, somewhere there was a way to come out on top. If not on top, at least away from the edge of the dreaded Abyss.

Sunday. Everything hinged on Sunday.

# Chapter Seventeen

Late Saturday afternoon, Roxanne walked home from a long, hectic day at the Acorn. Warm weather had brought customers into the café in droves. The day had passed quickly, but not without a hundred reminders of Spence. Each time she let her thoughts stray to his proclamation, that they would pick up where they left off in her office, her heart skipped a beat, and her palms dampened.

While her body had a clear notion of the physical aspects, her emotions were just as muddled today as when he left. Yes, they had to talk, but about what? Until she decided whether to take a chance on him or walk away, there was little to discuss. It wasn't that she didn't believe his assurances that he wanted more than sex. She did. Just how much more and for how long were questions neither of them could answer. She knew it was unfair to ask. But that didn't change her need for answers. She was caring far too much about Mr. Spencer Griffith.

Lost in speculation, she quickened her pace. The breeze rustled the leaves in the giant magnolias shading the street and sidewalk. The warmth of summer beamed in the splotches of sunlight dancing along the ground.

Matt met her on the front porch stairs. "About tomorrow, Rox-anne."

"I had a busy day, thank you for asking." Although she was tempted to goad him further, Roxanne noticed he was a wispy visage of his normal self and instead, refrained. Concerned, she sat on the stair beside him. "What's bothering you? Afraid Greg won't show?"

Matt turned his face to the sun. In a few minutes it would dip below the treetops. "I'm afraid he will and afraid he won't. I didn't realize what a winless situation I was in until recently."

"You're already dead. What's the worst that can happen either way?" she asked softly.

"I could fail completely." The flicker of his ectoplasm cast a dejected pall over the stairs.

For a fleeting instant Roxanne wanted to reach out to him— not as his daughter, but as someone who recognized abject misery and wanted to ease the pain. "Are there consequences attached to failure?"

"Yes. That's one of the lessons I've mastered this time. Dead or alive, there are consequences to everything. Often, you can't calculate how great they are, but you have to try for your dreams anyway."

"I thought what you did in life became a moot issue after you died. Isn't there white light and angels, then a final judgment where you have to answer for the good and bad things you did while you were alive?" She hadn't figured out the intricacies of living yet. The prospect of a new set of rules and exceptions after death was another good reason to hope for a long life.

"It doesn't work that way, nor is it instantaneous. Beyond the comprehension of infinity, time does not exist."

"Infinity," she murmured. "I never did grasp the concept out-side the context of the mathematical or scientific worlds."

"It's impossible to do so when you're alive. Look, Roxanne, regardless of what happens with Greg tomorrow, I'd like you to remember something."

The emotionalism of the topic made his aura visible. Blue spikes with lavender hearts leaped around the faint image of his body. It shook her to see the depth of his despair. "What should I remember?"

"First, remember that I'll love your mother for the rest of eter-nity. It took dying and coming back like this to realize how fortunate I was to be loved by such an extraordinary woman, even if my time with her was short."

Stunned by his statement, Roxanne's breath caught in her throat. Meeting his gaze, she nodded and murmured, "You loved her."

"Yes, and I still do, and will continue to love her until eternity claims the last bit of awareness from my soul."

Gooseflesh marched up and down her body.

"Regardless of my fate on my final judgment day, I've come out ahead even if I fail here. I've seen the self-sufficient woman you've become. I'm proud of you, Roxanne. I have no right to expect anything of you, and I don't. I see myself in you. Fortunately, I see your mother, too. I love you, daughter."

A lump formed in Roxanne's throat. "Twenty years ago my heart would have burst with joy if you'd returned, even as a ghost, and told me you loved me, that you were proud of me."

"The timing of my death and return wasn't my choice." His hand rose toward her cheek. His fingers curled into a fist, then retreated.

"I never thought it was." Emotion twisted as he faded a little more. "I know you'd like to hear those words from me, but I can't tell you I love you." She leaned against the back of the step and wondered just what she'd call the tender emotion growing in her heart for her ghost of a father. "If it's any consolation, I don't hate you anymore. Not that you're not a pain in the butt sometimes."

"Fortunately, I had an intelligent, sensitive, loving daughter."

She grinned, glad his wit hadn't disappeared. "There are those who might argue your assessment."

"Your mother wouldn't." His voice was a whisper on the breeze. "Neither would Spence."

"I don't know," she said slowly.

"He's a man who knows exactly what he wants."

"We agree on that at least." She stood and brushed the dust from her bottom, then tucked her fingers into the front pockets of her jeans.

"I'll be back in the morning," Matt said.

When she looked back, Matt had already faded into the stairs. The house lights, which he usually turned on at dusk, remained dark.

Before she turned to go up the stairs, a yellow taxi pulled into the driveway. Sure the driver had the wrong address, Roxanne stepped down to the concrete. To her surprise, the taxi pulled even with the front of the house. The back door opened and an old woman got out.

"Wait for me, Sammy," said the woman.

"Sure thing." He turned off the engine, tilted the driver's seat into a semi-reclining position, and picked up a paperback already opened to his place.

Brown eyes assessed Roxanne through thick lenses in wire frames. The elderly woman held the corner hinge of her glasses and adjusted the fit the way a biologist might tune a microscope for a better look. Thick, white hair framed an age-mapped face that hadn't known many smiles. The reed-thin woman clutched a brown vinyl pocketbook. The color matched her flowing, brown trousers and knit sweater with embroidered flowers and cotton lace at the neck and cuffs.

"Can I help you?" Roxanne pushed her hands deeper into her front pockets and started down the walkway.

The woman peered up at her for so long Roxanne repeated the question.

"You must be Roxanne. You look just like your mother," the old woman said with a quaver in her voice.

Surprised, Roxanne looked more closely at the woman. "You knew my mother?"

"I'm Janice Boyle."

"I'm sorry, I don't know . . . Janice Boyle?" Roxanne repeated, her throat suddenly dry, her brain on overload.

"Marian's mother," the elderly woman said, switching her pocketbook from one hand to the other. The ghost of a frown touched her pale, thin lips and crinkled her tissue-thin skin.

Roxanne stared at the woman, her mind reeling, her ears ringing. This was the woman who had abandoned them, who hadn't visited when her daughter lay dying in a hospital bed, and who hadn't attended her own daughter's funeral.

Her grandmother.

No, not her grandmother. Marian's mother. This woman had never bothered to step into the shoes of a grandmother.

"What do you want?" Roxanne asked in a whisper. The sound of the afternoon breeze registered as the ringing in her ears faded. Gradually the shock of facing Janice Boyle for the first time ebbed. The woman was a total stranger. She was family by circumstance, obviously not by choice.

"I'd like to know where my daughter is buried."

"High Oaks Cemetery beside the empty grave of her husband," Roxanne answered. She took a deep breath, then asked in a rush, "Why weren't you there for her? Why didn't you see my mother before she died? She loved you. No one should lay in a hospital and die alone. You could have held her hand during her last hours. You could . . ." Roxanne stopped and looked away. She had wanted those things. The woman standing before her had not. "You could have said good-bye," she whispered. Twenty-two-year-old scars reminded her just how deep the wounds were and how raw the emotions remained. Even Thelma had had someone in her hour of need. Thelma had had her.

"No, I couldn't have," Janice Boyle said, then turned away. "Not then."

"Why not?" Roxanne demanded. Someone should have sat with her mother during those precious, final hours.

"Back then, heroin controlled my life. The truth is, if Thelma Griffith would have offered me an ounce of the stuff to attend my daughter's funeral, I'd have come crawling on my knees. As it was, I didn't know Marian had died until it was much too late."

Roxanne stared at the woman. Her childhood expectations of Janice Boyle were very wide of the reality mark. Yet, Roxanne felt no disappointment. She felt nothing for the stranger in her front yard. "Thelma died last month."

"She was never alive. She had no heart," Janice said with enough venom to color her cheeks.

"You're speaking about the woman who raised me, who put clothes on my back, a roof over my head, and food in my mouth." *The woman who finally loved me,* she added silently. "When Thelma died, so did the last of my family."

Nodding, the elderly woman turned back to the yellow taxi. She paused with her hand on the door handle. "You look like Marian, but you're very different. Marian would have understood I had difficult times. She accepted the way things were, the way I was."

"You think so?" Roxanne asked, incredulous.

"Yes."

"Then I guess I'm not like my mother. I don't jump at the chance to forge familial bonds with someone who has ignored

my existence for twenty-eight years. Especially not with someone
who uses drug addiction as an excuse for abandoning her own
family."

Janice took a step toward Roxanne. "Can you find it in your
heart to forgive me, Roxanne?"

Dead or alive, with the exception of her mother, it seemed
everyone in her immediate family wanted forgiveness. Until her
father's unexpected return, she'd never contemplated forgiveness
from this side of the coin. She remained silent as Janice Boyle
got into the backseat of the taxi.

Sammy the cabby gave her a sour look as he backed down the
driveway.

Roxanne made it as far as the porch steps before her knees
gave out and she sat on the top riser and closed her eyes. She
was in the eye of an emotional hurricane.


As soon as Spence saw Roxanne sitting on the porch stairs, the
stress and fatigue of recovering the runaways in Ketchikan became raw desire and energy.

Although he knew better, his optimistic nature hoped she'd
been waiting for him.

Seeing his car, she crossed the lawn and stood at the edge of
the driveway. Spence got out of the car and closed the door.
Without a word he gathered her in his arms and held her close.
The scent of spring flowers and freshly baked bread lingered in
her hair. The woman in his arms was warmth and light, and simultaneously comforting and exciting. The delicious response of
her body compelled him to tighten the embrace. She flowed
against him, twining her arms around his neck, making small
noises that vibrated in his soul.

"Roxanne," he breathed, savoring the way their bodies fit. To
his hopeful heart, Roxanne was both a safe harbor and dangerous
waters. "I missed you. Did things quiet down at work after I left?"

She nodded against him, then kissed his neck. "Jenna is no
longer interested in dating you."

"Good. How did your date with the three-year-old go?" He
stroked the nape of her neck, which seemed to grow warmer with
each pass.

"He's crazy about me, but the only way he'd go to sleep was
if I laid down with him."

"Smart kid." He'd love to get her into bed, too. "Anything else happen while I was away?"

She hesitated a fraction of a second before shaking her head against him. He knew her subtle body language. The brief hesitation meant something had happened.

Spence was tempted to push her for clarification, then thought better of it. She was in his arms; eager, willing, and nibbling at his earlobe like it was an appetizer for a carnal meal. He'd anticipated this moment for what now seemed an eternity.

"You had a pretty rough time playing referee between parents and children, huh?" The inviting softness of her lips against his neck eased the lingering distaste of family discord, legal negotiations, and teenage tirades.

"It would have been rougher if I didn't have you to look forward to tonight." He kissed her slowly, his teeth nibbling at her in a blatantly sexual caress.

"Let's go inside," she suggested in a breathy voice.

"I have a better idea." He felt the trembling in her shoulders and the rapid pulse in her neck. He ran his thumb over the hollow at the base of her throat.

"Better than . . ." She let her voice fade and raised her eyebrows in a knowing question.

"Suppose we let the world take care of itself for a little while and go someplace neutral. No ghosts. No intrusions or problem-solving demands." The skin along her throat and beneath her chin invited his lips. He continued stroking with the pad of his thumb.

"Haven't you had enough traveling in the last couple of days?" The feel of her fingers in his hair reminded him of how good her hands felt roaming other parts of his body.

"I've had my fill of everything, except you, Roxanne. At this point the backseat of the car is starting to appeal to me."

An instant smile lit her face. "The house is ours tonight."

He glanced at the dark structure, then back to her. "How convenient. Did you arrange for the resident ghost's absence so we could play strip hide-and-seek?" Her spontaneous laughter made him grin, and he had to touch the corner of her blithe smile. Her head moved in the direction of his stroking. So did her hips.

"I have better uses for your energy than chasing you through the house," she warned. "Besides, Inez has started closing off the rooms we don't use, which is all but four, including the kitchen."

"In that case, I'll start undressing you right here."

• • •

Dazed by the euphoria after hard, fast, needy sex, Roxanne lay as limp as the sheets consigned to her bedroom floor. She and Spence had barely made it to her bedroom before coming together in a wild burst of passion.

Nestled in the crook of Spence's arm, her head on his shoulder, Roxanne closed her eyes. Rather than define the tumultuous emotions begging for examination, she focused on him.

She kissed his chest. "After you left my office the other day, I wished I'd planted a camera link on this sexy body of yours."

He shifted, pulling her up so she looked into his eyes. "Why would you want to do that?"

"To discover whether the plight of my teenage heroes was worthy of their ingenuity."

"You really admire those kids, don't you?" Puzzlement narrowed his shining blue gaze.

"I don't have to agree with their position to admire those who have the courage to act in accordance with their convictions and who are also willing to pay the price those convictions often demand." She folded her hands over his chest and tried to explain. "And I have great respect for creativity and ingenuity."

"Running away from home via cruise ship fits the bill on both counts. Unfortunately for Erin and Brian, once the cruise line became aware of the situation, they were eager to get rid of their teenage travelers." He cocked his head in warning. "In their defense, confronting Carolyn when she's really angry isn't a pleasant experience."

Carolyn's predictions concerning Spence's motives for dating her weren't a happy thought, either. "I'll bet she doesn't hold a candle to you in full fury, which is another reason to admire Erin and Brian. They knew you'd hunt them down, didn't they?"

"Hunt? You make me sound like Godzilla searching for his son."

"You hunted for them," she repeated. "There is no other way to describe what you went through last week."

The tip of his finger slid down the length of her nose. "Do I scare you?"

"Your single-minded pursuit of something you want disturbs me." She nipped his fingertip before it trailed over her bottom lip. Her heart beat a little faster. She had to learn the truth.

"Are you referring to finding the kids, or something else?" He twined his fingers with hers and brought her hand to his mouth.

She watched in rapt fascination as the electricity of desire tuned the orchestra of her hormones for their next symphony. "Why me, Spence?"

"Why you, for what?"

"You attention. Sex."

"Affection? Lovemaking?" In a quick motion he had her on her back and loomed over her. Passion and intelligence blazed in his dark, blue eyes. The seriousness of the moment sharpened the acute angles and planes of his rough-sculpted face. "You give me your body in the greatest intimacy two people can share and ask why? Jeezus, but you're a walking lesson in humility for me, Roxanne."

The intensity of his entire body conveyed the seriousness of he moment. "Humility? You? I don't get it."

His head lowered until his lips grazed hers. "No, you don't get it, do you?"

Before she could pursue the matter further, his mouth closed on hers. His intensity of a moment earlier converged in a slow, thorough kiss rife with passion and a new kind of hunger. As he probed and explored her mouth, it seemed the hunt was on full force.

*Hide-and-seek.*

He was definitely seeking, but she wasn't hiding. The heart beating so hard in every limb and under her heated skin was vulnerable to his kiss, his touch, and the whisper of her name on his lips. In a moment of insight she knew the depth of his longing, and the nature of the powerful something alive and breathing around them.

When he broke the kiss, his lips roamed her face. Reverent and hot, he avoided her hungry mouth. She lifted her shoulders from the pillows and craned her neck in search of another kiss. His hard, heavy body moved over hers. The weight pressed her into the mattress.

"Kiss me." She slid her ankles around his calves, urging him to give her more than a kiss.

"I will," he promised, then laid a heated trail of kisses and touches down the length of her neck and over the sensitive pulse point at the base of her throat.

The deliberate fever he created with each glide of his fingers and the play of his hot, moist mouth on her skin sent her arching against him.

"Think hard. You'll get it before you come again." The vibration of his lips against her sensitive, aroused nipple made her gasp.

"I can't think. Not now." All she could do was feel the molten honey of desire sluice through her. Whether his masterful touch and adventurous mouth were reward or punishment, she neither knew nor cared as he brought her close to climax.

They rocked with the primal rhythm of two lovers becoming familiar with the pulse of shared desire. Spence was relentless in his slow, reverent worship of her passion-heated body.

"Think," he said against her navel, then dipped the tip of his tongue into the well.

Think? "About . . . about what?" If breathing required thought, she'd suffocate.

His palms slid beneath her and supported her buttocks, his fingers kneading slowly, seductively. "Why this feels so good." His chin grazed the tender flesh between her hipbones, each pass lower and lower. "So right. Inside, where you live."

"Yes." What he did to her felt good, right, almost holy. Naked and hot against him, everything in the world was right. Taking him inside her body and becoming one with him was the only improvement possible.

Spence moved between her thighs, his fingertips gently parting her and revealing the treasure he sought. The intimacy of his mouth on her femininity dissolved another protective layer from around her heart. She cried out. The incredible pleasure carried her higher and higher until the tension in her burst into euphoria.

Reveling in the aftermath of bliss, the hard edges of sexual need vanished. She relaxed into a boneless mass of satisfaction. He moved over her, sliding up her body, kissing her into awareness.

"It feels this way because it *is* right." He cradled her head and looked down into her eyes with the same intensity controlling his every movement. "Because I love you, Roxanne."

Everything turned white. "Huh?" The inarticulate protest died against the pressure of his mouth on hers. Simultaneously he entered her, reached down, and drew her thigh up. She tasted herself on his lips, ran her hands over his back, then held him tightly and deepened the kiss. Thought fled. The world consisted of him, her, and the urgency of the moment.

Spence made love to her slowly, intensely, and more thoroughly than she thought possible to experience and remain conscious. Her heart pounded in her chest. Any second it would burst with the tempo of wanting the sweet release he promised. His deliberate, deep penetration tightened the coils of need until she thought the core of reason would snap and send her into oblivion.

Braced on his elbows, he framed her face in his big hands. Wild and dictated by need, his gaze bore into her soul. Never had she felt as passionately excited or as vulnerable as she did while looking up into the blue sea of roiling desire.

"I love you, Roxanne," he said in a raspy voice, then drove into her with a hard, barely controlled force that sent her over the edge before the full impact of his declaration registered. She flew with him into bliss beyond her imagination.

She savored each nuance of the amazing haven he'd created for them with patience and an iron will. She had always suspected the difference between having sex and making love was vast. However, she hadn't expected it to fall into the life-altering realm. With Spence, it did.

They lay in a tangle of arms and legs until the rapid pace of their harsh breathing softened and slowed. Holding Spence, stroking his back and shoulders until his tired body slipped the noose of his mind's control, she stared at the ceiling.

*"I love you, Roxanne."*

It was passion talking, not reason or even his heart. He didn't really mean he loved her. How could he?

The longer she thought about it, the heavier his sleeping body became, and the stronger panic gripped her. Careful not to awaken him, she coaxed him onto his side. Through a series of small movements, she freed her arm and leg, then slowly rolled away.

She spread the sheet and coverlet over the sexy body that made hers sing glorious arias. In the soft golden lights burning on the night tables the telltale stain of exhaustion showed beneath his closed eyes. He slept soundly.

She gathered her clothing and escaped into the shower. Even the pulsing water couldn't drown out the words or wash away the urge to get in her car and drive until she ran out of money, which wouldn't be in this lifetime.

Listless, uncertain why Spence's unabashed declaration disturbed her, Roxanne pulled on a mismatched sweat suit and ventured downstairs. In the darkness the house seemed larger. Emptier.

She sat on the bottom stair, hugged her legs, and rocked her forehead on the top of her knees. Buster curled up on her feet as though sharing her nocturnal unease.

Everything was upside down.

Spence had slept soundly. He couldn't recall the last time he'd slept until noon. After a quick shower he dressed in his jeans and sweatshirt and went downstairs. He found coffee in the kitchen and Roxanne in the backyard. He leaned against the sunroom door, sipped his morning coffee, and watched the woman he loved cut flowers in the garden.

He lifted his coffee mug when she glanced up and saw him.

"Good morning," she called, then resumed her task with the rosebushes.

A simple black knit top accentuated the richness of her sharply creased tan slacks. The last few flowers she cut filled the basket at her feet. She arranged the blooms, then picked up the basket and crossed the yard. The fragrance of roses, lilacs, and gardenias filled the air. She placed the flowers on the glass-topped patio table. "I trust you slept well?"

"Like the dead. Thanks for not calling the mortician." Right now he could take on the world and conquer it single-handed.

A smile quaked in the corners of her mouth. "Believe me, I understand crash and burn. My troops and I have met deadlines that had us working nonstop for weeks. When we finished, I'd sleep for an entire day." She fiddled with the locking mechanism on the garden shears. "I'll take work stress any day over what you've been doing, Spence." After the fourth time she'd opened, closed, and tested the lock on the shears, she set them on the table, then straightened the basket.

"What is it you think I've been doing?" He worked on finishing his coffee and speculating the reasons for her nervousness.

"Juggling two businesses with your family's needs and demands. You look good this morning." She played with her gloves, then removed them by repetitively tugging one finger at a time, starting at her thumb and working to her little finger.

Damn, she was as nervous as a mouse in a room full of cats. "What's going on here, Roxanne?"

"I cut flowers for my mother's grave." She picked up a big red rose from the top of the basket. "Today is the anniversary of her death. Twenty-two years."

"That's not why you're on edge." He closed the distance between them and set his mug beside the flowers. The rigidity of her posture served as an unspoken "Do Not Touch" warning.

"Greg Detweiler is coming over today. He left a message on the machine sometime yesterday." She looked back at the garden as though she'd left her personal peace among the manicured flowers and shrubs.

"Is he an old boyfriend?" That might explain things. Damn, maybe she was carrying a torch for Detweiler.

"Not hardly. I haven't seen him since my mother's service. He was a friend of my parents." She tossed the rose onto the table and turned away. "I asked him to come for Matt. He has some unfinished business."

"Is this a change of heart concerning your father?" he asked hopefully.

"Don't go there, Spence. My motives are purely selfish. This is a way to expedite Matt's departure from this house." She looked over her shoulder, her brown eyes sad and haunted by something other than her father's ghost. "Ironic, isn't it?"

"What?"

"This is really more my father's house than it ever was or will be mine. My name is on the deed. I maintain it. Sleep here. But it isn't really my home. The closest I came to feeling at home here was the last few months before Thelma died." She straightened and looked across the yard in front of her. "By then she was in the hospital more than she was here."

As gently as he could, he took her shoulders and turned her to face him. The brittleness of her stance became fragility in the brown eyes searching his face for answers he didn't have.

"I scared the hell out of you last night, didn't I?" The flat statement allowed no quarter.

"Yes." She looked away and shook her head. "No."

He waited for her to resolve her struggle.

"I don't know, Spence. Somehow, telling me what you told me changed things. I'm sure people say a lot of things when they're tired, or in a moment of passion, that they don't mean." Hope lifted her eyebrows a little and widened her eyes.

"I did mean it, Roxanne. I love you in bed, out of bed, at night, in the morning, in rush-hour traffic, or standing in your backyard."

Judging by her expression, he may as well have pronounced a death sentence. Desolation slackened her features and dented his optimism. Although she didn't pull away, he read her desire to retreat in her stiff body language.

"Let's get a few things clear, Roxanne." He opened his hands and held them away from her shoulders. She didn't step away, which he took as an encouraging sign. "My loving you places no obligation on you. No demands or expectations on your tightly guarded emotions. I don't know if you're afraid to let me inside your heart, or if I'm already there and you want me gone."

He lowered his hands, then stuck them in his pockets. All the while, he searched her eyes for something other than confusion. "You're worth the risk of hanging around to find out."

"I don't know what to say." She turned away and put distance between them. "Or what to do, Spence."

"Nothing is required of you, Roxanne. If you're willing, we'll take it a step at a time and see where it goes. If you're not, I'll back off." The set of her shoulders revealed her silent struggle. He'd laid his heart on the table; as long as she didn't kick it off, he'd stay.

The minutes dragged. The afternoon stillness settled on the yard. The muffled hum of the pool motor provided a background for the baby birds nested in the old trees shading the grass.

Determined not to push for something that wasn't there, Spence folded his ego around his aching heart and turned to leave. Silence was an answer, too.

"Don't go, Spence. Give me a little time to get used to . . ." Her voice faded; her shoulders sagged.

"To being loved?" Every fiber of his body wanted to eliminate the distance between them and hold her in his arms forever. He remained in place, unwilling to risk the frailty of what felt like the victory of a lifetime.

After a long, thoughtful moment, Roxanne nodded.

Oh, she was a shy heart. She'd retreat behind her defenses at the first sign of trouble. He'd tread carefully, keep it light and nonthreatening so as not to spook her.

"Suppose I fix breakfast for us?" He retrieved his coffee mug and picked up the flower basket. "I've heard it said that the best way to a woman's heart is through her stomach. Even if it isn't, I'm starved, so why don't you join me?"

When she faced him, she reminded him of a hungry, wide-eyed waif invited inside a bakery.

He hoped love was enough.

# Chapter Eighteen

Social platitudes failed Roxanne when she opened the front door for Greg Detweiler. She'd half-expected a man who looked fifty and wore pieces of a military uniform or the scruffy attire of the homeless who had entered the Mission District row house. Instead, a clean-shaven man in sharply pressed gray pants, a pale blue Oxford dress shirt, and a dark blue tie on her porch. He carried a windbreaker over his left arm.

The contrast between Matt's ageless specter in a tattered, Vietnam vintage flight suit standing beside his former best friend further rattled Roxanne's composure. Traces of the handsome young man who had loved her mother lingered around the leathery creases of Greg's face. Years of alcoholism and hard living had aged him prematurely. Now it seemed everything about him was gray: his hair, his eyes, even the pallor of his complexion.

"Mr. Detweiler, won't you come in?" She stepped aside and gestured him to enter. "It's been a long time since we last saw each other."

"You're all grown up and as pretty as your mother," Greg said wistfully, then fixed his gaze on the man standing beside her. "And you are?"

"Spencer Griffith. No relation." He offered his hand to Detweiler.

"Remembrance Foundation?" Greg asked, taking Spence's hand, his gray eyes narrowed into a scrutinizing squint.

Roxanne caught the glimmer of understanding shared by the two men as Spence nodded.

"I thought you looked familiar. The men from the Center and I attend the Memorial Day services. We're fewer in numbers every year. Pretty soon there won't be anyone left to remember." The sudden brightness of his eyes betrayed his emotion. Regret sculpted his thin lips into a frown.

Uncertain how Matt intended to proceed, Roxanne led them into the main parlor. With every lamp in the room lit, not a shadow hugged the corners.

Greg assessed the parlor. His slow movements were indicative of a man who remembered the past well and preferred being somewhere else. "I never expected to set foot in this house again." The tentative way he settled on the edge of a gold brocade love seat underscored his statement. He held his jacket like a man might hold a favorite hat. "Why did you want to meet me here instead of at Marian's grave?"

It was Roxanne's turn for discomfort. She sat beside Spence on the couch across a coffee table from Greg, swallowed hard, and plunged forward. "I have a story to tell you, Mr. Detweiler. You may find it preposterous, but I'd appreciate it if you'd hear me out before you say anything."

"A story?" Incredulity deepened the furrows plowed across his forehead and along the upper bridge of his nose. "I've come down here for a story?"

"I know it sounds a bit bizarre, but yes." She glanced at Matt, who gave encouragement with a nod and a forced smile.

"All right. I suppose I can indulge you. Am I correct in assuming we'll visit Marian's grave afterward?"

"I would be honored if you'd accompany me there," Roxanne told him. "You were her friend." Echoes of her own conflict rang in her awareness. "You loved her."

"Yes, I did." He took a deep breath, then let it out. "There are some things the years can't change." His nervous gray gaze darted around the room as though cataloging the changes through time. "I'm listening. Tell your story, then let's go to Marian's grave."

"All right." She breathed a small sigh of relief when he settled back, spread his arms over the top of the love seat, and rested his left ankle on his right knee. There seemed no graceful way to lead into a ghost story, particularly when said ghost watched her with silent intensity.

As she related the events of her father's ghostly return, she stood and begun pacing. Matt remained at her side during each pacing circuit. She appreciated the support, because Greg Detweiler had turned to stone. Halfway through her recounting of the events, she was tempted to check his breathing. All that moved were his expressionless gray eyes following her pattern across the parlor.

When finished, she sat beside Spence on the couch. He caught her hand and gave it a squeeze. In response, she twined her fingers with his. The contact fortified her and siphoned some of her nervousness. Until that moment she hadn't realized how much she wanted Matt to succeed for reasons totally unrelated to hastening his departure.

Throughout the storytelling, Greg's impassive expression remained fixed. Now he looked around the room without turning his head. "You're telling me Matt's here? In this room?"

Roxanne nodded.

"Can you see him?"

"Yes. He's standing beside you."

Greg turned his head, though he remained seated in his relaxed posture. "On the cushion?"

"He has a habit of standing in the furniture. It's rather disconcerting first thing in the morning." She directed the last remark to Matt. "I'm the only one who sees him."

"Trust us, Mr. Detweiler, Matthew Griffith's ghost is very real," Spence said softly.

"So are DTs. What does he want from me?"

"He's seeking atonement," she said. "Your forgiveness."

Detweiler straightened and dropped his foot to the floor. "Forgiveness? For what? Marian?"

The intensity of Matt's aura as he approached Roxanne stunned her. Reds, oranges, blues, greens, and a yellow so bright it hurt her eyes flared around his spectral image.

"Help me, Roxanne." He extended his hand, bidding her to stand, which she did reflexively.

"How? Tell me, and I'll do it for you." The raw pain he emanated wouldn't allow her refusal.

"Lend me your body."

"My body? Like at the beach?" Instinctively she tried to step back but lumped into the couch.

"Yes. I need your voice, too."

The conscious choice of allowing a ghost to take possession of her body required serious thought. A year or two debating the wisdom of doing such a rash thing was a good start. Unfortunately, Matt needed an answer now. "I owe you for saving me on the beach. I guess its payday."

"No. That was your father helping his daughter. This is different. You owe me nothing, Roxanne. I have no right to expect otherwise."

"Roxanne?" Spence rose beside her. "Tell us what's going on."

"He wants to use me. My body." For the first time since her father's arrival, she genuinely wanted to help him. This was crazy. A few minutes earlier she'd actually wanted him to succeed. Now she was contemplating helping him. She was getting soft. Sure, lending the use of her voice to make his peace with the man he'd grown up with was scary, but doable.

"Tell him no." Spence stood beside her. "There's something out of whack here. You're talking about possession." He took her by the shoulders, turning her away from Matt and Greg. "Don't do this, Roxanne. It's too risky."

She looked at Spence and then over at Matt. "I want this finished, Spence." Oddly, the dread in his expression deepened her conviction to help her father. "I want to do this."

"Is this reassurance? How do you know you'll separate? How do you know—"

"All I know is that I have to do this for him, Spence."

Becoming embroiled in another argument wouldn't change anything. She stepped out of the shelter of Spence's embrace, nodded at Matt, then braced herself. The next instant the tingle of a million padded needles ran like a current from her head to her toes, then back. An arctic chill enveloped her.

The person facing Greg Detweiler wasn't the same woman with whom Spence had made love. Her willingness to help her father in this gut-wrenching endeavor indicated a change Spence didn't understand. Damn, it seemed to be all or nothing with Roxanne. However, lending her body went beyond the pale and bothered him in more ways than he could define.

"Marian loved me, Greg. And I loved her so damn much, it didn't matter if I had to lie or screw over my best friend to have her." Roxanne/Matt rounded the coffee table and strode into the spacious openness of the living room.

Spence hadn't known what to expect, but it sure wasn't the change of voice inflection or the abrupt swagger in Roxanne's step.

Greg bolted to his feet, then stood rigid and swaying. His gray pallor turned a chalky white. "Matt? Jesus, is it really you?"

"Yeah. I've come to ask you the biggest favor ever, Buddy. Forgiveness."

"You can't forgive someone as a favor. What does it matter?"

"It matters a great deal." The inflection in Roxanne's voice assumed a satiny quality an octave lower than her normal tone. "This is a second chance for both of us to part friends."

Detweiler studied Roxanne as though he saw something Spence couldn't. "What do you want my forgiveness for? Lying to Marian about me, or screwing me over?"

"Both."

"I thought this was over and done with." Detweiler crossed the room to the French doors. "Damn near thirty years, and my gut still burns over it." He examined the toes of his shoes before continuing in his slow, deliberate baritone. "Go back to wherever you came from, Matt. It's all history. Done. You quit being my friend thirty years ago."

"I'll go, but not yet. I'm guilty of injuring your soul. I can't give you Marian, nor would I, no matter what it cost me. But maybe at this point in your life we can give each other peace." Roxanne/Matt followed Greg to the door.

"All you give me is bullshit and lies," Greg spat.

"He speaks the only truth he knows," Spence defended without considering the repercussions. "He can't lie." He felt like a fly on the wall of a confessional.

Distress narrowed Greg's gaze. "Then maybe the way we live our lives does dictate the kind of hell waiting at the end. Is that how it is, Matt? Hell? Forced to tell the truth for eternity? I'll bet Marian finds some irony in the situation."

Roxanne/Matt turned away from the French doors. "I suppose she would."

Spence didn't know whose misery pinched Roxanne's pale features: her own, Matt's, or both. Regardless of the source, the situation was detrimental to her. Spence wanted it over. A slow anger began festering.

"Nothing makes a man as vulnerable or crazy as love," Matt said. "I'd have given my right arm to spare you the hurt I caused by telling Marian you'd found someone new. And God knows, I'd have told her anything to win her over."

"Loyalty was Marian's strongest quality. You corrupted even that." Greg leaned against the French doors, his body facing Roxanne/Matt's, his face toward the window.

"Love was Marian's greatest strength, and her greatest vulnerability. She loved you as a friend. She wanted to talk to you before marrying me. She wanted to tell you in person how she and I felt about each other. Then my draft number came up.

"I didn't want to wait until you came home from flight school. So I did the most expedient thing—I talked her into eloping. We kept the marriage secret. I needed time to break it to my parents. But time slipped away and I wound up doing the same thing you did. I enlisted in the Air Force with hopes of flying instead of marching through the jungle."

"Remember when we soloed our first time? What were we? Fifteen?" Greg's memory-bright eyes lifted to the ceiling.

"Sixteen. We used Hal Kirchoff's Cessna 150 out of Reid-Hillview in San José." A crooked smile matched the gleam in Roxanne's eyes. For the instant her eyes appeared blue instead of brown, icy shivers rode up Spence's backbone.

The helplessness of watching Roxanne's strange body language and facial expressions galled Spence.

"Yeah. That was before they built that big mall, Eastridge, at the end of the runway." Trembling fingers plowed furrows through Greg's steely-gray hair. "In those days we never thought our love of flying would take us to the skies over Vietnam."

"Did we think?" An infectious grin accompanied the question.

The tattered and torn bonds of a twenty-five-year friendship snaked a frayed tendril across the gap of years. "We must have. We became pilots instead of ground troops."

"We were good pilots, too." Roxanne/Matt lounged against the doorjamb, shoved her fists into her pockets, and crossed her left ankle over her right.

"I was a good pilot. You were the Lone Ranger." Greg resumed studying his shoe tips. "I obeyed orders and stayed with my wingman. You . . . You always went looking for trouble." He glanced up. "And usually found it." Tears shimmered on Greg's lower lashes, then spilled down the fine web of his leathery cheeks.

Spencer remained immobile, every muscle aching to grab Roxanne and protect her from the emotions building between Matt and Greg. Beneath the civilities, an undercurrent crackled in the air. He kept telling himself that Roxanne had chosen her role in the confrontation. But silent support was becoming more difficult by the second.

"I *was* the Lone Ranger. Without Tonto. My fault, not yours."

"You had lots of friends. You were Good-Time Charlie. Everyone partied with you."

"Good-Time Charlie. Hear that, Roxanne?" The cocky shake of Roxanne/Matt's head punctuated the allusion to a private conversation.

"I had many acquaintances, Greg. Plenty of drinking buddies, especially when I picked up the tab. But I only had one friend, and I lost him.

"If I had it to do over, I'd do the honorable thing. I'd let Marian tell you the way she wanted to. Christ, I'd muster up some integrity." Self-loathing clipped Roxanne/Matt's words. The pacing resumed.

Spence met Greg's gaze then watched Roxanne/Matt follow the pacing circuit.

"I came here, to this house, after I got back from Nam—before I crawled into a bottle. I told Marian you were dead. She refused to believe it until she saw your body." Greg turned toward the window and lifted his face to the clear blue sky on the other side of the French doors. "I'd hoped she would turn to me, but she didn't. She loved you, Matt, the way I wanted her to love me. She sat with Roxanne on her lap and said she'd wait for you. It broke my heart all over. I knew you weren't coming back."

Greg folded his arms over his chest and looked over his shoulder at Matt pacing in Roxanne's body for a moment before continuing. "When Marian died, I held your daughter and cried with her. Soon after her death, I learned from Thelma that Marian had no estate. It didn't take a clairvoyant to see your aunt Thelma's attitude about raising your daughter. Knowing her as I did, I figured somebody ought to do something for Roxanne's future. I set up a trust fund for her college—in Marian's name.

"You should have taken care of them, Matt. You took that job when you married her, but you didn't do it. You didn't even bother to leave a will, did you? You had the whole world in your hand, everything a man could want, and you pissed it away."

"Like hell I did! I loved her."

"You loved yourself and our easy, freewheeling lifestyle more. You didn't want anything in the way of your good time.

"Remember who Marian ran to when you told her to get an abortion, Matt? To me!" Greg poked a bony finger at the center of his chest. "She came to me. Sobbing. At first, I told her to divorce you. I'd marry her and raise the baby as mine. But she said she'd never divorce you. She loved you too much for that."

The anguish of opening old wounds burned in Greg's gray eyes. The jut of his chin and rise of his white-knuckled, trembling fist reeked of accusation. "So don't pontificate on the lengths a man in love will go to, Matt. I know what it is to love, and how to love. I know what it is to lose at love, and how it rips out your guts to send the woman you love back to the man who betrayed you. She loved you, Matt. You won. I lost."

Roxanne/Matt sagged against the arm of a couch. Spence started forward, then stopped when she straightened and a strange fire burned in her eyes. It was damn near killing him to let her play out the exchange. The bottom line was that he didn't know how to stop the phenomenon and suspected it would be destructive to try.

Her shoulders straightened; her gaze sought, then fixed on Greg. "You have your life," came Matt's measured response.

"Yeah, I've learned to get up in the morning and do something constructive. I have a life. But you've haunted me day and night since your plane went down. Nothing got rid of you—not drugs, not booze. Don't it beat all? Now I'm sober, you've come back for real."

"It's not the same as being alive. You saw me go down. You were on the radio with me until I punched out."

Detweiler crossed the room like a summer storm in full fury. He snatched his jacket from the love seat, turned on his heel, and glared at Roxanne/Matt. "You couldn't follow orders, could you? You had to play Lone Ranger and go after the MIG. Hero for a day. Center of attention at the Officers' Club. God, you thrived on the glory. Was it more important than your life? Than being Marian's husband or your child's father? Did you even think about them?"

"Hell, yes! I thought about them all the time. I wanted to be home with them, but I wanted something else, too. Damned if I know what it was now. In the end, the pilot of the MIG put an end to it all."

"You bailed. I saw your chute."

"So did Charlie. I came down in the trees and popped out of my chute. I made it to a hole in the ground and pulled the dirt in after me. They came. They looked. When I realized how badly I was hurt, I knew I wasn't getting out alive."

"They found you," Greg said with a sad finality.

"No."

Greg swore under his breath, his entire body shaking.

"The napalm got me the next day. The hole I'd found wasn't deep enough to save me."

The instant tightening in Spence's gut kept him immobile.

"The MIG didn't shoot you down, Matt. When you disobeyed orders and went after him, you rose into my gun sights. I didn't let off the trigger fast enough. I shot you down. Goddamnit! *I* shot you down! Not the MIG."

Stunned, Spence watched Greg rush out of the room.

Roxanne's knees buckled and she collapsed onto the edge of the couch, then slid to the floor in a dazed heap.

Spence wanted to hurt somebody for hurting Roxanne. He scooped up her chilled, limp body and placed her on the couch.

"Don't ever do that again," he ground out through the war of emotion raging inside him. With hands trembling from anger, he framed Roxanne's tear-dampened face. Soulful brown eyes looked back at him with a desolate sorrow. Tears spilled down her cheeks. "Tell me you're all right, sweetheart."

She remained silent, the flood of confused sorrow flowing over her face. He gathered her shivering body against his chest and rocked her like a child.

After what seemed an eternity, her fingers wound into the shirt fabric at his shoulders. She held on as though her life depended on it.

Spence wanted to rage in anger and empathy. Instead, he continued holding her and his silence.

"I didn't want to know their history. I can't change what they've done to each other or themselves." Roxanne snatched a couple of tissues from the box on the side table. "Oh, Spence, I didn't expect to feel his emotions. I've never experienced anything as frightening, or morose, or, or, so wild and painful. I had no idea anyone could feel so much all at once. His emotions. Mine. Separate, but jumbled together at times."

"He had no right to do that to you, Roxanne."

"At the risk of being his defender, he asked and I agreed." But she hadn't known what she was in for, and she knew with unerring certainty Matt had not known either. The memories evoked by Greg's conversation had come from nowhere, flashed, then evaporated. Initially Roxanne had barely comprehended the content, but that had changed quickly.

"The weirdest part of it all was when I realized neither one of us was in charge of the images or memories rolling through my head."

"Are you sure you're all right now?"

Scarcely able to keep herself from crumbling under the weight of residual emotion, she had no solution for the sharp-eyed anger keeping Spence on the prowl.

Roxanne nodded, then blew her nose "I'll get over it. I have to. Don't worry, I won't be doing it again. For some things in life, once really *is* enough." The torment raging through her had eased to a tolerable level. The aftermath of the potent paranormal link would take a long time to fade. "I thought it would be like on the beach, except he'd use my voice. I should have asked questions. I should have—"

"Stop it. You can spend the rest of your life second-guessing what happened. Analyzing the things leading to Matt and Greg's confrontation doesn't fall on your shoulders." At the center of the room, Spence stood guard with the scowling ferocity of a cougar protecting his territory.

Roxanne rose and tucked the tissue box under her arm. "I'd like to go to my mother's grave now."

Spence reached for her arm and escorted her from the parlor. Roxanne retrieved the vase of flowers for her mother. Heaven help her if she ever owned the mountains of regret her father's ghost experienced every minute of every day, for what? Eternity?

Apprehension skimmed the top of her skin with a tingling that left gooseflesh rippling in its wake.

Tension filled the space between her and Spence inside the car. Roxanne didn't know how to handle the chaos lingering from her father's possession of her body. Helping Spence was even further out of reach, but she had to try. "Do you want to yell at me?"

"The last thing you need is for me to get angry at you because I was powerless to help you. Besides, yelling won't do any good. I'd rather hit something."

"My sense of volunteerism doesn't extend that far."

She bowed her head and inhaled the sweet perfume of the bouquet. "My mother loved flowers. She used to braid them in our hair. We'd pretend she was a queen and I was a princess. The red rosebuds were rubies; the gardenias were diamonds. Many of the rosebushes in the backyard came from slips of the bushes she and I planted."

She lifted the rose and inhaled the heady attar. It went to the heart of the past. "If I close my eyes, I can see my mother planting those rosebushes. Her favorites were the red ones. I think they were her favorites because they were my father's. Funny how people leave all types of legacies."

"Your parents left an irreplaceable legacy much better than monuments or rosebushes. They left you, their daughter. Bright and creative. Industrious and more self-sufficient than any woman should have to be. Or man, for that matter."

"They almost didn't," she whispered. Her father had wanted her mother to have an abortion, not a daughter. The inexplicable hurt of that admission made her wince. "Obviously, she took a stand. Thank God." The full memory of the situation and time rolled across her mind like a tidal wave. The price of understanding left no villains.

"Have you seen your father since he left you in the parlor?"

"No. I don't know what I'd say to him if I did right now." The manicured grounds of the cemetery spread among the tombstones passing outside the car window took on a surrealism. Designed to impart serenity, the trees, flowering shrubs, and richly colored bushes marked the road curving among the granite memorials rising from the lawn. Fresh flowers on a few graves bore evidence of other weekend visitors.

Spence parked the car against the curb and turned in his seat. "Pack a bag and move into my place, Roxanne."

Her head reeled with the implications couched in such a brazen suggestion. "I may be a bit discombobulated, but that sounds like you're rushing things."

"I'm not talking about moving in together."

"Sounded like it to me."

"Give yourself a few days away from the house. Distance usually helps find perspective. Stay at my place. I'll stay somewhere else."

Shaken by his concern, Roxanne slumped in the seat. "I know you mean well, Spence, but I need to see this through. Running away—"

"I wasn't suggesting you run away, just take some time for yourself." He removed the keys from the ignition and released his seat belt. "Of course, you could take a tip from Erin and Brian and do both on a cruise ship."

"Right. And desert my business and my staff. Not an option. I know you mean well, but copping out even for a few days is like jumping from the frying pan into the fire for me. Thanks anyway."

"Just remember, both burn. All I'm offering is the hot pads and an asbestos island." The back of his fingers stroked her cheek in an assuring caress. The action reflected the affection softening the hard angles of his face.

In that instant she felt loved; then the tender feeling fell victim to the tumult still swirling in her brain. "Thank you, Spence." *For loving me at this moment*, she added silently.

Since her mother's death Roxanne had longed for someone to love her. In the span of one weekend, she'd heard declarations of love from her father and Spence. Being loved wasn't what she'd expected. She'd never considered it might feel like a burden she didn't know how to shoulder.

Eager to escape Spence's worried gaze, she quit fiddling with the flowers and opened the car door. For a few seconds she pretended she was alone and the day's events were a distant nightmare. Eyes closed, she slowly inhaled the afternoon air deep into her lungs. She exhaled at the same slow rate and consciously tried to relax.

Today marked twenty-two years of separation. Neither death nor time had diminished her love for her mother. Aware she still saw her mother through the perspective of a six-year-old, she had no desire to change it. Some things should be left alone. Like the dead. Today's debacle reinforced her belief.

The day couldn't get worse, could it?

# Chapter Nineteen

Wild with raging emotion, Matt separated from Roxanne as gently as possible, then fled the house behind Greg.

He'd failed. Miserably. Selfishly. At the beginning of the encounter, Greg had pegged Matt's bankrupt character as the source for all their misery. Greg was right. The depth of Matt's self-centeredness ran as deep as the Abyss of Nothingness.

In a narrow-minded pursuit of reaching an understanding with Greg, Matt had taken the easiest, most expedient path. He'd given no real thought to the consequences Roxanne might suffer. The old habits of the past hadn't died. At the first sign of opportunity, they had roared back, and he abandoned the lessons he thought he'd relearned during his time as a ghost.

For the brief moment it had taken Roxanne to make the decision to allow the use of her body, she'd trusted him not to harm her. He'd rewarded her by proving unworthy of her faith, of anyone's trust.

God, he'd felt her struggle to keep his memories out, and he'd been powerless to shield her. He hadn't expected the sharp clarity or the deep bites of pain. Neither of them had been prepared for it. The best he could do for her now was to leave her alone with the tumult of emotions that had swamped them both. He'd shamelessly used his daughter as a means to avoid the dreaded pit.

Someone, somewhere, had said you didn't remember pain, just the experience of a pain-filled incident. If the axiom was true, the spirit world operated by different laws. A real, physical pain had accompanied the memories.

What he had feared most, he had left to fate rather than risk confrontation. By not explaining fully to Roxanne what had happened between him and Marian all those years ago, he'd acted the coward. Consequently, he destroyed the fragile acceptance he'd fostered since his arrival. Learning the way he'd planned to deal with the problem of Marian's unplanned pregnancy surely had shredded his daughter's goodwill.

He'd shared Roxanne's desolation. She'd never understand what a knee-jerk reaction pushing for an abortion had been. How could she?

Nearly thirty years ago he and Marian thought they had their whole lives ahead of them. Marian would have finished college by the time his tour in Nam ended. Riding the wave of change sweeping the country, they could have gone anywhere, done anything.

A baby changed those golden dreams.

His death revoked them.

Once again, Matt found himself in bleak circumstances of his own initiation with no way to make reparations to those he'd hurt. He said a prayer of thanks that Spencer Griffith remained with Roxanne.

Although he preferred retreating to the attic and brooding, Matt couldn't ignore the fallout from the debacle he'd created. Greg's despondency worried Matt. The tenuous bond of an old friendship they'd reconstructed in the parlor held. Matt used it to stay close during Greg's visit to Marian's grave.

"We were fools, Marian. All three of us." Greg knelt on one knee and traced the letters carved on Marian Boyle Griffith's granite gravestone with a calloused fingertip.

"Lies and deceit. The wonder is that any of our souls survive what we did to ourselves and each other."

Matt yearned to tell Greg that without forgiveness and love, his soul wouldn't survive. The truth settled on Matt with grim finality; he'd reaped what he'd sown.

Greg arranged the flowers he'd pilfered from the median gardens in a recess at the headstone base. "There's no way to know how different things might have turned out if I'd told you why I knew Matt was dead, not MIA. I didn't know how much you loved him until I came back and looked into your eyes. Right or wrong, I couldn't tell you the truth. You weren't ready to hear it, and I couldn't have stood the condemnation I'd have seen in your eyes. Besides, your heart was already breaking. Later . . . Later, it was too late.

"You have a fine daughter, Marian. She's a lot like you. If you're watching, you already know it, and you're proud of her. I wish so many things, Marian. I wish she could have been mine."

His head bowed into the web of his thumb and forefinger, Greg wept openly. "I wish I'd moved on with my life instead of crawling into a bottle and wasting all those years. More than anything, I wish Matt hadn't flown into my line of fire. I killed him, Marian. I killed our best friend."

Matt's anger played out with Greg's lament. The dull, aching reality of truth settled. Friendly fire hadn't brought him down and napalm hadn't finished him off. He'd died from the self-inflicted wound of arrogant stupidity.

"She is the magnet that draws us." Roxanne knelt beside Greg Detweiler. "I'm glad you came here, despite what happened at the house."

"What you did today took a lot of courage."

"I was thinking more along the lines of shortsightedness." And masochism.

Greg took a handkerchief from his back pocket and blew his nose. "I'm sorry. I said things best left in the past."

"It all just sort of happened." She refused to dwell on it and reached for the flowers in the granite well. "May I?"

Detweiler nodded. "That's a typical Matt Griffith event for you. It just happens. Later, you think about the consequences. Spontaneity was his middle name. It was one of the reasons I liked him so damn much. He was the Martha Stewart of a good time. He found humor in a rock. I envied him the ability to have fun in nearly any situation."

"He found no humor in today's . . . whatever we did." She took the flowers from her vase and poured some of the water into the recess holding Greg's purloined bouquet.

"I lured you here under false pretenses," she said with a sigh. "I wrote the letter because Matt asked me to. I genuinely wanted him to make his peace with you. I might have been less optimistic had I known the circumstances." She glanced over and saw his rapt attention. "He's been to your house, Mr. Detweiler. He tried contacting you on his own, but you couldn't see him. The ghosts wandering where you live limited what he could do." She mixed his flowers with those from her backyard, then filled the two vases.

"Hitting the wall of something he couldn't do must have made him desperate." Greg put his windbreaker on the ground, rocked back, and sat on it. "Where is he now?"

Roxanne made a slow search of the cemetery. Spence walked the path winding through the headstone forest but remained within sight. "I don't know. Does it make a difference?"

Greg stuffed the handkerchief into his pocket. "No. Whenever we had a row, we'd both say things without thinking. Afterward, we'd go off somewhere, talk, then apologize even if we didn't think we were wrong. Guess it was a carryover from our kindergarten days and our teacher, Miss Nathanson.

"Your mother didn't understand the rules of engagement with Matt."

Sensing his struggle through her own tumult, Roxanne put a hand on his forearm. "What are you trying to tell me?"

"God, you're like him, too. No preamble, just make the point."

Finished arranging the flowers, she sat cross-legged on the ground and faced Greg. "I prefer to think of myself as an autonomous woman who appreciates directness."

Greg nodded, then studied the headstone. After a moment of silence he spoke. "Look, I flew off the handle. I said some things I shouldn't have. It was cruel. Even worse, it fell a little short of the truth. I've been angry for thirty years. I wanted to hurt him, not you."

To Roxanne's left, Spence prowled the headstones and watched her with the intensity of an eagle ready to swoop down on a moment's notice. She looked back at Greg, understanding very well the consequence of lashing out and hurting the innocent unintentionally. "What part wasn't true?"

"He didn't mean it."

"Didn't mean what? To get killed?" Undoubtedly, Matt had thought he was invincible.

"He didn't push for Marian to get an abortion. After she told him she was pregnant, he flared. He hadn't thought it through.

That's how he was, Roxanne. At crucial times he acted or spoke first, and thought later."

"I'm living proof my mother won the no-abortion argument. You don't have to defend him." The acrimonious bite of such thorough rejection sunk its sharp teeth deeper into her psyche.

"There was no real argument. She'd taken a stand and nothing would have swayed her." He stroked the side of the headstone. "You'd never want to confuse Marian with facts or logic once she'd made up her mind. You'd go crazy and she wouldn't have changed her mind. So attempting was an exercise in futility. And frustration. Yours. She didn't take a stand often. Before she did, she'd learn as much about the issue or event as she could. But once she'd committed to it, the Pacific would have to dry up before she'd change her point of view.

"Despite everything else, Matt wanted her happy. He damn sure didn't want her turning to me. If having the baby made her happy, Matt wanted the baby, too. At the Officers' Club he'd show pictures of Marian in profile, her belly getting bigger and bigger. He named you, you know."

The revelations quickened the whirlpool of emotion swirling through her. "He named me Roxanne? Why Roxanne?"

"He chose it because in Persian, it means *dawn*. He once said your conception was the dawn of his adult life. You and Marian were his new life." Greg rested his hands on his knees. "And he liked the hard and soft sounds of your name. He gave it a lot of thought, which marked a significant change in his approach to things."

"Tell me about my mother," she asked with a heavy heart. "Tell me what Mom was like before she married him."

During the recounting, Roxanne sometimes laughed, sometimes cried while envisioning her mother's youth. When they pushed themselves to their feet and dusted themselves off an hour later, much of the rancor she'd experienced earlier had faded.

Roxanne threw her shoulders back, stretching, and looked around. A short distance away Spence leaned against a monument. Silent, vigilant, his patience and willingness to let her seek her own kind of peace with Greg Detweiler tugged at her. She smiled at him when he straightened; his attention focused on something behind her.

She turned and saw Janice Boyle approaching them.

"Hello, Greg," Janice said. "I see you've remembered Marian after all these years."

Greg gaped and grew paler by the moment. "Janice. I thought you'd be dead by now."

"With few exceptions, only the good die young, Greg. I hope you don't mind some company." Janice leaned against the edge of Hayden and Pauline Griffith's headstone. "Looks like I'm late for the gathering of Marian's friends and loved ones, but better late than never, right?"

Before Roxanne thought of a response, Spence spoke up. "Not necessarily. Sometimes, better never, Mrs. Boyle."

Roxanne wasn't sure which rocked her more: Janice Boyle's unexpected appearance or Spence's surly attitude toward the elderly woman. "I don't get it," Roxanne blurted. "Why did you pick this weekend to return here?"

"I admit the timing is questionable—"

"Questionable, Mrs. Boyle?" Spence's shoulders tensed into a steel cage around Roxanne.

"Spence?" Lost, Roxanne looked at the storm riding the small muscles of Spence's angular face. He knew something.

"Would you like to tell her, Mrs. Boyle, or shall I?"

"I didn't catch your name, young man," Janice said with the right blend of curiosity and imperialism to command an answer.

"Spencer No-Relation Griffith," Roxanne responded immediately.

"Are you questioning the timing of my return in relation to Thelma's death? One has nothing to do with the other. I'm getting old. If I was ever going to see Marian's daughter, I had to do it now or forget it. Traveling is difficult when your joints ache and a fast-food burger is out of the question."

"You've seen her." Spence tried to turn them both away from the frail old lady.

Roxanne had never seen this side of Spence. "She came by the house yesterday, Spence."

"She's a con artist, Roxanne. Surprise and timing form the backbone for her schemes."

"A con artist?" Roxanne asked, confused. The day's events were burying her in splintering emotion. "I thought you were a drug addict."

"Ask Matt," Greg said under his breath without moving his gaze. "He knows all about her."

Dimly Roxanne thought it strange for Greg to close ranks with the ghost of the man who had deceived him. She looked around. If Matt was near, he kept his presence a silent secret.

"I was both. For a while I was part of a confidence ring," Janice agreed, her white head bowed in shame. "That was a long, long time ago. People change, but the past has a way of following."

"How did you know, Spence?" Dazed, Roxanne continued staring at him.

"When we recover remains in Vietnam, there's an exhaustive effort to identify the soldier and the family. Through the investigation, we match up the families. Because of the name confusion at the onset, I was more involved than usual. As the sole survivors in Matthew Griffith's family, you and Thelma were easy to locate. We went a step further and checked Marian's family for possible notifications and found more than we expected."

"You tried to tell me you did this before . . ." Her mind refused to focus on anything except the angst in Spence's blue eyes. "When was that?"

"When I was telling you about the Remembrance Foundation." Spence took Roxanne's hand.

"Look, I didn't come out here to stir things up," Janice said, pushing away from the headstone. "I just came to see where Marian was laid to rest." She reached for Roxanne's arm. "And as I said yesterday, to see you, Roxanne."

Roxanne looked from Janice, to Greg, then to Spence as she pulled her hand from his. "I can't do this any more today. I'm sorry, Greg." Her defenses were shattered, her emotions a roiling sea of confusion between those genuinely hers and the residual ones from her father's possession.

She kissed her fingertips, then placed them atop her mother's headstone. "I have to go home. I need some Greta Garbo alone time."

"Roxanne," Greg said. "Thank you."

She reached for him, caught him in a hug, and held on until he hugged her back. "I never thanked you for holding me here twenty-two years ago and crying with me." She kissed his leathery cheek. "Thank you, Greg, from the bottom of my heart, for loving my mother and caring about me. I'm a big girl now. You can't disappear easily again. I'll find you."

"I'll be around." Flustered, he released her, then gave Janice Boyle a pointed look.

Spence put an arm around Roxanne shoulders and led her to the car. How comforting his silent strength was right now. How dangerous.

Roxanne lay in bed and stared at the ceiling. All the things she didn't want to think about marched through her mind with the rhythm of a chant. Nothing stopped long enough for her to focus on and resolve. Bits and pieces of strange memories bobbed and spun like carousel horses.

The sounds of her parents' laughter echoed in her ears.

Her mother's brown eyes gazed at her in adoration. Except she wasn't herself. The memory belonged to her father.

The realization evoked screaming outrage so consuming it made the hair at the nape of Roxanne's neck prickle.

In a dank, dark earthen tunnel, fear and an immobilizing physical pain came next. She could smell the dirt and the damp jungle, hear the calculated, deadly search a few feet away. The terror of discovery robbed her breath.

Bleak near-darkness stretched into infinity. The nothingness was impervious to anything in the sensory realm.

Visions of her parents making love with a soul-aching tenderness were the final straw.

Like many mistakes in life, she was powerless to obliterate the images she'd unknowingly and unwillingly acquired. Matt's memories of the things he and Greg had spoken about in the parlor were hers, too. The very idea plowed new grounds in the fields of abuse and mental cruelty. Ownership of someone's past, particularly his death, seemed a capital crime.

And what was she going to do about Janice Boyle? What were her real reasons for showing up now? The woman was a stranger who had turned her back on her own daughter. A drug addict who couldn't be bothered with a little matter like her daughter's death and an orphaned grandchild. A con artist, according to Remembrance Foundation's investigation.

Roxanne didn't want to think of Janice as family. Presently, she wished her mother had opted for artificial insemination, then moved to the Yukon.

Just before midnight Roxanne got out of bed and went downstairs. The lights blazed brightly.

*The great, unfeeling darkness,* she realized. *He fears it and craves the light.*

She grabbed towels from the nearest bathroom and kept walking until she reached the cabana beside the swimming pool. In seconds she stripped off her sleep shirt and panties, then dived into the heated water and swam. And swam. Until her limbs felt like lead and her lungs screamed for mercy.

Lacking the energy to stand, she crawled from the warm water into the cold night, where Buster greeted her with a chastising yowl. In the cabana, she curled into a shivering ball around Buster and the towels. At last, her body disengaged from the furious pace of her mind. She slept.

Matt covered his daughter with quilts and lowered the cabana screens as a barrier against the heavy dew gathering in the yard. He spent the night watching over her, determined to gather enough memories to last him until his soul disintegrated in the Abyss.

"Guardian? Are you there?" he asked in the small hours of the night.

"I am here, Matthew."

"I screwed up."

"The consequences of your actions haven't gone unnoticed."

"I thought I'd learned a lot, but when it came time to apply it, I resorted to the old ways of expediency."

The Guardian loosed a sigh so deep it filled the air and sent ripples across the top of the swimming pool. "Can a leopard change his stripes?"

"Thelma?" Matt brightened at the prospect of familiarity, even if it was Thelma. "I know that's you. You never got the leopard and tiger markings right."

"Answer the question," snapped the voice.

Thelma, he decided. "No. A leopard cannot change his spots, nor can a tiger change his stripes regardless of how hard he tries."

"Correct. They're animals governed by instinct. You are neither a leopard, nor a tiger, Matthew. You possess the gift of a fine intellect and free will. Granted, you have tried to make amends and change your approach with those you've harmed, but the results speak for themselves. The time grows very short. Memorial Day is two weeks away."

"I'm aware of the time." It felt like a guillotine built just for him.

"Then state quickly why you've summoned me now. I am not

the equivalent of a bartender. I will not pour liquor while listening to your tales of woe and enable you to continue deluding yourself."

Matt winced. The analogy hit too close to home. "I don't know what to do."

"Don't be a wimp. Buck up, Matthew. There's still time. Cherish this second chance. Few have the opportunity, and even fewer know how to capitalize on it for the good of their soul. Look deep inside yourself." The voice softened to an almost eerie quality. "The answers lie there. Trust yourself first. Rely on what you've learned these last weeks."

"What good is learning the error of my ways if I'm incapable of using it when the chips are down?"

"It has a far better chance of success than the self-pitying whining you're doing now. Make the most of the time remaining, Matthew. Take care of your daughter. God knows the Griffiths have done a miserable imitation of doing so in the past. Roxanne stands on the threshold of great happiness or abysmal loneliness. You cannot make the choice for her, but you can offer some fatherly guidance."

He seemed to have missed the boat when it came to learning about fatherhood. It was as daunting now as when Marian announced her pregnancy. "Guidance. Advice."

"She will choose her own path, Matthew, just as you've chosen yours. As for Mr. Detweiler, there is still the possibility of salvaging something."

"No man should carry the guilt Greg does," Matt murmured, dragging a quilt over Roxanne's bare foot. "It wasn't his fault. I broke right in front of his guns."

"Help him forgive himself, Matthew, then he can forgive you. It's the best you can do for all concerned. He has walked a long ways alone. He hasn't much farther to travel until he enters the light and comes home."

"He's dying?" The news neither surprised nor saddened him. Greg would do far better on the other side than he'd fared here.

"Godspeed, Matthew. Be his friend again. Be your daughter's father. Open your heart and put them first."

The air settled into the calm of early morning. In a few hours he would start anew, like the dawn.

His goals were becoming less attainable each day. Time to

change goals. This time he'd follow the advice of the Guardian to the letter. He vowed to do what he could for Roxanne and Greg. The oath was the only island of peace in the self-inflicted chaos.

# Chapter
# Twenty

"Roxanne Griffith is here to see you. She says she isn't family and she doesn't have an appointment."

"Send her in and cancel whatever I have for the rest of the day." Spence dropped the telephone receiver into the cradle. He rose from the desk chair and closed the folders in front of him.

The floor-to-ceiling double doors guarding the inner sanctum of Griffith Enterprises' CEO opened. The red blazer Roxanne wore with a black turtleneck and trousers was the only spot of color about her. When the doors closed, she brought a fragrant yellow rose from behind her back and offered it to him.

Big-eyed and pensive, she drew him across the expanse of his office. "From your rose gardens?"

"Yes. It's a way of saying thank you and a peace offering. I'm taking you to dinner, too." The way she glanced around the office showed her nervousness. "If you can get away, that is. You must have a lot to catch up on from last week."

He captured the rose and her hand in his, then lifted both to his face. The fine art of growing showy, fragrant blooms reached perfection in the rose they held between them. He inhaled, knowing he'd never see or smell a rose again without thinking of Roxanne.

"A peace offering?"

"For locking the front door on you when all you wanted to do was make sure I was all right. I couldn't deal with having anyone around me, Spence. I still don't know how to reconcile all that happened Sunday." A flash of emotion washed away some of her contrition. "I wasn't fair to you, Spence. You didn't deserve a cold shoulder when all you did was help me. You're a real friend." She couldn't help grinning. "And an exceptional lover."

"You don't want to lose me, so you've come with a gift"—he raised the flower—"promises of food, and flattery. I can be seduced, you know."

"I was counting on it." Her knowing expression made him smile.

"Yesterday was the most bizarre day of our lives," he said, trying to keep the conversation on a boardroom level. "Are you ready to tell me what happened between you and your father?"

Roxanne hesitated, lowered her gaze to the rose, then shook her head. "I don't have it all sorted out."

Her eyelids flew wide when he curled a finger beneath her chin and lifted so he could kiss her. The panic in her dark eyes stopped him. "What is it, Roxanne?"

"I thought it would be better if I was with you. It isn't. It's worse."

"What's worse?" Instead of kissing her, he cupped her neck and slid his thumb down the soft skin of her throat. The frantic rate of her pulse reminded him of a sparrow caught in a snare. "What happened when your father borrowed your voice?"

"Some of his memories became mine, Spence. I don't want them, and I don't know how to get rid of them." She swallowed hard, then turned away. "I wanted to ask him this morning, but he wasn't talking. Or manifesting, or doing any of the things he usually does."

"You're sure he was there?"

"Yes, he was there. I wanted to yell and scream at him. But part of the problem of sharing memories is the issue of ownership. Whether I like it or not, those memories are now part of my memory, too. It was the ultimate virtual reality trip, Spence.

"Most of the time I felt what he felt, saw what he saw. Most of the time I knew his surprise when he realized I was part of it. And his disappointment when he couldn't shield me." She sat on the arm of the leather couch and stared at the floor.

The depth of her despair rattled him. "There must be a way to block those memories." If Matt Griffith proved incapable of undoing the reprehensible mess he'd made in his daughter's mind, maybe hypnosis would help. The time wasn't right to speak of that option.

Roxanne raised her sad, dry gaze to focus on him. "How do you un-know something, Spence?"

Other than the possibility of hypnosis, he had no answer. The bitter realization of helplessness pervaded his mind. The woman he loved needed something. He had no idea of how to get it for her. All his life he'd fixed people and problems. Fixing trouble was his greatest talent. What Roxanne needed lay beyond his expertise.

If he couldn't help, he wasn't going to add to her problem. He prowled the office, pulled books off the bookshelves and leafed through them. He kept an eye on Roxanne as he flipped through one book after another. One by one, he lifted decorative awards and art off the shelves and checked beneath before putting them back. Finally he went to his desk and riffled the drawer contents.

"What are you doing?" she finally asked, her brow furrowed by concern.

"Looking for answers." He dropped the folders from his desktop into his center drawer and closed it. "No luck so far. What do you say we keep looking down on Fishermen's Wharf? Maybe we can dust a few off in the Wax Museum? Speaking of museums, there's always Ripley's Believe It Or Not. Under the circumstances, it might be the best place to look for answers. We'll start there."

Before she tried to beg off, he whisked his suit coat from the wooden valet in the corner of his office and grabbed her arm on the way to the door. "Let's go."

"Spence, I don't think—"

"That's the point, Roxanne. You don't have to think right now. Tomorrow, yes. Maybe even later tonight. Right now just go with the flow." He opened the office door.

"Hello, Roxanne. Would you give us a few minutes? Spence, we have to meet on this." Candice rounded his administrator's desk.

"Tomorrow," Spence said, then gave his efficient administrator a nod. "Put Candice at the top of the list."

"It can't wait."

The urgency in her voice stopped him.

"This was a bad idea." Roxanne discreetly tried to wiggle free of his grasp.

"Business or personal, Candice."

"Business." She held up a red folder with a competitor's logo in the corner.

"It can wait." Nothing was as important as lifting the eighteen-ton weight Roxanne carried. One genuine smile was worth more than a jump on any competitor. This afternoon, he aspired to laughter.

Roxanne felt as if she'd stepped through Alice's mirror and into a wonderland orchestrated by Spence. While they found no answers at the Ripley museum, they did find some of the most interesting art either had seen. The eight-foot-long scale model of a San Francisco cable car constructed from 270,836 matchsticks made them both question the existence of the creator's social life. An eight-foot-tall Stegosaurus made entirely from chrome car bumpers was a shining reminder of *Jurassic Park*. The real fine art was a portrait of Van Gogh made from toasted bread.

"We didn't find answers to your predicament, but we've filled an important gap in your cultural development." The matter-of-fact way Spence took her hand bespoke possession of a different sort.

"You're right. I might have lived my life without seeing an eight-legged pig or a two-headed calf. I'm sure I'm a better person for the experience." She laughed softly and glanced over her shoulder at the theater lights framing the Ripley's sign in a never-ending run. "Thank you for the laughter." She squeezed his hand. Before she walked into his office that afternoon, laughter was impossible. "Thank you for putting me first. I'm not sure what to say about that. Candice—"

"Business will wait until morning." He tilted his head toward the Bay. "The fog is rolling in."

"Don't change the subject, Spence. Being put first is new to me."

Spence guided them out of the stream of foot traffic on the Wharf and into the shelter of a building. "Get used to it, Roxanne."

*Not in a million years*. Being placed above self- or business interests was the grand prize in a contest she hadn't entered. She didn't deserve the honor. Each time she thought about the natural way he sloughed aside the responsibilities of a multimillion dollar business to do what? To make her laugh? Make her forget? Think of something other than what neither of them could change? It amazed her.

"Turn off the worry machine." Spence thumbed away the lock of hair the night breeze fluttered against her face. "You're more important to me than any business problem."

"You knew what Candice wanted, didn't you?" she demanded, sure she'd never have dropped everything to help him. Realizing she and her staff had done just that during the search for Erin and Brian, she groaned. This relationship was getting entirely too serious.

"It'll wait. You, on the other hand, were in desperate need of being kissed." He lowered his mouth to hers and brushed her lips.

"I was not—" Before she finished protesting, she was. "You're a magician."

"That's right, and if you spend the night with me, I'll make your clothes disappear."

Roxanne laughed and pushed him away. "It isn't my clothing I'd like to disappear."

"Neither is your father, metaphorically speaking. Looks like he's going to be part of our family." He slid a protective arm around her shoulders.

"Back up. What's this *our* family stuff? Are you adopting my father?"

"Sure. Speaking of him, let's clear up something."

She stared at the throng of spectators gathered around a juggler plying his talent for donations in the glow of a streetlight. "What?"

"I know you aren't attending the Memorial Day ceremony. That's your choice. I think I understand it a little better today than when you threw me out of your house."

"I did that, didn't I." Remembering made her frown. Thank heaven he had persisted. Spence was becoming the best friend she'd ever had.

"Where do you want him buried, Roxanne? He's entitled to a military ceremony, or you can place him beside your mother."

"I don't know anymore."

"What would your mother have wanted?"

Roxanne lifted her face to the damp air. "Put him beside her. Regardless of the way things turned out, they loved each other.

In the grand scheme of things, they had so little time together. This is the right thing." The decision finalized, she let it settle comfortably.

"Then our business is concluded. Let's get something to eat. What are you in the mood for?" The intimate way he looked at her revealed his greatest appetite.

A shiver of excitement ran over her skin. "Considering the exhibits we saw at Ripley's, anything but pork or beef!"

"You're in luck." He led her toward an open-air seafood market. "Neptune's bounty is at hand, and you're with a pro when it comes to picking the cream of the harvest."

The festive air he wove around selecting their dinner "victims" was contagious. She decided on the scallops—until he started naming them. Laughing, she clapped a hand over his mouth before he baptized the fillet of sole she decided on. Their dinner selection made, they entered the restaurant.

Spence's reputation preceded them. The maître d' personally escorted them to a window table overlooking the water. Moments later an excellent bottle of wine arrived as a courtesy from the management.

Roxanne relaxed and enjoyed the exchange of mutual compliments between Spence and the restaurant owner. The nods and acknowledging gestures proffered all the mystique of ancient ritual. She found it fascinating.

"I'm impressed," she said over the top of her wineglass. "If someone genuflects and grabs your hand, I'll know for sure I'm dining with the Don of Fisherman's Wharf."

"You are." The glint in his eyes made her question whether he was teasing or serious. She suspected the latter.

"I see. Do I want to know the particulars?"

"Of course you do, but we'd have to elope to Reno when we finish dinner. After we're married, I can tell you the smallest detail your curiosity craves for satiation." He lifted his wineglass and his left eyebrow as though waiting for agreement.

The eccentric direction of his answer astonished her into laughter. "Elope?" She laughed at the absurd notion. Not for a moment had she considered eloping. "Isn't the usual tact to give me a choice between knowing and death?"

"You're much too precious to threaten. You're made for love and loving. Besides, a wife cannot testify against her husband; I'd marry you." He set the glass down, folded his arms across the edge of the table, and then leaned forward. "Do you still want to know why I'm the Don of the Wharf?"

"Let me get this straight." She wondered if he was serious, then decided he couldn't be, but she'd play the game. "If I say yes, we elope to Reno? If I say no—"

"You forfeit an all-expenses-paid trip to beautiful downtown Reno and the pleasure of having me as your husband." His head tilted slightly. "And you lose the key to the Pandora's box of Fisherman's Wharf."

"Do I get to keep the fillet of sole I picked out for dinner?"

"Yes. I would never deprive you of sole food."

Roxanne groaned at his pun. The facets of his personality multiplied boundlessly. At first glance, the harsh angles of his features suggested a man equally hard. Whenever the door opened on his true nature, the depth of his heart and the richness of his unique sense of humor shone like beacons in a storm.

Mouthwatering aromas accompanied the arrival of their meal. "I'm actually hungry," she said, amazed.

Through dinner she paid close attention to his mannerisms and the subtle ways he telegraphed his moods. Over dessert she approached the delicate subject she hoped wouldn't ruin the evening.

"Tell me something, Spence."

"Maybe." He indulged in a courteous sampling of the Mud Pie, then abandoned it for coffee.

"What prompted you to investigate us so thoroughly?" Mentally she held her breath.

"If we made a mistake in identifying the remains of one of our soldiers, the government can't be sued. As a private organization straddling two governments, we can, so we have to cover ourselves. Juries have a tendency to award hefty punitive damages for pain and suffering if there's a mistake on the identification."

"I don't suppose anyone has ever sued you for being right," she suggested.

"You would be the first." The edge in his voice accentuated the sudden wariness behind his narrowed gaze.

"Hey, I was teasing." Sensitive area, she decided. "Not to worry, Spence. I'm allergic to courtrooms. Please, continue."

"There isn't much to add. We investigate so we notify the right people—it's usually the immediate family. Vietnam was a long time ago. Women remarried. Families moved. People died.

"Initially all we had was a dog tag so corroded all we could make out was the name Griffith. My brother was lost in the same general area. That's why we thought it was Mitch. The military investigators at Hickam Air Force Base in Hawaii made a positive ID of your father from the service number from the dog tag.

"When we started investigating Matthew Griffith, we located Thelma, then you. Few families reside at the home of record address a soldier used during the war."

He took her hand and ran his thumb over her knuckles. "Once we learned Thelma was in the final stages of leukemia, we thought you might need help in coping with what might be a double-whammy. We branched out and looked into your mother's family."

Thus far, it sounded logical. "And you found my grandmother."

"No, we didn't, but we learned a lot about her. Janice Boyle was a surprise." He gazed out the window long enough to make her uneasy. "How much do you know about your mother's family?"

"Nothing. The Griffiths detested them. I had no reason to look for them. They made their position clear when they didn't bother to show up for my mothers service." She turned her hand over and caught his fingers. "I recall how angry Thelma was at the time. The next day she started formal guardianship proceedings."

She daubed the corners of her mouth with her napkin. "Ahh, Spence, no kid wants to feel as alone as I was. I used to make up stories about why no one from my mother's family ever came to see me. I knew I had a grandmother. In my mind she was a Mrs. Santa Claus clone."

The flush of embarrassment crept up her neck and over her cheeks. "Silly, huh?"

"Not for a little girl with a fantasy heroine."

One glance at him confirmed the conviction of his belief. She supposed he was right. She recited the Litany of the Grateful Child according to Thelma Griffith. "I never missed a meal. I had clothes. I lived in a nice house in the best school district in the Valley. I wasn't on the street or shuffled around in foster care. And I was never physically abused."

"I didn't hear love in there," he said softly.

"By the time she died, Thelma and I loved each other." She squeezed his hand.

"Sounds miserable, but I think you had a better childhood with

Thelma than you would have had with Janice." Spence ran the pad of his thumb over her knuckles. "This is one of those times when absence is the best course. Leave the whole issue of Janice Boyle alone."

"I can't. She called me this afternoon. I'm having lunch with her Friday."

"Why?"

"If there's anything I've learned from you, Spence, it's the importance of family. I can't ignore her. Like it or not, she is my grandmother." A sharp laugh escaped her. "Some family? An absentee grandmother, a ghost for a father, and who else, Spence? Who else came out from under the rock you turned over?"

For the second night in a row, when the moon rose on Marian Griffith's grave, her husband's spirit huddled against the headstone.

Matt didn't know where to go, what to do, or how to undo the damage he'd unintentionally inflicted on their daughter. He'd never meant to share his pain with her. On the contrary, had he known she'd experienced his private hell, he'd have never considered borrowing her body.

The passage of time weighed heavily on his awareness. It did nothing to alleviate the guilt eating him.

He'd called upon the Guardian, and received silence.

There was no help for him, no divine revelation. He knew in his heart what he had to do. The path lay clear. The risk was the greatest he'd ever faced.

With a ghostly hand, he stroked the letters of Marian's name carved into the granite. Twenty-two years of exposure to the elements had softened the edges of the letters. Then again, Marian had had no rough or sharp edges, just softness and love. What he wouldn't give for a thimbleful of it now.

"I'm afraid, Marian. Doesn't that beat all? I've wronged her. Again." Being afraid of someone was a new experience he could have done without. How ironic that he hadn't experienced the helpless, hopeless fear of having his destiny in someone else's hands until now.

The boot of despair pressed hard on his spirit. In that dark moment, he knew he deserved to spend eternity disintegrating in the Abyss of Nothingness.

Suddenly, a spark of comprehension flared like a match striking in a storm.

If he gave up now, the Abyss had him forever. His inability to predict Roxanne's reaction might work in his favor. And it might not. Either way he had to face her.

The crushing fear of her judgment was secondary to the sorrow that had paralyzed him since he'd invaded her body. If child abuse had a poster boy, the face belonged to him. He owed her an apology, which he intended to deliver.

He couldn't wait any longer.

He said a silent prayer on the way back to Griffith Gables. By the time he entered the house, he understood the meaning of courage and bravery; if a man was unafraid to begin with, he required neither. He would need both when confronting his daughter.

In consideration for her electric bill, Matt restricted the blazing wattage to the kitchen. He waited in the center of the island for her to come home. When he sensed her approaching the house, he put on the teakettle and laid out the service.

He knew his actions were blatantly superficial and designed to ingratiate, but he couldn't help it. Such was his nature.

Dressed in a tailored business suit, Roxanne entered the kitchen juggling her purse, briefcase, and one shoe while trying to remove the other.

Matt collected her shoes and briefcase, then neatly arranged them on the island.

"You're back." She eyed the whistling teakettle suspiciously, then looked around the room

It took all Matt's courage to manifest so she could see him. He watched her from a stool at the island.

"What gives? You fix me tea and actually sit *on* the furniture in the same night? Are all the rest of the lightbulbs burned out?" She barely took her gaze off him while washing her hands.

"I'm sorry, Roxanne. From the bottom of my heart, I'm sorry for what happened Sunday. I never meant to hurt you . . . to have you feel what I felt . . . to experience the burden of the sins I can't atone for even now. I won't ask you to forgive me. I don't know if forgiveness is even possible for what I did to you. I just want you to know I am sorry." He had never meant anything as sincerely as this apology.

Roxanne poured boiling water over a tea bag in a mug. "Is that why you've stayed away? Afraid to face me?"

"Yes," he answered and swallowed, another lesson in humility.

"What did you expect me to do? Tell you to leave? I've already done that. Tell you to go to hell? You've already been there." When she faced him, the tea mug trembling in her hand, tears filled her eyes.

"I feared your rejection," he whispered, trying to slow the guilt and sorrow coloring his aura.

"Both of us wish things hadn't turned out the way they did. I sure as hell don't want your memories, your guilt, and certainly not your pain. But most of all, I didn't want to understand." Tears spilled over her lower lashes and flowed down her cheeks.

"I'm sorry," he managed in a raspy whisper. The last thing he expected was compassion.

"There's nothing for either one of us to apologize for. It seemed like a good idea at the time."

"You forgive me?" All his fear turned to a soul-pulverizing sorrow. He'd used her. Shamelessly. Without regard for the consequences she'd live with for the rest of her life.

Roxanne picked up her shoes with her free hand. "Forgiveness?" Her tear-filled brown eyes—so like Marian's—regarded him sympathetically. "For what? Part of having some of your memories and thoughts is knowing you had no idea this would happen. I can't deny it any more than I can blame you. It happened. We can't undo it, just deal with the way things are. Case closed."

"I'm still sorry."

"Well, while you're being so accommodating, how about turning on the lights so I can go upstairs? My hands are full." She headed for the kitchen door. "Leave them on, Matt."

"I . . ." The relief washing through him, dancing with vibrant color in his aura, robbed his ability to speak. The fear, uncertainty, and guilt he'd wallowed in at Marian's grave had been for naught. He'd spend the rest of the night trying to understand.

"Good night," she said from the door.

He turned on every light in the house.

"Leave them on," she repeated on her way out. "I bought stock in PG and E today."

When the awe faded and reality settled, he went to the rose garden and contemplated how best he could help his daughter during the twelve short days he had left with her.

● ● ●

"You invited that woman into our home?" Matt demanded from above the refrigerator.

Unknowingly, Inez had agreed with Matt's desire to blackball Janice Boyle from the Griffith home. The housekeeper had prepared the luncheon meal, then took the rest of the day off. The strong show of emotion from the normally amiable housekeeper spoke loudly.

But Roxanne had made up her mind. Now it was lunch time. Inez was gone. Matt sulked on the center of the dining room table. "You neglected to share any memories that justify turning my back on what may be the last living relative I have." The long lunch she'd scheduled for today suddenly seemed a questionable idea. Regardless, she was going to hear the other side of the story.

"You know, for a man in search of a second chance, you're pretty closed-minded when it comes to others looking for the same thing." She carried the salads into the dining room. "If you aren't going to be of help, stay out of sight and keep silent. I don't need any more surprises from you."

The doorbell rang before he responded. Roxanne expected him to disappear into the woodwork and brood.

She took a deep breath as she crossed the foyer and reached for the knob.

Clad in a flowery spring dress beneath a smart jersey jacket, two-inch heels, and a blue leather clutch, Janice Boyle didn't look like anyone's grandmother. Soft white curls framed her face. Despite the glasses, her cosmetics accentuated her eyes and managed to diminish the finer badges of age and hard living.

The two women survived the awkwardness of the first few minutes unscathed. Roxanne invited her grandmother into the house. She marveled at the unabashed curiosity Janice showed in the house.

"The house has undergone several remodelings over the years."

"It's Thelma all the way." As though satisfied with the assessment, Janice ended her perusal.

"Yes, it is." It was Roxanne's turn to examine the elegant furnishings, silk wallpaper, and the thick rugs on the highly polished wood and marble floors with a new eye.

"Lunch is ready. We'll be serving ourselves. Inez had to leave." Roxanne gestured toward the dining room.

"I'm too old for discretion, Roxanne. Inez left because she hates me." Janice settled into a chair at the exquisitely set table.

"But she still makes the best crab salad on the West Coast."

Roxanne draped her napkin over her lap. Her fickle appetite had fled. She picked up her fork, then set it down. Meanwhile, the elderly woman delved into the crab salad as though she hadn't eaten in days.

While Roxanne nibbled on fruit, cheese, and crackers, her mind ran in circles. She waited until her grandmother's plate was nearly empty before breaking the silence.

"We'll set diplomacy aside, Janice. Tell me what you want from me."

"I do want something from you, Roxanne." She reached for the coffeepot from the silver tray strategically placed between them. "It isn't what you think. Even the Griffith money can't turn the clock back for me." She smiled thinly and poured coffee into their cups.

"You're right. I can't turn the clock back. So you'll settle for money?" Given Janice's background, it seemed the logical conclusion. "How much?" Roxanne pushed aside her plate. At least this time Janice was asking for it up front. According to Matt, after he married Marian, Janice had solicited and received several large loans from the Griffiths, none of which she repaid.

Janice sat back in her chair. Her rheumy brown gaze never wavered from Roxanne's. "I deserved that."

"Just how much do you think you deserve?"

"I'm not here to extort money from you, Roxanne."

*A good con makes it your idea to part with what they want.* Spence's words rattled through her mind. So did all the things he'd told her about the Boyle family. "Well, why don't we start at the beginning. Why didn't you come to my mother's funeral?"

"Because I was serving time for armed robbery." Janice didn't even flinch.

Spence had forewarned her about Janice's past but hearing it from her grandmother's mouth rocked her. "I knew you'd . . . done time for a felony. I didn't realize it was during the time my mother died."

"If you already know my rap sheet, why ask?"

"Sometimes there are reasons. They don't right a wrong, just provide a glimmer of insight."

"Is that why you agreed to have lunch with me? To get a rundown of excuses for my rap sheet?" The steel backbone of a seasoned survivor was evident in her clipped words and abrupt demeanor.

"Soften her. Ask about Marian," Matt whispered in Roxanne's ear.

"The only thing we have in common is my mother," Roxanne said. "You knew Mom her whole life. I had her a short six years, most of which I was too young to recall. You must have loved her. You visited her grave."

Janice loaded her coffee with cream and sugar. The tinkle of the silver spoon against the fine porcelain marked the silence. Finally she laid her spoon in the saucer. "She was my daughter, but she was so unlike me. Unlike us. At times I thought she was a Changeling." She looked sharply at Roxanne. "You do know what a Changeling is, don't you?"

"Yes, if you're referring to medieval times and fairy legends where human babies were switched for weaker fairy children."

Janice nodded. "Marian was born with a moral streak that shunned anything on the gray side of righteousness. She was your basic, good person and no one or nothing could change her because she was true to herself. In our family that was the equivalent to having a severe birth defect.

"I didn't just love Marian, I worshipped her because I knew she was something good. Someone special." Janice sipped her coffee, then continued staring at the cup as she spoke; her mind focused on something Roxanne couldn't see. "But she didn't fit into the family. When she was fourteen, I rented a room for her in this school district. It was the only way I could give her a shot at what she wanted. She worked her tail off and stayed in school.

"When she graduated high school and started college, my sister Cheryl and I went to Los Angeles. Without Marian, our conscience, nagging us, things went down hill."

"Where is Cheryl now?" Roxanne asked as gently as possible.

"After I got out of prison, I was going to go straight. Cheryl was involved with a crowd too rough for me. But after a few hungry months of job hunting, I worked for Cheryl's drug dealers. She overdosed. I went off the deep end and tried to kill her dealer. I ended up doing hard time for attempted murder. That was eighteen years ago. I got out of prison six months ago."

Thank heaven Spence had prepared her for Janice's history. "A rehabilitated woman, huh?"

A more relaxed Janice poured more coffee for herself. "There are many forms of rehabilitation. They all start inside. I hit rock bottom when I was in prison. Since getting out, I had nowhere to go but up."

"Up?" Roxanne hadn't a clue what she meant.

"I joined the Army."

Nonplussed, Roxanne stared at her. "The Army. Weren't you a little old for boot camp?"

"The Salvation Army. I've been with them for six months, since I got out." She retrieved her purse, opened it, and withdrew a business card, which she placed on the table. A knowing smile deepened the wrinkles on her cheeks. "In case you ever want to get in touch with me in Tulsa, Oklahoma. Or check out my story. I know . . . it's hard to believe people can change. It's even harder to do it."

"Amen, sister," came Matt's voice from behind Roxanne.

The temptation to turn around and question him put her on pins and needles.

"What do I want from you, Roxanne? I want the most precious thing in the universe. A chance. Time. Just a little. Enough to know you even a little bit."

"A chance," Roxanne repeated slowly.

"It's a chance for you, too," Matt whispered. "Never turn your back on a chance to do something good. Even if it turns out wrong. You don't know how many chances are left for you or her."

"Are you all right, Roxanne?" Janice leaned toward her. "Or are you searching for a polite way to ask me to leave?"

"I'm just feeling a little crazy at the moment," she managed. Matt's about-face concerning his mother-in-law defied logic. Staring at Janice, she couldn't help wondering about her grandmother's life, what she'd seen, done, and the depth of her sincerity. Later, she would check out her story. But something about the woman wouldn't tolerate rejection.

Later, she assured herself. And she'd ask Spence for the investigative firm he'd used. If she was being conned, Janice was damn good.

But if it really was a chance . . .

Roxanne smiled, her decision made. "Would you like dessert?"

# *Chapter Twenty-one*

Suspended above the beach the last Sunday evening in May, Matt watched Roxanne stroll along the waterline. Overhead, gulls stalked the surf and shore for a final meal. Sand crabs scurried in the foamy kelp strands.

The time remaining to salvage his soul had run out. Tomorrow his six weeks were over. A strange peace settled over him. He might not escape the Abyss, but he suspected it wouldn't be as dark as before.

"How are my memories treating you?"

Roxanne's gaze searched, and then narrowed on him. "They're settling in, just as you seem to be wherever I go. They're a unique version of 'Getting to Know You' from the inside out. As for coping with your memories"—she shrugged and kicked at the spume lingering on the wet sand—"I don't have much choice. But don't ever ask to use my body or voice again."

"I won't. I don't expect you to forgive me for the way it turned out." He stilled, braced for rejection.

"Yeah. How can I not? You didn't know. Speaking of forgiveness, which seems heavy on your mind these days, how did it go with Greg last night?" Roxanne angled toward the cottage and dry sand.

Matt drank in her height and the natural grace of her walk. During the bleak eternity ahead, he'd picture his beautiful daughter walking along the ocean, her jeans rolled up and her bare feet coated with sand. The restless sea mirrored her personality: tranquil until roused, and always deep.

Dear God in heaven, how did he father such a magnificent woman?

"Each of us views reality through the lens of our own perception."

"You're turning philosopher?"

"Comes from being around Greg. Between the two of us, he was the philosopher, the heavy thinker."

"He's very insightful." She sat on a dune, hugged her knees, and met his gaze. Sand facets caught the long rays of the sun and shimmered on her skin. "Can he see you yet?"

"Yes. We spoke most of the night. I learned something, too."

"Really? What did you learn?" She brushed a lock of windblown hair from her eyes.

"Sometimes it is as important to forgive as to be forgiven. Greg wanted . . . No, he needed my forgiveness for shooting me down. Although it wasn't his fault, he still needed absolution." Finally, Greg was finding the peace he craved before he ventured into the light at the end of his life."

Roxanne nodded her head and threw a playful smile at her father. "That isn't a recurring problem for you, is it? Needing to forgive someone, I mean."

"No. I have too many real grievances against me." He winked at her. "I was a proactive sinner."

Roxanne laughed aloud. Matt had noticed that since deciding to get to know her grandmother, she seemed more relaxed. It gladdened his heart that Roxanne had taken the risk and opened her own heart before receiving a confirmation of Janice's story.

"At least you didn't sit on your hands," she said. "There are situations when I preferred doing something—even if it was the wrong thing—to doing nothing."

In this light she was the image of Marian. "You not only got your mother's physical beauty, you got her heart. She had an amazing capacity for love, patience, and perseverance. The ability to wait is a talent."

Roxanne laughed softly. "Then you have one very talented daughter. When I look back, it seems like as soon as I was born,

I was waiting for something and I just never stopped."

"How so?" It pained him to think of her wasting one precious minute not living her life to the fullest.

"I waited for you to come home from the war and make things right. I waited for Thelma to love me. So many foolish things seem possible in the mind of a child."

"But you weren't idle. You got an education and built a business. Even waiting has limits. If you exceed them, the chances for achieving your dreams pass by unnoticed. The dreams remain just that—dreams." When applied to his own life, the words became knives slicing guilty cuts into his flimsy character. Thank God, his daughter was made of sterner stuff. "However, your wait to be rid of me is almost at an end."

In a flurry of sand, she straightened her legs. "What do you mean? Are you going somewhere?"

Was that concern in her eyes? "Yes. Tomorrow." *A heartbeat away.*

"How do you know this?" she demanded as though expecting him to reverse a decision over which he had no control.

"The same way you know the sun in going down." Maybe she would miss him—a little. Selfishly, he hoped she would think about him occasionally. The prospect made him surprisingly happy.

"I mean, is there some sort of ghost train leaving at a set time?" The long shadows of dusk accented her confusion. Her dark gaze bored into him. His happiness bubble burst in the face of her distress.

"I was granted a final chance to make amends to those I've hurt. Now I realize the opportunity had an ulterior purpose."

She caught a handful of sand and let it slip through her fingers. "Which is?"

"Understanding. The chance to know the truth." And he wouldn't have missed the opportunity to know his daughter even if it meant instant consignment to the Abyss.

It was his last evening in the corporeal realm, and he was still learning. Genuine gratitude was new. He savored the heart-swelling emotion and offered a silent prayer of thanks.

"The truth? About what?" She leaned forward as though eager to hear his answer.

"My life. Ironically, it is different for each of us because of the choices we made and the ones we ignored." He laced his fingers behind his head and took a quick look at the sky. The first stars of night were winking into life. "I'm becoming maudlin."

"I won't see you again after tomorrow?" Disappointment knit her brow.

"You sound almost sad, Roxanne. Could it be you've gotten used to having your dear old dad around?"

An air of vulnerability softened her features. Sorrow darkened her eyes. "You have a way of growing on a person. If you have to go . . . Yeah, I'll miss you."

Sadly, Matt accepted the change without a challenge. "It isn't my choice."

Suddenly agitated, she checked her watch, then stood. "I have a pizza in the oven."

"Then you'd better get it out. He's coming," Matt said. The lights in the cottage burned brightly against the encroaching night. Judging by the way Roxanne hugged her arms, the temperature was dropping quickly.

"Who?" She peered up at the house. "Spence?"

"He's your future, if you aren't too afraid to take the chance." He retreated toward the troubled sea.

"Where are you going?"

He shrugged. "You'll see me tomorrow."

She stared at him for a moment before nodding.

"Meanwhile, Roxanne, think about the difference surviving life and living it. The path you choose makes a big difference to your soul."

For the small eternity she met his gaze, the sorrow in her eyes warmed his heart. When she turned away, her shoulders rigid with unspoken emotion, he retreated.

Hovering over the incessant waves, he watched her trudge through the sand toward the cottage. She looked back once. He remained motionless and waited until she was safely inside.

Instead of being relieved at the prospect of her ghost's departure, Roxanne felt strangely bereft. Matt emanated too much light and zest to return to the dark place he feared. But then, she had no idea of how things worked on the other side. Matt's presence assured there was indeed something after the years ended.

Pondering ramifications that expanded by the second, Roxanne left her shoes on the porch step and entered the beach cottage. The aroma of the pizza she'd left warming in the oven filled the

air. She checked on her dinner, turned off the oven, then brought
out the salad and a cold root beer.

She set everything on the counter, picked up the stereo remote,
and selected a soft rock station.

A sharp rap on the kitchen porch door brought her head up.
Before she crossed the room, the door opened.

"Spence," she breathed, delighted beyond words to see him.

"Actually, I'm not Spence. I'm a burglar dressed in Griffith's
clothing." He closed and locked the door. "Matt must be around,
huh?" He tossed his windbreaker at the hooks beside the door. It
caught neatly.

"He was here earlier." She studied him, wondering about
Matt's assertion that Spence was her future. "How about some
salad and pizza?"

"Sold." He washed up at the kitchen sink while she set another
place at the table.

"I didn't expect to see you until Tuesday evening at the earli-
est." The dismal prospect had made this the longest three-day
weekend in her personal history, and there was still another day
to go. "I'm glad you got away for a few minutes."

"I wanted to see you, even if it was to deliver papers I could
have mailed." He dropped the packet on the counter, then caught
her in his arms.

She shook the oven mitts from her hands and reached for him.
"Kiss me."

His body hard against hers and the wild, wonderful acceleration
of everything good and alive was what she wanted. His tender,
intoxicating lovemaking was exactly what she needed tonight, and
maybe next week. Maybe even longer.

Instead of kissing her, he surprised her by cupping her face in
his big hands. The pad of his thumb slid over her bottom lip and
whetted her appetite for a taste of him. The restless excitement
building in her had the tenacity of the ocean waves crashing
against the shore.

"I'm the one for you, Roxanne. Your heart knows it. So does
your body." Conviction burned brightly in his dark blue eyes. His
head moved closer and tilted slightly. Her arms tightened around
his waist. "You love me, Roxanne. Admit it."

Before she had a chance to admit or deny anything, his hand
slid around the back of her head. He claimed her mouth in a slow,
savage kiss. The sweet fire of anticipation flared so hot and fast

that she had to hold on to him to keep from crumbling into the flame. On a primal level she *felt* his body speak to hers. She let the emotions penetrate the depths of her heart, and welcomed them without question.

Only when the kiss ended did she experience a flicker of trepidation.

"Pizza, huh?" He released her slowly.

She held him, her body quaking with the same kind of sexual need that intensified each time they made love. For a split second, admitting her love for him seemed a good idea.

Reality struck with the force of a storm. She loved him, there was no undoing it.

"Ah, would you like a root beer?" she managed, then let go of him.

"I'll get it. You do the pizza." He went to the refrigerator, and she groped for a chair, then sat.

"Matt says you're my future, if I'm willing to take the chance." The words spilled into the room without thought. "He's leaving tomorrow."

Spence hesitated, then closed the refrigerator. "Let's take these one at a time."

"Pizza and salad first?" The quaking inside her increased with each step he took toward the table.

He twisted the top off the root beer bottle. "As for your father leaving, did he give you a reason?"

A small sigh of relief escaped that he hadn't pressed for some kind of commitment or agreement on their future. "No, he, ah, dropped the news on me, then left."

"I see. Has he finished whatever he had to do here?"

Staring into Spence's patient eyes, she shook her head. "From what I gather, I'd say he doesn't consider himself successful. Though, from what he's told me, he hasn't failed, either."

"I wonder if the timing of his departure is because you're burying him tomorrow," Spence mused.

"We aren't burying his remains tomorrow. That's next Saturday." She looked away. "Greg asked me to wait another week so he and some friends could attend. I didn't see any harm in a postponement. It doesn't affect your ceremony tomorrow."

"We located your father's CO. He's flying in tonight. He'll do the eulogy."

"He didn't even know my father. What about Greg?"

"Funny, he asked the same question about you."

She turned sideways in her chair.

The cell phone in his jacket warbled a summons. He rose from the table and retrieved the phone. "No one is asking anything of you, Roxanne. If you change your mind and decide to attend, you still have the choice of being a spectator or a participant. The door is open."

She didn't know if she could confront the disappointment of MIA families still searching for loved ones. That took more strength and courage than any human possessed. But to eulogize her father, to stand before his peers and verbally express what having his remains on American soil meant to her . . .

Fear shot through her. Again, the choice boiled down to waiting out the day by doing nothing and doing something.

Spence spoke on the phone for several minutes, then reached for his jacket. "I have to go. Seems your father's CO caught a military hop into Travis Air Force Base and saved the Foundation the price of the airfare. I have to pick him up in a couple of hours."

As though drawn on an invisible string, she rose and crossed the room to where he waited beside the door. "Two hours isn't much time in holiday traffic."

"No, it isn't." He kissed her lightly, then opened the door.

"In regard to the observation your father made about us, plain and simply put, I *am* your future, Roxanne. I love you. I want to marry you. Have children with you. Grow old with you. All I ask of you is to love me forever. There's no middle ground. It's simple."

He certainly made it sound that way. So why was she so afraid of following her heart? He already owned it. The thought of marrying him and having children with him excited and terrified her.

He pulled on his jacket. "I can fix a lot of things, but not your fear of loving me."

Her heart beat as though trying to escape her chest. God, was she that transparent? Gazing into his clear eyes, she knew he meant every word he'd spoken. Disoriented, totally at odds, she saw the same fiery need in his face that she felt. "Spence, I do love you. I . . ."

Hope brightened his smile. Excitement burned in his eyes. "I know. And I'm damn glad you do, too. We're so good together, Roxanne. So right. Think about it. All of it."

"I will. All of it," she promised, nearly overwhelmed by the prospect of marriage and children.

"Good." He caught her hand and brought it to his lips. "I wish the colonel had taken a commercial flight so we could make mad, passionate love on the beach. Tomorrow night, Roxanne."

"Me, too." Her fingertips brushed his smooth-shaved cheek. "If I come tomorrow . . ."

He kissed her with a tempered passion. Every nerve in her body answered his silent plea for a commitment to a future she could barely grasp.

When he broke the kiss, he squeezed her hand. "If you show up, you show up. Tell me what you want then."

After his car pulled away, she returned to the cottage and closed the door. In the dining room, the dinner neither of them had touched sat waiting.

Matt's words echoed inside her head. She had a choice between surviving life and actually living it by participating.

It was so simple.

All she had to do was take a chance and trust what was in her heart.

Roxanne let Janice take her cold, clammy hand. A May afternoon breeze teased with a promise of a hot summer. The manicured hills of Golden Gate National Cemetery rolled on a green-grass sea topped with precision whitecaps of military grave markers. Small flags fluttered beside each grave. Clusters of bright flowers hugged some of the headstones. In the distance a band played "America, The Beautiful." The American flag waved overhead as though beckoning the passersby on the freeway into the memorial.

They'd barely started down the walkway before the enormity of the cemetery crashed down on Roxanne. Her breath caught in her throat as she stared at the rows and rows of the nation's dead. "So many men," she finally breathed. "I've driven past this place a thousand times, but I'd never really looked at it."

"Take it from one who knows the true meaning of freedom, it doesn't come cheap. Whether you believe in a war or not, it makes no difference to the men under the markers." Janice patted her hand. "Come on. We're late."

Roxanne drew a deep breath. "Guess we follow the music."

"Or the signs." Janice pointed at a directional marker.

The music grew louder. A couple of old men in VFW caps and

khaki vests laden with pins and patches stood beside the headstone of a fallen comrade. Closer to the main gathering, two
younger women in their fifties placed flowers and a second small
flag beside a headstone. Somewhere a child laughed.

The band started a crisp rendition of "This Is My Country."

Roxanne stopped in her tracks. For a moment, she thought
she'd suffocate from the potent emotion rising from some unknown place inside her. Tears stung her eyes, though she had no
reason to cry. Then it struck her. All these men had served their
country. These men were resting in their final home. Their families and friends knew their whereabouts. They had their closure
and opportunity to grieve.

Her father's ghost was leaving today.

Six weeks ago the news of his imminent departure would have
called for a celebration. How things had changed in such a short
time.

"Do you know that woman?" Janice asked.

"Who?" Thick-throated and blurry-eyed, Roxanne turned in the
direction Janice indicated. "Oh. Yes. That's Candice Cathcart, one
of Spence's closest friends. She's also his Marketing VP at Griffith Enterprises." Thankful for the distraction, she tamped down
the jumble of inexplicable emotion and made the introductions.

"I'm glad you came," Candice said. Today, she was ethereal
in a long dress made of flowing white cotton. Her only adornment
was an American flag patch sewn above her left breast.

"I've changed my mind. I'm here as a participant." No sooner
were the words out than Matt materialized beside Candice.

"Come with me, daughter." Matt extended his hand to show
her the way.

Impervious to everything else around her, Roxanne stepped forward and walked beside him. She couldn't take her eyes off of
him. Suddenly she had a desperate need to memorize every detail
of his transparent face, and every frayed thread of his tattered
flight suit. He caught her gaze, then gave her a classic Matt Griffith smile.

She wanted to cry out at the injustice of his leaving before she
got to know him the way a father and daughter should know each
other. God, had she really spent all those years hating him?

"You're leaving very soon, aren't you?" she said when they
reached the staging area.

"It feels that way. You're the best part of your mother and me.

I'm proud of you." He hovered in front of her, effectively halting her. "Be happy, Roxanne."

She reached for him, and he disappeared. Another hand caught and clasped hers. When she looked up, it was into familiar, concerned blue eyes. The tumult tilting her world robbed her of her voice.

"I'm glad you changed your mind." Spence stood beside her at the bottom of the stairs. "Would you like to join Candice or some of the family?"

She struggled for a moment, then swallowed hard. "No. I'd like to join you on the platform," she whispered. "I've come to eulogize my father."

Spence's only reaction was the slight arch of his eyebrows. "Are you sure you want to do this?"

She'd never been surer of anything in her life. Today was the day she stopped waiting and started participating in life. In an almost surreal atmosphere, she took her place on the makeshift stage. Red, white, and blue bunting hid the plywood fronts and equipment boxes.

Roxanne went through the formalities of introductions to the dignitaries sharing the stage before she settled on the edge of her metal folding chair, her hands in her lap. Spence remained at her right side while she searched the crowd for familiar faces.

The speakers at the podium rotated, and the television cameramen prowled the stage. She studied the faces of the spectators. The men in wheelchairs were reminders of narrow escapes in the war machine. Neither race nor creed segregated them. The vintage of the war that changed their lives imposed their groupings. The men with Greg Detweiler were clean and polished today. In their midst wandered the ghost of Matthew Griffith. Greg caught her eye, then nodded encouragement.

When it was her turn to speak, she went to the podium and cleared her throat. "Six weeks ago Mr. Spencer No-Relation Griffith came to my door and gave me a gift. That gift was my father."

She looked across the sea of hats denoting battles and decorated with medals, Purple Hearts, and commemorative pins—and into the faces of patriotism.

"Captain Matthew Mayhew Griffith died before I was born. How can a daughter get to know her father so long after the jungle of Vietnam claimed him? I've spent the last six weeks on that journey."

She looked over her shoulder at Spence, who gave her a thumbs-up sign.

"Please, bear with me. I'd like to address you all as though *you* were my father, and say some of the things I'd like him to hear." She smiled at Matt's ghost poised beside Greg. "And maybe he will."

She took the microphone from the holder fixed to the podium and walked around a cameraman to the corner of the stage. "When I was a child, I didn't understand why you didn't come home, Dad. I'd found my doll's shoe after it had been missing for a year. Surely, something as big as a man couldn't stay missing for so long.

"That was before I knew how many ways there are to become lost." Her gaze drifted to Janice standing with Candice, Carolyn, Erin, and a man she assumed was Carolyn's husband.

"You were blessed with a special gift. You made people laugh. You knew how to have fun. According to my mother's letters and diaries, you weren't big on tending to details; and you seemed to have an allergy to long-range planning." She sought Matt and found him watching her with a peculiar intensity. "But there were no boundaries on her love for you, Dad. She waited and never gave up hope.

"You lived your life to the fullest and went from one grand adventure to the next as though you knew you had to take big bites because you weren't going to be at the banquet of life very long. Twenty-five is too young to die." She continued slowly pacing the stage. "I'm not ready to part with you without knowing you. Perhaps I'll never be ready. I still want the fun, the silliness, the laughter that always accompanied you." She blinked hard to keep the tears stinging her eyes from falling. "But death isn't a democracy.

"There are some things I want to thank you for, Dad. First and foremost, thank you for your choice of my mother. I understand why you loved each other."

"Amen," called Greg Detweiler. Laughter erupted around him, but he wasn't looking at her. He and Matt stood alone in a very different realm.

"Thank you for your choice of friends. Whenever I hear the term 'best friend,' I think of your best friend, Greg Detweiler. Preschool, right, Greg?" She pointed at him, then smiled when he nodded. "Your best friend, Dad, who loved us all enough to watch over me in a special way when Mom died. He started my college fund and let me think it was from Mom until I discovered the truth.

"Dad, I'd like to thank you for the gift of laughter, for some of your sense of humor flows through my veins. Thank you for your sense of adventure, and by example, giving me the courage to take a risk. A chance. You're proof we don't all get the same number of chances for the good stuff.

"Through the memories you leave behind, I've learned the value of forgiveness and the enrichment of keeping an open heart and mind. It's been a fast, whirlwind six weeks, Dad. But, I guess that's how it always was around you. That's why you were missed so very much.

"You had a reputation for doing the unexpected. So, I'll take that to heart. If you're in the neighborhood, stop by and say hello. I'll leave a light on for you." She shared a tremulous smile with Matt, then sniffed.

She returned to the podium and took a drink of water, then lifted her gaze and stared into Matt's blue eyes. "I love you, Dad," she whispered. "I'll always miss you, and I'll tell my children about you and Mom. So, go with God on the adventure you find on the other side."

Her chin quivered. Beside Greg, Matt began to fade. She wanted to reach out, call him back and make him stay. Her gaze locked on his. A veil of tears distorted him, then spilled down her cheeks. With each rapid heartbeat, his image grew fainter.

"I love you, too," came the sigh of his voice on the sudden afternoon breeze. She watched until he disappeared into the empty air. Greg stared at the empty space beside him and wept openly.

Just like that, it was over. Her father was gone.

She drew a ragged breath and looked across the sea of expectant faces. "I'd like to show my appreciation to the Remembrance Foundation by donating the proceeds from the sale of the house my father and I called home. I put it on the market this morning. It seems appropriate that the money go to supporting the cost of searching for other fathers, sons, brothers, and husbands still in Vietnam. It is a long journey."

Heart in hand, she turned away from the podium and found Spence at her side. Pride and love softened the harsh angles of his face and burned brightly in his eyes.

"You were right last night. I do love you. More than I thought it possible. Are you still willing to take a chance on me?"

"You bet. Are you using all your bravado in one place?"

She sniffed again, then took a handful of tissues from Senator Quinton Norton. "It seems so."

"Then finish it."

She looked up at him and sniffed. "I'll love you forever, Spence."

"And you'll marry me?" Spence asked.

"Yes."

He caught her in a crushing embrace and planted a big kiss on her mouth. Dimly she heard laughter, applause, then the brass band playing "I'm Gettin' Married in the Morning." Through it all she heard Matt's parting whisper in her ear, "He *will* love you forever, dear daughter. And so will I."

# Epilogue

Roxanne sat between her twin three-year-old boys and read the final bedtime story for the night. Earlier, Matthew and Mitchell had worn her to a frazzle at the Memorial Day ceremony. It seemed appropriate for the twin terrors named after the men lost in Vietnam to rule their corner of the ceremony.

They were growing up too fast. Already their blond locks were darkening. She tucked them in and kissed each good night. On the way out of their bedroom she adjusted the lamp on the dresser so it shone on Matt's bed but not Mitch's.

"Thanks, Mom," Matt said.

She chuckled at the ritual. Matt's first words were "light on," though he'd made his demand for a lighted room known the day he came home from the hospital by crying whenever the room turned dark. "You're welcome, son. Anytime."

The child with her father's name and eyes smiled his smile, and she smiled back at him, then exchanged a wink with Mitch. For the thousandth time she wondered if her father had found a way into her life in a manner that turned the tables.

She left the boys' bedroom door open a little. Before retiring, she and Spence would check on the boys again.

"They went down easy tonight," Spence said and took her

hand. He led her onto the terrace overlooking the ocean, then handed her a cup of hot tea.

"Only because they ran us ragged at the cemetery. Three-year-olds have no sense of tradition." She appreciated the hot tea in the cool evening. "Did you salvage the bathroom?"

"Yeah. If we keep playing submarine—"

"You're spoiling them."

". . . and they keep growing—"

"Unless you saw signs of shrinkage tonight, that's a given."

". . . we're going to need a swimming pool."

"No." She didn't want a pool until the children were much older.

"A hot tub? With a kid sensor system?"

"It'll have to be big," she said. "And tighter than Fort Knox on the security measures. Those two are going to be spending some time on their own in a while." The feel of Spence's arms around her was sheer heaven. "Your first baseman should be here before Thanksgiving."

"You're sure?" Spence's face lit up with delight.

"Positive." She kissed his chin.

"We'll leave the light on for her, too."

Roxanne smiled. She would love this man forever.